719

THE CLOISTER
AND THE HEARTH

THE CLOISTER
AND THE HEARTH

by CHARLES READE

Designed to be read as a modern novel

THE BOOK LEAGUE OF AMERICA

New York

PRINTED IN THE UNITED STATES OF AMERICA
AMERICAN BOOK–STRATFORD PRESS, INC., NEW YORK

THE CLOISTER AND THE HEARTH

CHAPTER I

IT WAS PAST the middle of the fifteenth century, Louis XI was sovereign of France, Edward IV was wrongful King of England, and Philip "the Good" reigned undisturbed this many years in Holland, where our tale begins.

Elias and Catherine his wife lived in the little town of Tergou. He traded, wholesale and retail, in cloth, silk, brown holland, and above all, in curried leather, a material highly valued by the middling people, because it would stand twenty years' wear, and turn an ordinary knife—no small virtue in a jerkin of that century, in which folk were so liberal of their steel. Even at dinner a man would leave his meat awhile and carve you his neighbor, on a very moderate difference of opinion.

The couple were well-to-do, and would have been free from all earthly care but for nine children. When these were coming into the world, one per annum, each was hailed with rejoicings, and the saints were thanked, not expostulated with; and when parents and children were all young together, the latter were looked upon as lovely little playthings invented by Heaven for the amusement, joy, and evening solace of people in business.

But as the olive branches shot up, and the parents grew older and saw with their own eyes the fate of large families, misgivings and care mingled with their love. They belonged to a singularly wise and provident people. In Holland reckless parents were as rare as disobedient children. So now when the huge loaf came in on a gigantic trencher, looked like a fortress in its moat, and, the tour of the table once made, seemed to have melted away, Elias and Catherine would look at one another and say, "Who is to find bread for them all when we are gone?"

At this observation the younger ones needed all their filial respect to keep their little Dutch countenances; for in their opinion dinner and supper came by nature like sunrise and sunset, and so long as that luminary should travel round the earth, so long *must* the brown loaf go round their family circle, and set in their stomachs only to rise again in the family oven. But the remark awakened the national thoughtfulness of the elder boys, and being often repeated, set several of the family thinking, some of them good thoughts, some ill thoughts, according to the nature of the thinkers.

"Kate, the children grow so, this table will soon be too small."

"We cannot afford it, Eli," replied Catherine, answering not his words, but his thought, after the manner of women.

Their anxiety for the future took at times a less dismal but more mortifying turn. The free burghers had their pride as well as the nobles, and these two could not bear that any of their blood should go down in the burgh after their decease. So by prudence and self-denial they managed to clothe all the little bodies, and feed all the great mouths, and yet put by a small hoard to meet the future; and as it grew, and grew, they felt a pleasure the miser hoarding for himself knows not.

One day the eldest boy but one, aged nineteen, came to his mother, and with that outward composure which has so misled some persons as to the real nature of this people begged her to intercede with his father to send him to Amsterdam, and place him with a merchant. "It is the way of life that likes me; merchants are wealthy; I am good at numbers; prithee, good Mother, take my part in this, and I shall ever be, as I am now, your debtor."

Catherine threw up her hands with dismay and incredulity. "What, leave Tergou!"

"What is one street to me more than another? If I can leave the folk of Tergou, I can surely leave the stones."

"What! Quit your poor father now he is no longer young?"

"Mother, if I can leave you, I can leave him."

"What, leave your poor brothers and sisters, that love you so dear?"

"There are enough in the house without me."

"What mean you, Richart? Who is more thought of than you? Stay, have I spoken sharp to you? Have I been unkind to you?"

"Never that I know of; and if you had, you should never hear of it from me. Mother," said Richart gravely, but the tear was in his eye, "it all lies in a word. And nothing can change my mind. There will be one mouth less for you to feed."

"There now, see what my tongue has done," said Catherine, and the next moment she began to cry. For she saw her first young bird on the edge of the nest trying his wings, to fly into the world. Richart had a calm, strong will, and she knew he never wasted a word. It ended as nature has willed all such discourse shall end. Young Richart went to Amsterdam with a face so long and sad as it had never been seen before, and a heart like granite.

That afternoon at supper there was one mouth less. Catherine looked at Richart's chair and wept bitterly. On this Elias shouted roughly and angrily to the children, "Sit wider, can't ye? Sit wider!" and turned his head away over the back of his seat awhile, and was silent.

Richart was launched, and never cost them another penny; but to fit him out and place him in the house of Vander Stegen the merchant took all the little hoard but one gold crown. They began again. Two years passed, Richart found a niche in commerce for his brother Jacob, and Jacob left

Tergou directly after dinner, which was at eleven in the forenoon. At supper that day Elias remembered what had happened the last time, so it was in a low whisper he said, "Sit wider, dears!"

The little coffer was empty again, and to fill it they gathered like ants. In those days speculation was pretty much confined to the card-and-dice business. Elias knew no way to wealth but the slow and sure one. "A penny saved is a penny gained," was his humble creed. All that was not required for the business and the necessaries of life went into the little coffer with steel bands and florid key. They denied themselves in turn the humblest luxuries, and then, catching one another's looks, smiled, perhaps with a greater joy than self-indulgence has to bestow. And so in three years more they had gleaned enough to set up their fourth son as a master tailor, and their eldest daughter as a robe-maker, in Tergou. Here were two more provided for. Their own trade would enable them to throw work into the hands of this pair. But the coffer was drained to the dregs, and this time the shop too bled a little in goods if not in coin.

Alas! there remained on hand two that were unable to get their bread, and two that were unwilling. The unable ones were 1, Giles, a dwarf, of the wrong sort, half stupidity, half malice, all head and claws and voice, run from by dogs and unprejudiced females, and sided with through thick and thin by his mother; 2, Little Catherine, a poor little girl that could only move on crutches. She lived in pain, but smiled through it, with her marble face and violet eyes and long silky lashes: and fretful or repining word never came from her lips. The unwilling ones were Sybrandt, the youngest, a ne'er-do-well, too much in love with play to work, and Cornelis, the eldest, who had made calculations and stuck to the hearth, waiting for dead men's shoes. Almost worn out by their repeated efforts, and above all dispirited by the moral and physical infirmities of those that now remained on hand, the anxious couple would often say, "What will become of all these when we shall be no longer here to take care of them?" But when they had said this a good many times, suddenly the domestic horizon cleared, and then they used still to say it, because a habit is a habit, but they uttered it half mechanically now, and added brightly and cheerfully, "But thanks to Saint Bavon and all the saints, there's Gerard."

Young Gerard was for many years of his life a son apart and distinct, object of no fears and no great hopes. No fears, for he was going into the Church, and the Church could always maintain her children by hook or by crook in those days. No great hopes, because his family had no interest with the great to get him a benefice, and the young man's own habits were frivolous, and indeed such as our cloth merchant would not have put up with in anyone but a clerk that was to be. His trivialities were reading and penmanship, and he was so wrapped up in them that often he could hardly be got away to his meals. The day was never long enough for him: and he carried ever a tinderbox and brimstone matches, and begged ends of candles of the neighbors, which he lighted at unreasonable hours—ay, even at eight of the clock at night in winter, when the very Burgomaster was abed.

Endured at home, his practices were encouraged by the monks of a neighboring convent. They had taught him penmanship, and continued to teach him, until one day they discovered in the middle of a lesson that he was teaching them. They pointed this out to him in a merry way. He hung his head and blushed. He had suspected as much himself, but mistrusted his judgment in so delicate a matter. "But, my son," said the elderly monk, "how is it that you, to whom God has given an eye so true, a hand so subtle yet firm, and a heart to love these beautiful crafts, how is it you do not color as well as write? A scroll looks but barren unless a border of fruit, and leaves, and rich arabesques surround the good words, and charm the senses as those do the soul and understanding—to say nothing of the pictures of holy men and women departed with which the several chapters should be adorned, and not alone the eye soothed with the brave and sweetly blended colors, but the heart lifted by effigies of the saints in glory. Answer me, my son."

At this Gerard was confused, and muttered that he had made several trials at illuminating, but had not succeeded well, and thus the matter rested.

Soon after this a fellow enthusiast came on the scene in the unwonted form of an old lady. Margaret, sister and survivor of the brothers Van Eyck, left Flanders and came to end her days in her native country. She bought a small house near Tergou. In course of time she heard of Gerard, and saw some of his handiwork. It pleased her so well that she sent her female servant, Reicht Heynes, to ask him to come to her. This led to an acquaintance. It could hardly be otherwise, for little Tergou had never held so many as two zealots of this sort before.

At first the old lady damped Gerard's courage terribly. At each visit she fished out of holes and corners drawings and paintings, some of them by her own hand, that seemed to him unapproachable; but if the artist over-powered him, the woman kept his heart up. She and Reicht soon turned him inside out like a glove. Among other things, they drew from him what the good monks had failed to hit upon, the reason why he did not illumi-nate, viz., that he could not afford the gold, the blue, and the red, but only the cheap earths; and that he was afraid to ask his mother to buy the choice colors, and was sure he should ask her in vain.

Then Margaret Van Eyck gave him a little brush gold, and some ver-milion and ultramarine, and a piece of good vellum to lay them on. He almost adored her. As he left the house Reicht ran after him with a candle and two quarters; he quite kissed her. But better even than the gold and lapis lazuli to the illuminator was the sympathy to the isolated enthusiast. That sympathy was always ready, and, as he returned it, an affection sprung up between the old painter and the young calligrapher that was doubly characteristic of the time. For this was a century in which the fine arts and the higher mechanical arts were not separated by any distinct boundary, nor were those who practiced them; and it was an age in which artists sought out and loved one another. Should this last statement stagger a painter or writer of our day, let me remind him that even Christians loved one another at first starting.

Backed by an acquaintance so venerable, and strengthened by female sympathy, Gerard advanced in learning and skill. His spirits, too, rose visibly: he still looked behind him when dragged to dinner in the middle of an initial G; but once seated, showed great social qualities: likewise a gay humor that had hitherto but peeped in him shone out, and often he set the table in a roar, and kept it there, sometimes with his own wit, sometimes with jests which were glossy-new to his family, being drawn from antiquity.

As a return for all he owed his friends the monks, he made them exquisite copies from two of their choicest MSS., viz., the life of their founder, and their *Comedies* of Terence, the monastery finding the vellum.

The high and puissant Prince, Philip "the Good"—Duke of Burgundy, Luxemburg, and Brabant, Earl of Holland and Zealand, Lord of Friesland, Count of Flanders, Artois, and Hainault, Lord of Salins and Macklyn—was versatile. He could fight as well as any king going, and he could lie as well as any, except the King of France. He was a mighty hunter, and could read and write. His tastes were wide and ardent. He loved jewels like a woman, and gorgeous apparel. He dearly loved maids of honor, and indeed paintings generally, in proof of which he ennobled Jan Van Eyck.

He had also a rage for giants, dwarfs, and Turks. These last stood ever planted about him, turbaned, and blazing with jewels. His agents inveigled them from Istambul with fair promises; but the moment he had got them, he baptized them by brute force in a large tub, and, this done, let them squat with their faces toward Mecca, and invoke Mahound as much as they pleased, laughing in his sleeve at their simplicity in fancying they were still infidels. He had lions in cages, and fleet leopards trained by Orientals to run down hares and deer. In short, he relished all rarities except the humdrum virtues. For any thing singularly pretty, or diabolically ugly, this was your customer.

The best of him was, he was openhanded to the poor; and the next best was, he fostered the arts in earnest, whereof he now gave a signal proof. He offered prizes for the best specimens of "orfévrerie" in two kinds, religious and secular; item for the best paintings in white of egg, oils and tempera—these to be on panel, silk, or metal, as the artists chose; item for the best transparent painting on glass; item for the best illuminating and border painting on vellum; item for the fairest writing on vellum. The burgomasters of the several towns were commanded to aid all the poorer competitors by receiving their specimens and sending them with due care to Rotterdam at the expense of their several burghs.

When this was cried by the bellman through the streets of Tergou, a thousand mouths opened, and one heart beat—Gerard's. He told his family timidly he would try for two of those prizes. They stared in silence, for their breath was gone at this audacity; but one horrid laugh exploded on the floor like a petard. Gerard looked down, and there was the dwarf, slit and fanged from ear to ear at his expense, and laughing like a lion. Nature, relenting at having made Giles so small, had given him as a set-off the biggest voice on record. His very whisper was a bassoon. He was like those stunted wide-mouth pieces of ordnance we see on fortifications; more like a flowerpot than a cannon, but ods tympana, how they bellow!

Gerard turned red with anger, and the more so as the others began to titter. White Catherine saw, and a pink tinge came on her cheeks. She said softly: "Why do you laugh? Is it because he is our brother you think he cannot be capable? Yes, Gerard, try with the rest. Many say you are skillful; and Mother and I will pray the Virgin to guide your hand."

"Thank you, Little Kate. You shall pray to our Lady, and our Mother shall buy me vellum and the colors to illuminate with."

"What will they cost, my lad?"

"Two gold crowns." (About three shillings and fourpence English money.)

"What?" screamed the housewife. "When the bushel of rye costs but a groat! What! Me spend a month's meal and meat and fire on such vanity as that? The lightning from Heaven would fall on me, and my children would all be beggars."

"Mother!" sighed little Catherine imploringly.

"Oh! it is in vain, Kate," said Gerard, with a sigh. "I shall have to give it up, or ask the Dame Van Eyck. She would give it me, but I think shame to be forever taking from her."

"It is not her affair," said Catherine very sharply. "What has she to do coming between me and my son?" And she left the room with a red face. Little Catherine smiled. Presently the housewife returned with a gracious, affectionate air and two little gold pieces in her hand.

"There, sweetheart," said she, "you won't have to trouble dame or demoiselle for two paltry crowns."

But on this Gerard fell a-thinking how he could spare her purse.

"One will do, Mother. I will ask the good monks to let me send my copy of their Terence. It is on snowy vellum, and I can write no better. So then I shall only need six sheets of vellum for my borders and miniatures, and gold for my ground, and prime colors—one crown will do."

"Never tyne the ship for want of a bit of tar, Gerard," said this changeable mother. But she added, "Well, there, I will put the crown in my pocket. That won't be like putting it back in the box. Going to the box to take out instead of putting in, it is like going to my heart with a knife for so many drops of blood. You will be sure to want it, Gerard. The house is never built for less than the builder counted on."

Sure enough, when the time came, Gerard longed to go to Rotterdam and see the Duke, and above all to see the work of his competitors and so get a lesson from defeat. And the crown came out of the housewife's pocket with a very good grace. Gerard would soon be a priest. It seemed hard if he might not enjoy the world a little before separating himself from it for life.

The night before he went, Margaret Van Eyck asked him to take a letter for her, and when he came to look at it, to his surprise he found it was addressed to the Princess Marie at the Stadthouse in Rotterdam.

The day before the prizes were to be distributed, Gerard started for Rotterdam in his holiday suit; to wit, a doublet of silver-gray cloth with sleeves, and a jerkin of the same over it, but without sleeves. From his waist to his heels he was clad in a pair of tight-fitting buckskin hose fastened by laces (called points) to his doublet. His shoes were pointed, in moderation, and secured by a strap that passed under the hollow of his foot. On his head and the back of his neck he wore his flowing hair, and pinned to his back between his shoulders was his hat; it was further secured by a purple silk ribbon little Kate had passed round him from the sides of the hat and knotted neatly on his breast. Below his hat, attached to the upper rim of his broad waist belt, was his leathern wallet.

When he got within a league of Rotterdam he was pretty tired, but he soon fell in with a pair that was more so. He found an old man sitting by the roadside quite worn out, and a comely young woman holding his hand, with a face brimful of concern. The country people trudged by and noticed nothing amiss, but Gerard as he passed drew conclusions. Even dress tells a tale to those who study it so closely as he did, being an illuminator. The old man wore a gown, and a fur tippet, and a velvet cap, sure signs of dignity; but the triangular purse at his girdle was lean, the gown rusty, the fur worn, sure signs of poverty. The young woman was dressed in plain russet cloth, yet snow-white lawn covered that part of her neck the gown left visible, and ended halfway up her white throat in a little band of gold embroidery. And her headdress was new to Gerard; instead of hiding her hair in a pile of linen or lawn, she wore an open network of silver cord with silver spangles at the interstices. In this her glossy auburn hair was rolled in front into two solid waves, and supported behind in a luxurious and shapely mass. His quick eye took in all this, and the old man's pallor, and the tears in the young woman's eyes. So when he had passed them a few yards, he reflected, and turned back, and came toward them bashfully.

"Father, I fear you are tired."

"Indeed, my son, I am," replied the old man, "and faint for lack of food."

Gerard's address did not appear so agreeable to the girl as to the old man. She seemed ashamed, and with much reserve in her manner said that it was her fault—she had underrated the distance and imprudently allowed her father to start too late in the day.

"No! no!" said the old man. "It is not the distance, it is the want of nourishment."

The girl put her arms round his neck with tender concern, but took that opportunity of whispering, "Father, a stranger—a young man!"

But it was too late. Gerard, with simplicity, and quite as a matter of course, fell to gathering sticks with great expedition. This done, he took down his wallet, out with the manchet of bread and the iron flask his careful mother had put up, and his everlasting tinderbox, lighted a match, then a candle end, then the sticks, and put his iron flask on it. Then down he went on his stomach and took a good blow. Then, looking up, he saw the girl's face had thawed, and she was looking down at him and his energy with a demure smile. He laughed back to her.

"Mind the pot," said he, "and don't let it spill, for Heaven's sake. There's a cleft stick to hold it safe with." And with this he set off running toward a cornfield at some distance. While he was gone, there came by, on a mule with rich purple housings, an old man redolent of wealth. The purse at his girdle was plethoric, the fur on his tippet was ermine, broad and new. It was Ghysbrecht van Swieten, the Burgomaster of Tergou. He was old, and his face furrowed. He was a notorious miser, and looked one generally. But the idea of supping with the Duke raised him just now into manifest complacency.

Yet at the sight of the faded old man and his bright daughter sitting by a fire of sticks, the smile died out of his face, and he wore a strange look of pain and uneasiness. He reined in his mule. "Why, Peter—Margaret—" said he almost fiercely. "What mummery is this!" Peter was going to answer, but Margaret interposed hastily, and said: "My father was exhausted, so I am warming something to give him strength before we go on." "What, reduced to feed by the roadside like the Bohemians?" said Ghysbrecht, and his hand went into his purse. But it did not seem at home there, it fumbled uncertainly, afraid too large a coin might stick to a finger and come out.

At this moment who should come bounding up but Gerard. He had two straws in his hand, and he threw himself down by the fire and relieved Margaret of the cooking part. Then, suddenly recognizing the Burgomaster, he colored all over. Ghysbrecht van Swieten started and glared at him, and took his hand out of his purse. "Oh," said he bitterly, "I am not wanted," and went slowly on, casting a long look of suspicion on Margaret and hostility on Gerard that was not very intelligible. However, there was something about it that Margaret could read enough to blush at, and almost toss her head. Gerard only stared with surprise. "By Saint Bavon, I think the old miser grudges us three our quart of soup," said he. When the young man put that interpretation on Ghysbrecht's strange and meaning look, Margaret was greatly relieved and smiled gaily on the speaker.

Meantime Ghysbrecht plodded on, more wretched in his wealth than these in their poverty. And the curious thing is that the mule, the purple housings, and one half the coin in that plethoric purse belonged not to Ghysbrecht van Swieten, but to that faded old man and that comely girl who sat by the roadside fire to be fed by a stranger. They did not know this, but Ghysbrecht knew it, and carried in his heart a scorpion of his own begetting. That scorpion is remorse—the remorse that, not being penitence, is incurable, and ready for fresh misdeeds upon a fresh temptation.

Twenty years ago, when Ghysbrecht was a hard and honest man, the touchstone opportunity came to him, and he did an act of heartless roguery. It seemed a safe one. It had hitherto proved a safe one, though he had never felt safe. Today he has seen youth, enterprise, and, above all, knowledge seated by fair Margaret and her father on terms that look familiar and loving. And the fiends are at his ear again.

CHAPTER II

"'The soup is hot," said Gerard.

"But how are we to get it to our mouths?" inquired the senior despondingly.

"Father, the young man has brought us straws." And Margaret smiled slyly.

"Ay, ay!" said the old man. "But my poor bones are stiff, and indeed the fire is too hot for a body to kneel over with these short straws. Saint John the Baptist, but the young man is adroit!"

For while he stated his difficulty Gerard removed it. He untied in a moment the knot on his breast, took his hat off, put a stone in each corner of it, then, wrapping his hand in the tail of his jerkin, whipped the flask off the fire, wedged it in between the stones, and put the hat under the old man's nose with a merry smile. The other tremulously inserted the pipe of rye straw and sucked. Lo and behold, his wan, drawn face was seen to light up more and more till it quite glowed. And as soon as he had drawn a long breath——

"Hippocrates and Galen," he cried, "'tis a *soupe au vin*—the restorative of restoratives! Blessed be the nation that invented it, and the woman that made it, and the young man who brings it to fainting folk."

The bread and soup being disposed of, the old scholar prepared to continue his journey. Then came a little difficulty. Gerard the adroit could not tie his ribbon again as Catherine had tied it. Margaret, after slyly eying his efforts for some time, offered to help him; for at her age girls love to be coy and tender, saucy and gentle, by turns, and she saw she had put him out of countenance but now. Then a fair head with its stately crown of auburn hair, glossy and glowing through silver, bowed sweetly toward him; and while it ravished his eye, two white supple hands played delicately upon the stubborn ribbon, and molded it with soft and airy touches. Then a heavenly thrill ran through the innocent young man, and vague glimpses of a new world of feeling and sentiment opened on him. And these new and exquisite sensations Margaret unwittingly prolonged. It is not natural to her sex to hurry aught that pertains to the sacred toilet. Nay, when the taper fingers had at last subjugated the ends of the knot, her mind was not quite easy till, by a maneuver peculiar to the female hand, she had made her palm convex, and so applied it with a gentle pressure to the center of the knot—a sweet little coaxing hand kiss, as much as to say, "Now be a good knot, and stay so." The palm kiss was bestowed on the ribbon, but the wearer's heart leaped to meet it.

"There, that is how it was," said Margaret, and drew back to take one last keen survey of her work. Then, looking up for simple approval of her skill, received full in her eyes a longing gaze of such ardent adoration as made her lower them quickly and color all over. An indescribable tremor seized her, and she retreated with downcast lashes and telltale cheeks and took her father's arm on the opposite side. Gerard, blushing at having scared her away with his eyes, took the other arm; and so the two young things went downcast and conscious, and propped the eagle along in silence.

They entered Rotterdam by the Schiedamze Poort; and, as Gerard was unacquainted with the town, Peter directed him the way to the Hoog Straet, in which the Stadthouse was. He himself was going with Margaret to his cousin in the Ooster-Waagen Straet, so, almost on entering the gate, their roads lay apart. They bade each other a friendly adieu, and Gerard dived into the great town. A profound sense of solitude fell upon him, yet the streets were crowded. Then he lamented too late that, out of delicacy, he had not asked his late companions who they were and where they lived.

He found the Hoog Straet, and it speedily led him to the Stadthouse. But when he got there he was refused, first at one door, then at another, till he came to the great gate of the courtyard. It was kept by soldiers, and superintended by a pompous major-domo, glittering in an embroidered collar and a gold chain of office and holding a white staff with a gold knob.

There was a crowd of persons at the gate endeavoring to soften this official rock. They came up in turn like ripples, and retired as such in turn. It cost Gerard a struggle to get near him, and when he was within four heads of the gate, he saw something that made his heart beat. There was Peter, with Margaret on his arm, soliciting humbly for entrance.

"My cousin the alderman is not at home. They say he is here."

"What is that to me, old man?"

"If you will not let us pass in to him, at least take this leaf from my tablet to my cousin. See, I have written his name. He will come out to us."

"For what do you take me? I carry no messages. I keep the gate." He then bawled, in a stentorian voice, inexorably: "No strangers enter here but the competitors and their companies."

"Come, old man," cried a voice in the crowd, "you have gotten your answer. Make way."

Margaret turned half round imploringly:

"Good people, we are come from far, and my father is old; and my cousin has a new servant that knows us not and would not let us sit in our cousin's house."

At this the crowd laughed hoarsely. Margaret shrank as if they had struck her. At that moment a hand grasped hers—a magic grasp. It felt like heart meeting heart, or magnet, steel. She turned quickly around at it, and it was Gerard. Such a little cry of joy and appeal came from her bosom, and she began to whimper prettily. They had hustled her and frightened her for one thing; and her cousin's thoughtlessness in not even telling his servant they were coming was cruel; and the servant's caution, however wise and faithful to her master, was bitterly mortifying to her father and her. And to her so mortified and anxious and jostled, came suddenly this kind hand and face. "*Hinc illae lacrimae.*"

"All is well now," remarked a coarse humorist. "She hath gotten her sweetheart."

"Haw! haw! haw!" went the crowd.

She dropped Gerard's hand directly, and turned round with eyes flashing through her tears.

"I have no sweetheart, you rude men. But I am friendless in your boorish town, and this is a friend; and one who knows, what you know not, how to treat the aged and the weak."

The crowd was dead silent. They had only been thoughtless, and now felt the rebuke, though severe, was just. The silence enabled Gerard to treat with the porter.

"I am a competitor, sir."

"What is your name?" And the man eyed him suspiciously.

"Gerard, the son of Elias."

The janitor inspected the slip of parchment he held in his hand.

"Gerard Eliassoen can enter."

"With my company, these two?"

"Nay, those are not your company. They came before you."

"What matter? They are my friends, and without them I go not in."

"Stay without, then."

"That will I not."

"That we will see."

"We will, and speedily." And with this, Gerard raised a voice of astounding volume and power and shouted, so that the whole street rang:

"*Ho! Philip Earl of Holland!*"

"Are you mad?" cried the porter.

"*Here is one of your varlets defies you.*"

"Hush, hush!"

"*And will not let your guests pass in.*"

"Hush! Murder! The Duke's there. I'm dead," cried the janitor, quaking.

Then suddenly trying to overpower Gerard's thunder, he shouted with all his lungs:

"*Open the gates, ye knaves! Way there for Gerard Eliassoen and his company!* (The fiends go with him!)"

The gate swung open as by magic. Eight soldiers lowered their pikes halfway and made an arch, under which the victorious three marched in triumphant. The moment they had passed, the pikes clashed together horizontally to bar the gateway.

Once passed the guarded portal, a few steps brought the trio upon a scene of Oriental luxury. The courtyard was laid out in tables loaded with rich meats and piled with gorgeous plate. Guests in rich and various costumes sat beneath a leafy canopy of fresh-cut branches fastened tastefully to golden, silver, and blue silken cords that traversed the area; and fruits of many hues, including some artificial ones of gold, silver, and wax, hung pendent or peeped like fair eyes among the green leaves of plane trees and lime trees. The Duke's minstrels swept their lutes at intervals, and a fountain played red Burgundy in six jets that met and battled in the air. The evening sun darted its fires through those bright and purple wine spouts, making them jets and cascades of molten rubies, then passing on, tinged with the blood of the grape, shed crimson glories here and there on fair faces, snowy beards, velvet, satin, jeweled hilts, glowing gold, gleaming silver, and sparkling glass.

Gerard and his friends stood dazzled, spellbound. Presently a whisper buzzed around them, "Salute the Duke! Salute the Duke!" They looked up, and there on high, under the dais, was their sovereign, bidding them welcome with a kindly wave of the hand. The men bowed low, and Margaret curtsied with a deep and graceful obeisance. The Duke's hand being up, he gave it another turn and pointed the newcomers out to a knot of valets. Instantly seven of his people, with an obedient start, went headlong at our friends, seated them at a table, and put fifteen many-colored soups before them in little silver bowls, and as many wines in crystal vases.

"Nay, Father, let us not eat until we have thanked our good friend," said Margaret, now first recovering from all this bustle.

"Girl, he is our guardian angel."

Gerard put his face into his hands.

"Tell me when you have done," said he, "and I will reappear and have my supper, for I am hungry. I know which of us three is the happiest at meeting again."

"Me?" inquired Margaret.

"No, guess again."

"Father?"

"No."

"Then I have no guess which it can be." And she gave a little crow of happiness and gaiety.

The soup was tasted, and vanished in a twirl of fourteen hands, and fish came on the table in a dozen forms, with patties of lobster and almonds mixed, and of almonds and cream, and an immense variety of "*brouets*," known to us as "rissoles." The next trifle was a wild boar, which smelt divine. Why, then, did Margaret start away from it with two shrieks of dismay, and pinch so good a friend as Gerard? Because the Duke's "cuisinier" had been too clever, had made this excellent dish too captivating to the sight as well as taste. He had restored to the animal, by elaborate mimicry with burnt sugar and other edible colors, the hair and bristles he had robbed him of by fire and water. To make him still more enticing, the huge tusks were carefully preserved in the brute's jaw, and gave his mouth the winning smile that comes of tusk in man or beast: and two eyes of coloured sugar glowed in his head. Saint Argus! what eyes! so bright, so bloodshot, so threatening—they followed a man and every movement of his knife and spoon—old Peter clasping both hands in pious admiration of it; Margaret wheeling round with horror-stricken eyes and her hand on Gerard's shoulder, squeaking and pinching; his face of unwise delight at being pinched; the grizzly brute glaring sulkily on all; and the guests grinning from ear to ear.

"What's to do?" shouted the Duke, hearing the signals of female distress. Seven of his people with a zealous start went headlong and told him. He laughed and said, "Give her of the beef stuffing, then, and bring me Sir Boar." Benevolent monarch! The beef stuffing was his own private dish. On these grand occasions an ox was roasted whole, and reserved for the poor. But this wise as well as charitable prince had discovered that whatever venison, hares, lamb, poultry, and so forth you skewered into that beef cavern got cooked to perfection, retaining their own juices and receiving those of the reeking ox. These he called his beef stuffing, and took delight therein, as did now our trio for, at his word, seven of his people went headlong and drove silver tridents into the steaming cave at random, and speared a kid, a cygnet, and a flock of wild fowl. These presently smoked before Gerard and company; and Peter's face, sad and slightly morose at the loss of the savage hog, expanded and shone.

After this, twenty different tarts of fruits and herbs, and last of all, confectionery on a titanic scale: cathedrals of sugar, all gilt and painted in the interstices of the bas-reliefs; castles and their moats and ditches, imitated to the life; elephants, camels, toads; knights on horseback, jousting; kings and princesses looking on; trumpeters blowing; and all these personages delicious eating, and their veins filled with sweet-scented juices—works of art made to be destroyed. The guests breached a bastion, crunched a Crusader and his horse and lance, or cracked a bishop, cope, chasuble, crosier and all, as remorselessly as we do a caraway comfit; sipping, meanwhile, hippocras and other spiced drinks, and Greek and Corsican wines, while every now and then little Turkish boys, turbaned, spangled, jeweled, and gilt, came offering on bended knee golden troughs of rosewater and orange water to keep the guests' hands cool and perfumed.

But long before our party arrived at this final stage, appetite had succumbed, and Gerard had suddenly remembered he was the bearer of a letter to the Princess Marie, and in an undertone had asked one of the servants if he would undertake to deliver it. The man took it with a deep obeisance. He could not deliver it himself, but would instantly give it one of the Princess's suite, several of whom were about.

It may be remembered that Peter and Margaret came here not to dine, but to find their cousin. Well, the old gentleman ate heartily and being much fatigued, dropped asleep and forgot all about his cousin. Meantime, that cousin was seated within a few feet of them, at their backs, and discovered them when Margaret turned round and screamed at the boar. But he forbore to speak to them, for municipal reasons. Margaret was very plainly dressed and Peter inclined to be threadbare. So the alderman said to himself:

" 'Twill be time to make up to them when the sun sets and the company disperses. Then I will take my poor relations to my house, and none will be the wiser."

Half the courses were lost on Gerard and Margaret. They were no great eaters, and just now were feeding on sweet thoughts that have ever been unfavorable to appetite. But there is a delicate kind of sensuality, to whose influence these two were perhaps more sensitive than any other pair in that assembly—the delights of color, music, and perfume, all of which blended so fascinatingly here. Margaret leaned back and half closed her eyes, and murmured to Gerard:

"What a lovely scene! The warm sun, the green shade, the rich dresses, the bright music of the lutes and the cool music of the fountain, and all faces so happy and gay! And then, it is to you we owe it."

Gerard was silent, all but his eyes, observing which—

"Now, speak not to me," said Margaret languidly. "Let me listen to the fountain. What are you a competitor for?"

He told her.

"Very well! You will gain one prize, at least."

"Which? Which? Have you seen any of my work?"

"I? No. But you will gain a prize."

"I hope so, but what makes you think so?"

"Because you were so good to my father."

Gerard smiled at the feminine logic, and hung his head at the sweet praise, and was silent.

"Speak not," murmured Margaret. "They say this is a world of sin and misery. Can that be? What is your opinion?"

"No! That is all a silly old song," explained Gerard. " 'Tis a byword our elders keep repeating, out of custom. It is not true."

"How can you know? You are but a child," said Margaret, with pensive dignity.

"Why, only look round! And then I thought I had lost you forever, and you are by my side. And now the minstrels are going to play again. Sin and misery? Stuff and nonsense!"

The lutes burst out. The courtyard rang again with their delicate harmony.

"What do you admire most of all these beautiful things, Gerard?"

"You know my name? How is that?"

"White magic. I am a witch."

"Angels are never witches. But I can't think how you—"

"Foolish boy! Was it not cried at the gate loud enough to deave one?"

"So it was. Where is my head? What do I admire most? If you will sit a little more that way, I'll tell you."

"This way?"

"Yes, so that the light may fall on you. There. I see many fair things here, fairer than I could have conceived; but the bravest of all to my eye is your lovely hair in its silver frame, and the setting sun kissing it. It reminds me of what the Vulgate praises for beauty, 'an apple of gold in a network of silver,' and oh, what a pity I did not know you before I sent in my poor endeavors at illuminating! I could illuminate so much better now. I could do everything better. There, now the sun is full on it, it is like an aureole. So our Lady looked, and none since her until today."

"Oh, fie! It is wicked to talk so. Compare a poor, coarse-favored girl like me with the Queen of Heaven? Oh, Gerard, I thought you were a good young man!" And Margaret was shocked, apparently.

Gerard tried to explain. "I am no worse than the rest. But how can I help having eyes, and a heart—Margaret!"

"Gerard?"

"Be not angry now!"

"Now, is it likely?"

"I love you."

"Oh, for shame! You must not say that to me." And Margaret colored furiously at this sudden assault.

"I can't help it. I love you. I love you."

"Hush, hush, for pity's sake! I must not listen to such words from a stranger. I am ungrateful to call you a stranger. Oh, how one may be mistaken! If I had known you were so bold—" And Margaret's bosom began to heave, and her cheeks were covered with blushes, and she looked toward her sleeping father very much like a timid thing that meditates actual flight.

Then Gerard was frightened at the alarm he caused. "Forgive me," said he imploringly. "How could anyone help loving you?"

"Well, sir, I will *try* and forgive you—you are so good in other respects. But then you must promise me never to say you—to say *that* again."

"Give me your hand, then, or you don't forgive me."

She hesitated, but eventually put out her hand a very little way, very slowly, and with seeming reluctance. He took it, and held it prisoner. When she thought it had been there long enough, she tried gently to draw it away. He held it tight. It submitted quite patiently to force. What *is* the use resisting force? She turned her head away, and her long eyelashes drooped sweetly. Gerard lost nothing by his promise. Words were not heeded here, and silence was more eloquent.

Nature was in that day what she is in ours, but manners were somewhat freer. Then, as now, virgins drew back alarmed at the first words of love; but of prudery and artificial coquetry there was little, and the young soon read one another's hearts. Everything was on Gerard's side: his good looks, her belief in his goodness, her gratitude; and opportunity, for at the Duke's banquet this mellow summer eve all things disposed the female nature to tenderness—the avenues to the heart lay open; the senses were so soothed and subdued with lovely colors, gentle sounds, and delicate odors; the sun gently sinking, the warm air, the green canopy, the cool music of the now violet fountain.

Gerard and Margaret sat hand in hand in silence. And Gerard's eyes sought hers lovingly; and hers now and then turned on him timidly and imploringly; and presently two sweet unreasonable tears rolled down her cheeks, and she smiled deliciously while they were drying—yet they did not take long.

And the sun declined, and the air cooled, and the fountain plashed more gently; and the pair throbbed in unison, and silence, and this weary world looked Heaven to them.

CHAPTER III

A GRAVE white-haired seneschal came to their table and inquired courteously whether Gerard Eliassoen was of their company. Upon Gerard's answer, he said:

"The Princess Marie would confer with you, young sir. I am to conduct you to her presence."

Instantly all faces within hearing turned sharp round and were bent with curiosity and envy on the man that was to go to a Princess. Gerard rose to obey.

"I wager we shall not see you again," said Margaret calmly, but coloring a little.

"That will you," was the reply. Then he whispered in her ear: "This is my good Princess, but you are my queen." He added aloud: "Wait for me, I pray you. I will presently return."

"Ay, ay!" said Peter, awaking and speaking at one and the same moment.

Gerard gone, the pair whose dress was so homely, yet they were with the man whom the Princess sent for, became "the cynosure of neighboring eyes," observing which, William Johnson came forward, acted surprised and claimed his relations.

"And to think that there was I at your backs and you saw me not."

"Nay, Cousin Johnson, I saw you long syne," said Margaret coldly.

"You saw me, and spoke not to me?"

"Cousin, it was for you to welcome us to Rotterdam, as it is for us to welcome you at Sevenbergen. Your servant denied us a seat in your house."

"The idiot!"

"And I had in mind to see whether it was 'like maid like master,' for there is sooth in bywords."

William Johnson blushed purple. He saw Margaret was keen, and suspected him. He did the wisest thing under the circumstances—trusted to deeds, not words. He insisted on their coming home with him at once, and he would show them whether they were welcome to Rotterdam or not.

"Who doubts it, Cousin? Who doubts it?" said the scholar.

Margaret thanked him graciously, but demurred to go just now; said she wanted to hear the minstrels again. In about a quarter of an hour Johnson renewed his proposal, and bade her observe that many of the guests had left. Then her real reason came out.

"It were ill manners to our friend, and he will lose us. He knows not where we lodge in Rotterdam, and the city is large, and we have parted company once already."

"Oh," said Johnson, "we will provide for that! My young man—ahem! I mean my secretary shall sit here and wait and bring him on to my house. He shall lodge with me and with no other."

"Cousin, we shall be too burdensome."

"Nay, nay, you shall see whether you are welcome or not, you and your friends, and your friend's friends if need be. And I shall hear what the Princess would with him."

Margaret felt a thrill of joy that Gerard should be lodged under the same roof with her; then she had a slight misgiving. "But if your young man should be thoughtless, and go play, and Gerard miss him?"

"He go play? He leave that spot where I put him and bid him stay? Ho! Stand forth, Hans Cloterman."

A figure clad in black serge and dark violet hose arose and took two steps and stood before them without moving a muscle: a solemn, precise young man, the very statue of gravity and starched propriety. At his aspect Margaret, being very happy, could hardly keep her countenance. But she whispered Johnson: "I would put my hand in the fire for him. We are at your command, Cousin, as soon as you have given him his orders."

Hans was then instructed to sit at the table and wait for Gerard and conduct him to Ooster-Waagen Straet. He replied not in words, but by calmly taking the seat indicated, and Margaret, Peter, and William Johnson went away together.

"And indeed it is time you were abed, Father, after all your travel," said Margaret. This had been in her mind all along.

Hans Cloterman sat waiting for Gerard, solemn and businesslike. The minutes flew by, but excited no impatience in that perfect young man. Johnson did him no more than justice when he laughed to scorn the idea of his secretary leaving his post, or neglecting his duty, in pursuit of sport or out of youthful hilarity and frivolity.

As Gerard was long in coming, the patient Hans—his employer's eye being no longer on him—improved the time by quaffing solemnly, silently, and at short but accurately measured intervals goblets of Corsican wine. The wine was strong, so was Cloterman's head; and Gerard had been gone a good hour ere the model secretary imbibed the notion that Creation expected Cloterman to drink the health of all good fellows, and "*nommément*" of the Duke of Burgundy there present. With this view he filled bumper nine, and rose gingerly, but solemnly and slowly. Having reached his full height, he instantly rolled upon the grass, goblet in hand, spilling the cold liquor on more than one ankle—but not disturbing a muscle in his own long face, which, in the total eclipse of reason, retained its gravity, primness, and infallibility.

The seneschal led Gerard through several passages to the door of the pavilion, where some young noblemen, embroidered and feathered, sat sentinel, guarding the heir apparent and playing cards by the red light of torches their servants held. A whisper from the seneschal and one of them rose reluctantly, stared at Gerard with haughty surprise, and entered the pavilion. He presently returned and, beckoning the pair, led them through a passage or two and landed them in an antechamber, where sat three more young gentlemen, feathered, furred, and embroidered like pieces of fancy-work, and deep in that instructive and edifying branch of learning, dice.

"You can't see the Princess—it is too late," said one.

Another followed suit:

"She passed this way but now with her nurse. She is gone to bed, doll and all. Deuce-ace again!"

Gerard prepared to retire. The seneschal, with an incredulous smile, replied:

"The young man is here by the Countess's orders. Be so good as conduct him to her ladies."

On this a superb Adonis rose, with an injured look, and led Gerard into a room where sat or lolloped eleven ladies, chattering like magpies. A duenna said, severely, "Mesdames!" and they were all abashed at once as though a modesty string had been pulled. This same duenna took Gerard and marched before him in solemn silence, suddenly introducing him into a room where three ladies sat working, and a pretty little girl tuning a lute. The ladies were richly but not showily dressed, and the duenna went up to the one who was hemming a kerchief and said a few words in a low tone. This lady then turned toward Gerard with a smile, and beckoned him to come near her. She did not rise, but she laid aside her work, and her manner of turning toward him, slight as the movement was, was full of grace and ease and courtesy. She began a conversation at once.

"Margaret Van Eyck is an old friend of mine, sir, and I am right glad to have a letter from her hand, and thankful to you, sir, for bringing it to me safely. Marie, my love, this is the young gentleman who brought you that pretty miniature."

"Sir, I thank you a thousand times," said the young lady.

"I am glad you feel her debtor, sweetheart, for our friend could have us to do him a little service in return."

"I will do anything on earth for him," replied the young lady with ardor.

"Anything on earth is nothing in the world," said the Countess of Charolois quietly.

"Well, then, I will—— What would you have me to do, sir?"

Gerard had just found out what high society he was in. "My sovereign Demoiselle," said he, gently and a little tremulously, "where there have been no pains there needs no reward."

"But we must obey Mamma. All the world must obey Mamma."

"That is true. Then, our Demoiselle, reward me, if you will, by letting me hear the stave you were going to sing and I did interrupt it."

"What, you love music, sir?"

"I adore it."

The little Princess looked inquiringly at her mother, and received a smile of assent. She then took her lute and sang a romaunt of the day. Although but twelve years old, she was a well-taught and painstaking musician. Her little claw swept the chords with courage and precision, and struck out the notes of the arpeggio clear and distinct and bright, like twinkling stars; but the main charm was her voice. It was not mighty, but it was round, clear, full, and ringing like a bell. She sang with a certain modest eloquence, though she knew none of the tricks of feeling. She was too young to be theatrical, or even sentimental, so nothing was forced.

While the pure and tender strain was flowing from the pure young throat, Gerard's eyes filled. The Countess watched him with interest, for it was usual to applaud the Princess loudly, but not with cheek and eye. So when the voice ceased, and the glasses left off ringing, she asked demurely, Was he content? Gerard gave a little start. The spoken voice broke the charm, and brought him back to earth.

"Oh, madam," he cried, "surely it is thus that cherubs and seraphs sing, and charm the saints in Heaven!"

"I am somewhat of your opinion, my young friend," said the Countess with emotion; and she bent a look of love and gentle pride upon her girl— a heavenly look, such as, they say, is given to the eye of the short-lived resting on the short-lived. The Countess resumed: "My old friend requests me to be serviceable to you. It is the first favor she has done us the honor of asking us, and the request is sacred. You are in holy orders, sir?"

Gerard bowed.

"I fear you are not a priest, you look too young."

"Oh, no, madam, I am not even a subdeacon. I am only a lector; but next month I shall be an exorcist, and before long an acolyth."

"Well, Monsieur Gerard, with your accomplishments you can soon pass through the inferior orders. And let me beg you to do so. For the day after you have said your first mass I shall have the pleasure of appointing you to a benefice."

"Oh, madam!"

"And, Marie, remember I make this promise in your name as well as my own."

"Fear not, Mamma, I will not forget. But if he will take my advice, what he will be is Bishop of Liége. The Bishop of Liége is a beautiful bishop. What! Do you not remember him, Mamma, that day we were at Liége? He was braver than Grandpa himself. He had on a crown, a high one, and it was cut in the middle, and it was full of oh! such beautiful jewels. And his gown stiff with gold, and his mantle, too; and it had a broad border, all pictures. But above all, his gloves; you have no such gloves, Mamma. They were embroidered and covered with jewels, and scented with such lovely scent. I smelt them all the time he was giving me his blessing on my head with them. Dear old man! I dare say he will die soon—most old people do—and then, sir, you can be bishop, you know, and wear——"

"Gently, Marie, gently. Bishoprics are for old gentlemen, and this is a young gentleman."

"Mamma, he is not so very young!"

"Not compared with you, Marie, eh?"

"He is a good bigth, dear Mamma, and I am sure he is *good* enough for a bishop."

"Alas, mademoiselle, you are mistaken!"

"I know not that, Monsieur Gerard; but I am a little puzzled to know on what grounds mademoiselle there pronounces your character so boldly."

"Alas, Mamma," said the Princess, "you have not looked at his face, then." And she raised her eyebrows at her mother's simplicity.

"I beg your pardon," said the Countess, "I have. Well, sir, if I cannot go quite so fast as my daughter, attribute it to my age, not to a want of interest in your welfare. A benefice will do to begin your career with; and I must take care it is not too far from—what call you the place?"

"Tergou, madam."

"A priest gives up much," continued the Countess; "often, I fear, he learns too late how much." And her woman's eye rested a moment on Gerard with mild pity and half surprise at his resigning her sex, and all that Heaven they can bestow, and the great parental joys. "At least you shall be near your friends. Have you a mother?"

"Yes, madam, thanks be to God!"

"Good! You shall have a church near Tergou. She will thank me. And now, sir, we must not detain you too long from those who have a better claim on your society than we have. Duchess, oblige me by bidding one of the pages conduct him to the hall of banquet. The way is hard to find."

Gerard bowed low to the Countess and the Princess and backed toward the door.

"I hope it will be a nice benefice," said the Princess to him with a pretty smile as he was going out; then, shaking her head with an air of solemn misgiving, "But you had better have been Bishop of Liége."

Gerard followed his new conductor, his heart warm with gratitude; but ere he reached the banquet hall a chill came over him. The mind of one who has led a quiet, uneventful life is not apt to take in contradictory feelings at the same moment and balance them, but rather to be overpowered by each in turn. While Gerard was with the Countess, the excitement of so new a situation, the unlooked-for promise, the joy and pride it would cause at home, possessed him wholly. But now it was passion's turn to be heard again. What, give up Margaret, whose soft hand he still felt in his, and her deep eyes in his heart? Resign her and all the world of love and joy she had opened on him today? The revulsion, when it did come, was so strong that he hastily resolved to say nothing at home about the offered benefice.

"The Countess is so good," thought he. "She has a hundred ways of aiding a young man's fortune. She will not compel me to be a priest when she shall learn I love one of her sex—one would almost think she does know it, for she cast a strange look on me and said, 'A priest gives up much, too much.' I dare say she will give me a place about the palace."

And with this hopeful reflection his mind was eased and, being now at the entrance of the banqueting hall, he thanked his conductor and ran hastily with joyful eyes to Margaret. He came in sight of her table—she was gone. Peter was gone too. Nobody was at the table at all—only a citizen in sober garments had just tumbled under it dead drunk, and several persons were raising him to carry him away. Gerard never guessed how important this solemn drunkard was to him. He was looking for "Beauty," and let the "Beast" lie. He ran wildly round the hall, which was now comparatively empty. She was not there. He left the palace. Outside he found a crowd gaping at two great fanlights just lighted over the gate. He asked them earnestly if they had seen an old man in a gown and a lovely girl pass out. They laughed at the question. They were staring at these new lights that turn night into day. They didn't trouble their heads about old men and young wenches, everyday sights. From another group he learned there was a Mystery being played under canvas hard by, and all the world gone to see it. This revived his hopes, and he went and saw the Mystery. Margaret was nowhere in the crowd, and Gerard could not enjoy the performance. He actually went away in Act 2, in the midst of a much-admired piece of dialogue in which Justice outquibbled Satan. He walked through many streets, but could not find her he sought. At last, fairly worn out, he went to a hostelry and slept till daybreak.

All that day, heavy and heartsick, he sought her, but could never fall in with her or her father, nor ever obtain the slightest clue. Then he felt she was false, or had changed her mind. He was irritated now, as well as sad. More good fortune fell on him; he almost hated it. At last, on the third day, after he had once more been through every street, he said: "She is not in the town, and I shall never see her again. I will go home." He started for Tergou with a royal favor promised, with fifteen golden angels in his purse, a golden medal on his bosom, and a heart like a lump of lead.

CHAPTER IV

IT WAS near four o'clock in the afternoon. Eli was in the shop. His eldest and youngest sons were abroad. Catherine and her little crippled daughter had long been anxious about Gerard, and now they were gone a little way down the road, to see if by good luck he might be visible in the distance. Giles was alone in the sitting-room, which I will sketch, furniture and dwarf included.

The Hollanders were always an original and leading people. They claim to have invented printing (wooden type), oil painting, liberty, banking, gardening, and so on. Above all, years before my tale, they invented cleanliness. So while the English gentry, in velvet jerkins, and chicken-toed shoes, trod floors of stale rushes, foul receptacle of bones, decomposing morsels, spittle, dogs' eggs, and all abominations, this hosier's sitting-room at Tergou was floored with Dutch tiles so highly glazed and constantly washed that you could eat off them. There was one large window; the cross stonework in the center of it was very massive, and stood in relief, looking like an actual cross to the inmates, and was eyed as such in their devotions. The panes were very small and lozenge-shaped, and soldered to one another with strips of lead—the like you may see to this day in our rural cottages.

The chairs were rude and primitive, all but the armchair, whose back, at right angles with its seat, was so high that the sitter's head stopped two feet short of the top. This chair was of oak and carved at the summit. There was a copper pail that went in at the waist holding holy water; and a little hand besom to sprinkle it far and wide; and a long, narrow but massive oak table, and a dwarf sticking to its rim by his teeth, his eyes glaring, and his claws in the air like a pouncing vampire. His center was anything but his center of gravity. Bisected, upper Giles would have outweighed three lower Giles.

But this very disproportion enabled him to do feats that would have baffled Milo. His brawny arms had no weight to draw after them, so he could go up a vertical pole like a squirrel, and hang for hours from a bough by one hand, like a cherry by its stalk. If he could have made a vacuum with his hands, as the lizard is said to do with its feet, he would have gone along a ceiling. Now this pocket athlete was insanely fond of gripping the dinner table with both hands, and so swinging, and then—climax of delight!—he would seize it with his teeth, and taking off his hands, hold on like grim death by his huge ivories.

But all our joys, however elevating, suffer interruption. Little Kate caught

Sampsonet in this posture, and stood aghast. She was her mother's daughter, and her heart was with the furniture, not with the 12mo gymnast.

"Oh, Giles, how can you? Mother is at hand. It dents the table."

"Go and tell her, little talebearer," snarled Giles. "You are the one for making mischief."

"Am I?" inquired Kate calmly. "That is news to me."

"The biggest in Tergou," growled Giles, fastening on again.

"Oh, indeed?" said Kate dryly.

This piece of unwonted satire launched, and Giles not visibly blasted, she sat down quietly and cried. Her mother came in almost at that moment, and Giles hurled himself under the table, and there glared.

"What is to do now?" said the dame, sharply. Then, turning her experienced eye from Kate to Giles and observing the position he had taken up, and a sheepish expression, she hinted at cuffing of ears.

"Nay, Mother," said the girl, "it was but a foolish word Giles spoke. I had not noticed it at another time, but I was tired and in care for Gerard, you know."

"Let no one be in care for me," said a faint voice at the door, and in tottered Gerard, pale, dusty, and worn-out; and amidst uplifted hands and cries of delight, curiosity, and anxiety mingled, dropped exhausted into the nearest chair.

Beating Rotterdam like a covert for Margaret, and the long journey afterward, had fairly knocked Gerard up. But elastic youth soon revived, and behold him the center of an eager circle. First of all they must hear about the prizes. Then Gerard told them he had been admitted to see the competitors' works all laid out in an enormous hall before the judges pronounced.

"Oh, Mother! oh, Kate, when I saw the goldsmith's work, I had like to have fallen on the floor. I had thought not all the goldsmiths on earth had so much gold, silver, jewels, and craft of design and facture. But in sooth all the arts are divine."

Then, to please the females, he described to them the reliquaries, feretories, chalices, crosiers, crosses, pyxes, monstrances, and other wonders ecclesiastical, and the goblets, hanaps, watches, clocks, chains, brooches, and so on, so that their mouths watered.

"But, Kate, when I came to the illuminated work from Ghent and Bruges, my heart sank. Mine was dirt by the side of it. For the first minute I could almost have cried; but I prayed for a better spirit, and presently I was able to enjoy them, and thank God for those lovely works and for those skillful, patient craftsmen, whom I own my masters. Well, the colored work was so beautiful I forgot all about the black-and-white. But next day, when all the other prizes had been given, they came to the writing, and whose name think you was called first?"

"Yours," said Kate.

The others laughed her to scorn.

"You may well laugh," said Gerard, "but for all that Gerard Eliassoen of Tergou was the name the herald shouted. I stood stupid; they thrust me forward. Everything swam before my eyes. I found myself kneeling on a cushion at the feet of the Duke. He said something to me, but I was so fluttered I could not answer him. So then he put his hand to his side and did not draw a glaive and cut off my dull head, but gave me a gold medal, and there it is." There was a yell and almost a scramble. "And then he gave me fifteen great bright golden angels. I had seen one before, but I never handled one. Here they are."

"Oh, Gerard! oh, Gerard!"

"There is one for you, our eldest; and one for you Sybrandt, and for you, Little Mischief; and two for thee, Little Lily, because God hath afflicted thee; and one for myself to buy colors and vellum; and nine for her that nursed us all and risked the two crowns upon poor Gerard's hand."

The gold drew out their characters. Cornelis and Sybrandt clutched each his coin with one glare of greediness and another glare of envy at Kate who had got two pieces. Giles seized his and rolled it along the floor and gamboled after it. Kate put down her crutches and sat down and held out her little arms to Gerard with a heavenly gesture of love and tenderness; and the mother, fairly benumbed at first by the shower of gold that fell on her apron, now cried out: "Leave kissing him, Kate, he is my son, not yours. Ah, Gerard, my boy! I have not loved you as you deserved." Then Gerard threw himself on his knees beside her, and she flung her arms round him and wept for joy and pride upon his neck.

"Good lad! Good lad!" cried the hosier, with some emotion. "I must go and tell the neighbors. Lend me the medal, Gerard. I'll show it my good friend Peter Buyskens. He is ever regaling me with how his son Jorian won the tin mug a-shooting at the butts."

"Ay, do, my man, and show Peter Buyskens one of the angels. Tell him there are fourteen more where that came from. Mind you bring it me back!"

"Stay a minute, Father, there is better news behind," said Gerard, flushing with joy at the joy he caused.

"Better! Better than this?"

Then Gerard told his interview with the Countess, and the house rang with joy.

"Now God bless the good lady and bless the Dame Van Eyck! A benefice? Our son! My cares are at an end. Eli, my good friend and master, now we two can die happy whenever our time comes. This dear boy will take our place, and none of these loved ones will want a home or friend."

From that hour Gerard was looked upon as the stay of the family. He was a son apart, but in another sense. He was always in the right, and nothing was too good for him. Cornelis and Sybrandt became more and more jealous of him, and longed for the day he should go to his benefice. They would get rid of the favorite, and His Reverence's purse would be open to them. With these views he co-operated. The wound love had given him throbbed duller and duller. His success and the affection and admiration of his parents made him think more highly of himself, and resent with more spirit Margaret's ingratitude and discourtesy.

For all that, she had power to cool him toward the rest of her sex, and now for every reason he wished to be ordained priest as soon as he could pass the intermediate orders. He knew the Vulgate already better than most of the clergy, and studied the rubric and the dogmas of the Church with his friends the monks; and, the first time the Bishop came that way, he applied to be admitted "exorcist," the third step in holy orders. The Bishop questioned him, and ordained him at once. He had to kneel, and after a short prayer, the Bishop delivered to him a little MS. full of exorcisms, and said: "Take this, Gerard, and have power to lay hands on the possessed, whether baptized or catechumens!" And he took it reverently, and went home invested by the Church with power to cast out demons.

Returning home from the church, he was met by Little Kate on her crutches.

"Oh, Gerard! Who think you hath sent to our house seeking you?—the Burgomaster himself."

"Ghysbrecht van Swieten? What would he with me?"

"Nay, Gerard, I know not. But he seems urgent to see you. You are to go to his house on the instant."

"Well, he is the Burgomaster. I will go, but it likes me not. Kate, I have seen him cast such a look on me as no friend casts. No matter; such looks forewarn the wise. To be sure, he knows—"

"Knows what, Gerard?"

"Nothing."

"Nothing?"

"Kate, I'll go."

CHAPTER V

GHYSBRECHT VAN SWIETEN was an artful man. He opened on the novice with something quite wide of the mark he was really aiming at. "The town records," said he, "are crabbedly written, and the ink is rusty with age." He offered Gerard the honor of transcribing them fair. Gerard inquired what he was to be paid. Ghysbrecht offered a sum that would have just purchased the pens, ink, and parchment.

"But, Burgomaster, my labor? Here is a year's work."

"Your labor? Call you marking parchment labor? Little sweat goes to that, I trow."

" 'Tis labor, and skilled labor to boot; and that is better paid in all crafts than rude labor, sweat or no sweat. Beside, there's my time."

"Your time? Why, what is time to you, at two-and-twenty?" Then, fixing his eyes keenly on Gerard, to mark the effect of his words, he said: "Say rather, you are idle grown. You are in love. Your body is with these chanting monks, but your heart is with Peter Brandt and his red-haired girl."

"I know no Peter Brandt."

This denial confirmed Ghysbrecht's suspicion that the caster-out of demons was playing a deep game.

"Ye lie!" he shouted. "Did I not find you at her elbow on the road to Rotterdam?"

"Ah!"

"Ah. And you were seen at Sevenbergen but t'other day."

"Was I?"

"Ay; and at Peter's house."

"At Sevenbergen?"

"Ay, at Sevenbergen."

Now this was what in modern days is called a draw. It was a guess, put boldly forth as fact, to elicit by the young man's answer whether he had been there lately or not. The result of the artifice surprised the crafty one. Gerard started up in a strange state of nervous excitement. "Burgomaster," said he, with trembling voice, "I have not been at Sevenbergen this three years, and I knew not the name of those you saw me with, nor where they dwelt; but as my time is precious, though you value it not, give you good day."

And he darted out with his eyes sparkling. Ghysbrecht started up in huge ire; but he sank into his chair again.

"He fears me not. He knows something, if not all." Then he called hastily to his trusty servant, and almost dragged him to a window.

"See you yon man?" he cried. "Haste! Follow him! But let him not see you. He is young, but old in craft. Keep him in sight all day. Let me know whither he goes and what he does."

It was night when the servant returned.

"Well? Well?" cried Van Swieten, eagerly.

"Master, the young man went from you to Sevenbergen." Ghysbrecht groaned. "To the house of Peter the Magician."

CHAPTER VI

HALFWAY to Sevenbergen Gerard looked into his own heart and asked it why he was going to Sevenbergen. His heart replied without a moment's hesitation: "We are going out of curiosity to know why she jilted us, and to show her it has not broken our hearts, and that we are quite content with our honors and our benefice in prospectu, and don't want her nor any of her fickle sex."

He soon found out Peter Brandt's cottage, and there sat a girl in the doorway, plying her needle, and a stalwart figure leaned on a long bow and talked to her. Gerard felt an unaccountable pang at the sight of him. However, the man turned out to be past fifty years of age, an old soldier whom Gerard remembered to have seen shoot at the butts with admirable force and skill. Another minute and the youth stood before them. Margaret looked up and dropped her work, and uttered a faint cry, and was white and red by turns. But these signs of emotion were swiftly dismissed, and she turned far more chill and indifferent than she would if she had not betrayed this agitation.

"What! Is it you, Master Gerard? What on earth brings you here, I wonder?"

"I was passing by and saw you, so I thought I would give you good day and ask after your father."

"My father is well. He will be here anon."

"Then I may as well stay till he comes."

"As you will. Good Martin, step into the village and tell my father here is a friend of his."

"And not of yours?"

"My father's friends are mine."

"That is doubtful. It was not like a friend to promise to wait for me, and then make off the moment my back was turned. Cruel Margaret! You little know how I searched the town for you, how for want of you nothing was pleasant to me."

"These are idle words. If you had desired my father's company, or mine, you would have come back. There I had a bed laid for you, sir, at my cousin's, and he would have made much of you, and, who knows? I might have made much of you too. I was in the humor that day. You will not catch me in the same mind again, neither you nor any young man, I warrant me."

"Margaret, I came back the moment the Countess let me go, but you were not there."

"Nay, you did not, or you had seen Hans Cloterman at our table. We left him to bring you on."

"I saw no one there, but only a drunken man that had just tumbled down."

"At our table? How was he clad?"

"Nay, I took little heed—in sad-colored garb."

At this Margaret's face gradually warmed; but presently, assuming incredulity and severity, she put many shrewd questions, all of which Gerard answered most loyally. Finally the clouds cleared, and they guessed how the misunderstanding had come about. Then came a revulsion of tenderness, all the more powerful that they had done each other wrong; and then, more dangerous still, came mutual confessions. Neither had been happy since, neither ever would have been happy but for this fortunate meeting.

And Gerard found a MS. Vulgate lying open on the table and pounced upon it like a hawk—MSS. were his delight. But before he could get to it two white hands quickly came flat upon the page, and a red face over them.

"Nay, take away your hands, Margaret, that I may see where you are reading, and I will read there too at home; so shall my soul meet yours in the sacred page. You will not? Nay, then I must kiss them away." And he kissed them so often that for very shame they were fain to withdraw, and, lo! the sacred book lay open at

An apple of gold in a network of silver.

"There, now," said she, "I had been hunting for it ever so long, and found it but even now—and to be caught!" and with a touch of inconsistency she pointed it out to Gerard with her white finger.

"Ay," said he, "but today it is all hidden in that great cap."

"It is a comely cap, I'm told by some."

"Maybe, but what it hides is beautiful."

"It is not—it is hideous."

"Well, it was beautiful at Rotterdam."

"Ay, everything was beautiful that day"—— with a little sigh.

And now Peter came in and welcomed Gerard cordially, and would have him stay to supper. And Margaret disappeared; and Gerard had a nice learned chat with Peter; and Margaret reappeared with her hair in a silver net, and shot a glance half-arch half-coy, and glided about them, and spread supper, and beamed bright with gaiety and happiness. And in the cool evening Gerard coaxed her out, and she objected, and came; and coaxed her on to the road to Tergou, and she declined, and came, and there they strolled up and down, hand in hand. And when he must go they pledged each other never to quarrel or misunderstand one another again; and they sealed the promise with a long loving kiss, and Gerard went home on wings.

From that day Gerard spent most of his evenings with Margaret, and the attachment deepened and deepened on both sides till the hours they spent together were the hours they lived; the rest they counted and underwent. And at the outset of this deep attachment all went smoothly. Obstacles there were, but they seemed distant and small to the eyes of hope, youth, and love. The feelings and passions of so many persons that this attachment would thwart gave no warning smoke to show their volcanic nature and power.

The course of true love ran smoothly, placidly, until it had drawn these two young hearts into its current for ever.

And then—

CHAPTER VII

One bright morning unwonted velvet shone, unwonted feathers waved, and horses' hoofs glinted and rang through the streets of Tergou, and the windows and balconies were studded with wondering faces. The French Ambassador was riding through to sport in the neighboring forest.

Besides his own suite, he was attended by several servants of the Duke of Burgundy, lent to do him honor and minister to his pleasure. The Duke's tumbler rode before him with a grave, sedate majesty that made his more noble companions seem light, frivolous persons. But ever and anon, when respect and awe neared the oppressive, he rolled off his horse so ignobly and funnily that even the Ambassador was fain to burst out laughing. He also climbed up again by the tail in a way provocative of mirth, and so he played his part. Toward the rear of the pageant rode one that excited more attention still—the Duke's leopard. A huntsman mounted on a Flemish horse of prodigious size and power carried a long box fastened to the rider's loins by straps curiously contrived, and on this box sat a bright leopard crouching. She was chained to the huntsman. The people admired her glossy hide and spots, and pressed near, and one or two were for feeling her, and pulling her tail. Then the huntsman shouted in a terrible voice, "Beware! At Antwerp one did but throw a handful of dust at her, and the Duke made dust of him."

"Gramercy!"

"I speak sooth. The good Duke shut him up in prison, in a cell under ground, and the rats cleaned the flesh off his bones in a night. Served him right for molesting the poor thing."

There was a murmur of fear, and the Tergovians shrank from tickling the leopard of their sovereign. But an incident followed that raised their spirits again. The Duke's giant, a Hungarian seven feet four inches high, brought up the rear. This enormous creature had, like some other giants, a treble, fluty voice of little power. He was a vain fellow, and not conscious of this nor any defect. Now it happened he caught sight of Giles sitting on top of the balcony, so he stopped and began to make fun of him.

"Hallo, Brother!" squeaked he. "I had nearly passed without seeing thee."

"*You* are plain enough to see," bellowed Giles in his bass tones.

"Come on my shoulder, Brother," squeaked Titan, and held out a shoulder of mutton fist to help him down.

"If I do I'll cuff your ears," roared the dwarf.

The giant saw the homuncule was irascible, and played upon him, being encouraged thereto by the shouts of laughter. For he did not see that the people were laughing not at his wit, but at the ridiculous incongruity of the two voices—the gigantic feeble fife, and the petty, deep, loud drum, the mountain delivered of a squeak and the molehill belching thunder.

The singular duet came to as singular an end. Giles lost all patience and self-command, and being a creature devoid of fear, and in a rage to boot, he actually dropped upon the giant's neck, seized his hair with one hand, and punched his head with the other. The giant's first impulse was to laugh, but the weight and rapidity of the blows soon corrected that inclination.

"He, he! Ah, ah! Hallo! Oh, oh! Holy saints! Here! Help, or I must throttle the imp. I can't! I'll split your skull against the——" And he made a wild run backwards at the balcony. Giles saw his danger, seized the balcony in time with both hands, and whipped over it just as the giant's head came against it with a stunning crack. The people roared with laughter and exultation at the address of their little champion. The indignant giant seized two of the laughers, knocked them together like dumbbells, shook them and strewed them flat—(Catherine shrieked and threw her apron over Giles)— then strode wrathfully away after the party.

This incident had consequences no one then present foresaw. Its immediate results were agreeable. The Tergovians turned proud of Giles, and listened with more affability to his prayers for parchment. For he drove a regular trade with his brother Gerard in this article. Went about and begged it gratis, and Gerard gave him coppers for it.

On the afternoon of the same day, Catherine and her daughter were chatting together about their favorite theme, Gerard—his goodness, his benefice, and the brightened prospects of the whole family. Their good luck had come to them in the very shape they would have chosen; besides the advantages of a benefice such as the Countess Charolois would not disdain to give, there was the feminine delight at having a priest, a holy man, in their own family. "He will marry Cornelis, and Sybrandt: for they can wed (good housewives) now if they will. Gerard will take care of you and Giles when we are gone."

"Yes, Mother, and we can confess to him instead of to a stranger," said Kate.

"Ay, girl! and he can give the sacred oil to your father and me, and close our eyes when our time comes."

"Oh, Mother, not for many, many years I do pray Heaven! Pray speak not of that, it always makes me sad. I hope to go before you, Mother dear. No, let us be gay today. I am out of pain, Mother, quite out of all pain. It does seem so strange, and I feel so bright and happy, that—Mother, can you keep a secret?"

"Nobody better, child. Why, you know I can."

"Then I will show you something so beautiful. You never saw the like, I trow. Only Gerard must never know; for sure he means to surprise us with it—he covers it up so, and sometimes he carries it away altogether."

Kate took her crutches and moved slowly away, leaving her mother in an exalted state of curiosity. She soon returned with something in a cloth, uncovered it, and there was a lovely picture of the Virgin, with all her insignia and wearing her tiara over a wealth of beautiful hair, which flowed loose over her shoulders. Catherine at first was struck with awe.

"It is herself!" she cried. "It is the Queen of Heaven. I never saw one like her to my mind before."

"And her eyes, Mother—lifted to the sky, as if they belonged there, and not to a mortal creature. And her beautiful hair of burning gold."

"And to think I have a son that can make the saints live again upon a piece of wood!"

"The reason is, he is a young saint himself, Mother. He is too good for this world. He is here to portray the blessed, and then to go away and be with them forever."

Ere they had half done admiring it, a strange voice was heard at the door. By one of the furtive instincts of their sex they hastily hid the picture in the cloth, though there was no need. And the next moment in came, casting his eyes furtively around, a man that had not entered the house this ten years—Ghysbrecht van Swieten. The two women were so taken by surprise that they merely stared at him and at one another, and said, "The Burgomaster!" in a tone so expressive that Ghysbrecht felt compelled to answer it.

"Yes! I own the last time I came here was not on a friendly errand. Men love their own interest—Eli's and mine were contrary. Well, let this visit atone for the last. Today I come on your business, and none of mine."

Catherine and her daughter exchanged a swift glance of contemptuous incredulity. They knew the man better than he thought.

"It is about your son Gerard."

"Ay! ay! You want him to work for the town all for nothing. He told us."

"I come on no such errand. It is to let you know he has fallen into bad hands."

"Now Heaven and the saints forbid! Man, torture not a mother! Speak out, and quickly. Speak ere you have time to coin a falsehood—we know thee."

Ghysbrecht turned pale at this affront, and spite mingled with the other motives that brought him here. "Thus it is, then," said he, grinding his teeth and speaking very fast. "Your son Gerard is more like to be the father of a family than a priest. He is forever with Margaret, Peter Brandt's red-haired girl, and he loves her like a cow her calf."

Mother and daughter both burst out laughing. Ghysbrecht stared at them. "What, you knew it?"

"Carry this tale to those who know not my son Gerard. Women are naught to him."

"Other women, mayhap. But this one is the apple of his eye to him, or will be if you part them not, and soon. Come, dame, make me not waste time and friendly counsel. My servant has seen them together a score of times, handed, and reading babies in one another's eyes like—you know, dame—you have been young too."

"Girl, I am ill at ease. Yea, I have been young, and know how blind and foolish the young are. My heart! He has turned me sick in a moment. Kate, if it should be true."

"Nay, nay!" cried Kate eagerly. "Gerard might love a young woman. All young men do—I can't find what they see in them to love so—but if he did he would let us know, he would not deceive us. You wicked man! No, dear Mother, look not so! Gerard is too good to love a creature of earth. His love is for our Lady and the saints. Ah! I will show you the picture—there. If his heart was earthly, could he paint the Queen of Heaven like that —look! look!" and she held the picture out triumphantly, and more radiant and beautiful in this moment of enthusiasm than ever dead picture was or will be, overpowered the Burgomaster with her eloquence and her feminine proof of Gerard's purity. His eyes and mouth opened, and remained open, in which state they kept turning, face and all, as if on a pivot, from the picture to the women and from the women to the picture.

"Why, it is herself," he gasped.

"Isn't it?" cried Kate, and her hostility was softened. "You admire it? I forgive you for frightening us."

"Am I in a madhouse?" said Ghysbrecht van Swieten, thoroughly puzzled. "You show me a picture of the girl, and you say he painted it, and that is proof he cannot love her. Why, they all paint their sweethearts, painters do."

"A picture of the girl?" exclaimed Kate, shocked. "Fie! This is no girl, this is our Blessed Lady."

"No, no—it is Margaret Brandt."

"Oh, blind! It is the Queen of Heaven."

"No, only of Sevenbergen village."

"Profane man! Behold her crown!"

"Silly child! Look at her red hair! Would the Virgin be seen in red hair? She who had the pick of all the colors ten thousand years before the world began?"

At this moment an anxious face was insinuated round the edge of the open door. It was their neighbor Peter Buyskens.

"What is to do?" said he in a cautious whisper. "We can hear you all across the street. What on earth is to do?"

"Oh, neighbor! What is to do? Why here is the Burgomaster blackening our Gerard."

"Stop!" cried Van Swieten. "Peter Buyskens is come in the nick of time. He knows father and daughter both. They cast their glamour on him."

"What, is she a witch, too?"

"Else the egg takes not after the bird. Why is her father called the magician? I tell you they bewitched this very Peter here; they cast unholy spells on him, and cured him of the colic. Now, Peter, look and tell me, who is that? And you be silent, women, for a moment, if you can. Who is it, Peter?"

"Well, to be sure!" said Peter in reply, and his eye seemed fascinated by the picture.

"Who is it?" repeated Ghysbrecht impetuously.

Peter Buyskens smiled. "Why, you know as well as I do; but what have they put a crown on her for? I never saw her in a crown, for my part."

"Man alive! Can't you open your great jaws and just speak a wench's name plain out to oblige three people?"

"I'd do a great deal more to oblige one of you than that, Burgomaster. If it isn't as natural as life!"

"Curse the man! He won't, he won't—curse him!"

"Why, what have I done now?"

"Oh, sir!" said Little Kate, "for pity's sake tell us—are these the features of a living woman, of—of—Margaret Brandt?"

"A mirror is not truer, my little maid."

"But is it she, sir, for very certain?"

"Why, who else should it be?"

"Now why couldn't you say so at once?" snarled Ghysbrecht.

"I did say so, as plain as I could speak," snapped Peter; and they growled over this small bone of contention so zealously that they did not see Catherine and her daughter had thrown their aprons over their heads, and were rocking to and fro in deep distress. The next moment Elias came in from the shop and stood aghast. Catherine, though her face was covered, knew his footstep.

"This is my poor man," she sobbed. "Tell him, good Peter Buyskens, for I have not the courage."

Elias turned pale. The presence of the Burgomaster in his house after so many years of coolness, coupled with his wife's and daughter's distress, made him fear some heavy misfortune.

"Richart! Jacob!" he gasped.

"No! No!" said the Burgomaster. "It is nearer home, and nobody is dead or dying, old friend."

"God bless you, Burgomaster! Ah, something is gone off my breast that was like to choke me. Now, what is the matter?"

Ghysbrecht then told him all that he told the women, and showed the picture in evidence.

"Is that all?" said Eli, profoundly relieved. "What are ye roaring and bellowing for? It is vexing, it is angering, but it is not like death nor even sickness. Boys will be boys. He will outgrow that disease—'tis but skin-deep."

But when Ghysbrecht told him that Margaret was a girl of good character, that it was not to be supposed she would be so intimate if marriage had not been spoken of between them, his brow darkened.

"Marriage? That shall never be," said he sternly. "I'll stay that, ay, by force if need be, as I would his hand lifted to cut his throat. I'd do what old John Koestein did t'other day."

"And what is that, in heaven's name?" asked the mother, suddenly removing her apron.

It was the Burgomaster who replied:

"He made me shut young Albert Koestein up in the prison of the Stadthouse till he knocked under—it was not long. Forty-eight hours all alone, on bread and water, cooled his hot stomach. 'Tell my father I am his humble servant,' says he, 'and let me into the sun once more—the sun is worth all the wenches in the world.'"

"Oh, the cruelty of men!" sighed Catherine.

"As to that, the Burgomaster has no choice. It is the law. And if a father says, 'Burgomaster, lock up my son,' he must do it. A fine thing it would be if a father might not lock up his own son."

"Well, well! It won't come to that with me and my son. He never disobeyed me in his life; he never shall. Where is he? It is past suppertime. Where is he, Kate?"

"Alas, I know not, Father."

"I know," said Ghysbrecht. "He is at Sevenbergen. My servant met him on the road."

Supper passed in gloomy silence. Evening descended—no Gerard. Eight o'clock came—no Gerard. Then the father sent all to bed except Catherine.

"You and I will walk abroad, wife, and talk over this new care."

"Abroad, my man, at this time? Whither?"

"Why, on the road to Sevenbergen."

"Oh, no, no hasty words, Father. Poor Gerard! He never vexed you before."

"Fear not. But it must end, and I am not one that trusts tomorrow with today's work."

The old pair sauntered on a long time in silence. The night was clear and balmy. The moon was bright, but they were in the shadow of some trees and their son did not see them. He came singing in the moonlight, and his face shining.

CHAPTER VIII

WHILE the Burgomaster was exposing Gerard at Tergou, Margaret had a trouble of her own at Sevenbergen. It was a housewife's distress, but deeper than we can well conceive. She came to Martin Wittenhaagen, the old soldier, with tears in her eyes.

"Martin, there's nothing in the house, and Gerard is coming, and he is so thoughtless. He forgets to sup at home. When he gives over work, then he runs to me straight, poor soul, and often he comes quite faint. And to think I have nothing to set before my servant that loves me so dear."

Martin scratched his head. "What can I do?"

"It is Thursday. It is your day to shoot—sooth to say, I counted on you today."

"Nay," said the soldier, "I may not shoot when the Duke or his friends are at the chase—read else. I am no scholar." And he took out of his pouch a parchment with a grand seal. It purported to be a stipend and a license given by Philip Duke of Burgundy to Martin Wittenhaagen, one of his archers, in return for services in the wars, and for a wound received at the Duke's side. The stipend was four marks yearly to be paid by the Duke's almoner, and the license was to shoot three arrows once a week, viz., on Thursday, and no other day, in any of the Duke's forests in Holland, at any game but a seven-year-old buck or a doe carrying fawn; proviso, that the Duke should not be hunting on that day, or any of his friends. In this case Martin was not to go and disturb the woods on peril of his salary, and his head, and a fine of a penny. Margaret sighed and was silent.

"Come, cheer up, mistress," said he. "For your sake I'll peril my carcass. I have done that for many a one that was not worth your forefinger. It is no such mighty risk, either. I'll but step into the skirts of the forest here. It is odds but they drive a hare or a fawn within reach of my arrow."

"Well, if I let you go you must promise me not to go far, and not to be seen. Far better Gerard went supperless than ill should come to you, faithful Martin."

The required promise given, Martin took his bow and three arrows, and stole cautiously into the wood—it was scarce a furlong distant. The horns were heard faintly in the distance, and all the game was afoot. "Come," thought Martin, "I shall soon fill the pot and no one be the wiser." He took his stand behind a thick oak that commanded a view of an open glade, and strung his bow, a truly formidable weapon. It was of English yew, six feet two inches high, and thick in proportion: and Martin, broad-chested, with arms all iron and cord, and used to the bow from infancy, could draw a three-foot arrow to the head, and when it flew, the eye could scarce follow it, and the bowstring twanged as musical as a harp.

Presently he heard a bustle behind him, and turned round just in time to see a noble buck cross the open, but too late to shoot at him. At that moment a long, spotted animal glided swiftly across after the deer; its belly seemed to touch the ground as it went. Martin recognized the Duke's leopard. "The hunters will not be far from her," said he, "and I must not be seen. Gerard must go supperless this night."

He plunged into the wood, following the buck and leopard, for that was his way home. He had not gone far when he heard an unusual sound ahead of him—leaves rustling violently, and the ground trampled. He hurried in the direction. He found the leopard on the buck's back, tearing him with teeth and claw, and the buck running in a circle and bounding convulsively, with the blood pouring down his hide. Then Martin formed a desperate resolution to have the venison for Margaret. He drew his arrow to the head and buried it in the deer, who, spite of the creature on his back, bounded high into the air, and fell dead. The leopard went on tearing him as if nothing had happened.

Martin hoped that the creature would gorge itself with blood, and then let him take the meat. He waited some minutes, then walked resolutely up, and laid his hand on the buck's leg. The leopard gave a frightful growl, and left off sucking blood, flew at his head with a frightful yell, flaming eyes, and jaws and claws distended. He had but just time to catch her by the throat before her teeth could crush his face. One of her claws seized his shoulder and rent it, the other, aimed at his cheek, would have been more deadly still but Martin was old-fashioned, and wore no hat, but a scapulary of the same stuff as his jerkin, and this scapulary he had brought over his head like a hood; the brute's claw caught in the loose leather. Martin kept her teeth off his face with great difficulty, and gripped her throat fiercely, and she kept rending his shoulder. It was like blunt reaping hooks grinding and tearing. The pain was fearful; but instead of cowing the old soldier, it put his blood up, and he gnashed his teeth with rage almost as fierce as hers, and squeezed her neck with iron force.

The two pairs of eyes flared at one another—and now the man's were almost as furious as the brute's. She found he was throttling her, and made a wild attempt to free herself, in which she dragged his cowl all over his face and blinded him, and tore her claw out of his shoulder, flesh and all. But still he throttled her with hand and arm of iron. Presently her long tail, that was high in the air, went down. "Aha!" cried Martin, joyfully, and gripped her like death; next, her body lost its elasticity, and he held a choked and powerless thing. He gripped it till all motion ceased, then dashed it to the earth; then, panting, removed his cowl.

The leopard lay mute at his feet with tongue protruding and bloody paw, and for the first time terror fell on Martin. "I am a dead man. I have slain the Duke's leopard." He hastily seized a few handfuls of leaves and threw them over her, then shouldered the buck and staggered away, leaving a trail of blood all the way—his own and the buck's. He burst into Peter's house a horrible figure, bleeding and bloodstained, and flung the deer's carcass down.

"There, no questions," said he. "But broil me a steak on't, for I am faint."

Margaret did not see he was wounded. She thought the blood was all from the deer. She busied herself at the fire, and the stout soldier stanched and bound his own wound apart, and soon he and Gerard and Margaret were supping royally on broiled venison.

They were very merry. Gerard, with wonderful thoughtfulness, had brought a flask of Schiedam, and under its influence Martin revived, and told them how the venison was got; and they all made merry over the exploit. Their mirth was strangely interrupted. Margaret's eye became fixed and fascinated, and her cheek pale with fear. She gasped, and could not speak, but pointed to the window with trembling finger. Their eyes followed hers, and there in the twilight crouched a dark form with eyes like glowworms.

It was the leopard. While they stood petrified, fascinated by the eyes of green fire, there sounded in the wood a single deep bay. Martin trembled at it.

"They have lost her, and laid muzzled bloodhounds on her scent. They will find her here, and the venison. Good-by, friends. Martin Wittenhaagen ends here."

Gerard seized his bow and put it into the soldier's hands.

"Be a man!" he cried. "Shoot her, and fling her into the wood ere they come up. Who will know?"

More voices of hounds broke out, and nearer.

"Curse her!" cried Martin. "I spared her once. Now she must die, or I, or both, more likely." And he reared his bow and drew his arrow to the head.

"Nay, nay!" cried Margaret, and seized the arrow. It broke in half; the pieces fell on each side of the bow. The air at the same time filled with the tongues of the hounds. They were hot upon the scent.

"What have you done, wench? You have put the halter round my throat."

"No!" cried Margaret. "I have saved you. Stand back from the window, both! Your knife, quick!"

She seized his long-pointed knife, almost tore it out of his girdle, and darted from the room. The house was now surrounded with baying dogs and shouting men. The glowworm eyes moved not.

CHAPTER IX

MARGARET cut off a huge piece of venison, and ran to the window, and threw
it out to the green eyes of fire. They darted on it with a savage snarl, and
there was a sound of rending and crunching. At this moment a hound
uttered a bay so near and loud it rang through the house, and the three at
the window shrank together. Then the leopard feared for her supper, and
glided swiftly and stealthily away with it toward the woods, and the very
next moment horses and men and dogs came helter-skelter past the window,
and followed her full-cry. Martin and his companions breathed again. The
leopard was swift and would not be caught within a league of their house.
They grasped hands. Margaret seized this opportunity and cried a little.
Gerard kissed the tears away. To table once more and Gerard drank to
woman's wit.

"'Tis stronger than man's force," said he.

"Ay," said Margaret, "when those she loves are in danger, not else."

Tonight Gerard stayed with her longer than usual, and went home
prouder than ever of her, and happy as a prince. Some little distance from
home, under the shadow of some trees, he encountered two figures: they
almost barred his way. It was his father and mother. Out so late—what could
be the cause? A chill fell on him. He stopped and looked at them. They
stood grim and silent. He stammered out some word of inquiry.

"Why ask?" said his father. "You know why we are here."

"Oh, Gerard!" said his mother, with a voice full of reproach and yet of
affection.

Gerard's heart quaked. He was silent. Then his father pitied his confusion,
and said to him:

"Nay, you need not to hang your head. You are not the first young fool
that has been caught by a red cheek and a pair of blue eyes."

"Nay, nay!" put in Catherine. "It was witchcraft. Peter the Magician is
well known for that."

"Come, Sir Priest," resumed his father, "you know you must not meddle
with womenfolk. But give us your promise to go no more to Sevenbergen
and here all ends. We won't be hard on you for one fault."

"I cannot promise that, Father."

"Not promise it, you young hypocrite?"

"Nay, Father, miscall me not. I lacked courage to tell you what I knew
would vex you, and right grateful am I to that good friend, whoever he be,
that has let you wot. 'Tis a load off my mind. Yes, Father, I love Margaret.
And call me not a priest, for a priest I will never be. I will die sooner."

"That we shall see, young man. Come, gainsay me no more. You will learn what 'tis to disrespect a father."

Gerard held his peace, and the three walked home in gloomy silence, broken only by a deep sigh or two from Catherine.

From that hour the little house at Tergou was no longer the abode of peace. Gerard was taken to task next day before the whole family, and every voice was loud against him except Little Kate's, and the dwarf's, who was apt to take his cue from her without knowing why. As for Cornelis and Sybrandt, they were bitterer than their father. Gerard was dismayed at finding so many enemies, and looked wistfully into his little sister's face. Her eyes were brimming at the harsh words showered on one who but yesterday was the universal pet. But she gave him no encouragement. She turned her head away from him, and said:

"Dear, dear Gerard, pray to Heaven to cure you of this folly!"

"What, are you against me too?" said Gerard sadly, and he rose with a deep sigh and left the house, and went to Sevenbergen.

The combatants were unequally matched. Elias was angry, Cornelis and Sybrandt spiteful; but Gerard, having a larger and more cultivated mind, saw both sides where they saw but one, and had fits of irresolution, and was not wroth, but unhappy. He was lonely too in this struggle. He could open his heart to no one. Margaret was a high-spirited girl. He dared not tell her what he had to endure at home. She was capable of siding with his relations by resigning him, though at the cost of her own happiness. Margaret Van Eyck had been a great comfort to him on another occasion, but now he dared not make her his confidante. Her own history was well known. In early life she had many offers of marriage, but refused them all for the sake of that art to which a wife's and mother's duties are so fatal. Thus she remained single and painted with her brothers. How could he tell her that he declined the benefice she had got him, and declined it for the sake of that which at his age she had despised and sacrificed so lightly?

Gerard at this period bade fair to succumb. But the other side had a horrible ally in Catherine Senior. This goodhearted but uneducated woman could not, like her daughter, act quietly and firmly; still less could she act upon a plan. She irritated Gerard at times, and so helped him; for anger is a great sustainer of the courage. At others, she turned round in a moment and made onslaughts on her own forces.

But at last, after more than six months of irritation, came the climax. The father told the son before the whole family he had ordered the Burgomaster to imprison him in the Stadthouse rather than let him marry Margaret. Gerard turned pale with anger at this, but by a great effort held his peace. His father went on to say, "And a priest you shall be before the year is out, nilly-willy."

"It is so?" cried Gerard. "Then hear me, all. By God and Saint Bavon I swear I will never be a priest while Margaret lives. Since force is to decide it, and not love and duty, try force, Father. But force shall not serve you, for the day I see the Burgomaster come for me, I leave Tergou forever, and Holland too, and my father's house, where it seems I have been valued all these years not for myself, but for what is to be got out of me."

And he flung out of the room white with anger and desperation.

"There!" cried Catherine. "That comes of driving young folk too hard. But men are crueler than tigers, even to their own flesh and blood. Now, Heaven forbid he should ever leave us, married or single."

As Gerard came out of the house, his cheeks pale and his heart panting, he met Reicht Heynes. She had a message for him—Margaret Van Eyck desired to see him. He found the old lady seated grim as a judge. She wasted no time in preliminaries, but inquired coldly why he had not visited her of late. But before he could answer, she said in a sarcastic tone, "I thought we had been friends, young sir."

At this Gerard looked the picture of doubt and consternation.

"It is because you never told her you were in love," said Reicht Heynes, pitying his confusion.

"Silence, wench! Why should he tell us his affairs? We are not his friends. We have not deserved his confidence."

"Alas! my second mother," said Gerard, "I did not dare to tell you my folly."

"What folly? Is it folly to love?"

"I am told so every day of my life."

"You need not have been afraid to tell my mistress. She is always kind to true lovers."

"Madam—Reicht—I was afraid because I was told—"

"Well? You were told—?"

"That in your youth you scorned love, preferring art."

"I did, boy, and what is the end of it? Behold me here a barren stock while the women of my youth have a troop of children at their side and grandchildren at their knee. I gave up the sweet joys of wifehood and motherhood for what? For my dear brothers. They have gone and left me long ago. For my art. It has all but left me too. I have the knowledge still, but what avails that when the hand trembles? No, Gerard, I look on you as my son. You are good, you are handsome, you are a painter, though not like some I have known. I will not let you throw your youth away as I did mine. You shall marry this Margaret. I have inquired, and she is a good daughter. Reicht here is a gossip. She has told me all about it. But that need not hinder *you* to tell me."

Poor Gerard was overjoyed to be permitted to praise Margaret aloud, and to one who could understand what he loved in her. Soon there were two pairs of wet eyes over his story, and when the poor boy saw that, there were three.

Margaret and Reicht were agreed that *a man* should always take the bull by the horns. Gerard's only course was to marry Margaret Brandt offhand. The old people would come to after a while, the deed once done. Whereas the longer this misunderstanding continued on its present footing, the worse for all parties, especially for Gerard.

"See how pale and thin they have made him among them."

"Indeed you are, Master Gerard," said Reicht. "It makes a body sad to see a young man so wasted and worn. Mistress, when I met him in the street today, I had like to have burst out crying, he was so changed."

"And I'll be bound the others keep their color, eh, Reicht? Such as it is."

"Oh, I see no odds in them."

"Of course not. We painters are no match for boors. We are glass, they are stone. We can't stand the worry, worry, worry of little minds; and it is not for the good of mankind we should be exposed to it. It is hard enough, heaven knows, to design and paint a masterpiece, without having gnats and flies stinging us to death into the bargain."

Exasperated as Gerard was by his father's threat of violence, he listened to these friendly voices telling him the prudent course was rebellion. But though he listened, he was not convinced.

"I do not fear my father's violence," he said, "but I do fear his anger. When it came to the point he would not imprison me. I would marry Margaret tomorrow if that was my only fear. No, he would disown me. I should take Margaret from her father, and give her a poor husband who would never thrive weighed down by his parent's curse. Madam! I sometimes think if I could but marry her secretly and then take her away to some country where my craft is better paid than in this; and after a year or two, when the storm had blown over, you know, could come back with money in my purse, and say 'My dear parents, we do not seek your substance, we but ask you to love us once more as you used, and as we have never ceased to love you'—but alas! I shall be told these are the dreams of an inexperienced young man."

The old lady's eyes sparkled.

"It is no dream, but a piece of wonderful common sense in a boy. It remains to be seen whether you have spirit to carry out your own thought. There is a country, Gerard, where certain fortune awaits you at this moment. Here the arts freeze, but there they flourish, as they never yet flourished in any age or land."

"It is Italy!" cried Gerard. "It is Italy!"

"Ay, Italy! Where painters are honored like princes, and scribes are paid three hundred crowns for copying a single manuscript. Know you not that his Holiness the Pope has written to every land for skillful scribes to copy the hundreds of precious manuscripts that are pouring into that favored land from Constantinople, whence learning and learned men are driven by the barbarian Turks?"

"Nay, I know not that. But it has been the dream and hope of my life to visit Italy, the queen of all the arts, oh, madam! But the journey, and we are all so poor."

"Find you the heart to go, I'll find the means. I know where to lay my hands on ten golden angels. They will take you to Rome, and the girl with you if she loves you as she ought."

They sat till midnight over this theme. And, after that day, Gerard recovered his spirits, and seemed to carry a secret talisman against all the gibes and the harsh words that flew about his ears at home.

Besides the money she procured him for the journey, Margaret Van Eyck gave him money's worth. Said she:

"I will tell you secrets that I learned from masters that are gone from me, and have left no fellow behind. Even the Italians know them not; and what I tell you now in Tergou you shall sell dear in Florence. Note my brother Jan's pictures. Time, which fades all other paintings, leaves his colors bright as the day they left the easel. The reason is, he did nothing blindly, nothing in a hurry. He trusted to no hireling to grind his colors; he did it himself, or saw it done. His panel was prepared, and prepared again—I will show you how—a year before he laid his color on. Most of them are quite content to have their work sucked up and lost, sooner than not be in a hurry. Bad painters are always in a hurry.

"Above all, Gerard, I warn you use but little oil, and never boil it. Boiling it melts that vegetable dross into its very heart, which it is our business to clear away; for impure oil is death to color. No, take your oil and pour it into a bottle with water. In a day or two, the water will turn muddy—that is muck from the oil. Pour the dirty water carefully away, and add fresh. When that is poured away, you will fancy the oil is clear. You are mistaken. Reicht, fetch me *that!*" Reicht brought a glass trough with a glass lid fitting tight. "When your oil has been washed in bottle, put it into this trough with water, and put the trough in the sun all day. You will soon see the water turbid again. But mark, you must not carry this game too far, or the sun will turn your oil to varnish. When it is as clear as crystal, not too luscious, drain carefully, and cork it up tight. Grind your own prime colors and lay them on with this oil, and they shall live. Hubert would put sand or salt in the water to clear the oil quicker. But Jan used to say, 'Water will do it best, give water time.' Jan Van Eyck was never in a hurry, and that is why the world will not forget *him* in a hurry."

This and several other receipts Margaret gave him with sparkling eyes, and Gerard received them like a legacy from Heaven, so interesting are some things that read uninteresting. Thus provided with money and knowledge,

Gerard decided to marry, and fly with his wife to Italy. Nothing remained now but to inform Margaret Brandt of his resolution, and to publish the banns as quietly as possible. He went to Sevenbergen earlier than usual on both these errands. He began with Margaret; told her of the Dame Van Eyck's goodness, and the resolution he had come to at last; and invited her co-operation. She refused it plump.

"No, Gerard. You and I have never spoken of your family, but when you come to marriage—" She stopped, then began again. "I do think your father has no ill will to me more than to another. He told Peter Buyskens as much, and Peter told me. But so long as he is bent on your being a priest (you ought to have told me this instead of I you), I could not marry you, Gerard, dearly as I love you."

Gerard strove in vain to shake this resolution. He found it very easy to make her cry, but impossible to make her yield. Then Gerard was impatient and unjust.

"Very well!" he cried. "Then you are on their side, and you will drive me to be a priest, for this must end one way or another. My parents hate me in earnest, but my lover only loves me in jest."

And with this wild, bitter speech, he flung away home again and left Margaret weeping.

When a man misbehaves, the effect is curious on a girl who loves him sincerely. It makes her pity him. This, to some of us males, seems anything but logical. The fault is in our own eye; the logic is too swift for us. The girl argues thus: "How unhappy, how vexed, poor —— must be. *Him* to misbehave! Poor thing!"

Margaret was full of this sweet womanly pity when, to her great surprise, scarce an hour and a half after he left her Gerard came running back to her with the fragments of a picture in his hand, and panting with anger and grief.

"There Margaret! See, see! The wretches! Look at their spite! They have cut your portrait to pieces."

Margaret looked. And sure enough, some malicious hand had cut her portrait into five pieces. She was a good girl, but she was not ice; she turned red to her very forehead.

"Who did it?"

"Nay, I know not. I dared not ask, for I should hate the hand that did it, ay, till my dying day. My poor Margaret! The butchers, the ruffians! Six months' work cut out of my life, and nothing to show for it now. See, they have hacked through your very face, the sweet face that everyone loves who knows it. Oh, heartless, merciless vipers!"

"Never mind, Gerard," said Margaret, panting. "Since this is how they treat you for my sake— Ye rob him of my portrait, do ye? Well, then he shall have the face itself, such as it is."

"Oh, Margaret!"

"Yes, Gerard. Since they are so cruel, I will be the kinder. Forgive me for refusing you. I will be your wife: tomorrow, if it is your pleasure."

Gerard kissed her hands with rapture and then her lips, and in a tumult of joy ran for Peter and Martin. They came and witnessed the betrothal—a solemn ceremony in those days, and indeed for more than a century later, though now abolished.

CHAPTER X

THE BANNS of marriage had to be read three times, as in our days; with this difference, that they were commonly read on weekdays, and the young couple easily persuaded the curé to do the three readings in twenty-four hours. He was new to the place, and their looks spoke volumes in their favor. They were cried on Monday at matins and at vespers, and, to their great delight, nobody from Tergou was in the church. The next morning they were both there palpitating with anxiety when, to their horror, a stranger stood up and forbade the banns, on the score that the parties were not of age, and their parents not consenting.

Outside the church door, Margaret and Gerard held a trembling and almost despairing consultation. But before they could settle anything, the man who had done them so ill a turn approached, and gave them to understand that he was very sorry to interfere; that his inclination was to further the happiness of the young; but that in point of fact his only means of getting a living was by forbidding banns. "The young people give me a crown, and I undo my work handsomely, tell the curé I was misinformed, and all goes smoothly."

"A crown? I will give you a golden angel to do this," said Gerard eagerly. The man consented as eagerly, and went with Gerard to the curé, and told him he had made a ridiculous mistake, which a sight of the parties had rectified. On this the curé agreed to marry the young couple next day at ten, and the professional obstructor of bliss went home with Gerard's angel. Like most of these very clever knaves, he was a fool, and proceeded to drink his angel at a certain hostelry in Tergou, where was a green devoted to archery and the common sports of the day. There, being drunk, he bragged of his day's exploit. And who should be there, imbibing every word, but a great frequenter of the spot, the ne'er-do-well Sybrandt. Sybrandt ran home to tell his father. His father was not at home; he was gone to Rotterdam to buy cloth of the merchants. Catching his elder brother's eye, he made him a signal to come out, and told him what he had heard.

There are black sheep in nearly every large family, and these two were Gerard's black brothers. Idleness is vitiating. Waiting for the death of those we ought to love is vitiating. And these two one-ideaed curs were ready to tear anyone to death who should interfere with that miserable inheritance, which was their thought by day and their dream by night. They put their heads together, and agreed not to tell their mother, whose sentiments were so uncertain, but to go first to the Burgomaster. They were cunning enough to see that he was averse to the match, though they could not divine why.

Ghysbrecht van Swieten saw through them at once, but he took care not to let them see through him. He heard their story, and putting on magisterial dignity and coldness, he said:

"Since the father of the family is not here, his duty falleth on me, who am the father of the town. I know your father's mind. Leave all to me, and above all, tell not a woman a word of this, least of all the women that are in your own house, for chattering tongues mar wisest counsels."

So he dismissed them a little superciliously. He was ashamed of his confederates.

On their return home they found their brother Gerard seated on a low stool at their mother's knee. She was caressing his hair with her hand, speaking very kindly to him, and promising to take his part with his father and thwart his love no more. The main cause of this change of mind was characteristic of the woman. She it was who in a moment of female irritation had cut Margaret's picture to pieces. She had watched the effect with some misgivings, and had seen Gerard turn pale as death, and sit motionless like a bereaved creature, with the pieces in his hands, and his eyes fixed on them till tears came and blinded them. Then she was terrified at what she had done; and next her heart smote her bitterly; and she wept sore apart. But she dared not own it, but said to herself, "I'll not say a word, but I'll make it up to him."

The next morning, at ten o'clock, Gerard and Margaret were in the church at Sevenbergen, he radiant with joy, she with blushes. Peter was also there, and Martin Wittenhaagen, but no other friend. Secrecy was everything. Margaret had declined Italy. She could not leave her father; he was too learned and too helpless. But it was settled they should retire into Flanders for a few weeks until the storm should be blown over at Tergou. The curé did not keep them waiting long, though it seemed an age. Presently he stood at the altar, and called them to him. They went hand in hand, the happiest in Holland. The curé opened his book.

But ere he uttered a single word of the sacred rite, a harsh voice cried "Forbear!" And the constables of Tergou came up the aisle and seized Gerard in the name of the law. Martin's long knife flashed out directly.

"Forbear, man!" cried the priest. "What! Draw your weapon in a church? And ye who interrupt this holy sacrament, what means this impiety?"

"There is no impiety," said the Burgomaster's servant respectfully. "This young man would marry against his father's will, and his father has prayed our Burgomaster to deal with him according to the law. Let him deny it if he can."

"Is this so, young man?"

Gerard hung his head.

"We take him to Rotterdam to abide the sentence of the Duke."

At this Margaret uttered a cry of despair, and the young creatures, who were so happy a moment ago, fell to sobbing in one another's arms so piteously that the instruments of oppression drew back a step, and were ashamed. But one of them that was good-natured stepped up under pretense of separating them and whispered to Margaret:

"Rotterdam? It is a lie. We but take him to our Stadthouse."

They took him away on horseback, on the road to Rotterdam, and after a dozen halts, and by sly detours, to Tergou. Just outside the town they were met by a rude vehicle covered with canvas. Gerard was put into this, and about five in the evening was secretly conveyed into the prison of the Stadthouse. He was taken up several flights of stairs and thrust into a small room lighted only by a narrow window, with a vertical iron bar. The whole furniture was a huge oak chest.

Gerard felt he was in the hands of an enemy. "Oh, the look that man gave me on the road to Rotterdam! There is more here than my father's wrath. I doubt I shall see no more the light of day." And he knelt down and commended his soul to God.

Presently he rose and sprang at the iron bar of the window and clutched it. This enabled him to look out by pressing his knees against the wall. It was but for a minute, but in that minute he saw a sight such as none but a captive can appreciate. Martin Wittenhaagen's back. Martin was sitting quietly fishing in the brook near the Stadthouse. Gerard sprang at the window and whistled. Martin instantly showed that he was watching much harder than fishing. He turned hastily round and saw Gerard, made him a signal, and taking up his line and bow, went quickly off.

Gerard saw by this that his friends were not idle, yet he had rather Martin had stayed. The very sight of him was a comfort. He held on, looking at the soldier's retiring form, as long as he could, then falling back somewhat heavily, wrenched the rusty iron bar, held only by rusty nails, away from the stonework just as Ghysbrecht van Swieten opened the door stealthily behind him. The Burgomaster's eye fell instantly on the iron, and then glanced at the window; but he said nothing. The window was a hundred feet from the ground, and if Gerard had a fancy for jumping out, why should he balk it? He brought a brown loaf and a pitcher of water, and set them on the chest in solemn silence. Gerard's first impulse was to brain him with the iron bar and fly down the stairs; but the Burgomaster, seeing something wicked in his eye, gave a little cough and three stout fellows, armed, showed themselves directly at the door.

"My orders are to keep you thus until you shall bind yourself by an oath to leave Margaret Brandt and return to the Church to which you have belonged from your cradle."

"Death sooner."

"With all my heart." And the Burgomaster retired.

Martin went with all speed to Sevenbergen. There he found Margaret pale and agitated, but full of resolution and energy. She was just finishing a letter to the Countess Charolois, appealing to her against the violence and treachery of Ghysbrecht.

"Courage!" cried Martin on entering. "I have found him. He is in the haunted tower, right at the top of it. Ay! I know the place. Many a poor fellow has gone up there straight and come down feet foremost."

He then told them how he had looked up and seen Gerard's face at a window that was like a slit in the wall.

"Oh, Martin! How did he look?"

"What mean you? He looked like Gerard Eliassoen."

"But was he pale?"

"A little."

"Looked he anxious? Looked he like one doomed?"

"Nay, nay, as bright as a pewter pot."

"You mock me. Stay! Then that must have been at sight of you. He counts on us. Oh, what shall we do? Martin, good friend, take this at once to Rotterdam."

Martin held out his hand for the letter. Peter had sat silent all this time, but pondering, and yet, contrary to custom, keenly attentive to what was going on around him.

"Put not your trust in princes," said he.

"Alas! What else have we to trust in?"

"Knowledge."

"Welladay, Father! Your learning will not serve us here."

"How know you that? Wit has been too strong for iron bars ere today."

"Ay, Father, but nature is stronger than wit, and she is against us. Think of the height! No ladder in Holland might reach him."

"I need no ladder. What I need is a gold crown."

"Nay, I have money for that matter. I have nine angels. Gerard gave them me to keep. But what do they avail? The Burgomaster will not be bribed to let Gerard free."

"What do they avail? Give me but one crown and the young man shall sup with us this night."

Peter spoke so eagerly and confidently that for a moment Margaret felt hopeful; but she caught Martin's eye dwelling upon him with an expression of benevolent contempt.

"It passes the powers of man's invention," said she with a deep sigh.

"Invention?" cried the old man. "A fig for invention. What need we invention at this time of day? Everything has been said that is to be said and done that ever will be done. I shall tell you how a Florentine knight was shut up in a tower higher than Gerard's, yet did his faithful squire stand at the tower foot and get him out, with no other engine than that in your hand, Martin, and certain kickshaws I shall buy for a crown."

Martin looked at his bow and turned it round in his hand, and seemed to interrogate it. But the examination left him as incredulous as before.

Then Peter told them his story, how the faithful squire got the knight out of a high tower at Brescia. The maneuver, like most things that are really scientific, was so simple that now their wonder was they had taken for impossible what was not even difficult. The letter never went to Rotterdam. They trusted to Peter's learning and their own dexterity.

It was nine o'clock on a clear moonlight night. Elias, senior, was still away, the rest of his little family had been sometime abed. A figure stood by the dwarf's bed. It was white, and the moonlight shone on it. With an unearthly noise between a yell and a snarl the gymnast rolled off his bed and under it by a single unbroken movement. A soft voice followed him in his retreat.

"Why, Giles, are you afeard of me?"

At this, Giles's head peeped cautiously up, and he saw it was only his sister Kate. She put her finger to her lips. "Hush! lest the wicked Cornelis or the wicked Sybrandt hear us." Giles's claws seized the side of the bed, and he returned to his place by one undivided gymnastic.

Kate then revealed to Giles that she had heard Cornelis and Sybrandt mention Gerard's name; and being herself in great anxiety at his not coming home all day, had listened at their door, and had made a fearful discovery. Gerard was in prison, in the haunted tower of the Stadthouse. He was there, it seemed, by their father's authority. But here must be some treachery, for how could their father have ordered this cruel act? He was at Rotterdam. She ended by entreating Giles to bear her company to the foot of the haunted tower, to say a word of comfort to poor Gerard, and let him know their father was absent, and would be sure to release him on his return.

"Dear Giles, I would go alone but I am afeard of the spirits that men say do haunt the tower. But with you I shall not be afeard."

"Nor I with you," said Giles. "I don't believe there are any spirits in Tergou. I never saw one. This last was the likest one ever I saw, and it was but you, Kate, after all."

In less than half an hour Giles and Kate opened the house door cautiously and issued forth. She made him carry a lantern, though the night was bright. "The lantern gives me more courage against the evil spirits," said she.

As the sun declined, Gerard's heart too sank and sank. With the waning light even the embers of hope went out. He was faint, too, with hunger, for he was afraid to eat the food Ghysbrecht had brought him, and hunger alone cows men. He sat upon the chest, his arms and his head drooping before him, a picture of despondency. Suddenly something struck the wall beyond him very sharply, and then rattled on the floor at his feet. It was an arrow; he saw the white feather. A chill ran through him—they meant then to assassinate him from the outside. He crouched. No more missiles came. He crawled on all fours, and took up the arrow. There was no head to it. He uttered a cry of hope. Had a friendly hand shot it? He took it up and felt it all over; he found a soft substance attached to it. Then one of his eccentricities was of grand use to him. His tinderbox enabled him to strike a light. It showed him two things that made his heart bound with delight, none the less thrilling for being somewhat vague. Attached to the arrow was a skein of silk; and on the arrow itself were words written. How his eyes devoured them, his heart panting the while!

Well beloved, make fast the silk to thy knife and lower to us: but hold thine end fast. Then count a hundred and draw up.

Gerard seized the oak chest and with almost superhuman energy dragged it to the window—a moment ago he could not have moved it. Standing on the chest and looking down, he saw figures at the tower foot. They were so indistinct they looked like one huge form. He waved his bonnet to them with trembling hand. Then he undid the silk rapidly but carefully, and made one end fast to his knife and lowered it till it ceased to draw. Then he counted a hundred. Then pulled the silk carefully up; it came up a little heavier. At last he came to a large knot, and by that knot a stout whipcord was attached to the silk.

What could this mean? While he was puzzling himself, Margaret's voice came up to him, low but clear. "Draw up, Gerard, till you see liberty." At the word Gerard drew the whipcord line up, and drew and drew till he came to another knot, and found a cord of some thickness take the place of the whipcord. He had no sooner begun to draw this up than he found that he had now a heavy weight to deal with. Then the truth suddenly flashed on him, and he went to work and pulled and pulled till the perspiration rolled down him. The weight got heavier and heavier, and at last he was well-nigh exhausted. Looking down, he saw in the moonlight a sight that revived him. It was as it were a great snake coming up to him out of the deep shadow cast by the tower.

He gave a shout of joy, and a score more wild pulls, and lo! a stout new rope touched his hand. He hauled and hauled, and dragged the end into his prison and instantly passed it through both handles of the chest in succession, and knotted it firmly, then sat for moment to recover his breath and collect his courage. The first thing was to make sure that the chest was sound, and capable of resisting his weight poised in mid air. He jumped with all his force upon it. At the third jump the whole side burst open, and out scuttled the contents, a host of parchments.

After the first start and misgiving this gave him, Gerard comprehended that the chest had not burst, but opened. He had doubtless jumped upon some secret spring. Still it shook in some degree his confidence in the chest's powers of resistance, so he gave it an ally. He took the iron bar and fastened it with the small rope across the large rope, and across the window. He now mounted the chest, and from the chest put his foot through the window, and sat half in and half out, with one hand on that part of the rope which was inside. In the silent night he heard his own heart beat.

The free air breathed on his face, and gave him the courage to risk what we must all lose one day—for liberty. Many dangers awaited him, but the greatest was the first getting onto the rope outside. Gerard reflected. Finally he put himself in the attitude of a swimmer, his body to the waist being in the prison, his legs outside. Then, holding the inside rope with both hands, he felt anxiously with his feet for the outside rope, and when he had got it, he worked it in between the palms of his feet, and kept it there tight. Then he uttered a short prayer and, all the calmer for it, put his left hand on the sill and gradually wriggled out. Then he seized the iron bar, and for one fearful moment hung outside from it by his right hand while his left hand felt for the rope down at his knees. It was too tight against the wall for his fingers to get round it higher up.

The moment he had fairly grasped it, he left the bar and swiftly seized the rope with the right hand too; but in this maneuver his body necessarily fell about a yard. A stifled cry came up from below. Gerard hung in mid-air. He clenched his teeth and nipped the rope tight with his feet and gripped it with his hands, and went down slowly hand below hand. He passed by one huge rough stone after another. He looked up and he looked down. The moon shone into his prison window; it seemed very near. The fluttering figures below seemed an awful distance. It made him dizzy to look down, so he fixed his eyes steadily on the wall close to him, and went slowly down, down, down.

He passed a rusty, slimy, streak on the wall. It was some ten feet long. The rope made his hands very hot. He stole another look up. The prison window was a good way off now. Down—down—down—down. The rope made his hands sore. He looked up. The window was so distant, he ventured now to turn his eyes downward again, and there not more than thirty feet below him were Margaret and Martin, their faithful hands upstretched to catch him should he fall. He could see their eyes and their teeth shine in the moonlight. For their mouths were open, and they were breathing hard.

"Take care, Gerard! Oh, take care! Look not down."

"Fear me not," cried Gerard joyfully, and eyed the wall, but came down faster.

In another moment his feet were at their hands. They seized him ere he touched the ground, and all three clung together in one embrace.

"Hush! Away in silence, dear one."

They stole along the shadow of the wall. Now ere they had gone many yards, suddenly a stream of light shot from an angle of the building and lay across their path like a barrier of fire, and they heard whispers and footsteps close at hand.

"Back!" hissed Martin. "Keep in the shade."

They hurried back, passed the dangling rope, and made for a little square projecting tower. They had barely rounded it when the light shot trembling past them, and flickered uncertainly into the distance.

"A lantern!" groaned Martin, in a whisper. "They are after us."

"Give me my knife," whispered Gerard. "I'll never be taken alive."

"No, no!" murmured Margaret. "Is there no way out where we are?"

"None, none. But I carry six lives at my shoulder." And with the word, Martin strung his bow and fitted an arrow to the string. "In war, never wait to be struck. I will kill one or two ere they shall know where their death comes from." Then, motioning his companions to be quiet, he began to draw his bow, and ere the arrow was quite drawn to the head, he glided round the corner ready to loose the string the moment the enemy should offer a mark.

Gerard and Margaret held their breath in horrible expectation. They had never seen a human being killed.

And now a wild hope, but half repressed, thrilled through Gerard, that this watchful enemy might be the Burgomaster in person. The soldier, he knew, would send an arrow through a burgher or burgomaster as he would through a boar in a wood.

But who may foretell the future, however near? The bow, instead of remaining firm and loosing the deadly shaft, was seen to waver first, then shake violently, and the stout soldier staggered back to them, his knees knocking and his cheeks blanched with fear. He let his arrow fall and clutched Gerard's shoulder.

"Let me feel flesh and blood," he gasped. "The haunted tower! The haunted tower!"

His terror communicated itself to Margaret and Gerard. They gasped, rather than uttered, an inquiry.

"Hush!" he cried. "It will hear you. *Up* the wall! It is going *up* the wall! Its head is on fire. *Up* the wall, as mortal creatures walk upon greensward. If you know a prayer say it! For hell is loose tonight."

"I have power to exorcise spirits," said Gerard, trembling. "I will venture forth."

"Go alone, then!" said Martin. "I have looked on't once and live."

CHAPTER XI

THE STRANGE GLANCE of hatred the Burgomaster had cast on Gerard, coupled with his imprisonment, had filled the young man with a persuasion that Ghysbrecht was his enemy to the death, and he glided round the angle of the tower fully expecting to see no supernatural appearance, but some cruel and treacherous contrivance of a bad man to do him mischief in that prison, his escape from which could hardly be known. As he stole forth, a soft but brave hand crept into his, and Margaret was by his side to share this new peril.

No sooner was the haunted tower visible than a sight struck their eyes that benumbed them as they stood. More than halfway up the tower a creature with a fiery head, like an enormous glowworm, was steadily mounting the wall. The body was dark, but its outline visible through the glare from the head, and the whole creature not much less than four feet long. At the foot of the tower stood a thing in white that looked exactly like the figure of a female. Gerard and Margaret palpitated with awe.

"The rope, the rope! It is going up the rope," gasped Gerard.

As they gazed, the glowworm disappeared in Gerard's late prison, but its light illuminated the cell inside and reddened the window. The white figure stood motionless below.

Margaret put down Gerard's hand quietly, and stood bewildered, then, all in a moment, with a wild cry darted toward the specter. Gerard never doubted the evil one was drawing her to her perdition. He fell on his knees.

"*Exorcizo vos. In nomine beatae Mariae, exorcizo vos.*"

While the exorcist was shrieking his incantations in extremity of terror, to his infinite relief he heard the specter utter a feeble cry of fear. To find that Hell had also its little weaknesses was encouraging. He redoubled his exorcisms, and presently he saw the ghastly shape kneeling at Margaret's knees and heard it praying piteously for mercy.

Kate and Giles soon reached the haunted tower. Judge their surprise when they found a new rope dangling from the prisoner's window to the ground.

"I see how it is," said the inferior intelligence, taking facts as they came. "Our Gerard has come down this rope. He has got clear. Up I go, and see."

"No, Giles, no!" said the superior intelligence, blinded by prejudice. "See you not this is glamour? This rope is a line the evil one casts out to wile thee to destruction. He knows the weaknesses of all our hearts; he has seen how fond you are of going up things. Where should our Gerard procure a rope? How fasten it in the sky like this? It is not in nature. Holy saints protect us this night, for Hell is abroad."

"Stuff!" said the dwarf. "The way to Hell is down, and this rope leads up. I never had the luck to go up such a long rope. It may be years ere I fall in with such a long rope all ready hung for me. As well be knocked on the head at once as never know happiness."

And he sprang onto the rope with a cry of delight, as a cat jumps with a mew onto a table where fish is. All the gymnast was on fire, and the only concession Kate could gain from him was permission to fasten the lantern on his neck first.

"A light scares the ill spirits," said she.

And so, with his huge arms and his legs like feathers, Giles went up the rope faster than his brother came down it. The light at the nape of his neck made a glowworm of him. His sister watched his progress with trembling anxiety. Suddenly a female figure started out of the solid masonry and came flying at her with more than mortal velocity. Kate uttered a feeble cry. It was all she could, for her tongue clove to her palate with terror. Then she dropped her crutches, and sank upon her knees, hiding her face and moaning:

"Take my body, but spare my soul!"

Margaret (panting). "Why, it is a woman."

Kate (quivering). "Why, it is a woman."

Margaret. "How you scared me!"

Kate. "I am scared enough myself. Oh! oh! oh!"

"This is strange. But the fiery-headed thing? Yet it was with you, and you are harmless. But why are you here at this time of night?"

"Nay, why are *you?*"

"Perhaps we are on the same errand? Ah, you are his *good* sister, Kate."

"And you are Margaret Brandt."

"Yea."

"All the better. You love him, you are here. Then Giles was right. He has won free."

Gerard came forward and put the question at rest. But all further explanation was cut short by a horrible, unearthly noise, like a sepulchre ventriloquizing.

"*Parchment!—parchment!—parchment!*"

At each repetition it rose in intensity. They looked up, and there was the dwarf with his hands full of parchments, and his face lighted with fiendish joy and lurid with diabolical fire. The light being at his neck, a more infernal "transparency" never startled mortal eye. With the word the awful imp hurled parchment at the astonished heads below. Down came records, like wounded wild ducks, some collapsed, others fluttering and others spread out and wheeling slowly down in airy circles. They had hardly settled when again the sepulchral roar was heard: "Parchment—parchment!" and down pattered and sailed another flock of documents; another followed; they whitened the grass. Finally the fire-headed imp with his light body and horny hands slid down the rope like a falling star and (business before sentiment) proposed to his rescued brother an immediate settlement for the merchandise he had just delivered.

"Hush!" said Gerard. "You speak too loud. Gather them up and follow us to a safer place than this."

"Will you not come home with me, Gerard?" said Little Kate.

"I have no home."

"You shall not say so. Who is more welcome than you will be, after this cruel wrong, to your father's house?"

"Father? I have no father," said Gerard sternly. "He that was my father is turned my gaoler. I have escaped from his hands. I will never come within their reach again."

"An enemy did this, and not our father."

And she told him what she had overheard Cornelis and Sybrandt say. But the injury was too recent to be soothed. Gerard showed a bitterness of indignation he had hitherto seemed incapable of.

"Cornelis and Sybrandt are two curs that have shown me their teeth and their heart a long while, but they could do no more. My father it is that gave the Burgomaster authority, or he durst not have laid a finger on me that am a free burgher of this town. So be it, then. I was his son. I am his prisoner. He has played his part. I shall play mine. Farewell the burgh where I was born and lived honestly, and was put in prison. While there is another town left in creation, I'll never trouble you again, Tergou."

"Oh, Gerard! Gerard!"

Margaret whispered her: "Do not gainsay him now. Give his choler time to cool!"

Kate turned quickly toward her. "Let me look at your face!" The inspection was favorable, it seemed, for she whispered: "It is a comely face, and no mischiefmaker's."

"Fear me not," said Margaret in the same tone. "I could not be happy without your love as well as Gerard's."

"These are comfortable words," sobbed Kate. Then, looking up, she said: "I little thought to like you so well. My heart is willing, but my infirmity will not let me embrace you."

At this hint, Margaret wound gently round Gerard's sister and kissed her lovingly.

"Often he has spoken of you to me, Kate, and often I longed for this."

"You too, Gerard," said Kate. "Kiss me ere you go, for my heart lies heavy at parting with you this night."

Gerard kissed her, and she went on her crutches home. The last thing they heard of her was a little patient sigh. Then the tears came and stood thick in Margaret's eyes; but Gerard was a man and noticed not his sister's sigh.

As they turned to go to Sevenbergen, the dwarf nudged Gerard with his bundle of parchments, and held out a concave claw. Margaret dissuaded Gerard.

"Why take what is not ours?"

"Oh, spoil an enemy how you can!"

"But may they not make this a handle for fresh violence?"

"How can they? Think you I shall stay in Tergou after this? The Burgomaster robbed me of my liberty. I doubt I should take his life for it if I could."

"Oh, fie, Gerard!"

"What? Is life worth more than liberty? Well, I can't take his life, so I take the first thing that comes to hand."

He gave Giles a few small coins, with which the urchin was gladdened and shuffled after his sister. Margaret and Gerard were speedily joined by Martin, and away to Sevenbergen.

CHAPTER XII

GHYSBRECHT VAN SWIETEN kept the key of Gerard's prison in his pouch. He waited till ten of the clock ere he visited him, for he said to himself, "A little hunger sometimes does well; it breaks 'em." At ten he crept up the stairs with a loaf and pitcher, followed by his trusty servant well armed. Ghysbrecht listened at the door. There was no sound inside. A grim smile stole over his features. "By this time he will be as downhearted as Albert Koestein was," thought he. He opened the door. No Gerard. Ghysbrecht stood stupefied.

Although his face was not visible, his body seemed to lose all motion in so peculiar a way, and then after a little he fell a-trembling so, that the servant behind him saw there was something amiss, and crept close to him and peeped over his shoulder. At sight of the empty cell and the rope and iron bar, he uttered a loud exclamation of wonder. But his surprise doubled when his master, disregarding all else, suddenly flung himself on his knees before the empty chest and felt wildly all over it with quivering hands, as if unwilling to trust his eyes in a matter so important. The servant gazed at him in utter bewilderment.

"Why, master, what is the matter?"

Ghysbrecht's pale lips worked as if he was going to answer, but they uttered no sound. His hands fell by his side, and he stared into the chest.

"Why, master, what avails glaring into that empty box? The lad is not there. See here! Note the cunning of the young rogue. He hath taken out the bar, and—"

"*Gone! Gone! Gone!*"

"Gone? What is gone? Holy saints! He is planet-struck."

"*Stop thief!*" shrieked Ghysbrecht, and suddenly turned on his servant and collared him and shook him with rage. "D'ye stand there, knave, and see your master robbed? Run! Fly! A hundred crowns to him that finds it me again! No, no! 'Tis in vain. Oh, fool, fool, to leave that in the same room with him! But none ever found the secret spring before. None ever would but he. It was to be. It is to be. Lost! lost!" and his years and infirmity now gained the better of his short-lived frenzy and he sank on the chest muttering "Lost! lost!"

"What is lost, master?" asked the servant kindly.

"House and lands and good name," groaned Ghysbrecht, and wrung his hands feebly.

"*What?*" cried the servant.

This emphatic word, and the tone of eager curiosity, struck on Ghysbrecht's ear and revived his natural cunning.

"I have lost the town records," stammered he, and he looked askant at the man like a fox caught near a henroost.

"Oh, is that all?"

"Is't not enough? What will the burghers say to me? What will the burgh do?" Then he suddenly burst out again. "A hundred crowns to him who shall recover them! All, mind, all that were in this box. If one be missing, I give nothing."

" 'Tis a bargain, master. The hundred crowns are in my pouch. See you not that where Gerard Eliassoen is, there are the pieces of sheepskin you rate so high?"

"That is true, that is true, good Dierich, good faithful Dierich. All, mind, all, that were in the chest."

"Master, I will take the constables to Gerard's house and seize him for the theft."

"The theft? Ay! Good, very good. It is theft. I forgot that. So, as he is a thief now, we will put him in the dungeons below where the toads are and the rats. Dierich, that man must never see daylight again. 'Tis his own fault, he must be prying. Quick, quick! Ere he has time to talk, you know, time to talk."

In less than half an hour Dierich Brower and four constables entered the hosier's house and demanded young Gerard of the panic-stricken Catherine.

"Alas! What has he done now?" cried she. "That boy will break my heart."

"Nay, dame, but a trick of youth," said Dierich. "He hath but made off with certain skins of parchment, in a frolic doubtless; but the Burgomaster is answerable to the burgh for their safekeeping, so he is in care about them. As for the youth, he will doubtless be quit for a reprimand."

This smooth speech completely imposed on Catherine: but her daughter was more suspicious, and that suspicion was strengthened by the disproportionate anger and disappointment Dierich showed the moment he learned Gerard was not at home, had not been at home that night.

"Come away, then," said he roughly. "We are wasting time." He added vehemently, "I'll find him if he is above ground."

Affection sharpens the wits, and often it has made an innocent person more than a match for the wily. As Dierich was going out, Kate made him a signal she would speak with him privately. He bade his men go on and waited outside the door. She joined him.

"Hush!" said she. "My mother knows not. Gerard has left Tergou."

"How?"

"I saw him last night."

"Ay? Where?" cried Dierich eagerly.

"At the foot of the haunted tower."

"How did he get the rope?"

"I know not, but this I know: My brother Gerard bade me there farewell, and he is many leagues from Tergou ere this. The town, you know, was always unworthy of him, and when it imprisoned him, he vowed never to set foot in it again. Let the Burgomaster be content, then. He has imprisoned him, and he has driven him from his birthplace and from his native land. What need now to rob him and us of our good name?"

This might at another moment have struck Dierich as good sense, but he was too mortified at this escape of Gerard and the loss of a hundred crowns.

"What need had he to steal?" retorted he, bitterly.

"Gerard stole not the trash, he but *took* it to spite the Burgomaster, who stole his liberty. But he shall answer to the Duke for it, he shall. As for these skins of parchment you keep such a coil about, look in the nearest brook, or sty, and 'tis odds but you find them."

"Think ye so, mistress?—Think ye so?" And Dierich's eyes flashed. "Mayhap you know 'tis so."

"This I know, that Gerard is too good to steal, and too wise to load himself with rubbish, going a journey."

"Give you good day, then," said Dierich sharply. "The sheepskin you scorn I value more than the skin of any he in Tergou."

And he went off hastily on a false scent. Kate returned into the house and drew Giles aside.

"Giles, my heart misgives me. Breathe not to a soul what I say to you. I have told Dirk Brower that Gerard is out of Holland, but much I doubt he is not a league from Tergou."

"Why, where is he, then?"

"Where should he be but with her he loves? But if so, he must not loiter. These be deep and dark and wicked men that seek him. Giles, I see that in Dirk Brower's eye makes me tremble. Oh, why cannot I fly to Sevenbergen and bid him away? Why am I not lusty and active like other girls? God forgive me for fretting at His will, but I never felt till now what it is to be lame and weak and useless. But you are strong, dear Giles," added she coaxingly, "you are very strong."

"Yes, I am strong," thundered Perpusillus. Then, catching sight of her meaning, "But I hate to go on foot," he added, sulkily.

"Alas! alas! Who will help me if you will not? Dear Giles, do you not love Gerard?"

"Yes, I like him best of the lot. I'll go to Sevenbergen on Peter Buyskens his mule. Ask you him, for he won't lend her me."

Kate remonstrated. The whole town would follow him. It would be known whither he was gone, and Gerard be in worse danger than before. Giles parried this by promising to ride out of the town the opposite way, and not turn the mule's head toward Sevenbergen till he had got rid of the curious. Kate then assented, and borrowed the mule. She charged Giles with a short but meaning message, and made him repeat it after her, over and over, till he could say it word for word.

Giles started on the mule, and little Kate retired, and did the last thing now in her power for her beloved brother—prayed on her knees long and earnestly for his safety.

CHAPTER XIII

GERARD and Margaret went gaily to Sevenbergen in the first flush of recovered liberty and successful adventure. But these soon yielded to sadder thoughts. Gerard was an escaped prisoner, and liable to be retaken and perhaps punished, and therefore he and Margaret would have to part for a time. Moreover, he had conceived a hatred to his native place. Margaret wished him to leave the country for a while, but at the thought of his going to Italy her heart fainted. Gerard, on the contrary, was reconciled to leaving Margaret only by his desire to visit Italy, and his strong conviction that there he should earn money and reputation, and remove every obstacle to their marriage. He had already told her all that the Demoiselle Van Eyck had said to him. He repeated it, and reminded Margaret that the gold pieces were only given him to go to Italy with.

The journey was clearly for Gerard's interest. He was a craftsman and an artist, lost in this boorish place. In Italy they would know how to value him. On this ground above all the unselfish girl gave her consent. But many tender tears came with it, and at that Gerard, young and loving as herself, cried bitterly with her, and often they asked one another what they had done that so many different persons should be their enemies, and combine, as it seemed, to part them.

They sat hand in hand till midnight, now deploring their hard fate, now drawing bright and hopeful pictures of the future, in the midst of which Margaret's tears would suddenly flow, and then poor Gerard's eloquence would die away in a sigh.

The morning found them resigned to part, but neither had the courage to say when, and much I doubt whether the hour of parting ever would have struck. But about three in the afternoon, Giles, who had made a circuit of many miles to avoid suspicion, rode up to the door. They both ran out to him, eager with curiosity.

"Brother Gerard," cried he in his tremendous tones, "Kate bids you run for your life. They charge you with theft. You have given them a handle. Think not to explain. Hope not for justice in Tergou. The parchments you took, they are but a blind. She hath seen your death in the men's eyes —a price is on your head. Fly! For Margaret's sake and all who love you, loiter not life away, but fly!"

It was a thunderclap, and left two white faces looking at one another and at the terrible messenger. Then Giles, who had hitherto but uttered by rote what Catherine bade him, put in a word of his own.

"All the constables were at our house after you, and so was Dirk Brower. Kate is wise, Gerard. Best give ear to her rede, and fly."

"Oh, yes, Gerard!" cried Margaret wildly. "Fly on the instant. Ah! those parchments! My mind misgave me—why did I let you take them?"

"Margaret, they are but a blind, Giles says so. No matter, the old caitiff shall never see them again. I will not go till I have hidden his treasure where he shall never find it." Gerard then, after thanking Giles warmly, bade him farewell and told him to go back and tell Kate he was gone. "For I shall be gone ere you reach home," said he. He then shouted for Martin, and told him what had happened, and begged him to go a little way toward Tergou, and watch the road.

"Ay," said Martin, "and if I see Dirk Brower, or any of his men, I will shoot an arrow into the oak tree that is in our garden; and on that you must run into the forest hard-by, and meet me at the weird hunter's spring. Then I will guide you through the wood."

Surprise thus provided against, Gerard breathed again. He went with Margaret, and, while she watched the oak tree tremblingly, fearing every moment to see an arrow strike among the branches, Gerard dug a deep hole to bury the parchments in. He threw them in, one by one. They were nearly all charters and records of the burgh, but one appeared to be a private deed between Floris Brandt, father of Peter, and Ghysbrecht.

"Why, this is as much yours as his," said Gerard. "I will read this."

"Oh, not now, Gerard, not now!" cried Margaret. "Every moment you lose fills me with fear. And see, large drops of rain are beginning to fall, and the clouds lower."

Gerard yielded to this remonstrance, but he put the deed into his bosom, and threw the earth in over the others and stamped it down. While thus employed there came a flash of lightning followed by a peal of distant thunder, and the rain came down heavily. Margaret and Gerard ran into the house, whither they were speedily followed by Martin.

"The road is clear," said he, "and a heavy storm coming on."

His words proved true. The thunder came nearer and nearer till it crashed overhead: the flashes followed one another close, like the strokes of a whip, and the rain fell in torrents. Margaret hid her face not to see the lightning. On this, Gerard put up the rough shutter, and lighted a candle. The lovers consulted together, and Gerard blessed the storm that gave him a few hours more with Margaret. The sun set unperceived, and still the thunder pealed and the lightning flashed and the rain poured.

Supper was set, but Gerard and Margaret could not eat. The thought that this was the last time they should sup together choked them. The storm lulled a little. Peter retired to rest. But Gerard was to go at peep of day, and neither he nor Margaret could afford to lose an hour in sleep. Martin sat a while, too, for he was fitting a new string to his bow, a matter in which he was very nice. The lovers murmured their sorrows and their love beside him.

Suddenly the old man held up his hand to them to be silent. They were quiet and listened, and heard nothing. But the next moment a footstep crackled faintly upon autumn leaves that lay strewn in the garden at the back door of the house. To those who had nothing to fear such a step would have said nothing, but to those who had enemies it was terrible. For it was a foot trying to be noiseless.

Martin fitted an arrow to his string and hastily blew out the candle. At this moment, to their horror, they heard more than one footstep approach the other door of the cottage, not quite so noiselessly as the other, but very stealthily—and then a dead pause. Their blood froze in their veins.

"Oh! Kate! Oh, Kate! You said, 'Fly on the instant.'" And Margaret moaned and wrung her hands in anguish and terror, and wild remorse for having kept Gerard.

"Hush, girl!" said Martin in a stern whisper.

A heavy knock fell on the door. And on the hearts within.

CHAPTER XIV

As IF THIS had been a concerted signal, the back door was struck as rudely the next instant. They were hemmed in. But at these alarming sounds Margaret seemed to recover some share of self-possession. She whispered, "Say he *was* here, but is gone." And with this she seized Gerard and almost dragged him up the rude steps that led to her father's sleeping-room. Her own lay next beyond it. The blows on the door were repeated.

"Who knocks at this hour?"

"Open, and you will see!"

"I open not to thieves—honest men are all abed now."

"Open to the law, Martin Wittenhaagen, or you shall rue it."

"Why, that is Dirk Brower's voice, I trow. What make you so far from Tergou?"

"Open, and you will know."

Martin drew the bolt, very slowly, and in rushed Dierich and four more. They let in their companion who was at the back door.

"Now, Martin, where is Gerard Eliassoen?"

"Gerard Eliassoen? Why, he was here but now!"

"Was here?" Dierich's countenance fell. "And where is he now?"

"They say he has gone to Italy. Why? What is to do?"

"No matter. When did he go? Tell me not that he went in such a storm as this!"

"Here is a coil about Gerard Eliassoen," said Martin contemptuously. Then he lighted the candle and, seating himself coolly by the fire, proceeded to whip some fine silk round his bowstring at the place where the nick of the arrow frets it. "I'll tell you," said he carelessly. "Know you his brother Giles—a little misbegotten imp all head and arms? Well, he came tearing over here on a mule, and bawled out something. I was too far off to hear the creature's words, but only its noise. Anyway, he started Gerard. For as soon as he was gone, there was such crying and kissing, and then Gerard went away. They do tell me he has gone to Italy—maybe you know where that is; for I don't."

Dierich's countenance fell lower and lower at this account. There was no flaw in it. A cunninger man than Martin would perhaps have told a lie too many, and raised suspicion. But Martin did his task well. He only told the one falsehood he was bade to tell, and of his own head invented nothing.

"Mates," said Dierich, "I doubt he speaks sooth. I told the Burgomaster how 'twould be. He met the dwarf galloping Peter Buyskens' mule from

Sevenbergen. 'They have sent that imp to Gerard,' says he, 'so, then, Gerard is at Sevenbergen.' 'Ah, master!' says I, ' 'tis too late now. We should have thought of Sevenbergen before instead of wasting our time hunting all the odd corners of Tergou for those cursed parchments that we shall never find till we find the man that took 'em. If he was at Sevenbergen,' quoth I, 'and they sent the dwarf to him, it must have been to warn him we are after him. He is leagues away by now,' quoth I. Confound that chalk-faced girl! she has outwitted us bearded men, and so I told the Burgomaster, but he would not hear to reason. A wet jerkin apiece, that is all we shall get, mates, by this job."

Martin grinned coolly in Dierich's face.

"However," added the latter, "to content the Burgomaster, we will search the house."

Martin turned grave directly. This change of countenance did not escape Dierich. He reflected a moment.

"Watch outside, two of you, one on each side of the house, that no one jump from the upper windows. The rest come with me."

And he took the candle and mounted the stairs, followed by three of his comrades. Martin was left alone. The stout soldier hung his head. All had gone so well at first, and now this fatal turn! Suddenly it occurred to him that all was not yet lost. Gerard must be either in Peter's room or Margaret's. They were not so very high from the ground. Gerard would leap out. Dierich had left a man below, but what then? For half a minute Gerard and he would be two to one, and in that brief space, what might not be done?

Martin then held the back door ajar and watched. The light shone in Peter's room. "Curse the fool!" said he. "Is he going to let them take him like a girl?" The light now passed into Margaret's bedroom. Still no window was opened. Had Gerard intended escape that way, he would not have waited till the men were in the room. Martin saw that at once and left the door and came to the foot stair and listened. He began to think Gerard must have escaped by the window while all the men were in the house. The longer the silence continued, the stronger grew this conviction. But it was suddenly and rudely dissipated.

Faint cries issued from the inner bedroom—Margaret's.

"They have taken him," groaned Martin. "They have got him."

It now flashed across Martin's mind that if they took Gerard away his life was not worth a button; and that if evil befell him, Margaret's heart would break. He cast his eyes wildly round like some savage beast seeking an escape, and in a twinkling formed a resolution terribly characteristic of those iron times and of a soldier driven to bay. He stepped to each door in turn, and imitating Dirk Brower's voice, said sharply, "Watch the window!" He then quietly closed and bolted both doors. He then took up his bow and six arrows; one he fitted to his string, the others he put into his quiver. His knife he placed upon a chair behind him, the hilt toward him; and there he waited at the foot of the stair with the calm determination to slay those four men, or be slain by them. Two, he knew, he could dispose of by his arrows ere they could get near him, and Gerard and he must take their chance, hand to hand, with the remaining pair. Besides, he had seen men panic-stricken by a sudden attack of this sort. Should Brower and his men hesitate but an instant before closing with him, he should shoot three instead of two, and then the odds would be on the right side.

He had not long to wait. The heavy steps sounded in Margaret's room, and came nearer and nearer. The light also approached, and voices. Martin's heart, stout as it was, beat hard to hear men coming thus to their death, and perhaps to his—more likely so than not, for four is long odds in a battlefield of ten feet square, and Gerard might be bound, perhaps, and powerless to help. But this man, whom we have seen shake in his shoes at a Giles-o'-lanthorn, never wavered in this awful moment of real danger, but stood there, his body all braced for combat, and his eyes glowing, equally ready to take life and lose it. Desperate game! to win which was exile instant and for life, and to lose it was to die that moment upon that floor he stood on.

Dierich Brower and his men found Peter in his first sleep. They opened his cupboards; they ran their knives into an alligator he had nailed to his wall; they looked under his bed. It was a large room, and apparently full of hiding-places, but they found no Gerard.

Then they went on to Margaret's room, and the very sight of it was discouraging—it was small and bare, and not a cupboard in it. There was, however, a large fireplace and chimney. Dierich's eye fell on these directly. Here they found the beauty of Sevenbergen sleeping on an old chest, not a foot high, and no attempt made to cover it; but the sheets were snowy white, and so was Margaret's own linen. And there she lay, looking like a lily fallen into a rut. Presently she awoke, and sat up in the bed, like one amazed; then, seeing the men, began to scream faintly, and pray for mercy. She made Dierich Brower ashamed of his errand.

"Here is a to-do," said he, a little confused. "We are not going to hurt you, my pretty maid. Lie you still, and shut your eyes, and think of your wedding night while I look up this chimney to see if Master Gerard is there."

"Gerard! In my room?"

"Why not? They say that you and he—"

"Cruel, you know they have driven him away from me—driven him from his native place. This is a blind. You are thieves, you are wicked men. You are not men of Sevenbergen, or you would know Margaret

Brandt better than to look for her lover in this room of all others in the world. Oh, brave! Four great hulking men to come, armed to the teeth, to insult one poor honest girl! The women that live in your own houses must be naught, or you would respect them too much to insult a girl of good character."

"There, come away before we hear worse," said Dierich hastily. "He is not in the chimney. Plaster will mend what a cudgel breaks, but a woman's tongue is a double-edged dagger, and a girl is a woman with her mother's milk still in her." And he beat a hasty retreat. "I told the Burgomaster how 'twould be."

CHAPTER XV

WHERE is the woman that cannot act a part? Where is she who will not do it, and do it well, to save the man she loves? Nature on these great occasions comes to the aid of the simplest of the sex, and teaches her to throw dust in Solomon's eyes. The men had no sooner retired than Margaret stepped out of bed and opened the long chest on which she had been lying down in her skirt and petticoat and stockings, and nightdress over all; and put the lid, bedclothes and all, against the wall; then glided to the door and listened. The footsteps died away through her father's room, and down the stairs.

Now in that chest there was a peculiarity that it was almost impossible for a stranger to detect. A part of the boarding of the room had been broken, and Gerard, being applied to to make it look neater, and being short of materials, had ingeniously sawed away a space sufficient just to admit Margaret's *soi-disant* bed, and with the materials thus acquired he had repaired the whole room. As for the bed or chest, it really rested on the rafters a foot below the boards. Consequently it was full two feet deep, though it looked scarce one.

All was quiet. Margaret knelt and gave thanks to Heaven. Then she glided from the door and leaned over the chest, and whispered tenderly, "Gerard!" Gerard did not reply.

She then whispered, a little louder: "Gerard, all is safe, thank heaven! You may rise, but, oh, be cautious!" Gerard made no reply. She laid her hand upon his shoulder—"Gerard!" No reply.

"Oh, what is this?" she cried, and her hands ran wildly over his face and his bosom. She took him by the shoulders; she shook him; she lifted him; but he escaped from her trembling hands and fell back not like a man, but like a body. A great dread fell on her. The lid had been down. She had lain upon it. The men had been some time in the room. With all the strength of frenzy she tore him out of the chest. She bore him in her arms to the window. She dashed the window open. The sweet air came in. She laid him in it and in the moonlight. His face was the color of ashes, his body was all limp and motionless. She felt his heart. Horror! It was as still as the rest! Horror of horrors! She had stifled him with her own body.

The mind cannot all at once believe so great and sudden and strange a calamity. Gerard, who had got alive into that chest scarce five minutes ago, how could he be dead? She called him by all the endearing names that heart could think or tongue could frame. She kissed him and fondled him and coaxed him and implored him to speak to her. No answer to words of love such as she had never uttered to him before, nor thought she could utter. Then the poor creature, trembling all over, began to say over that ashy face little foolish things that were at once terrible and pitiable.

"Oh, Gerard! I am very sorry you are dead. I am very sorry I have killed you. Forgive me for not letting the men take you, it would have been better than this. Oh, Gerard! I am very, very sorry for what I have done." Then she began suddenly to rave. "No! no! such things can't be, or there is no God. It is monstrous. How can my Gerard be dead? How can I have killed my Gerard? I love him. Oh, God, You know how I love him! He does not. I never told him. If he knew my heart, he would speak to me, he would not be so deaf to his poor Margaret. It is all a trick to make me cry out and betray him. But, no, I love him too well for that. I'll choke first." And she seized her own throat, to check her wild desire to scream in her terror and anguish.

"If he would but say one word! Oh, Gerard! Don't die without a word. Have mercy on me and scold me, but speak to me. If you are angry with me, scold me! Curse me! I deserve it, the idiot that killed the man she loved better than herself. Ah! I am a murderess. The worst in all the world. Help, help! I have murdered him. Ah, ah, ah, ah, ah!"

She tore her hair and uttered shriek after shriek so wild, so piercing, they fell like a knell upon the ears of Dierich Brower and his men. All started to their feet and looked at one another.

Martin Wittenhaagen, standing at the foot of the stairs with his arrow drawn nearly to the head and his knife behind him, was struck with amazement to see the men come back without Gerard. He lowered his bow and looked open-mouthed at them. They for their part were equally puzzled at the attitude they had caught him in.

"Why, mates, was the old fellow making ready to shoot at *us?*"

"Stuff!" said Martin, recovering his stolid composure. "I was but trying my new string. There, I'll unstring my bow if you think that."

"Humph!" said Dierich suspiciously. "There is something more in you than I understand. Put a log on, and let us dry our hides a bit ere we go."

A blazing fire was soon made and the men gathered round it, and their clothes and long hair were soon smoking from the cheerful blaze. Then it was that the shrieks were heard in Margaret's room. They all started up, and one of them seized the candle and ran up the steps that led to the bedrooms. Martin rose hastily, too, and being confused by these sudden screams, and apprehending danger from the man's curiosity, tried to prevent him from going there.

At this Dierich threw his arms round him from behind, and called on the others to keep him. The man that had the candle got clear away, and all the rest fell upon Martin, and after a long and fierce struggle, in the course of which they were more than once all rolling on the floor, with Martin in the middle, they succeeded in mastering the old Samson, and binding him hand and foot with a rope they had brought for Gerard.

Martin groaned aloud. He saw the man had made his way to Margaret's room during the struggle, and here was he powerless.

"Ay, grind your teeth, you old rogue," said Dierich, panting with the struggle. "You shan't use them."

"It is my belief, mates, that our lives were scarce safe while this old fellow's bones were free."

"He makes me think this Gerard is not far off," put in another.

"No such luck," replied Dierich. "Hallo, mates. Jorian Ketel is a long time in that girl's bedroom. Best go and see after him, some of us."

The rude laugh caused by this remark had hardly subsided when hasty footsteps were heard running along overhead.

"Oh, here he comes, at last! Well, Jorian, what is to do now up there?"

CHAPTER XVI

JORIAN KETEL went straight to Margaret's room and there, to his infinite surprise, he found the man he had been in search of, pale and motionless, his head in Margaret's lap and she kneeling over him, mute now, and stricken to stone. Her eyes were dilated, yet glazed, and she neither saw the light nor heard the man, nor cared for anything on earth but the white face in her lap. Jorian stood awe-struck, the candle shaking in his hand.

"Why, where was he, then, all the time?"

Margaret heeded him not. Jorian went to the empty chest and inspected it. He began to comprehend. The girl's dumb and frozen despair moved him.

"This is a sorry sight," said he. "It is a black night's work—all for a few skins! Better have gone with us than so. She is past answering me, poor wench. Stop—let us try whether—"

He took down a little round mirror, no bigger than his hand, and put it to Gerard's mouth and nostrils, and held it there. When he withdrew it it was dull.

"*There is life in him!*" said Jorian Ketel to himself.

Margaret caught the words instantly, though only muttered, and it was as if a statue should start into life and passion. She rose and flung her arms round Jorian's neck.

"Oh, bless the tongue that tells me so!" and she clasped the great rough fellow again and again, eagerly, almost fiercely.

"There, there! Let us lay him warm," said Jorian; and in a moment he raised Gerard and laid him on the bedclothes. Then he took out a flask he carried, and filled his hand twice with Schiedamze, and flung it sharply each time in Gerard's face. The pungent liquor co-operated with his recovery—he gave a faint sigh. Oh, never was sound so joyful to human ear! She flew toward him, but then stopped, quivering for fear she should hurt him. She had lost all confidence in herself.

"That is right—let him alone," said Jorian. "Don't go cuddling him as you did me, or you'll drive his breath back again. Let him alone, he is sure to come to. 'Tisn't like as if he was an old man."

Gerard sighed deeply, and a faint streak of color stole to his lips. Jorian made for the door. He had hardly reached it, when he found his legs seized from behind.

It was Margaret! She curled round his knees like a serpent, and kissed his hand, and fawned on him. "You won't tell? You have saved his life; you have not the heart to thrust him back into his grave, to undo your own good work?"

"No, no! It is not the first time I've done you two a good turn. 'Twas I told you in the church whither we had to take him. Besides, what is Dirk Brower to me? I'll see him hanged ere I'll tell him. But I wish you'd tell *me* where the parchments are. There are a hundred crowns offered for them. That would be a good windfall for my Joan and the children, you know."

"Ah, they shall have those hundred crowns!"

"What! Are the things in the house?" asked Jorian eagerly.

"No, but I know where they are. And by God and Saint Bavon I swear you shall have them tomorrow. Come to me for them when you will, but come alone."

"I were mad else. What! Share the hundred crowns with Dirk Brower? And now may my bones rot in my skin if I let a soul know the poor boy is here."

He then ran off, lest by staying longer he should excite suspicion and have them all after him. And Margaret knelt, quivering from head to foot, and prayed beside Gerard, and for Gerard.

"What is to do?" replied Jorian, to Dierich Brower's query. "Why, we have scared the girl out of her wits. She was in a kind of fit."

"We had better all go and doctor her, then."

"Oh, yes! And frighten her into the churchyard. Her father is a doctor, and I have roused him and set him to bring her round. Let us see the fire, will ye?"

His offhand way disarmed all suspicion. And soon after the party agreed that the kitchen of the Three Kings was much warmer than Peter's house, and they departed, having first untied Martin.

"Take note, mate, that I was right and the Burgomaster wrong," said Dierich Brower, at the door. "I said we should be too late to catch him, and we were too late."

Thus Gerard, in one terrible night, grazed prison and the grave.

I should try in vain to convey what bliss unspeakable settled now upon these persecuted lovers. Even to those who have joyed greatly, and greatly suffered, my feeble art can present but a pale reflection of Margaret's and Gerard's ecstasy.

To sit and see a beloved face come back from the grave to the world, to health and beauty by swift gradations, this was Margaret's—a joy to balance years of sorrow. It was Gerard's to awake from a trance and find his head pillowed on Margaret's arm; to hear the woman he adored murmur new words of eloquent love, and shower tears and tender kisses and caresses on him. He never knew, till this sweet moment, how ardently, how tenderly, she loved him. He thanked his enemies. They wreathed their arms sweetly round each other, and trouble and danger seemed a world, an age, behind them. They called each other husband and wife. Were they not solemnly betrothed? And had they not stood before the altar together? Was not the blessing of Holy Church upon their union, her curse on all who would part them?

Poor things! They were happy. Tomorrow they must part. But that was nothing to them now. They had seen Death, and all other troubles seemed light as air. While there is life there is hope; while there is hope there is joy. Separation for a year or two—what was it to them, who were so young, and had caught a glimpse of the grave? The future was bright, the present was Heaven; so passed the blissful hours.

Alas! their innocence ran other risks besides the prison and the grave. They were in most danger from their own hearts and their inexperience, now that visible danger there was none.

Ghysbrecht Van Swieten could not sleep all night for anxiety. He was afraid of thunder and lightning: or he would have made one of the party that searched Peter's house. As soon as the storm ceased altogether, he crept down stairs, saddled his mule, and rode to the Three Kings at Sevenbergen.

There he found his men sleeping, some on chairs, some on the tables, some on the floor. He roused them furiously, and heard the story of their unsuccessful search, interlarded with praises of their zeal.

"Fool! to let you go without me," cried the Burgomaster. "My life on't he was there all the time. Looked ye under the girl's bed?"

"No, there was no room for a man there."

"How know ye that if ye looked not?" snarled Ghysbrecht. "Ye should have looked under her bed and in it, too, and sounded all the panels with your knives. Come now, get up, and I shall show ye how to search."

Dierich Brower got up and shook himself. "If you find him, call me a horse and no man."

In a few minutes Peter's house was again surrounded. The fiery old man left his mule in the hands of Jorian Ketel, and with Dierich Brower and the others entered the house. The house was empty.

Not a creature to be seen, not even Peter. They went upstairs, and then suddenly one of the men gave a shout and pointed through Peter's window, which was open. The others looked, and there, at some little distance, walking quietly across the fields with Margaret and Martin, was the man they sought. Ghysbrecht with an exulting yell descended the stairs, and flung himself on his mule, and he and his men set off in hot pursuit.

CHAPTER XVII

GERARD, warned by recent peril, rose before daybreak, and waked Martin. The old soldier was astonished. He thought Gerard had escaped by the window last night. Being consulted as to the best way for him to leave the country and elude pursuit, he said there was but one road safe.

"I must guide you through the great forest to a bridle road I know of. This will take you speedily to a hostelry, where they will lend you a swift horse; and then a day's gallop will take you out of Holland. But let us start ere the folk here quit their beds."

Peter's house was but a furlong and a half from the forest. They started, Martin with his bow and three arrows, for it was Thursday, Gerard with nothing but a stout oak staff Peter gave him for the journey. Margaret pinned up her kirtle and farthingale, for the road was wet. Peter went as far as his garden hedge with them, and then, with more emotion than he often bestowed on passing events, gave the young man his blessing.

The sun was peeping above the horizon as they crossed the stony field and made for the wood. They had crossed about half when Margaret, who kept nervously looking back every now and then, uttered a cry and, following her instinct, began to run toward the wood, screaming with terror all the way. Ghysbrecht and his men were in hot pursuit.

Resistance would have been madness. Martin and Gerard followed Margaret's example. The pursuers gained slightly on them, but Martin kept shouting, "Only win the wood! Only win the wood!" They had too good a start for the men on foot, and their hearts bounded with hope at Martin's words, for the great trees seemed now to stretch their branches like friendly arms toward them, and their leaves like a screen.

But an unforeseen danger attacked them. The fiery old Burgomaster flung himself on his mule and, spurring him to a gallop, he headed not his own men only but the fugitives. His object was to cut them off. The old man came galloping in a semicircle and got on the edge of the wood right in front of Gerard—the others might escape for ought he cared. Margaret shrieked and tried to protect Gerard by clasping him, but he shook her off without ceremony. Ghysbrecht in his ardor forgot that hunted animals turn on the hunter, and that two men can hate, and two can long to kill the thing they hate.

Instead of attempting to dodge him, as the Burgomaster made sure he would, Gerard flew right at him, with a savage, exulting cry, and struck at him with all his heart and soul and strength. The oak staff came down on Ghysbrecht's face with a frightful crash, and laid him under his mule's tail beating the devil's tattoo with his heels, his face streaming, and his collar spattered with blood. The next moment, the three were in the wood. The yell of dismay and vengeance that burst from Ghysbrecht's men at that terrible blow which felled their leader told the fugitives that it was now a race for life or death.

"Why run?" cried Gerard, panting. "You have your bow, and I have this." And he shook his bloody staff.

"Boy!" roared Martin; "The *gallows!* Follow me!" And he fled into the wood. Soon they heard a cry like a pack of hounds opening on sight of the game. The men were in the wood, and saw them flitting among the trees. Margaret moaned and panted as she ran, and Gerard clenched his teeth, and grasped his staff. The next minute they came to a stiff hazel coppice. Martin dashed into it, and shouldered the young wood aside as if it were standing corn.

Ere they had gone fifty yards in it they came to four blind paths. Martin took one. "Bend low," said he, and half creeping, they glided along. Presently their path was again intersected with other little tortuous paths. They took one of them. It seemed to lead back, but it soon took a turn, and after a while brought them to a thick pine grove where the walking was good and hard. There were no paths here, and the young fir trees were so thick you could not see three yards before your nose.

When they had gone some way in this, Martin sat down and, having learned in war to lose all impression of danger with the danger itself, took a piece of bread and a slice of ham out of his wallet and began quietly to eat his breakfast. The young ones looked at him with dismay. He replied to their looks.

"All Sevenbergen could not find you now. You will lose your purse, Gerard, long before you get to Italy. Is that the way to carry a purse?"

Gerard looked, and there was a large triangular purse entangled by its chains to the buckle and strap of his wallet.

"This is none of mine," said he. "What is in it, I wonder?" He tried to detach it, but in passing through the coppice it had become inextricably entangled in his strap and buckle. "It seems loath to leave me," said Gerard, and he had to cut it loose with his knife. The purse, on examination, proved to be well provided with silver coins of all sizes, but its bloated appearance was greatly owing to a number of pieces of brown paper folded and doubled. A light burst on Gerard. "Why, it must be that old thief's! And see—stuffed with paper to deceive the world!"

The wonder was, how the Burgomaster's purse came on Gerard. They hit at last upon the right solution. The purse must have been at Ghysbrecht's saddlebow, and Gerard, rushing at his enemy, had unconsciously torn it away, thus felling his enemy and robbing him with a single gesture. Gerard was delighted at this feat, but Margaret was uneasy.

"Throw it away, Gerard, or let Martin take it back. Already they call you a thief. I cannot bear it."

"Throw it away? Give it him back? Not a stiver. This is spoil lawfully won in battle from an enemy. Is it not, Martin?"

"Why, of course. Send him back the brown paper an you will, but the purse or the coin—that were a sin."

"Oh, Gerard," said Margaret, "you are going to a distant land. We need the goodwill of Heaven. How can we hope for that if we take what is not ours?"

But Gerard saw it in a different light.

"It is Heaven that gives it me by a miracle, and I shall cherish it accordingly," said this pious youth. "Thus the favored people spoiled the Egyptians and were blessed."

"Take your own way," said Margaret, humbly. "You are wiser than I am. You are my husband," added she in a low murmuring voice. "Is it for me to gainsay you?"

These humble words from Margaret, who till that day had held the whip hand, rather surprised Martin for the moment. They recurred to him some time afterward and then they surprised him less. Gerard kissed her tenderly in return for her wifelike docility, and they pursued their journey hand in hand, Martin leading the way, into the depths of the huge forest. The farther they went, the more absolutely secure from pursuit they felt.

Indeed the townspeople never ventured so far as this into the trackless part of the forest.

Impetuous natures repent quickly. Gerard was no sooner out of all danger than his conscience began to prick him.

"Martin, would I had not struck quite so hard."

"Whom? Oh, let that pass! He is cheap served."

"Martin, I saw his gray hairs as my stick fell on him. I doubt they will not from my sight this while."

Martin grunted with contempt. "Who spares a badger for his gray hairs? The grayer your enemy is, the older; and the older, the craftier; and the craftier, the better for a little killing."

"Killing? Killing, Martin? Speak not of killing!" And Gerard shook all over.

"I am much mistook if you have not," said Martin cheerfully.

"Now Heaven forbid!"

"The old vagabond's skull cracked like a walnut. Aha!"

"Heaven and the saints forbid it!"

"He rolled off his mule like a stone shot out of a cart. Said I to myself, 'There is one wiped out.'" And the iron old soldier grinned ruthlessly.

Gerard fell on his knees, and began to pray for his enemy's life. At this Martin lost his patience.

"Here's mummery. What, you that set up for learning, know you not that a wise man never strikes his enemy but to kill him? And what is all this coil about killing of old men? If it had been a young one now, with the joys of life waiting for him, wine, women, and pillage? But an old fellow at the edge of the grave, why *not* shove him in? Go he must, today or tomorrow—and what better place for graybeards? Now if ever I should be so mischancy as to last so long as Ghysbrecht did, and have to go on a mule's legs instead of Martin Wittenhaagen's, and a back like this"—striking the wood of his bow—"instead of this"—striking the string—"I'll thank and bless any young fellow who will knock me on the head, as you have done that old shopkeeper, malison on his memory!"

"Oh, *culpa mea, culpa mea!*" cried Gerard, and smote upon his breast.

"Look there," said Martin to Margaret scornfully, "*he is a priest at heart still.* And when he is not in ire, Saint Paul, what a milksop!"

"Tush, Martin!" cried Margaret reproachfully. Then she wreathed her arms round Gerard and comforted him with the double magic of a woman's sense and a woman's voice.

"Sweetheart," murmured she, "you forget! You went not a step out of the way to harm him who hunted you to your death. You fled from him. He it was who spurred on you. Then did you strike, but in self-defense, and a single blow, and with that which was in your hand. Malice had drawn knife, or struck again and again. How often have men been smitten with staves not one but many blows, yet no lives lost! If then your enemy has fallen, it is through his own malice, not yours, and by the will of God."

"Bless you, Margaret, bless you for thinking so!"

"Yes, but, beloved one, if you have had the *misfortune* to kill that wicked man, the more need is there that you fly with haste from Holland. Oh, let us on!"

"Nay, Margaret," said Gerard. "I fear not man's vengeance, thanks to Martin here, and this thick wood. Only Him I fear whose eye pierces the forest, and reads the heart of man. If I but struck in self-defense, 'tis well, but if in hate, He may bid the avenger of blood follow me to Italy. To Italy? Ay, to earth's remotest bounds."

"Hush!" said Martin, peevishly. "I can't hear for your chat."

"What is it?"

"Do you hear nothing, Margaret? My ears are getting old."

Margaret listened, and presently she heard a tuneful sound, like a single stroke upon a deep ringing bell. She described it so to Martin.

"Nay, I heard it," said he.

"And so did I," said Gerard. "It was beautiful. Ah, there it is again! How sweetly it blends with the air. It is a long way off. It is before us, is it not?"

"No, no! The echoes of this wood confound the ear of a stranger. It comes from the pine grove."

"What, the one we passed?"

"The one we passed."

"Why, Martin, is this *anything?* You look pale."

"Wonderful!" said Martin, with a sickly sneer. "He asks me is it *anything?* Come on, on! At any rate, let us reach a better place than this."

"A better place—for what?"

"To stand at bay, Gerard," said Martin gravely, "and die like soldiers, killing three for one."

"What's that sound?"

"*It is the avenger of blood.*"

"Oh, Martin, save him! Oh, Heaven be merciful! What new mysterious peril is this?"

"*Girl, it's a bloodhound.*"

CHAPTER XVIII

THE COURAGE, like the talent, of common men runs in a narrow groove. Take them but an inch out of that, and they are done. Martin's courage was perfect as far as it went. He had met and baffled many dangers in the course of his rude life, and these familiar dangers he could face with Spartan fortitude, almost with indifference. But he had never been hunted by a bloodhound; nor had he ever seen that brute's unerring instinct baffled by human cunning. Here, then, a sense of the supernatural combined with novelty to unsteel his heart. After going a few steps he leaned on his bow, and energy and hope oozed out of him. Gerard, to whom the danger appeared slight in proportion as it was distant, urged him to flight.

"What avails it?" said Martin sadly. "If we get clear of the wood we shall die cheap. Here, hard by, I know a place where we may die dear."

"Alas, good Martin!" cried Gerard. "Despair not so quickly. There must be some way to escape."

"Oh, Martin," cried Margaret, "what if we were to part company? Gerard's life alone is forfeit. Is there no way to draw the pursuit on us twain and let him go safe? Take us to some thick place where numbers will not avail our foes."

"I am going," said Martin sulkily. "Hurry avails not. We cannot shun the hound, and the place is hard by."

Then, turning to the left, he led the way, as men go to execution. He soon brought them to a thick hazel coppice, like the one that had favored their escape in the morning. "There," said he, "this is but a furlong broad, but it will serve our turn."

"What are we to do?"

"Get through this, and wait on the other side. Then as they come straggling through, shoot three, knock two on the head, and the rest will kill us."

"Is that all you can think of?" said Gerard.

"That is all."

"Then, Martin Wittenhaagen, I take the lead, for you have lost your head. Come, can you obey so young a man as I am?"

"Oh, yes, Martin!" cried Margaret. "Do not gainsay Gerard. He is wiser than his years."

Martin yielded a sullen assent.

"Do then as you see me do," said Gerard, and drawing his huge knife, he cut at every step a hazel shoot or two close by the ground, and turning round twisted them breast-high behind him among the standing shoots. Martin did the same, but with a dogged, hopeless air. When they had thus painfully traveled through the greater part of the coppice, the bloodhound's deep bay came nearer, and nearer, less and less musical, louder, and sterner. Margaret trembled. Martin went down on his stomach and listened.

"I hear a horse's feet."

"No," said Gerard. "I doubt it is a mule's. That cursed Ghysbrecht is still alive. None other would follow me up so bitterly."

"Never strike your enemy but to slay him," said Martin gloomily.

"I'll hit harder this time, if Heaven gives me the chance," said Gerard.

At last they worked through the coppice, and there was an open wood. The trees were large, but far apart, and no escape possible that way. And now with the hound's bay mingled a score of voices, whooping and hallooing.

"The whole village is out after us," said Martin.

"I care not," said Gerard. "Listen, Martin. I have made the track smooth to the dog but rough to the men, that we may deal with them apart. Thus the hound will gain on the men, and as soon as he comes out of the coppice we must kill him."

"The hound? There are more than one."

"I hear but one."

"Ay, but one speaks, the others run mute. But let the leading hound lose the scent, then another shall give tongue. There will be two dogs at least, or devils in dogs' hides."

"Then we must kill two instead of one. The moment they are dead, into the coppice again, and go right back."

"That is a good thought, Gerard!" said Martin, plucking up heart.

"Hush! The men are in the wood." Gerard now gave his orders in a whisper. "Stand you with your bow by the side of the coppice—there, in the ditch. I will go but a few yards to yon oak tree and hide behind it. The dogs will follow me, and as they come out, shoot as many as you can. The rest will I brain as they come round the tree."

Martin's eye flashed. They took up their places. The whooping and hallooing came closer and closer, and soon even the rustling of the young wood was heard, and every now and then the unerring bloodhound gave a single bay. It was terrible! the branches rustling nearer and nearer, and the inevitable struggle for life and death coming on minute by minute, and that death knell leading it. A trembling hand was laid on Gerard's shoulder. It made him start violently, strung up as he was.

"Martin says if we are forced to part company, make for that high ash tree we came in by."

"Yes! yes! yes! But go back, for Heaven's sake! Don't come here, all out in the open!"

She ran back toward Martin, but ere she could get to him, suddenly a huge dog burst out of the coppice and stood erect a moment. Margaret cowered with fear, but he never noticed her. Scent was to him what sight is to us. He lowered his nose an instant, and the next moment, with an awful yell, sprang straight at Gerard's tree, and rolled head over heels dead as a stone, literally spitted by an arrow from the bow that twanged beside the coppice in Martin's hand. That same moment out came another hound and smelt his dead comrade. Gerard rushed out at him, but ere he could use his cudgel, a streak of white lightning seemed to strike the hound, and he groveled in the dust, wounded desperately but not killed, and howling piteously.

Gerard had not time to dispatch him. The coppice rustled too near, it seemed alive. Pointing wildly to Martin to go back, Gerard ran a few yards to the right, then crept cautiously into the thick coppice just as three men burst out. These had headed their comrades considerably, the rest were following at various distances. Gerard crawled back almost on all fours. Instinct taught Martin and Margaret to do the same upon their line of retreat. Thus, within the distance of a few yards, the pursuers and pursued were passing one another upon opposite tracks.

A loud cry announced the discovery of the dead and wounded hound. Then followed a babble of voices, still swelling as fresh pursuers reached the spot. The hunters, as usual on a surprise, were wasting time, and the hunted ones were making the most of it.

"I hear no more hounds," whispered Martin to Margaret, and he was himself again.

It was Margaret's turn to tremble and despair.

"Oh, why did we part with Gerard! They will kill my Gerard, and I not near him."

"Nay, nay! The head to catch him is not on their shoulders. You bade him meet us at the ash tree?"

"And so I did. Bless you, Martin, for thinking of that. To the ash tree!"

"Ay, but with less noise."

They were now nearly at the edge of the coppice when suddenly they heard whooping and hallooing behind them. The men had satisfied themselves the fugitives were in the coppice, and were beating back.

"No matter," whispered Martin to his trembling companion. "We shall have time to win clear and slip out of sight by hard running."

"Ah!"

He stopped suddenly, for just as he was going to burst out of the brushwood, his eye caught a figure keeping sentinel. It was Ghysbrecht van Swieten seated on his mule. A bloody bandage was across his nose, the bridge of which was broken; but over this his eyes peered keenly, and it was plain by their expression he had heard the fugitives rustle and was looking out for them. Martin muttered a terrible oath and cautiously strung his bow, then with equal caution fitted his last arrow to the string. Margaret put her hands to her face, but said nothing. She saw this man must die or Gerard. After the first impulse she peered through her fingers, her heart panting to her throat.

The bow was raised, and the deadly arrow steadily drawn to its head, when at that moment an active figure leaped on Ghysbrecht from behind so swiftly it was like a hawk swooping on a pigeon. A kerchief went over the Burgomaster, in a turn of the hand his head was muffled in it, and he was whirled from his seat and fell heavily upon the ground, where he lay groaning with terror, and Gerard jumped down after him.

"Hist, Martin! Martin!"

Martin and Margaret came out, the former open-mouthed, crying: "Now fly, fly! While they are all in the thicket. We are saved."

At this crisis, when safety seemed at hand, as fate would have it Margaret, who had borne up so bravely till now, began to succumb.

"Oh, my beloved, fly!" she gasped. "Leave me, for I am faint."

"No! No!" cried Gerard. "Death together, or safety. Ah, the mule! Mount her, you, and I'll run by your side."

In a moment Martin was on Ghysbrecht's mule, and Gerard raised the fainting girl in his arms and placed her on the saddle, and relieved Martin of his bow.

"Help! Treason! Murder! Murder!" shrieked Ghysbrecht, suddenly rising on his hams.

"Silence, cur," roared Gerard, and trod him down again by the throat as men crush an adder.

"Now, have you got her firm? Then fly! For our lives, for our lives!"

But even as the mule, urged suddenly by Martin's heel, scattered the flints with his hind hoofs ere he got into a canter, and even as Gerard withdrew his foot from Ghysbrecht's throat to run, Dierich Brower and his five men, who had come back for orders and heard the Burgomaster's cries, burst roaring out of the coppice on them.

CHAPTER XIX

There was something terrible and truly animal, both in the roar of triumph with which the pursuers burst out of the thicket on our fugitives and the sharp cry of terror with which these latter darted away. The pursuers' hands clutched the empty air scarce two feet behind them as they fled for life. Confused for a moment, like lions that miss their spring, Dierich and his men let Gerard and the mule put ten yards between them. Then they flew after with uplifted weapons. They were sure of catching them, for this was not the first time the parties had measured speed. In the open ground they had gained visibly on the three this morning, and now at last it was a fair race again, to be settled by speed alone. A hundred yards were covered in no time. Yet still there remained these ten yards between the pursuers and the pursued.

This increase of speed since the morning puzzled Dierich Brower. The reason was this. When three run in company, the pace is that of the slowest of the three. From Peter's house to the edge of the forest Gerard ran Margaret's pace, but now he ran his own; for the mule was fleet, and could have left them all far behind. Moreover, youth and chaste living began to tell. Daylight grew imperceptibly between the hunted ones and the hunters. The pursuers began to curse. Martin heard, and his face lighted up.

"Courage, Gerard! Courage, brave lad! They are straggling."

It was so. Dierich was now headed by one of his men, and another dropped into the rear altogether. They came to a rising ground, not sharp, but long; and here youth, and grit, and sober living told more than ever. Ere he reached the top, Dierich's forty years weighed him down like forty bullets.

"Our cake is dough," he gasped. "Take him dead, if you can't alive." And he left running and followed at a foot's pace. Jorian Ketel tailed off next, and then another, and so, one by one, Gerard ran them all to a standstill, except one who kept on stanch as a bloodhound, though losing ground every minute. His name, if I am not mistaken, was Eric Wouverman. Followed by him, they came to a rise in the wood, shorter but much steeper than the last.

"Hand on mane!" cried Martin.

Gerard obeyed, and the mule helped him up the hill faster even than he was running before. At the sight of this maneuver Dierich's man lost heart and, being now full eighty yards behind Gerard, and rather more than that in advance of his nearest comrade, he pulled up short, and, in obedience to Dierich's order, took down his crossbow, leveled it deliberately, and just as the trio was sinking out of sight over the crest of the hill, sent the bolt whizzing among them.

There was a cry of dismay, and next moment, as if a thunderbolt had fallen on them, they were lying on the ground, mule and all.

The effect was so sudden and magical that the shooter himself was stupefied for an instant. Then he hailed his companions to join him in effecting the capture, and himself set off up the hill. But ere he had got halfway, up rose the figure of Martin Wittenhaagen with a bent bow in his hand. Eric Wouverman no sooner saw him in this attitude than he darted behind a tree, and made himself as small as possible. Martin's skill with that weapon was well known, and the slain dog was a keen reminder of it.

Wouverman peered round the bark cautiously. There was the arrow's point still aimed at him. He saw it shine. He dared not move from his shelter. When he had been at peep-bo some minutes, his companions came up in great force. Then with a scornful laugh Martin vanished, and presently was heard to ride off on the mule.

All the men ran up together. The high ground commanded a view of a narrow but almost interminable glade. They saw Gerard and Margaret running along at a prodigious distance—they looked like gnats—and Martin galloping after them *ventre à terre.*

The hunters were outwitted as well as outrun. The Burgomaster's mule put her foot in a rabbit hole at or about the time the crossbow bolt whizzed innocuous over her head. She fell and threw both her riders. Gerard caught Margaret, but was carried down by her weight and impetus. The docile mule was up again directly, and stood trembling. Martin was next and, looking round, saw there was but one in pursuit. On this he made the young lovers fly on foot while he checked the enemy as I have recorded.

He now galloped after his companions, and when after a long race he caught them, he instantly put Gerard and Margaret on the mule, and ran by their side till his breath failed, then took his turn to ride, and so in rotation. Thus the runner was always fresh, and long ere they relaxed their speed, all sound and trace of them was hopelessly lost to Dierich and his men. These latter went crestfallen back to look after their chief, and their winged bloodhound.

CHAPTER XX

THUS Gerard and Margaret, though they started at every leaf that rustled louder than its fellows, glowed all over with joy and thankfulness as they glided among the friendly trees in safety and deep tranquil silence, baying dogs and brutal voices yet ringing in their mind's ears. Suddenly they emerged upon a beaten path and Martin stopped.

"This is the bridle road I spoke of," said he, hanging his head, "and there away lies the hostelry."

Margaret and Gerard cast a scared look at one another.

"Come a step with me, Martin," whispered Gerard. When he had drawn him aside, he said to him in a broken voice: "Good Martin, watch over her for me! She is my wife, yet I leave her. See Martin, here is gold—it was for my journey. It is no use my asking her to take it—she would not—but you will for her, will you not? Oh, Heaven, and is this all I can do for her? Money? But poverty is a curse. You will not let her want for anything, dear Martin? The Burgomaster's silver is enough for me."

"Thou art a good lad, Gerard. Neither want nor harm shall come to her. I care more for her little finger than for all the world. And were she naught to me, even for thy sake would I be a father to her. Go with a stout heart, and God be with thee going and coming." And the rough soldier wrung Gerard's hand and turned his head away, with unwonted feeling. After a moment's silence, he was for going back to Margaret, but Gerard stopped him.

"No, good Martin. Prithee, stay here behind this thicket, and turn your head away from us while I—Oh, Martin, Martin!"

By this means Gerard escaped a witness of his anguish at leaving her he loved, and Martin escaped a piteous sight. He did not see the poor young things kneel and renew before Heaven those holy vows cruel men had interrupted. He did not see them cling together like one, and then try to part and fail, and return to one another, and cling again, like drowning, despairing creatures. But he heard Gerard sob, and sob, and Margaret moan. At last there was a hoarse cry, and feet pattered on the hard road.

He started up, and there was Gerard running wildly, with both hands clasped above his head in prayer, and Margaret tottering back toward him with palms extended piteously, as if for help, and ashy cheek, and eyes fixed on vacancy.

He caught her in his arms, and spoke words of comfort to her, but her mind could not take them in; only at the sound of his voice she moaned and held him tight, and trembled violently. He got her on the mule and put his arms round her, and so, supporting her frame, which, from being strung like a bow, had now turned all relaxed and powerless, he took her slowly and sadly home. She did not shed one tear, nor speak one word. At the edge of the wood he took her off the mule, and bade her go across to her father's house. She did as she was bid.

Martin went to Rotterdam. Sevenbergen was too hot for him.

Gerard, severed from her he loved, went like one in a dream. He hired a horse and guide at the little hostelry, and rode swiftly toward the German frontier. But all was mechanical. His senses felt blunted; trees and houses and men moved by him like objects seen through a veil. His companion spoke to him twice, but he did not answer. Only once he cried out savagely, "Shall we never be out of this hateful country?" After many hours' riding they came to the brow of a steep hill; a small brook ran at the bottom.

"Halt!" cried the guide, and pointed across the valley. "Here is Germany."

"Where?"

"On t'other side of the bourn. No need to ride down the hill, I trow."

Gerard dismounted without a word, and took the Burgomaster's purse from his girdle. While he opened it, "You will soon be out of this hateful country," said the guide, half sulkily. "Mayhap the one you are going to will like you no better. Anyway, though it be a church you have robbed, they cannot take you, once across that bourn."

These words at another time would have earned the speaker an admonition, or a cuff. They fell on Gerard now like idle air. He paid the lad in silence, and descended the hill alone. The brook was silvery. It ran murmuring over little pebbles that glittered, varnished by the clear water.

He sat down and looked stupidly at them. Then he drank of the brook, then he laved his hot feet and hands in it. It was very cold, it waked him. He rose, and taking a run, leaped across it into Germany. Even as he touched the strange land he turned suddenly and looked back.

"Farewell, ungrateful country!" he cried. "But for *her* it would cost me naught to leave you forever, and all my kith and kin, and—the mother that bore me, and—my playmates, and my little native town. Farewell, fatherland—welcome the wide world!" And with these brave words in his mouth he dropped suddenly with arms and legs all weak, and sat down and sobbed bitterly upon the foreign soil.

When the young exile had sat a while bowed down, he rose and dashed the tears from his eyes like a man and, not casting a single glance more behind him to weaken his heart, stepped out into the wide world.

All nations meet in a convent, so thanks to his good friends the monks, and his own thirst of knowledge, he could speak most of the languages needed on that long road. He said to himself: "I will soon be at Rome. The sooner the better, now."

After walking a good league, he came to a place where four ways met. Being country roads and serpentine, they had puzzled many an inexperienced neighbor passing from village to village. Gerard took out a little dial Peter had given him and set it in the autumn sun, and by this compass steered unhesitatingly for Rome.

Eight leagues he walked that day, and in the afternoon came upon a huge building with an enormous arched gateway and a postern by its side.

"A monastery!" cried he joyfully; "I go no further lest I fare worse." He applied at the postern, and, on stating whence he came and whither bound, was instantly admitted and directed to the guest chamber, a large and lofty room where travelers were fed and lodged gratis by the charity of the monastic orders. Soon the bell tinkled for vespers, and Gerard entered the church of the convent and from his place heard a service sung so exquisitely it seemed the choir of Heaven. But one thing was wanting—Margaret was not there to hear it with him, and this made him sigh bitterly amid rapture. At supper, plain but wholesome and abundant food, and good beer, brewed in the convent, were set before him and his fellows, and at an early hour they were ushered into a large dormitory, and, the number being moderate, had each a truckle bed, and for covering sheepskins dressed with the fleece on.

But previously to this a monk, struck by his youth and beauty, questioned him, and soon drew out his projects and his heart. When he was found to be convent-bred and going alone to Rome, he became a personage, and in the morning they showed him over the convent and made him stay and dine in the refectory. They also pricked him a route on a slip of parchment, and the Prior gave him a silver gulden to help him on the road, and advised him to join the first honest company he should fall in with, "and not face alone the manifold perils of the way."

"Perils?" said Gerard to himself.

That evening he came to a small straggling town where was one inn. It had no sign, but being now better versed in the customs of the country he detected it at once by the coats of arms on its walls. These belonged to the distinguished visitors who had slept in it at different epochs since its foundation, and left these customary tokens of their patronage. At present it looked more like a mausoleum than a hotel. Nothing moved nor sounded either in it, or about it. Gerard hammered on the great oak door. No answer. He hallooed. No reply. After a while he hallooed louder, and at last a little round window, or rather hole in the wall, opened, a man's head protruded cautiously, like a tortoise's from its shell, and eyed Gerard stolidly, but never uttered a syllable.

"Is this an inn?" asked Gerard with a covert sneer.

The head seemed to fall into a brown study. Eventually it nodded, but lazily.

"Can I have entertainment here?"

Again the head pondered and ended by nodding, but sullenly, and seemed a skull overburdened with catchpenny interrogatories.

"How am I to get within, an't please you?"

At this the head popped in and a hand popped out, pointed round the corner of the building, and slammed the window. Gerard followed the indication, and after some research discovered that the fortification had one vulnerable part, a small, low door on its flank. As for the main entrance, that was used to keep out thieves and customers, except once or twice in a year, when they entered together—when some duke or count arrived in pomp with his train of gaudy ruffians.

Gerard, having penetrated the outer fort, soon found his way to the stove (as the public room was called from the principal article in it), and sat down near the oven, in which were only a few live embers that diffused a mild and grateful heat.

They brought in the tablecloths, but oh, so brown, so dirty, and so coarse! They seemed like sacks that had been worn out in agriculture and come down to this, or like shreds from the mainsail of some worn-out ship. The Hollander, who had never seen such linen even in nightmare, uttered a faint cry.

"What is to do?" inquired a traveler. Gerard pointed ruefully to the dirty sackcloth. The other looked at it with lackluster eye, and comprehended naught.

A Burgundian soldier with his arbalest at his back came peeping over Gerard's shoulder, and seeing what was amiss, laughed so loud that the room rang again, then slapped him on the back and cried, "*Courage! Le diable est mort.*"

Gerard stared. He doubted alike the good tidings and their relevancy, but the tones were so hearty and the arbalestrier's face, notwithstanding a formidable beard, was so gay and genial, that he smiled, and after a pause said dryly, "*Il a bien fait. Avec l'eau et linge du pays on allait le noircir à ne se reconnaître plus.*"

"*Tiens, tiens!*" cried the soldier. "*V'là qui parle Français, peu s'en faut.*" And he seated himself by Gerard, and in a moment was talking volubly of war, women, and pillage, interlarding his discourse with curious oaths, at which Gerard drew away from him more or less.

At peep of day Gerard rose and went in search of milk and air. A cheerful voice hailed him in French.

"What ho! You are up with the sun, comrade."

"He rises betimes that lies in a dog's lair," answered Gerard crossly.

"*Courage, l'ami! Le diable est mort,*" was the instant reply. The soldier then told him his name was Denys, and he was passing from Flushing in Zealand to the Duke's French dominions. "And who are you, and whither bound?"

"My name is Gerard, and I am going to Rome," said the more reserved Hollander, and in a way that invited no further confidences.

"All the better. We will go together as far as Burgundy."

"That is not my road."

"All roads take to Rome."

"Ay, but the shortest road thither is my way."

"Well, then, it is I who must go out of my way a step for the sake of good company, for thy face likes me, and thou speakest French, or nearly."

"There go two words to that bargain," said Gerard coldly. "I steer by proverbs too. They do put old heads on young men's shoulders. '*Bon loup mauvais compagnon, dit le brebis,*' and a soldier, they say, is near a kin to a wolf."

"They lie," said Denys. "Besides, if he is, '*Les loups ne se mangent pas entre eux.*'"

"Ay, but, Sir Soldier, I am not a wolf. And, thou knowest, '*A bien petite occasion se saisit le loup du mouton.*'"

"Let us drop wolves and sheep, being men. My meaning is that a good soldier never pillages—a comrade. Come, young man, too much suspicion becomes not your years. They who travel should learn to read faces. Methinks you might see lealty in mine, sith I have seen it in yours. Is it yon fat purse at your girdle you fear for?" Gerard turned pale. "Look hither!" And he undid his belt and poured out of it a double handful of gold pieces, then returned them to their hiding-place. "There is a hostage for you," said he. "Carry you that, and let us be comrades"—and handed him his belt, gold and all.

Gerard stared. "If I am overprudent, you have not enow." But he flushed, and looked pleased at the other's trust in him.

"Bah, I can read faces! And so must you, or you'll never take your four bones safe to Rome."

"Soldier, you would find me a dull companion, for my heart is very heavy," said Gerard, yielding.

"I'll cheer you, *mon gars*."

"I think you would," said Gerard sweetly, "and sore need have I of a kindly voice in mine ear this day."

"Oh, no soul is sad alongside me! I lift up their poor little hearts with my consigne: '*Courage, tout le monde! Le diable est mort.*' Ha, ha!"

"So be it, then," said Gerard. "But take back your belt, for I could never trust by halves. We will go together as far as the Rhine, and God go with us both!"

"Amen!" said Denys, and lifted his cap. "*En avant!*"

CHAPTER XXI

One day, being in a forest a few leagues from Dusseldorf, as Gerard was walking like one in a dream thinking of Margaret and scarce seeing the road he trod, his companion laid a hand on his shoulder and strung his crossbow with glittering eye. "Hush!" said he in a low whisper that startled Gerard more than thunder. Gerard grasped his ax tight and shook a little. He heard a rustling in the wood hard by and at the same moment Denys sprang into the wood and his crossbow went to his shoulder even as he jumped. Twang! went the metal string and after an instant's suspense he roared: "Run forward, guard the road. He is hit! He is hit!"

Gerard darted forward, and as he ran a young bear burst out of the wood right upon him. Finding itself intercepted it went up on its hind legs with a snarl, and, though not half-grown, opened formidable jaws and long claws. Gerard in a fury of excitement and agitation flung himself on it and delivered a tremendous blow on its nose with his ax, and the creature staggered. Another, and it lay groveling with Gerard hacking it.

"Hallo! Stop! You are mad to spoil the meat."

"I took it for a robber," said Gerard, panting. "I mean I had made ready for a robber, so I could not hold my hand."

"Ay, these chattering travelers have stuffed your head full of thieves and assassins. They have not got a real live robber in their whole nation. Nay, I'll carry the beast; bear thou my crossbow."

"We will carry it by turns, then," said Gerard, "for 'tis a heavy load. Poor thing, how its blood drips. Why did we slay it?"

"For supper, and the reward the baillie of the next town shall give us."

Gerard sighed. "In sooth I love not to think of this Dusseldorf, where we are apt to part company, good friend." They walked silently, each thinking of the separation at hand. The thought checked trifling conversation, and at these moments it is a relief to do something, however insignificant. Gerard asked Denys to lend him a bolt. "I have often shot with a longbow, but never with one of these!"

"Draw thy knife and cut this one out of the cub," said Denys slyly.

"Nay, nay, I want a clean one."

Denys gave him three out of his quiver. Gerard strung the bow and leveled it at a bough that had fallen into the road at some distance. The power of the instrument surprised him; the short but thick steel bow jarred him to the very heel as it went off, and the swift steel shaft was invisible in its passage. Only the dead leaves with which November had carpeted the narrow road flew about on the other side of the bough.

"Ye aimed a thought too high," said Denys.

"What a deadly thing! No wonder it is driving out the longbow—to Martin's much discontent."

"Ay, lad," said Denys triumphantly, "it gains ground every day, in spite of their laws and their proclamations to keep up the yewen bow because forsooth their grandsires shot with it, knowing no better. You see, Gerard, war is not pastime. Men will shoot at their enemies with the hittingest arm and the killingest, not with the longest and missingest."

Gerard did not answer, for his ear was attracted by a sound behind them. It was a peculiar sound, too, like something heavy, but not hard, rushing softly over the dead leaves. He turned round with some little curiosity. A colossal creature was coming down the road at about sixty paces distance. He looked at it in a sort of calm stupor at first, but the next moment he turned ashy-pale.

"Denys!" he cried. "Oh, God! Denys!"

Denys whirled round. It was a bear as big as a cart horse.

It was tearing along with its huge head down, running on a hot scent. The very moment he saw it Denys said in a sickening whisper:

"*The cub!*"

Oh, the concentrated horror of that one word, whispered hoarsely, with dilating eyes! For in that syllable it all flashed upon them both like a sudden stroke of lightning in the dark—the bloody trail, the murdered cub, the mother upon them, *and it. Death.*

All this in a moment of time. The next, she saw them. Huge as she was, she seemed to double herself (it was her long hair bristling with rage). She raised her head big as a bull's, her swine-shaped jaws opened wide at them, her eyes turned to blood and flame, and she rushed upon them, scattering the leaves about her like a whirlwind as she came.

"Shoot!" screamed Denys, but Gerard stood shaking from head to foot, useless.

"Shoot, man! Ten thousand devils, shoot! Too late! Tree, tree!" and he dropped the cub, pushed Gerard across the road, and flew to the first tree and climbed it, Gerard the same on his side. And as they fled both men uttered inhuman howls like savage creatures grazed by death.

With all their speed one or other would have been torn to fragments at the foot of his tree, but the bear stopped a moment at the cub. Without taking her bloodshot eyes off those she was hunting, she smelt it all round, and found—how, her Creator only knows—that it was dead, quite dead. She gave a yell such as neither of the hunted ones had ever heard, nor dreamed to be in nature, and flew after Denys. She reared and struck at him as he climbed. He was just out of reach. Instantly she seized the tree, and with her huge teeth tore a great piece out of it. Then she reared again, dug her claws deep into the bark, and began to mount it slowly, but as surely as a monkey.

Denys's evil star had led him to a dead tree, a mere shaft, and of no very great height. He climbed faster than his pursuer, and was soon at the top. He looked this way and that for some bough of another tree to spring to. There was none, and if he jumped down, he knew the bear would be upon him ere he could recover the fall, and make short work of him. Moreover, Denys was little used to turning his back on danger, and his blood was rising at being hunted. He turned at bay.

"My hour is come," thought he. "Let me meet death like a man." He knelt down and grasped a small shoot to steady himself, drew his long knife, and clenching his teeth, prepared to jab the huge brute as soon as it should mount within reach. Of this combat the result was not doubtful. The monster's head and neck was scarce vulnerable for bone and masses of hair. The man was going to sting the bear, and the bear to crack the man like a nut.

Gerard's heart was better than his nerves. He saw his friend's mortal danger, and passed at once from fear to blinding rage. He slipped down his tree in a moment, caught up the crossbow, which he had dropped in the road, and running furiously up, sent a bolt into the bear's body with a loud shout. The bear gave a snarl of rage and pain, and turned its head irresolutely.

"Keep aloof," cried Denys, "or you are a dead man!"

"I care not." And in a moment he had another bolt ready and shot it fiercely into the bear, screaming, "Take that! Take that!"

Denys poured a volley of oaths down at him. "Get away, idiot!"

He was right. The bear, finding so formidable and noisy a foe behind her, slipped growling down the tree, rending deep furrows in it as she slipped. Gerard ran back to his tree and climbed it swiftly. But while his legs were dangling some eight feet from the ground, the bear came rearing and struck with her forepaw, and out flew a piece of bloody cloth from Gerard's hose. He climbed, and climbed, and presently he heard as it were in the air a voice say, "Go out on the bough!" He looked, and there was a long massive branch before him shooting upward at a slight angle. He threw his body across it, and by a series of convulsive efforts worked up it to the end. Then he looked round panting.

The bear was mounting the tree on the other side. He heard her claws scrape, and saw her bulge on both sides of the massive tree. Her eye not being very quick, she reached the fork and passed it, mounting the main stem. Gerard drew breath more freely. The bear either heard him, or found by scent she was wrong. She paused; presently she caught sight of him. She eyed him steadily, then quietly descended to the fork.

Slowly and cautiously she stretched out a paw and tried the bough. It was a stiff oak branch, sound as iron. Instinct taught the creature this. It crawled carefully out on the bough, growling savagely as it came.

Gerard looked wildly down. He was forty feet from the ground. Death below. Death moving slow but sure on him in a still more horrible form. His hair bristled. The sweat poured from him. He sat helpless, fascinated, tongue-tied. As the fearful monster crawled growling toward him, incongruous thoughts coursed through his mind. Margaret—the Vulgate where it speaks of the rage of a she-bear robbed of her whelps—Rome—Eternity.

The bear crawled on. And now the stupor of death fell on the doomed man. He saw the open jaws and bloodshot eyes coming, but in a mist. As in a mist he heard a twang. He glanced down. Denys, white and silent as death, was shooting up at the bear. The bear snarled at the twang, but crawled on. Again the crossbow twanged, and the bear snarled, and came nearer. Again the crossbow twanged, and the next moment the bear was close upon Gerard where he sat with hair standing stiff on end, and eyes starting from their sockets, palsied.

The bear opened her jaws like a grave, and hot blood spouted from them upon Gerard as from a pump. The bough rocked. The wounded monster was reeling. It clung, it stuck its sickles of claws deep into the wood; it toppled, its claws held firm, but its body rolled off, and the sudden shock to the branch shook Gerard forward on his stomach with his face upon one of the bear's straining paws. At this, by a convulsive effort, she raised her head up, up, till he felt her hot fetid breath. Then huge teeth snapped together loudly close below him in the air, with a last effort of baffled hate. The ponderous carcass rent the claws out of the bough, pounded the earth with a tremendous thump. There was a shout of triumph below, and the very next instant a cry of dismay; for Gerard had swooned and, without an attempt to save himself, rolled headlong from the perilous height.

Denys caught at Gerard and somewhat checked his fall; but it may be doubted whether this alone would have saved him from breaking his neck or a limb. His best friend now was the dying bear, on whose hairy carcass his head and shoulders descended. Denys tore him off her. It was needless. She panted still, and her limbs quivered, but a hare was not so harmless; and soon she breathed her last, and the judicious Denys propped Gerard up against her, being soft, and fanned him. He came to by degrees, but confused, and feeling the bear all around him, rolled away yelling.

"*Courage!*" cried Denys. "*Le diable est mort.*"

"Is it dead? Quite dead?" inquired Gerard from behind a tree; for his courage was feverish, and the cold fit was on him just now, and had been for some time.

"Behold," said Denys, and pulled the brute's ear playfully and opened her jaws and put in his head, with other insulting antics, in the midst of which Gerard was violently sick.

Denys laughed at him.

"What is the matter now?" said he. "Also why tumble off your perch just when we had won the day?"

"I swooned, I trow."

"But *why?*" Not receiving an answer, he continued: "Green girls faint as soon as look at you, but then they choose time and place. What woman ever fainted up a tree?"

"She sent her nasty blood all over me. I think the smell must have overpowered me. Faugh! I hate blood."

"I do believe it potently." Ere they had taken two steps, he stopped. "By-the-by, the cub!"

"Oh, no, no!" cried Gerard.

"You are right. It is late. We have lost time climbing trees, and tumbling off 'em, and swooning, and vomiting, and praying, and the brute is heavy to carry. And, now I think on't, we shall have Papa after it next. These bears make such a coil about an odd cub."

CHAPTER XXII

THEY CAME to a huge building.

"Courage!" cried Denys. "I think I know this convent. Ay, it is. We are in the see of Juliers."

The next moment they were safe within the walls. Here Gerard made acquaintance with a monk who had constructed the great dial in the Prior's garden, and a wheel for drawing water, and a winnowing machine for the grain, and had ever some ingenious mechanism on hand. He had made several psalteries and two dulcimers, and was now attempting a set of regalles, or little organ for the choir.

Now Gerard played the humble psaltery a little, but the monk touched that instrument divinely, and showed him most agreeably what a novice he was in music. He also illuminated finely, but could not write so beautifully as Gerard. Comparing their acquirements with the earnestness and simplicity of an age in which accomplishments implied a true natural bent, Youth and Age soon became like brothers, and Gerard was pressed hard to stay that night. He consulted Denys, who assented with a rueful shrug.

Gerard told his old new friend whither he was going, and described their late adventures.

"Alack!" said the good old man, "I have been a great traveler in my day, but none molested me." He then told him to avoid inns; they were always haunted by rogues and roysterers, whence his soul might take harm even did his body escape; and to manage each day's journey so as to lie at some peaceful monastery. Then, suddenly breaking off and looking as sharp as a needle at Gerard, he asked him how long since he had been shriven. Gerard colored up and replied feebly:

"Better than a fortnight."

"No wonder perils have overtaken thee. Come, thou must be assoiled out of hand."

"Yes, Father," said Gerard, "and with all mine heart," and was sinking down to his knees, with his hands joined, but the monk stopped him half fretfully:

"Not to me! Not to me! Not to me! I am as full of the world as thou or any he that lives in't. My whole soul it is in these wooden pipes, and sorry leathern stops, which shall perish—with them whose minds are fixed on such-like vanities."

"Where shall I find a confessor more holy?"

"In each of these cells," replied the monk simply (they were now in the corridor). "There, go to Brother Anselm, yonder."

Father Anselm was a venerable monk, with an ample head, and a face all dignity and love. Therefore Gerard in confessing to him, and replying to his gentle though searching questions, could not help thinking, "Here is a head!—Oh, dear! oh, dear! I wonder whether you will let me draw it when I have done confessing." And so his own head got confused, and he forgot a crime or two.

The penance inflicted was this: He was to enter the convent church and, prostrating himself, kiss the lowest step of the altar three times. Then, kneeling on the floor, to say three paternosters and a credo. "This done, come back to me on the instant." Accordingly, his short mortification performed, Gerard returned and found Father Anselm spreading plaster.

"After the soul the body," said he. "Know that I am the chirurgeon here, for want of a better. This is going on thy leg, to cool it, not to burn it, the saints forbid."

During the operation, the monastic leech rather sided with Denys upon "bleeding." "We Dominicans seldom let blood nowadays. The lay leeches say 'tis from timidity and want of skill, but in sooth we have long found that simples will cure most of the ills that can be cured at all.

"Thy wound is cared for. In three days 'twill be but a scar. And now God speed thee, and the saints make thee as good, and as happy, as thou art beautiful and gracious."

At the next town they came to, suddenly an arbalestrier ran out of a tavern after them, and in a moment his beard and Denys's were like two brushes stuck together. It was a comrade. He insisted on their coming into the tavern with him, and breaking a bottle of wine. In course of conversation, he told Denys there was an insurrection in the Duke's Flemish provinces, and soldiers were ordered thither from all parts of Burgundy. "Indeed I marveled to see thy face turned this way."

"I go to embrace my folk that I have not seen these three years. Ye can quell a bit of rising without me, I trow."

Suddenly Denys gave a start. "Dost hear, Gerard? This comrade is bound for Holland."

"What then? Ah, a letter! A letter to Margaret! But will he be so good, so kind?"

The soldier with a torrent of blasphemy informed him he would not only take it, but go a league or two out of his way to do it.

In an instant out came inkhorn and paper from Gerard's wallet, and he wrote a long letter to Margaret, and dwelt most on the bear, and the character of Denys, whom he painted to the life. And with many endearing expressions bade her be of good cheer. Some trouble and peril there had been, but all that was over now, and his only grief was that he could not hope to have a word from her hand till he should reach Rome. He ended with comforting her again as hard as he could. And so absorbed was he in his love and his work that he did not see all the people in the room were standing peeping, to watch the nimble and true finger execute such rare penmanship.

Denys, proud of his friend's skill, let him alone till presently the scalding tears began to run down his young cheeks, one after another, on the paper where he was then writing comfort, comfort. Then Denys rudely repulsed the curious, and asked his comrade with a faltering voice whether he had the heart to let so sweet a love letter miscarry. The other swore by the face of Saint Luke he would lose the forefinger of his right hand sooner.

Seeing him so ready, Gerard charged him also with a short, cold letter to his parents, and in it he drew hastily with his pen two hands grasping each other, to signify farewell.

"I am no general lover, Denys. There is room in my heart for one sweet-

heart, and for one friend. I am far from my dear mistress, and my friend—
a few leagues more and I must lose him too. Oh, let me drink thy friendship
pure while I may."

"And shalt, honey pot, and shalt," said Denys kindly. "But as to my leaving thee, reckon thou not on that! For"—three consecutive oaths—"if I do."

"Denys! Denys!"

"Denys not me! 'Tis settled. Gainsay me not, or I'll go with thee to Rome!
Why not? His Holiness the Pope hath ever some little merry pleasant war
toward, and a Burgundian soldier is still welcome in his ranks."

On this Gerard opened his heart. "Denys, ere I fell in with thee, I used
often to halt on the road, unable to go farther. My puny heart so pulled me
back, and then, after a short prayer to the saints for aid, would I rise and
drag my most unwilling body onward. But since I joined company with
thee, great is my courage. I have found the saying of the ancients true, that
better is a bright comrade on the weary road than a horse litter. And, dear
brother, when I do think of what we have done and suffered together!
Savedst my life from the bear, and from yet more savage thieves. How many
ties tender and strong between us! Had I my will, I'd never, never, never,
part with my Denys on this side the grave. Welladay! God His will be
done."

"No, my will shall be done this time!" shouted Denys. "*Le bon Dieu* has
bigger fish to fry than you or me. I'll go with thee to Rome. There is my
hand on it."

They shook hands over it. Then Gerard said nothing, for his heart was
too full; but he ran twice round his companion as he walked, then danced
backward in front of him, and finally took his hand, and so on they went
hand in hand like sweethearts, till a company of mounted soldiers, about
fifty in number, rose to sight on the brow of a hill.

"See the banner of Burgundy," said Denys, joyfully. "I shall look out for
a comrade among these."

"How gorgeous is the standard in the sun," said Gerard, "and how brave
are the leaders with velvet and feathers, and steel breastplates like glassy
mirrors!"

When they came near enough to distinguish faces, Denys uttered an exclamation: "Why 'tis the Bastard of Burgundy, as I live. Nay, then, there is
fighting afoot, since he is out—a gallant leader, Gerard, rates his life no
higher than a private soldier's, and a soldier's no higher than a tomtit's, and
that is the captain for me."

"And see, Denys, the very mules, with their great brass frontlets and trap-
pings, seem proud to carry them. No wonder men itch to be soldiers." And
in the midst of this innocent admiration the troop came up with them.

"Halt!" cried a stentorian voice. The troop halted. The Bastard of Burgundy bent his brow gloomily on Denys: "How now, arbalestrier, how

comes it thy face is turned southward when every good hand and heart is hurrying northward?"

Denys replied respectfully that he was going on leave, after some years of service, to see his kindred.

"Good. But this is not the time for't, the Duchy is disturbed. Ho! bring that dead soldier's mule to the front, and thou mount her and forward with us to Flanders."

"So please Your Highness," said Denys, firmly, "that may not be. My home is close at hand. I have not seen it these three years and, above all, I have this poor youth in charge, whom I may not, cannot leave till I see him shipped for Rome."

"Dost bandy words with me?" said the chief, with amazement turning fast to wrath. "Art weary o' thy life? Let go the youth's hand, and into the saddle without more idle words."

Denys made no reply, but he held Gerard's hand the tighter, and looked defiance. At this the Bastard roared: "Jarnac, dismount six of thy archers, and shoot me this white-livered cur dead where he stands—for an example."

The young Count de Jarnac, second in command, gave the order, and the men dismounted to execute it.

"Strip him naked," said the Bastard, in the cold tone of military business, "and put his arms and accouterments on the spare mule. We'll maybe find some clown worthier to wear them."

Denys groaned aloud, "Am I to be shamed as well as slain?"

"Oh, nay, nay, nay!" cried Gerard, awaking from the stupor into which this thunderbolt of tyranny had thrown him. "He shall go with you on the instant. I'd liever part with him forever than see a hair of his dear head harmed. Oh, sir, oh, my lord, give a poor boy but a minute to bid his only friend farewell! He will go with you. I swear he shall go with you."

The stern leader nodded a cold, contemptuous assent. "Thou, Jarnac, stay with them, and bring him on alive or dead—Forward!" And he resumed his march, followed by all the band but the young Count and six archers, one of whom held the spare mule.

Denys and Gerard gazed at one another haggardly. Oh, what a look! And after this mute interchange of anguish, they spoke hurriedly, for the moments were flying by.

"Thou goest to Holland. Thou knowest where she bides. Tell her all. She will be kind to thee for my sake."

"Oh, sorry tale that I shall carry her! For God's sake go back to the Tête d'Or. I am mad."

"Hush! Let me think—have I naught to say to thee, Denys? My head! My head!"

"Ah! I have it. Make for the Rhine, Gerard! Strasbourg. 'Tis but a step.

And down the current to Rotterdam. Margaret is there, I go thither. I'll tell her thou art coming. We shall all be together."

"My lads, haste ye, or you will get us into trouble," said the Count firmly, but not harshly now.

"Oh, sir, one moment! One little moment!" panted Gerard.

"Cursed be the land I was born in, cursed be the race of man, and He that made them what they are!" screamed Denys.

"Hush, Denys, hush! Blaspheme not! Oh, God, forgive him, he wots not what he says. Be patient, Denys—be patient! Though we meet no more on earth, let us meet in a better world, where no blasphemer may enter. To my heart, lost friend, for what are words now?" He held out his arms, and they locked one another in a close embrace. They kissed one another again and again, speechless, and the tears rained down their cheeks. Then at a signal from Jarnac, with kind force and words of rude consolation, they almost lifted Denys onto the mule and, putting him in the middle of them, spurred after their leader. And Gerard ran wildly after (for the lane turned), to see the very last of him. And the last glimpse he caught, Denys was rocking to and fro on his mule, and tearing his hair out. But at this sight something rose in Gerard's throat so high, so high, he could run no more nor breathe, but gasped, and leaned against the snow-clad hedge, seizing it, and choking piteously.

Denys, placed in the middle of his companions lest he should be so mad as attempt escape, was carried off in an agony of grief and remorse. For his sake Gerard had abandoned the German route to Rome, and what was his reward? Left all alone in the center of Burgundy. This was the thought which maddened Denys most, and made him now rave at Heaven and earth, now fall into a gloomy silence so savage and sinister that it was deemed prudent to disarm him. They caught up their leader just outside the town, and the whole cavalcade drew up and baited at the Tête d'Or.

CHAPTER XXIII

JORIAN KETEL came to Peter's house to claim Margaret's promise; but Margaret was ill in bed, and Peter, on hearing his errand, affronted him and warned him off the premises, and one or two that stood by were for ducking him; for both father and daughter were favorites, and the whole story was in every mouth, and the Sevenbergens in that state of hot, undiscriminating, irritation which accompanies popular sympathy. So Jorian Ketel went off in dudgeon, and repented him of his good deed.

The little family at Tergou wore still the same outward features, but within was no longer the simple happy family this tale opened with. Little

Kate knew the share Cornelis and Sybrandt had in banishing Gerard, and though, for fear of making more mischief still, she never told her mother, yet there were times she shuddered at the bare sight of them, and blushed at their hypocritical regrets. Catherine, with a woman's vigilance, noticed this, and with a woman's subtlety said nothing, but quietly pondered it, and went on watching for more.

The black sheep themselves, in their efforts to partake in the general gloom and sorrow, succeeded so far as to impose upon their father and Giles: but the demure satisfaction that lay at their bottom could not escape these feminine eyes—

"That, noting all, seem'd nought to note."

Thus mistrust and suspicion sat at the table, poor substitutes for Gerard's intelligent face that had brightened the whole circle unobserved till it was gone. As for the old hosier, his pride had been wounded by his son's disobedience, and so he bore stiffly up, and did his best never to mention Gerard's name. But underneath his Spartan cloak Nature might be seen tugging at his heartstrings. One anxiety he never affected to conceal. "If I but knew where the boy is, and that his life and health are in no danger, small would be my care," would he say, and then a deep sigh would follow. I cannot help thinking that if Gerard had opened the door just then and walked in, there would have been many tears and embraces for him, and few reproaches, or none.

One thing took the old couple quite by surprise—publicity. Ere Gerard had been gone a week, his adventures were in every mouth; and to make matters worse, the popular sympathy declared itself warmly on the side of the lovers, and against Gerard's cruel parents, and that old busybody the Burgomaster, "who must put his nose into a business that nowise concerned him."

"Mother," said Kate, "it is all over town that Margaret is down with a fever—a burning fever. Her father fears her sadly."

"Margaret? What Margaret?" inquired Catherine, with a treacherous assumption of calmness and indifference.

"Oh, Mother, whom should I mean? Why, Gerard's Margaret."

"Gerard's Margaret!" screamed Catherine. "How dare you say such a word to me? And I rede you never mention that hussy's name in this house that she has laid bare. She is the ruin of my poor boy, the flower of all my flock. She is the cause that he is not a holy priest in the midst of us, but is roaming the world, and I a desolate brokenhearted mother. There, do not cry, my girl, I do ill to speak harsh to you. But, oh, Kate, you know not what passes in a mother's heart. I bear up before you all, it behooves me swallow my fears. But at night I see him in my dreams and still some trouble or other near him. Sometimes he is torn by wild beasts; other times he is in the hands of robbers, and their cruel knives uplifted to strike his poor pale face, that one should think would move a stone. Oh, when I remember that while I sit here in comfort perhaps my poor boy lies dead in some savage place, and all along of that girl! There, her very name is ratsbane to me. I tremble all over when I hear it."

"I'll not say anything nor do anything to grieve you worse, Mother," said Kate tenderly, but she sighed.

She whose name was so fiercely interdicted in this house was much spoken of, and even pitied, elsewhere. All Sevenbergen was sorry for her, and the young men and maidens cast many a pitying glance, as they passed, at the little window where the beauty of the village lay "dying for love." Physical and mental excitement had brought on an attack of fever so violent that nothing but youth and constitution saved her. The malady left her at last, but in that terrible state of bodily weakness in which the patient feels life a burden.

Then it is that love and friendship by the bedside are mortal angels with comfort in their voices, and healing in their palms. But this poor girl had to come back to life and vigor how she could. Many days she lay alone, and the heavy hours rolled like leaden waves over her. In her enfeebled state existence seemed a burden, and life a thing gone by. She could not try her best to get well. Gerard was gone. She had not him to get well for. Often she lay for hours quite still, with the tears welling gently out of her eyes.

One day, waking from an uneasy slumber, she found two women in her room. One was a servant, the other by the deep fur on her collar and sleeves was a person of consideration. A narrow band of silvery hair, being spared by her coiffure, showed her to be past the age when women of sense conceal their years. The looks of both were kind and friendly. Margaret tried to raise herself in the bed, but the old lady placed a hand very gently on her.

"Lie still, sweetheart. We come not here to put you about, but to comfort you, God willing. Now cheer up a bit, and tell us, first, who think you we are."

"Nay, madam, I know you, though I never saw you before. You are the Demoiselle Van Eyck, and this is Reicht Heynes. Gerard has oft spoken of you, and of your goodness to him. Madam, he has no friend like you near him now." And at this thought she lay back and the tears welled out of her eyes in a moment.

The good-natured Reicht Heynes began to cry for company, but her mistress scolded her. "Well, you are a pretty one for a sickroom," said she. And she put out a world of innocent art to cheer the patient: and not without some little success. An old woman that has seen life and all its troubles is a sovereign blessing by a sorrowful young woman's side. She knows what to say, and what to avoid. She knows how to soothe her and interest her. Ere she had been there an hour, she had Margaret's head lying on her shoulder instead of on the pillow, and Margaret's soft eyes dwelling on her with gentle gratitude.

"Ah, this is hair!" said the old lady, running her fingers through it. "Come and look at it, Reicht!"

Reicht came and handled it, and praised it unaffectedly. The poor girl that owned it was not quite out of the reach of flattery, owing doubtless to not being dead.

"In sooth, madam, I did use to think it hideous; but *he* praised it, and ever since then I have been almost vain of it, saints forgive me. You know how foolish those are that love."

"They are greater fools that don't," said the old lady sharply.

This was only the first of many visits. In fact either Margaret Van Eyck or Reicht came nearly every day until their patient was convalescent, and she improved rapidly under their hands. Reicht attributed this principally to certain nourishing dishes she prepared in Peter's kitchen, but Margaret herself thought more of the kind words and eyes that kept telling her she had friends to live for.

Martin Wittenhaagen went straight to Rotterdam, to take the bull by the horns. The bull was a biped, with a crown for horns. It was Philip the Good, Duke of this, Earl of that, Lord of the other. Arrived at Rotterdam, Martin found the court was at Ghent. To Ghent he went, and sought an audience, but was put off and baffled by lackeys and pages. So he threw himself in his sovereign's way out hunting and, contrary to all court precedents, commenced the conversation—by roaring lustily for mercy.

"Why, where is the peril, man?" said the Duke, looking all round and laughing.

"Grace for an old soldier hunted down by burghers!"

Now kings differ in character like other folk, but there is one trait they have in common—they are mightily inclined to be affable to men of very low estate. These do not vie with them in anything whatever, so jealousy cannot creep in; and they amuse them by their bluntness and novelty, and refresh the poor things with a touch of nature—a rarity in courts. So Philip the Good reined in his horse and gave Martin almost a tête-à-tête and Martin reminded him of a certain battlefield where he had received an arrow intended for his sovereign. The Duke remembered the incident perfectly, and was graciously pleased to take a cheerful view of it. He could afford to, not having been the one hit.

Then Martin told His Majesty of Gerard's first capture in the church, his imprisonment in the tower, and the maneuver by which they got him out, and all the details of the hunt. And, whether he told it better than I have, or the Duke had not heard so many good stories as you have, certain it is that sovereign got so wrapt up in it that when a number of courtiers came galloping up and interrupted Martin, he swore like a costermonger, and threatened, only half in jest, to cut off the next head that should come between him and a good story. And when Martin had done, he cried out:

"Saint Luke! What sport goeth on in this mine Earldom, ay, in my own woods, and I see it not! You base fellows have all the luck." And he was indignant at the partiality of Fortune. "Lo, you now! This was a man hunt," said he. "*I* never had the luck to be at a man hunt."

"My luck was none so great," replied Martin bluntly. "I was on the wrong side of the dogs' noses."

"Ah, so you were! I forgot that." And royalty was more reconciled to its lot. "What would you, then?"

"A free pardon, Your Highness, for myself and Gerard."

"For what?"

"For prison-breaking."

"Go to. The bird will fly from the cage. 'Tis instinct. Besides, coop a young man up for loving a young woman? These burgomasters must be void of common sense. What else?"

"For striking down the Burgomaster."

"Oh, the hunted boar will turn to bay. 'Tis his right, and I hold him less than man that grudges it him. What else?"

"For killing of the bloodhounds."

The Duke's countenance fell.

" 'Twas their life or mine," said Martin eagerly.

"Ay, but I can't have my bloodhounds, my beautiful bloodhounds, sacrificed to—"

"No, no, no! They were not your dogs."

"Whose dogs, then?"

"The ranger's."

"Oh. Well, I am very sorry for him, but, as I was saying, I can't have my old soldiers sacrificed to his bloodhounds. Thou shalt have thy free pardon."

"And poor Gerard."

"And poor Gerard too, for thy sake. And more, tell thou this Burgomaster his doings mislike me. This is to set up for a king, not a burgomaster. I'll have no kings in Holland but one. Bid him be more humble, or by Saint Jude I'll hang him before his own door, as I hanged the Burgomaster of—what's the name, some town or other in Flanders it was—no, 'twas somewhere in Brabant—no matter—I hanged him, I remember that much—for oppressing the poor folk."

The Duke then beckoned his chancellor, a pursy old fellow that rode like a sack, and bade him write out a free pardon for Martin and one Gerard. This precious document was drawn up in form, and signed next day, and Martin hastened home with it. Margaret had left her bed some days, and was sitting pale and pensive by the fireside when he burst in, waving the parchment, and crying, "A free pardon, girl, for Gerard as well as me! Send for him back when you will. All the burgomasters on earth daren't lay a finger on him."

She flushed all over with joy, and her hands trembled with eagerness as she took the parchment and devoured it with her eyes, and kissed it again and again, and flung her arms round Martin's neck, and kissed *him*. When she was calmer, she told him Heaven had raised her up a friend in the Dame Van Eyck. "And I would fain consult her on this good news."

It was nearly dusk, so Margaret ventured, and about seven in the evening she astonished and gladdened her new but ardent friend by arriving at her house with unwonted roses on her cheeks, and Gerard's pardon in her bosom.

Some are old in heart at forty, some are young at eighty. Margaret Van Eyck's heart was an evergreen. She loved her young namesake with youthful ardor. Nor was this new sentiment a mere caprice. She was quick at reading character, and saw in Margaret Brandt that which in one of her own sex goes far with an intelligent woman—genuineness. But besides her own sterling qualities, Margaret had from the first a potent ally in the old artist's bosom. Human nature.

Now Margaret Van Eyck had been wonderfully kind to Margaret Brandt; had broken through her own habits to go and see her; had nursed her, and soothed her, and petted her, and cured her more than all the medicine in the world. So her heart opened to the recipient of her goodness, and she loved her now far more tenderly than she had ever loved Gerard, though in truth it was purely out of regard for Gerard she had visited her in the first instance. When, therefore, she saw the roses on Margaret's cheek, and read the bit of parchment that had brought them there, she gave up her own views without a murmur.

"Sweetheart," said she, "I did desire he should stay in Italy five or six years, and come back rich, and above all an artist. But your happiness is before all, and I see you cannot live without him, so we must have him home as fast as may be."

"Ah, madam, you see my very thoughts." And the young woman hung her head a moment and blushed. "But how to let him know, madam? That passes my skill. He is gone to Italy, but what part, that I know not. Stay! He named the cities he should visit. Florence was one, and Rome. But then—"

Finally, being a sensible girl, she divined that a letter addressed "My Gerard—Italy" might chance to miscarry, and she looked imploringly at her friend for counsel.

"You are come to the right place, and at the right time," said the old lady. "Here was this Hans Memling with me today. He is going to Italy, girl, no later than next week, 'to improve his hand,' he says. Not before 'twas needed, I do assure you."

"But how is he to find my Gerard?"

"Why, he knows your Gerard, child. They have supped here more than once, and were like hand and glove. Now, as his business is the same as Gerard's—"

"What! He is a painter, then?"

"He passes for one. He will visit the same places as Gerard, and soon or late he must fall in with him. Wherefore, get you a long letter written, and copy out this pardon into it, and I'll answer for the messenger. In six months at farthest Gerard shall get it; and when he shall get it, then will he kiss it, and put it in his bosom, and come flying home. What are you smiling at? And now what makes your cheeks so red? And what you are smothering me for, I cannot think. Yes! Happy days are coming to my little pearl."

The letter was duly written, and left with Margaret Van Eyck; and the following week, sure enough, Hans Memling returned from Flanders. Margaret Van Eyck gave him the letter, and a piece of gold toward his traveling expenses. He seemed in a hurry to be off.

"All the better," said the old artist. "He will be the sooner in Italy."

But as there are horses who burn and rage to start, and after the first yard or two want the whip, so all this hurry cooled into inaction when Hans got as far as the principal hostelry of Tergou, and saw two of his boon companions sitting in the bay window. He went in for a parting glass with them; but when he offered to pay, they would not hear of it. No; he was going a long journey, they would treat him; everybody must treat him, the landlord and all.

It resulted from this treatment that his tongue got as loose as if the wine had been oil; and he confided to the convivial crew that he was going to show the Italians how to paint. Next he sang his exploits in battle, for he had handled a pike; and his amorous successes with females, not present to oppose their version of the incidents. And among the miscellaneous matters that oozed out, he must blab that he was entrusted with a letter to a townsman of theirs, one Gerard, a good fellow. He added, "You are all good fellows," and to impress his eulogy, slapped Sybrandt on the back so heartily as to drive the breath out of his body.

Sybrandt got round the table to avoid this muscular approval, but listened to every word, and learned for the first time that Gerard was gone to Italy. However, to make sure, he affected to doubt it.

"My brother Gerard is never in Italy."

"Ye lie, ye cur!" roared Hans, taking instantly the irascible turn, and not being clear enough to see that he who now sat opposite him was the same he had praised, and hit, when beside him. "If he is ten times your brother, he is in Italy. What call ye this? There, read me that superscription!" And he flung down a letter on the table.

Sybrandt took it up and examined it gravely, but eventually laid it down, with the remark that he could not read. However, one of the company, by some immense fortuity, could read and, proud of so rare an accomplishment, took it, and read it out: "To Gerard Eliassoen, of Tergou. These by the hand of the trusty Hans Memling, with all speed."

" 'Tis excellently well writ," said the reader, examining every letter.

"Ay," said Hans bombastically, "and small wonder. 'Tis writ by a famous hand, by Margaret, sister of Jan Van Eyck. Blessed and honored be his memory! She is an old friend of mine, is Margaret Van Eyck."

Miscellaneous Hans then diverged into forty topics. Sybrandt stole out of the company and went in search of Cornelis. They put their heads together over the news. Italy was an immense distance off. If they could only keep him there!

"Keep him there? Nothing would keep him long from his Margaret."

"Curse her!" said Sybrandt. "Why didn't she die when she was about it?"

"*She die?* She would outlive the pest to vex us." And Cornelis was wroth at her selfishness in not dying, to oblige.

These two black sheep kept putting their heads together, and tainting each other worse and worse, till at last their corrupt hearts conceived a plan for keeping Gerard in Italy all his life, and so securing his share of their father's substance.

But when they had planned it, they were no nearer the execution, for that required talent. So iniquity came to a standstill. But presently, as if Satan had come between the two heads and whispered into the right ear of one and the left of the other simultaneously, they both burst out:

"*The Burgomaster!*"

They went to Ghysbrecht van Swieten, and he received them at once, for the man who is under the torture of suspense catches eagerly at knowledge. Certainty is often painful, but seldom, like suspense, intolerable.

"You have news of Gerard?" said he eagerly.

Then they told about the letter and Hans Memling. He listened with restless eye. "Who writ the letter?"

"Margaret Van Eyck," was the reply, for they naturally thought the contents were by the same hand as the superscription.

"Are ye sure?" And he went to a drawer and drew out a paper written by Margaret Van Eyck while treating with the burgh for her house. "Was it writ like this?"

"Yes. 'Tis the same writing," said Sybrandt boldly.

"Good. And now what would ye of me?" said Ghysbrecht, with beating heart, but a carelessness so well feigned that it staggered them. They fumbled with their bonnets, and stammered and spoke a word or two, then hesitated and beat about the bush, and let out by degrees that they wanted a letter written to say something that might keep Gerard in Italy. And this letter they proposed to substitute in Hans Memling's wallet for the one he carried.

While these fumbled with their bonnets and their iniquity, and vacillated between respect for a burgomaster and suspicion that this one was as great a rogue as themselves, and, somehow or other, on their side against Gerard, pros and cons were coursing one another to and fro in the keen old man's spirit. Vengeance said let Gerard come back and feel the weight of the law. Prudence said keep him a thousand miles off. But then prudence said also, why do dirty work on a doubtful chance? Why put it in the power of these two rogues to tarnish your name? Finally, his strong persuasion that Gerard was in possession of a secret by means of which he could wound him to the quick, coupled with his caution, found words thus:

"It is my duty to aid the citizens that cannot write. But for their matter I will not be responsible. Tell me, then, what I shall write."

"Something about this Margaret."

"Ay, ay, that she is false, that she is married to another, I'll go bail."

"Nay, Burgomaster, nay! Not for all the world!" cried Sybrandt. "Gerard would not believe it, or but half, and then he would come back to see. No, say that she is dead."

"Dead! What, at her age? Will he credit that?"

"Sooner than the other. Why she was *nearly* dead, so it is not to say a downright lie, after all."

"Humph. And you think that will keep him in Italy?"

"We are sure of it, are we not, Cornelis?"

"Ay," said Cornelis, "our Gerard will never leave Italy now he is there. It was always his dream to get there. He would come back for his Margaret, but not for us. What cares he for us? He despises his own family, always did."

"Well, tell me what to write for you, and I must write it, but take notice, you bear the blame if aught turns amiss. Not the hand which writes, but the tongue which dictates, doth the deed."

The brothers assented warmly, sneering within. Ghysbrecht then drew his inkhorn toward him, and laid the specimen of Margaret Van Eyck's writing before him, and made some inquiries as to the size and shape of the letter. An unlooked-for interruption occurred. Jorian Ketel burst hastily into the room, and looked vexed at not finding him alone.

"Thou seest I have matter on hand, good fellow."

"Ay, but this is grave. I bring good news, but 'tis not for every ear."

The Burgomaster rose and drew Jorian aside into the embrasure of his deep window, and then the brothers heard them converse in low but eager tones. It ended by Ghysbrecht sending Jorian out to saddle his mule. He then addressed the black sheep with a sudden coldness that amazed them.

"I prize the peace of households, but this is not a thing to be done in a hurry. We will see about it, we will see."

"But, Burgomaster, the man will be gone. It will be too late."

"Where is he?"

"At the hostelry, drinking."

"Well, keep him drinking! We will see, we will see." And he sent them off discomfited.

To explain this we must retrograde a step. This very morning, then, Margaret Brandt had met Jorian Ketel near her own door. He passed her with a scowl. This struck her, and she remembered him.

"Stay," said she. "Yes, it is the good man who saved him! Oh, why have you not been near me since? And why have you not come for the parchments? Was it not true about the hundred crowns?"

Jorian gave a snort; but, seeing her face that looked so candid, began to think there might be some mistake. He told her he had come, and how he had been received.

"Alas!" said she. "I knew naught of this. I lay at death's door." She then invited him to follow her, and took him into the garden and showed him the spot where the parchments were buried. "Martin was for taking them up, but I would not let him. *He* put them there, and I said none should move them but you, who had earned them so well of him and me."

"Give me a spade!" cried Jorian eagerly. "But stay! No, he is a suspicious man. You are sure they are there still?"

"I will openly take the blame if human hand hath touched them."

"Then keep them but two hours more, I prithee, good Margaret," said Jorian, and ran off to the Stadthouse of Tergou a joyful man.

The Burgomaster jogged along toward Sevenbergen, with Jorian striding beside him, giving him assurance that in an hour's time the missing parchments would be in his hand. When they came to Peter's gate, he felt uneasy.

"I wish it had been anywhere but here."

Jorian reassured him.

"The girl is honest and friendly," said he. "She had nothing to do with taking them, I'll be sworn." And he led him into the garden. "There, master, if a face is to be believed, here they lie, and, see, the mold *is* loose."

He ran for a spade which was stuck up in the ground at some distance, and soon went to work and uncovered a parchment. Ghysbrecht saw it and thrust him aside and went down on his knees and tore it out of the hole. His hands trembled and his face shone. He threw out parchment after parchment, and Jorian dusted them and cleaned them and shook them. Now when Ghysbrecht had thrown out a great many, his face began to darken and lengthen, and when he came to the last, he put his hands to his temples and seemed to be all amazed.

"What mystery lies here?" he gasped. "Are fiends mocking me? Dig deeper! There *must* be another."

Jorian drove the spade in and threw out quantities of hard mold. In vain. And even while he dug, his master's mood had changed.

"Treason! Treachery!" he cried. "You knew of this."

"Knew what, master, in heaven's name?"

"Caitiff, you knew there was another one worth all these twice-told."

" 'Tis false," cried Jorian, made suspicious by the other's suspicion. " 'Tis a trick to rob me of my hundred crowns. Oh, I know you, Burgomaster."

A mellow voice fell on them both like oil upon the waves. "No, good man, it is not false, nor yet is it quite true. There was another parchment."

"There, there, there! Where is it?"

"But," continued Margaret calmly, "it was not a town record (so you have gained your hundred crowns, good man). It was but a private deed between the Burgomaster here and my grandfather Flor——"

"Hush, hush!"

"—is Brandt."

"Where is it, girl? That is all we want to know."

"Have patience and I shall tell you. Gerard read the title of it, and he said, 'This is as much yours as the Burgomaster's,' and he put it apart to read it with me at his leisure."

"It is in the house, then?" said the Burgomaster, recovering his calmness.

"No, sir," said Margaret, bravely, "it is not." Then, in a voice that faltered suddenly; "You hunted—my poor Gerard—so hard—and so close—that you gave him—no time—to think of aught—but his life—and his grief.—The parchment was in his bosom, and he hath ta'en it with him."

"Whither, whither?"

"Ask me no more, sir. What right is yours to question me thus? It was for *your sake*, good man, I put force upon my heart and came out here, and bore to speak at all to this hard old man. For when I think of the misery he has brought on *him* and me, the sight of him is more than I can bear." And she gave an involuntary shudder, and went slowly in, with her hand to her head, crying bitterly.

Remorse for the past, and dread of the future—the slow, but, as he now felt, the inevitable future—avarice, and fear, all tugged in one short moment at Ghysbrecht's tough heart. He hung his head, and his arms fell listless by his sides.

"My mule! My mule!" screamed Ghysbrecht.

Jorian helped the old man up, trembling in every joint. Once in the saddle, he seemed to gather in a moment unnatural vigor, and the figure that went flying to Tergou was truly weirdlike and terrible—so old and wizened the face, so white and reverend the streaming hair, so baleful the eye, so fierce the fury which shook the bent frame that went spurring like mad while the quavering voice yelled: "I'll make their hearts ache.—I'll make their hearts ache.—I'll make their hearts ache.—I'll make their hearts ache. All of them. All—all—all!"

The black sheep sat disconsolate amidst the convivial crew and eyed Hans Memling's wallet. For more ease he had taken it off and flung it on the table. How readily they could have slipped out that letter and put in another. For the first time in their lives they were sorry they had not learned to write, like their brother. And now Hans began to talk of going, and the brothers agreed in a whisper to abandon their project for the time. They had scarcely resolved this when Dierich Brower stood suddenly in the doorway and gave them a wink. They went out to him.

"Come to the Burgomaster with all speed," said he.

They found Ghysbrecht seated at a table, pale and agitated. Before him lay Margaret Van Eyck's handwriting.

"I have written what you desired," said he. "Now for the superscription. What were the words? Did ye see?"

"We cannot read," said Cornelis.

"Then is all this labor lost," cried Ghysbrecht angrily. "Dolts!"

"Nay, but," said Sybrandt, "I heard the words read, and I have not lost them. They were, 'To Gerard Eliassoen, these by the hand of the trusty Hans Memling with all speed.'"

"'Tis well. Now, how was the letter folded? How big was it?"

"Longer than that one, and not so long as this."

"'Tis well. Where is he?"

"At the hostelry."

"Come, then, take you this groat, and treat him. Then ask to see the letter, and put this in place of it. Come to me with the other letter."

The brothers assented, took the letter, and went to the hostelry. They had not been gone a minute when Dierich Brower issued from the Stadthouse and followed them. He had his orders not to let them out of his sight till the true letter was in his master's hands. He watched outside the hostelry. He had not long to wait. They came out almost immediately, with downcast looks. Dierich made up to them.

"Too late!" they cried. "Too late! He is gone."

"Gone? How long?"

"Scarce five minutes. Cursed chance!"

"You must go back to the Burgomaster at once," said Dierich Brower.

"To what end?"

"No matter, come," and he hurried them to the Stadthouse.

Ghysbrecht van Swieten was not the man to accept a defeat. "Well," said he on hearing the ill news, "suppose he is gone. Is he mounted?"

"No."

"Then what hinders you to come up with him?"

"But what avails coming up with him? There are no hostelries on the road he is gone."

"Fools!" said Ghysbrecht. "Is there no way of emptying a man's pockets but liquor and sleight of hand?"

A meaning look that passed between Ghysbrecht and Dierich aided the brothers' comprehension. They changed color, and lost all zeal for the business.

"No, no! We don't hate our brother. We won't get ourselves hanged to spite him," said Sybrandt. "That would be a fool's trick."

"Hanged?" cried Ghysbrecht. "Am I not the Burgomaster? How can ye be hanged? I see how 'tis—ye fear to tackle one man, being two, hearts of hare that ye are! Oh, why cannot I be young again? I'd do it single-handed."

The old man now threw off all disguise and showed them his heart was in this deed. He then flattered and besought and jeered them alternately, but he found no eloquence could move them to an action, however dishonorable, which was attended with danger. At last he opened a drawer and showed them a pile of silver coins.

"Change but those letters for me," he said, "and each of you shall thrust one hand into this drawer, and take away as many of them as you can hold."

The effect was magical. Their eyes glittered with desire. Their whole bodies seemed to swell, and rise into male energy.

"Swear it, then," said Sybrandt.

"I swear it."

"No—on the crucifix."

Ghysbrecht swore upon the crucifix. The next minute the brothers were on the road, in pursuit of Hans Memling. They came in sight of him about two leagues from Tergou, but though they knew he had no weapon but his staff, they were too prudent to venture on him in daylight, so they fell back.

But being now three leagues and more from the town, and on a grassy road—sun down, moon not yet up—honest Hans suddenly found himself attacked before and behind at once by men with uplifted knives, who cried in loud though somewhat shaky voices, "Stand and deliver!" The attack was so sudden, and so well planned, that Hans was dismayed.

"Slay me not, good fellows!" he cried. "I am but a poor man, and ye shall have my all."

"So be it then. Live! But empty thy wallet."

"There is naught in my wallet, good friends, but one letter."

"That we shall see," said Sybrandt, who was the one in front. "Well—it *is* a letter."

"Take it not from me, I pray you. 'Tis worth naught, and the good dame would fret that writ it."

"There," said Sybrandt, "take back thy letter. And now empty thy pouch. Come, tarry not!"

But by this time Hans had recovered his confusion, and from a certain flutter in Sybrandt, and hard breathing of Cornelis, felt sure the pair he had to deal with were no heroes. He pretended to fumble for his money, then suddenly thrust his staff fiercely into Sybrandt's face and drove him staggering, and lent Cornelis a backhand slash on the ear that sent him twirling like a weathercock in March, then whirled his weapon over his head and danced about the road like a figure on springs, shouting, "Come on, ye thieving loons! Come on!"

It was a plain invitation, yet they misunderstood it so utterly as to take to their heels, with Hans after them, he shouting "Stop thieves!" and they howling with fear and pain as they ran.

CHAPTER XXIV

A CHANGE came over Margaret Brandt. She went about her household duties like one in a dream. If Peter did but speak a little quickly to her, she started and fixed two terrified eyes on him. She went less often to her friend Margaret Van Eyck, and was ill at her ease when there. Instead of meeting her warm old friend's caresses, she used to receive them passive and trembling, and sometimes almost shrink from them. But the most extraordinary thing was, she never would go outside her own house in daylight. When she went to Tergou it was after dusk, and she returned before daybreak. She would not even go to matins. At last Peter, unobservant as he was, noticed it, and asked her the reason.

"The folk all look at me so."

One day Margaret Van Eyck asked her what was the matter. A scared look and a flood of tears were all the reply. The old lady expostulated gently. "What, sweetheart, afraid to confide your sorrows to me?"

"I have no sorrows, madam, but of my own making. I am kinder treated than I deserve, especially in this house."

"Then why not come oftener, my dear?"

"I come oftener than I deserve." And she sighed deeply.

About a month after this a soldier of the Dalgetty tribe, returning from service in Burgundy, brought a letter one evening to the hosier's house. He was away on business: but the rest of the family sat at supper. The soldier laid the letter on the table by Catherine and, refusing all guerdon for bringing it, went off to Sevenbergen. The letter was unfolded and spread out, and curiously enough, though not one of them could read, they could all tell it was Gerard's handwriting.

"And your father must be away!" cried Catherine. "Are ye not ashamed of yourselves? Not one that can read your brother's letter?"

How to get the words read to them? They were loath to show their ignorance and their emotion to a stranger.

"The Dame Van Eyck?" said Kate timidly.

"And so I will, Kate. She has a good heart. She loves Gerard, too. She will be glad to hear of him. And she will tell me what my poor child says to me."

She was soon at Margaret Van Eyck's house. Reicht took her into a room, and said: "Bide a minute. She is at her orisons."

There was a young woman in the room seated pensively by the stove, but she rose and courteously made way for the visitor.

"Thank you, young lady. The winter nights are cold, and your stove is a treat." Catherine then, while warming her hands, inspected her companion furtively from head to foot, both inclusive. The young person wore an ordinary wimple, but her gown was trimmed with fur, which was in those days almost a sign of superior rank or wealth. But what most struck Catherine was the candor and modesty of the face. She felt sure of sympathy from so good a countenance, and began to gossip.

"Now what think you brings me here, young lady? It is a letter—a letter from my poor boy that is far away in some savage part or other. And I take shame to say that none of us can read it. I wonder whether you can read?"

"Yes."

"Can ye, now? It is much to your credit, my dear. I dare say she won't be long, but every minute is an hour to a poor longing mother."

"I will read it to you."

"Bless you, my dear, bless you!"

In her unfeigned eagerness she never noticed the suppressed eagerness with which the hand was slowly put out to take the letter. She did not see the tremor with which the fingers closed on it.

"Come then, read it to me, prithee. I am wearying for it."

"The first words are, 'To my honoured parents.'"

"Ay, and he always did honor us, poor soul."

"'God and the saints have you in his holy keeping, and bless you by night and by day. Your one harsh deed is forgotten, your years of love remembered.'"

Catherine laid her hand on her bosom and sank back in her chair with one long sob.

"Then comes this, madam. It doth speak for itself—'a long farewell.'"

"Ay, go on. Bless you, girl, you give me sorry comfort. Still 'tis comfort."

"'To my brothers Cornelis and Sybrandt: Be content, you will see me no more!'"

"What does that mean? Ah."

"'To my sister Kate, little angel of my father's house. Be kind to *her*—' Ah!"

"That is Margaret Brandt, my dear—his sweetheart, poor soul. I've not been kind to her, my dear. Forgive me, Gerard!"

" '—for poor Gerard's sake, since grief to her is death—to—me——' Ah!"
And nature, resenting the poor girl's struggle for unnatural composure,
suddenly gave way, and she sank from her chair and lay insensible, with
the letter in her hand and her head on Catherine's knees.

Experienced women are not frightened when a woman faints, nor do they
hastily attribute it to anything but physical causes, which they have often
seen produce it. Catherine bustled about, laid the girl down with her head
on the floor quite flat, opened the window, and unloosed her dress as she
lay. Not till she had done all this did she step to the door and say, rather
loudly:

"Come here, if you please."

Margaret Van Eyck and Reicht came and found Margaret lying quite
flat, and Catherine beating her hands.

"Oh, my poor girl! What have you done to her?"

"Me?" said Catherine angrily.

"What has happened, then?"

"Nothing, madam, nothing more than is natural in her situation."

Margaret Van Eyck colored with ire.

"You do well to speak so coolly," said she, "you that are the cause of her
situation."

"That I am not," said Catherine, bluntly, "nor any woman born."

"What? Was it not you and your husband that kept them apart? And
now he is gone to Italy all alone. Situation, indeed! You have broken her
heart among you."

"Why, madam? Who is it, then, in heaven's name? To hear you one
would think this was my Gerard's lass. But that can't be. This fur never cost
less than five crowns the ell. Besides, this young gentlewoman is a wife, or
ought to be."

"Of course she ought. And who is the cause she is none? Who came between them at the very altar?"

"God forgive them, whoever it was," said Catherine, gravely. "Me it was
not, nor my man."

"Well," said the other, a little softened, "now you have seen her perhaps
you will not be quite so bitter against her, madam. She is coming to, thank
heaven."

"Me bitter against her?" said Catherine. "No, that is all over. Poor soul!
Trouble behind her and trouble afore her. And to think of my setting her,
of all living women, to read Gerard's letter to me. Ay, and that was what
made her go off, I'll be sworn. She is coming to. What, sweetheart? Be not
afeard, none are here but friends."

They seated her in an easy chair. As the color was creeping back to her
face and lips, Catherine drew Margaret Van Eyck aside.

"Is she staying with you, if you please?"

"No, madam."

"I wouldn't let her go back to Sevenbergen tonight, then."

"That is as she pleases. She still refuses to bide the night."

"Ay, but you are older than she is, you can make her. There, she is beginning to notice." Catherine then put her mouth to Margaret Van Eyck's ear for half a moment. It did not seem time enough to whisper a word, far less a sentence. But on some topics female can flash communication to female like lightning, or thought itself. The old lady started, and whispered back.

"It's false! It is a calumny! It is monstrous! Look at her face. It is blasphemy to accuse such a face."

"Tut, tut, tut!" said the other. "You might as well say this is not my hand. I ought to know, and I tell ye it is *so*."

Then, much to Margaret Van Eyck's surprise, she went up to the girl and, taking her round the neck, kissed her warmly. "I suffered for Gerard. His own words show me I have been to blame, the very words you have read to me. Ay, Gerard, my child, I have held aloof from her. But I'll make it up to her, once I begin. You are my daughter from this hour."

Another warm embrace sealed this hasty compact, and the woman of impulse was gone. Margaret lay back in her chair, and a feeble smile stole over her face. Gerard's mother had kissed her and called her daughter; but the next moment she saw her old friend looking at her with a vexed air.

"I wonder you let that woman kiss you."

"His mother!" murmured Margaret, half-reproachfully.

"Mother or no mother, you would not let her touch you if you knew what she whispered in my ear about you."

"About me?" said Margaret faintly.

"Ay, about you whom she never saw till tonight."

The old lady was proceeding, with some hesitation and choice of language, to make Margaret share her indignation when an unlooked-for interruption closed her lips. The young woman slid from her chair to her knees, and began to pray piteously to her for pardon. From the words and the manner of her penitence a bystander would have gathered she had inflicted some cruel wrong, some intolerable insult, upon her venerable friend.

CHAPTER XXV

The little party at the hosier's house sat at table discussing the recent event when their mother returned and, casting a piercing glance all round the little circle, laid the letter flat on the table. She repeated every word of it by memory, following the lines with her finger, to cheat herself and hearers into the notion that she could read the words, or nearly. Then, suddenly lifting her head, she cast another keen look on Cornelis and Sybrandt. Their eyes fell. On this the storm that had long been brewing burst on their heads.

Catherine seemed to swell like an angry hen ruffling her feathers, and out of her mouth came a Rhone and Saône of wisdom and twaddle, of great and mean invective, such as no male that ever was born could utter in one current, and not many women.

Cornelis and Sybrandt slunk out, aching with remorse, and impenitence, and hate. They avoided her eye as much as ever they could, and for many days she never spoke a word, good, bad, or indifferent, to either of them.

Catherine was a good housewife who seldom left home for a day, and then one thing or another always went amiss. She was keenly conscious of this and, watching for a slack tide in things domestic, put off her visit to Sevenbergen from day to day. At last, one day Eli asked her before all the family whether it was true she had thought of visiting Margaret Brandt.

"Ay, my man."

"Then I do forbid you."

"Oh, do you?"

"I do."

"Then there is no more to be said, I suppose," said she, coloring.

"Not a word," replied Eli, sternly.

When she was alone with her daughter she was very severe, not upon Eli, but upon herself.

"Behooved me rather go thither like a cat at a robin. But this was me all over. I am like a silly hen that can lay no egg without cackling, and convening all the house to rob her on't. Next time you and I are after aught the least amiss, let's do't, in heaven's name, then and there, and not take time to think about it, far less talk. So then if they take us to task we can say, alack we knew naught, we thought no ill, now, who'd ever? and so forth. For two pins I'd go thither in all their teeth."

"Mother," said Kate timidly.

"Well, what is a-coming now? No good news, though, by the look of you. What on earth can make the poor wench so scared?"

"An avowal she hath to make," faltered Kate faintly.

"Now there is a noble word for ye," said Catherine proudly. "Our Gerard taught thee that, I'll go bail. Come then, out with thy vowel."

"Well then, sooth to say, I have seen her."

"Anan?"

"And spoken with her to boot."

"And never told me? After this marvels are dirt."

"Mother, you were so hot against her. I waited till I could tell you without angering you worse."

"Ay," said Catherine, half sadly, half bitterly, "like mother like daughter. Cowardice it is our bane. The others I whiles buffet, or how would the house fare? But did you, Kate, ever have harsh word or look from your poor mother, that you—— Nay, I will not have ye cry, girl. Ten to one ye had your reason, so rise up, brave heart, and tell me all—better late than ne'er. And first and foremost whenever, and however, wond you to Sevenbergen wi' your poor crutches, and I not know?"

"I never was there in my life. And Mammy, dear, to say that I ne'er wished to see her that I will not, but I ne'er went, nor sought, to see her."

"There, now," said Catherine, disputatively, "said I not 'twas all unlike my girl to seek her unbeknown to me? Come now, for I'm all agog."

"Then thus 'twas. It came to my ears, no matter how, and prithee, good Mother, on my knees ne'er ask me how, that Gerard was a prisoner in the Stadthouse tower."

"Ah!"

"By Father's behest, as 'twas pretended."

Catherine uttered a sigh that was almost a moan. "Blacker than I thought," she muttered faintly.

"Giles and I went out at night to bid him be of good cheer. And there at the tower foot was a brave lass, quite strange to me, I vow, on the same errand."

"Lookee there now, Kate."

"At first we did properly frighten one another, through the place his bad name, and our poor heads being so full o' divels, and we whitened a bit in moonshine. But next moment, quo' I, 'You are Margaret.' 'And you are Kate,' quo' she. Think on't!"

"Did one ever?—'Twas Gerard! He will have been talking backward and forrard of thee to her, and her to thee. Now then, speak thy mind, child. Gerard is not here. Alas, what am I saying? Would to heaven he were."

"Well then, Mother, she is comely, and wrongs her picture but little."

"Eh, dear, hark to young folk! I am for good acts, not good looks. Loves she my boy as he did ought to be loved?"

"Sevenbergen is farther from the Stadthouse than we are," said Kate, thoughtfully, "yet she was there afore me."

Catherine nodded intelligence.

"Nay, more, she had got him out ere I came. Ay, down from the captives' tower."

Catherine shook her head incredulously. "The highest tower for miles! It is not feasible."

"'Tis sooth, though. She and an old man she brought found means and wit to send him up a rope. There 'twas dangling from his prison, and our Giles went up it. When first I saw it hang, I said, 'This is glamour.' But when the frank lass's arms came round me, and her bosom did beat on mine, and her cheeks wet, then said I, ''Tis not glamour, 'tis love.' For she is not like me, but lusty and able; and, dear heart, even I, poor frail creature, do feel sometimes as I could move the world for them I love. I love *you*, Mother. And she loves Gerard."

"God bless her for't! God bless her!"

"But—"

"But what, lamb?"

"Her love, is it for very certain honest? 'Tis most strange, but that very thing which hath warmed your heart hath somewhat cooled mine toward her, poor soul. She is no wife, you know, Mother, when all is done."

"Humph! They have stood at th' altar together."

"Ay, but they went as they came, maid and bachelor."

"The Parson, saith he so?"

"Nay, for that I know not."

"Then I'll take no man's word but his in such a tangled skein." After some reflection she added: "Natheless art right, girl. I'll to Sevenbergen alone. A wife I am, but not a slave. We are all in the dark here. And she holds the clue. I must question her, and no one by, least of all you. I'll not take my lily to a house wi' a spot, no, not to a palace o' gold and silver."

The more Catherine pondered this conversation, the more she felt drawn toward Margaret, and moreover she was "all agog" with curiosity. At last one fine day, after dinner she whispered to Kate, "Keep the house from going to pieces, an ye can," and donned her best kirtle and hood, and her scarlet clocked hose and her new shoes, and trudged briskly off to Sevenbergen, troubling no man's mule.

When she got there she inquired where Margaret Brandt lived. The first person she asked shook his head, and said, "The name is strange to me." She went a little farther and asked a girl of about fifteen who was standing at a door. "Father," said the girl, speaking into the house, "here is another after that magician's daughter." The man came out and told Catherine Peter Brandt's cottage was just outside the town on the east side. "You may see the chimney hence," and he pointed it out to her. "But you will not find them there, neither father nor daughter. They have left the town this week, bless you."

"Say not so, good man, and me walken all the way from Tergou."

"From Tergou? Then you must ha' met the soldier."

"What soldier? Ay, I did meet a soldier."

"Well, then, yon soldier was here seeking that selfsame Margaret."

"Ay, and warn't a mad with us because she was gone?" put in the girl. "His long beard and her cheek are no strangers, I warrant."

"Say no more than ye know," said Catherine sharply. "You are young to take to slandering your elders. Stay! Tell me more about this soldier, good man."

"Nay, I know no more than that he came hither seeking Margaret Brandt, and I told him she and her father had made a moonlight flit on't this day sennight, and that some thought the Devil had flown away with them, being magicians. And he seemed quiet and sad-like, didn't he now, wench?"

"That a did," said the young woman warmly. "And, dame, he was just as pretty a man as ever I clapped eyes on. Cheeks like a rose, and shining beard, and eyes in his head like sloes."

"I saw he was well bearded," said Catherine, "but for the rest, at my age I scan them not as when I was young and foolish. But he seemed right civil —doffed his bonnet to me as I had been a queen, and I did drop him my best reverence, for manners beget manners. But little I wist he had been her light-o'-love."

Kate met her outside the town with beaming eyes.

"Well, Kate lass, it is a happy thing I went. I am heartbroken. Gerard has been sore abused. The child is none of ourn, nor the mother from this hour."

"Alas, Mother, I fathom not your meaning."

"Ask me no more, girl, but never mention her name to me again. That is all."

Kate acquiesced with a humble sigh, and they went home together. They found a soldier seated tranquilly by their fire. The moment they entered the door, he rose and saluted them civilly. They stood and looked at him, Kate with some little surprise, but Catherine with a great deal, and with rising indignation.

"What make you here?" was Catherine's greeting.

"I came to seek after Margaret."

"Well, we know no such person."

"Say not so, dame. Sure you know her by name, Margaret Brandt."

"We have heard of her for that matter—to our cost."

"Come, dame, prithee tell me at least where she bides."

"I know not where she bides, and care not."

Denys felt sure this was a deliberate untruth. He bit his lip. "Well, I looked to find myself in an enemy's country at this Tergou, but maybe if ye knew all ye would not be so dour."

"I do know all," replied Catherine bitterly. "This morn I knew naught." Then, suddenly setting her arms akimbo, she told him with a raised voice and flashing eyes she wondered at his cheek sitting down by that hearth of all hearths in the world.

"May Satan fly away with your hearth to the lake of fire and brimstone!" shouted Denys, who could speak Flemish fluently. "Your own servant bade me sit there till you came, else I had ne'er troubled your hearth. My malison on it, and on the churlish rooftree that greets an unoffending stranger this way." And he strode scowling to the door.

"Oh, oh!" ejaculated Catherine, frightened and also a little conscience-stricken; and the virago sat suddenly down and burst into tears. Her daughter followed suit quietly, but without loss of time.

Denys stood at the door looking ruefully at the havoc his thunderbolt of eloquence had made.

"Nay, wife," said he, "weep not neither for a soldier's hasty word. I mean not all I said. Why, your house is your own, and what right in it have I? There now, I'll go."

"What is to do?" said a grave manly voice. It was Eli; he had come in from the shop.

"Here is a ruffian been a-scolding of your womenfolk and making them cry," explained Denys.

"Little Kate, what is't? For ruffians do not use to call themselves ruffians," said Eli the sensible.

Ere she could explain, "Hold your tongue, girl," said Catherine. "Muriel bade him sit down, and I knew not that, and wyted on him; and he was going and leaving his malison on us, root and branch. I was never so becursed in all my days, oh, oh, oh!"

"You were both somewhat to blame, both you and he," said Eli calmly. "However, what the servant says the master should still stand to. We keep not open house, but yet we are not poor enough to grudge a seat at our hearth in a cold day to a wayfarer with an honest face, and as, I think, a wounded man. So end all malice, and sit ye down!"

"Wounded?" cried mother and daughter in a breath.

"Think you a soldier slings his arm for sport?"

"Nay, 'tis but an arrow," said Denys cheerfully.

"But an arrow?" said Kate with concentrated horror. "Where were our eyes, Mother?"

"Nay, in good sooth, a trifle. Which however I will pray mesdames to accept as an excuse for my vivacity. 'Tis these little foolish trifling wounds that fret a man, worthy sir. Why, look ye now, sweeter temper than our Gerard never breathed, yet when the bear did but strike a piece no bigger than a crown out of his calf, he turned so hot and choleric y'had said he was no son of yours, but got by the good knight Sir John Pepper on his wife dame Mustard. Who is this? A dwarf? Your servant, Master Giles."

"Your servant, soldier," roared the newcomer. Denys started. He had not counted on exchanging greetings with a petard.

Denys's words had surprised his hosts, but hardly more than their deportment now did him. They all three came creeping up to where he sat, and looked down into him with their lips parted as if he had been some strange phenomenon. And growing agitation succeeded to amazement.

"Now hush!" said Eli. "Let none speak but I. Young man," said he solemnly, "in God's name who are you that know us though we know you not, and that shake our hearts speaking to us of—the absent—our poor rebellious son, whom Heaven forgive and bless?"

"What, master," said Denys lowering his voice, "hath he not writ to you? Hath he not told you of me, Denys of Burgundy?"

"He hath writ but three lines, and named not Denys of Burgundy, nor any stranger."

"Ay, I mind the long letter was to his sweetheart, this Margaret, and she has decamped, plague take her, and how I am to find her Heaven knows."

"What, she is not your sweetheart, then?"

"Who, dame, an't please you?"

"Why, Margaret Brandt."

"How can my comrade's sweetheart be mine? I know her not from Noah's niece. How should I? I never saw her."

"Whist with this idle chat, Kate," said Eli impatiently, "and let the young man answer me. How came you to know Gerard, our son? Prithee now think on a parent's cares, and answer me straightforward, like a soldier as thou art."

"And shall. I was paid off at Flushing, and started for Burgundy. On the German frontier I lay at the same inn with Gerard. I fancied him. I said 'Be my comrade.' He was loath at first, consented presently. Many a weary league we trod together. Never were truer comrades, never will be while earth shall last. First I left my route a bit to be with him, then he his to be with me. We talked of Sevenbergen, and Tergou, a thousand times, and of all in this house.

"We had our troubles on the road: but battling them together made them light. But just when all was fair, and I was to see him safe aboard ship for Rome, if not to Rome itself, met us that son of a —— the Lord Anthony of Burgundy, and his men, making for Flanders, then in insurrection, tore us by force apart, took me where I got some broad pieces in hand, and a broad arrow in my shoulder, and left my poor Gerard lonesome. At that sad parting, soldier though I be, these eyes did rain salt scalding tears, and so did his, poor soul. His last word to me was 'Go comfort Margaret!' So here I be. Mine to him was 'Think no more of Rome. Make for Rhine, and downstream home.' Now say, for you know best, did I advise him well or ill?"

"Soldier, take my hand," said Eli. "God bless thee! God bless thee!" And his lip quivered. It was all his reply, but more eloquent than many words.

They could not make enough of Denys. They stuffed him, and crammed him, and then gathered round him and kept filling his glass in turn while by that genial blaze of fire and ruby wine and eager eyes he told all that I have related, and a vast number of minor details.

Catherine had never felt so kindly toward the truant Margaret as now, and she was fully as anxious to find her and be kind to her before Gerard's return as Denys was. But she could not agree with him that anything was to be gained by leaving this neighborhood to search for her.

"She must have told somebody whither she was going. It is not as though they were dishonest folk flying the country. They owe not a stiver in Sevenbergen, and dear heart, Denys, you can't hunt all Holland for her."

"Can I not?" said Denys grimly. "That we shall see." He added, after some reflection, that they must divide their forces—she stay here with eyes and ears wide-open, and he ransack every town in Holland for her, if need be. "But she will not be many leagues from here. They be three. Three fly not so fast, nor far, as one."

"That is sense," said Catherine. But she insisted on his going first to the Demoiselle Van Eyck. "She and our Margaret were bosom friends. She knows where the girl is gone, if she will but tell us."

Denys was for going to her that instant, so Catherine, in a turn of the hand, made herself one shade neater and took him with her. She was received graciously by the old lady sitting in a richly furnished room, and opened her business. The tapestry dropped out of Margaret Van Eyck's hands.

"Gone? Gone from Sevenbergen and not told me? The thankless girl."

This turn greatly surprised the visitors. "What, you knew not? When was she here last?"

"Maybe ten days a-gone. I had ta'en out my brushes, after so many years, to paint her portrait. I did not do it though, for reasons."

Catherine remarked it was "a most strange thing she should go away bag and baggage like this, without with your leave or by your leave, or wherefore. Was ever aught so untoward—just when all our hearts are warm to her. And here is Gerard's mate come from the ends o' the earth with comfort for her from Gerard, and can't find her, and Gerard himself expected. What to do I know not. But sure she is not parted like this without a reason. Can ye not give us the clue, my good Demoiselle? Prithee, now."

"I have it not to give," said the elder lady rather peevishly.

"Then I can," said Reicht Heynes, showing herself in the doorway, with color somewhat heightened.

"So you have been hearkening all the time, eh?"

"What are my ears for, mistress?"

"True. Well throw us the light of thy wisdom on this dark matter."

"There is no darkness that I see," said Reicht. "And the clue, why an' ye call't a two-ply twine, and the ends on't in this room e'en now, ye'll not be far out. Oh, mistress, I wonder at you sitting there pretending."

"Marry, come up!" And the mistress's cheek was now nearly as red as the servant's. "So 'twas I drove the foolish girl away."

"You did your share, mistress. What sort of greeting gave you her last time she came? Think you she could miss to notice it, and she all friendless? And you said, 'I have altered my mind about painting of you,' says you, a-turning up your nose at her."

"I did not turn up my nose. It is not shaped like yours for looking heavenward."

"Oh, all our nosen can follow our heart's bent, for that matter. Poor soul. She did come into the kitchen to me. 'I am not to be painted now,' said she, and the tears in her eyes. She said no more. But I knew well what she did mean. I had seen ye."

"Well," said Margaret Van Eyck, "I do confess so much, and I make you the judge, madam."

She went on to tell them how from step to step she had been led on to promise to resume the art she had laid aside with a sigh when her brothers died, and to paint the Madonna once more—with Margaret for model. Incidentally she even revealed how girls are turned into saints. "'Thy hair is adorable,' said I. 'Why, 'tis red,' quoth she. 'Ay,' quoth I, 'but what a red! How brown! How glossy! Most hair is not worth a straw to us painters; thine the artist's very hue. But thy violet eyes, which smack of earth, being now languid for lack of one Gerard, now full of fire in hopes of the same Gerard, these will I lift to Heaven in fixed and holy meditation, and thy nose, which doth already somewhat aspire that way (though not so piously as Reicht's), will I debase a trifle, and somewhat enfeeble thy chin.'"

"Enfeeble her chin? Alack, what may that mean? Ye go beyond me, mistress."

"'Tis a resolute chin. Not a jot too resolute for this wicked world, but when ye come to a Madonna? No, thank you."

"Well, I never. A resolute chin."

"And now comes the rub. When you told me she was—the way she is, it gave me a shock. I dropped my brushes. Was I going to turn a girl that couldn't keep her lover at a distance into the Virgin Mary, at my time of life?—I love the poor ninny still. But I adore our blessed Lady."

"Well, you know, dame," observed Catherine, "you must think it would go to the poor girl's heart, and she so fond of ye."

Margaret Van Eyck only sighed. The Frisian girl, after biting her lips impatiently a little while, turned upon Catherine.

"Why, dame, think you 'twas for that alone Margaret and Peter hath left Sevenbergen? Nay."

"For what else, then?"

"What else? Why because Gerard's people slight her so cruel. Who would bide among hardhearted folk that ha' driven her lad t'Italy, and now he is gone, relent not, but face it out, and ne'er come anigh her that is left?"

"Alack, Reicht, I did go but yestreen, and had gone before, but one plaguy thing or t'other did still come and hinder me."

Catherine and Denys bade the Van Eyck adieu, and that same afternoon Denys set out on a wild-goose chase. His plan, like all great things, was simple. He should go to a hundred towns and villages, and ask in each after an old physician with a fair daughter and an old longbow soldier. He should inquire of the burgomasters about all newcomers, and should go to the fountains and watch the women and girls as they came with their pitchers for water. And away he went, and was months and months on the tramp and could not find her.

CHAPTER XXVI

THE goodhearted Catherine was not happy. Not that she reproached herself very deeply for not having gone quickly enough to Sevenbergen, whither she was not bound to go at all—except on the score of having excited false hopes in Margaret. But she was in dismay when she reflected that Gerard must reach home in another month at farthest, more likely in a week. And how should she tell him she had not even kept an eye upon his betrothed? Then there was the uncertainty as to the girl's fate, and this uncertainty sometimes took a sickening form.

"Oh, Kate," she groaned, "if she should have gone and made herself away!"

"Mother, she would never be so wicked."

"Ah, my lass, you know not what hasty fools young lasses be, that have no mothers to keep 'em straight. They will fling themselves into the water for a man that the next man they meet would ha' cured 'em of in a week. I have known 'em to jump in like brass one moment and scream for help in the next. Couldn't know their own minds, ye see, even such a trifle as yon. And then there's times when their bodies ail like no other living creatures ever I could hear of, and that strings up their feelings so, the patience that belongs to them at other times beyond all living souls, barring an ass, seems all to jump out of 'em at one turn, and into the water they go.

"They do forget all these things in a moment o' despair, when the very sky seems black above them. I place more faith in him that is unborn than on him that is ripe for the grave, to keep her out o' mischief. For certes it do go sore against us to die when there's a little innocent a-pulling at our hearts to let un live, and feeding at our very veins."

"Well, then, keep up a good heart, Mother." She added that very likely all these fears were exaggerated.

All these anxieties were shortly suspended by an incident that struck nearer home, made Tergou furiously jealous of Catherine, and Catherine weep. Marched up to Eli's door a pageant brave to the eye of sense, and to the vulgar judgment noble, but to the philosophic, pitiable more or less.

It looked one animal, a centaur, but on severe analysis proved two. The human half was sadly bedizened with those two metals to clothe his carcass with which and line his pouch man has now and then disposed of his soul. Still, the horse was the vainer brute of the two; he was far worse beflounced, bebonneted, and bemantled than any fair lady *regnante crinolinâ*. For the man, under the color of a warming pan, retained Nature's outline, but scarce a pennyweight of honest horseflesh to be seen. This poor animal from stem to stern was swamped in finery. His ears were hid in great sheaths of white linen tipped with silver and blue. His body swaddled in stiff gorgeous cloths descending to the ground, except just in front, where they left him room to mince. His tail, though dear to memory, no doubt, was lost to sight, being tucked in heaven knows how. Only his eyes shone out like goggles, through two holes pierced in the wall of haberdashery, and his little front hoofs peeped in and out like rats.

Yet did this compound, gorgeous and irrational, represent power, absolute power. It came straight from a tournament at the Duke's court, which, being on a progress, lay last night at a neighboring town—to execute the behests of royalty.

"What ho!" cried the upper half, and on Eli emerging, with his wife behind him, saluted them. "Peace be with you, good people. Rejoice! I am come for your dwarf."

Eli looked amazed, and said nothing. But Catherine screamed over his shoulder: "You have mistook your road, good man. Here abides no dwarf."

"Nay, wife, he means our Giles, who is somewhat small of stature. Why gainsay what gainsayed may not be?"

"Ay," cried the pageant, "that is he, and discourseth like the big tabor!"

"His breast is sound, for that matter," said Catherine sharply.

"And prompt with his fists, though at long odds."

"Else how would the poor thing keep his head in such a world as this?"

" 'Tis well said, dame. Art as ready with thy weapon as he—art his mother, likely. So bring him forth and that presently. See, they lead a stunted mule for him. The Duke hath need of him, sore need. We are clean out o' dwarven, and tiger cats, which may not be whiles earth them yieldeth. Our last hop-o'-my-thumb tumbled down the well t'other day."

"And think you I'll let my darling go to such an ill-guided house as yon, where the reckless trollops of servants close not the well mouth, but leave it open to trap innocents like wolven?"

The representative of autocracy lost patience at this unwonted opposition, and with stern look and voice bade her bethink her whether it was the better of the two "to have your abortion at court fed like a bishop and put on like a prince, or to have all your heads stricken off and borne on poles, with the bellman crying, 'Behold the heads of hardy rebels, which having by good luck a misgotten son, did traitorously grudge him to the Duke, who is the true father of all his folk, little or mickle'?"

"Nay," said Eli, sadly, "miscall us not. We be true folk, and neither rebels nor traitors. But 'tis sudden, and the poor lad is our true flesh and blood, and hath of late given proof of more sense than heretofore."

"Avails not threatening our lives," whimpered Catherine. "We grudge him not to the Duke. But in sooth he cannot go, his linen is all in holes. So there is an end."

But the male mind resisted this crusher.

"Think you the Duke will not find linen, and cloth of gold to boot? None so brave, none so affected, at court as our monsters, big or wee."

How long the dispute might have lasted before the iron arguments of despotism achieved the inevitable victory, I know not; but it was cut short by a party whom neither disputant had deigned to consult. The bone of contention walked out of the house, and sided with monarchy.

"If my folk are mad, I am not," he roared. "I'll go with you, and on the instant."

At this Catherine set up a piteous cry. She saw another of her brood escaping from under her wing into some unknown element. Giles was not quite insensible to her distress, so simple yet so eloquent. He said:

"Nay, take not on, Mother! Why, 'tis a godsend. And I am sick of this ever since Gerard left it."

"Ah, cruel Giles! Should ye not rather say she is bereaved of Gerard, the more need of you to stay aside her and comfort her!"

"Oh, I am not going to Rome! Not such a fool. I shall never be farther than Rotterdam, and I'll often come and see you, and if I like not the place, who shall keep me there? Not all the dukes in Christendom."

"Good sense lies in little bulk," said the emissary approvingly. "Therefore, Master Giles, buss the old folk, and thank them for misbegetting of thee, and—ho! you—bring hither his mule!"

One of his retinue brought up the dwarf mule. Giles refused it with scorn. And on being asked the reason, said it was not just. "What, would ye throw all into one scale? Put muckle to muckle, and little to wee? Besides, I hate and scorn small things. I'll go on the highest horse here, or not at all."

The pursuivant eyed him attentively a moment. He then adopted a courteous manner. "I shall study your will in all things reasonable. (Dismount, Eric, yours is the highest horse.) And if you would halt in the town an hour or so while you bid them farewell, say but the word, and your pleasure shall be my delight."

Giles reflected.

"Master," said he, "if we wait a month 'twill be still the same. My mother is a good soul, but her body is bigger than her spirit. We shall not part without a tear or two, and the quicker 'tis done, the fewer. So bring yon horse to me."

Catherine threw her apron over her face and sobbed. The high horse was brought, and Giles was for swarming up his tail, like a rope, but one of the servants cried out hastily, "Forbear, for he kicketh." "I'll kick him," said Giles. "Bring him close beneath this window, and I'll learn you all how to mount a horse which kicketh, and will not be clomb by the tail, the staircase of a horse." And he dashed into the house and almost immediately reappeared at an upper window with a rope in his hand. He fastened an end somehow and, holding the other, descended as swift and smooth as an oiled thunderbolt in a groove and lighted astride his high horse as unperceived by that animal as a fly settling on him.

The official lifted his hands to heaven in mawkish admiration. "I have gotten a pearl," thought he, "and wow, but this will be a good day's work for me!"

"Come, Father, come, Mother, buss me, and bless me, and off I go."

Eli gave him his blessing, and bade him be honest and true, and a credit to his folk. Catherine could not speak, but clung to him with many sobs and embraces.

And so the dwarf mounted the high horse and rode away complacent, with the old hand laying the court butter on his back with a trowel. Little recked Perpusillus of two poor silly females that sat by the bereaved hearth rocking themselves, and weeping, and discussing all his virtues, and how his mind had opened lately, and blind as two beetles to his faults who rode away from them jocund and bold.

Arrived at court, he speedily became a great favorite. One strange propensity of his electrified the palace; but, on account of his small size, and for variety's sake, and as a monster, he was indulged on it. In a word, he was let speak the truth. It is an unpopular thing. He made it an intolerable one. Bawled it.

CHAPTER XXVII

Margaret Brandt had always held herself apart from Sevenbergen, and her reserve had passed for pride. This had come to her ears, and she knew many hearts were swelling with jealousy and malevolence. How would they triumph over her when her condition could no longer be concealed! This thought gnawed her night and day. For some time it had made her bury herself in the house, and shun daylight even on those rare occasions when she went abroad.

Not that in her secret heart and conscience she mistook her moral situation. Though not acquainted with the nice distinctions of the contemporary law, she knew that betrothal was a marriage contract, and could no more be legally broken on either side than any other compact written and witnessed; and that marriage with another party than the betrothed had been formally annulled both by Church and State; and that betrothed couples often came together without any further ceremony, and their children were legitimate.

But what weighed down her simple medieval mind was this: That very contract of betrothal was not forthcoming. Instead of her keeping it, Gerard had got it, and Gerard was far, far away. She hated and despised herself for the miserable oversight which had placed her at the mercy of false opinion.

Her marriage lines being out of sight, and in Italy, would never prevail to balance her visible pregnancy, and the sight of her child when born. What sort of a tale was this to stop slanderous tongues? "I have got my marriage lines, but I cannot show them you." What woman would believe her? Or even pretend to believe her? And as she was in reality one of the most modest girls in Holland, it was women's good opinion she wanted, not men's.

The wish to fly from this neighborhood began to grow and gnaw upon her till it became a wild and passionate desire. But how persuade her father to this? Old people cling to places. He was very old and infirm to change his abode. There was no course but to make him her confidant. Better so than to run away from him, and she felt that would be the alternative. And now between her uncontrollable desire to fly and hide, and her invincible aversion to speak out to a man, even to her father, she vibrated in a suspense full of lively torture. And presently betwixt these two came in one day the fatal thought "End all!" Things foolishly worded are not always foolish. One of poor Catherine's bugbears, these numerous canals, did sorely tempt this poor fluctuating girl. She stood on the bank one afternoon and eyed the calm deep water. It seemed an image of repose, and she was so harassed. No more trouble. No more fear of shame. If Gerard had not loved her, I doubt she had ended there.

As it was, she knelt by the waterside and prayed fervently to God to keep such wicked thoughts from her. "Oh, selfish wretch," said she, "to leave thy father! Oh, wicked wretch to kill thy child, and make thy poor Gerard lose all his pain and peril undertaken for thy sake! I will tell Father all, ay, ere this sun shall set." And she went home with eager haste lest her good resolution should ooze out ere she got there.

Now in matters domestic the learned Peter was simple as a child, and Margaret from the age of sixteen had governed the house, gently but absolutely. It was therefore a strange thing in this house, the faltering irresolute way in which its young but despotic mistress addressed that person who in a domestic sense was less important than Martin Wittenhaagen, or even than the little girl who came in the morning and for a pittance washed the vessels, and so on, and went home at night.

"Father, I would speak to thee."

"Speak on, girl."

"Wilt listen to me? And—and—not—and try to excuse my faults?"

"We have all our faults, Margaret, thou no more than the rest of us—but fewer, unless parental feelings blinds me."

"Alas, no, Father. I am a poor foolish girl, and would fain do well, but have done ill, most ill, most unwisely, and now must bear the shame. But, Father, I love you, with all my faults, and will not you forgive my folly, and still love your motherless girl?"

"That ye may count on," said Peter cheerfully.

"Oh, well, smile not. For then how can I speak and make you sad?"

"Why, what is the matter?"

"Father, disgrace is coming on this house—it is at the door. And I the culprit. Oh, Father, turn your head away. I—I—Father, I have let Gerard take away my marriage lines."

"Is that all? 'Twas an oversight."

" 'Twas the deed of a madwoman. But woe is me! That is not the worst." Peter interrupted her. "The youth is honest, and loves you dear. You are young. What is a year or two to you? Gerard will assuredly come back and keep troth."

"And meantime, know you what is coming?"

"Not I, except that I shall be gone first for one."

"Worse than that. There is worse pain than death. Nay, for pity's sake, turn away your head, Father."

"Foolish wench!" muttered Peter, but turned his head.

She trembled violently, and with her cheeks on fire began to falter out: "I did look on Gerard as my husband—we being betrothed—and he was in so sore danger, and I thought I had killed him, and I—Oh, if you were but my mother I might find courage, you would question me. But you say not a word."

"Why, Margaret, what is all this coil about? And why are thy cheeks crimson, speaking to no stranger but to thy old father?"

"Why are my cheeks on fire? Because—because—Father, kill me! send me to Heaven! Bid Martin shoot me with his arrow! And then the gossips will come and tell you why I blush so this day. And then, when I am dead, I hope you will love your girl again for her mother's sake."

"Give me thy hand, mistress," said Peter, a little sternly.

She put it out to him trembling. He took it gently, and began with some anxiety in his face to feel her pulse.

"Alas, nay!" said she. "'Tis my soul that burns, not my body with fever. I cannot, will not, bide in Sevenbergen." And she wrung her hands impatiently.

"Be calm now," said the old man, soothingly, "nor torment thyself for naught. Not bide in Sevenbergen? What need to bide a day, as it vexes thee, and puts thee in a fever—for fevered thou art, deny it not."

"What!" cried Margaret. "Would you yield to go hence, and—and ask no reason but my longing to be gone?" And suddenly throwing herself on her knees beside him, in a fervor of supplication she clutched his sleeve, and then his arm, and then his shoulder while imploring him to quit this place, and not ask her why. "Alas! What needs it? You will soon see it. And I could never say it. I would liever die."

"Foolish child! Who seeks thy girlish secrets? Is it I, whose life hath been spent in searching Nature's? And, for leaving Sevenbergen, what is there to keep me in it? Am I not yclept quacksalver by those that come not near thee unwilling—— Is there respect for me here, or gratitude?—and wizard by those I heal? And give they not the guerdon and the honor they deny me to the empirics that slaughter them? Besides, what is't to me where we sojourn? Choose thou that, as did thy mother before thee."

Margaret embraced him tenderly, and wept upon his shoulder. She was respited. Yet as she wept, respited, she almost wished she had had the courage to tell him. After a while nothing would content him but her taking a medicament he went and brought her. She took it submissively, to please him. It was the least she could do. It was a composing draught, and though administered under an error, and a common one, did her more good than harm. She awoke calmed by a long sleep, and that very day began her preparations.

Next week they went to Rotterdam, bag and baggage, and lodged above a tailor's shop in the Brede-Kirk Straet. Only one person in Tergou knew whither they were gone. The Burgomaster. He locked the information in his own breast. The use he made of it ere long, my reader will not easily divine, for he did not divine it himself. But time will show.

Among strangers Margaret Brandt was comparatively happy. And soon a new and unexpected cause of content arose. A civic dignitary being ill, and fanciful in proportion, went from doctor to doctor, and having arrived at death's door, sent for Peter. Peter found him bled and purged to nothing. He flung a battalion of bottles out of the window, and left it open; beat up yolks of eggs in neat Schiedam, and administered it in small doses; followed this up by meat stewed in red wine and water, shredding into both mild febrifugal herbs that did no harm. Finally, his patient got about again, looking something between a man and a pillowcase, and being a voluble dignitary, spread Peter's fame in every street; and that artist, who had long merited a reputation in vain, made one rapidly by luck. Things looked bright. The old man's pride was cheered at last, and his purse began to fill. He spent much of his gain, however, in sovereign herbs and choice drugs, and would have so invested them all, but Margaret whitemailed a part.

The victory came too late. Its happy excitement was fatal. One evening, in bidding her good night, his voice seemed rather inarticulate. The next morning he was found speechless, and only just sensible.

Margaret, who had been for years her father's attentive pupil, saw at once that he had had a paralytic stroke. But not trusting to herself, she ran for a doctor. One of those who, obstructed by Peter, had not killed the civic dignitary came, and cheerfully confirmed her views. He was for bleeding the patient. She declined. "He was always against blooding," said she, "especially the old." Peter lived, but was never the same man again. His memory became much affected, and of course he was not to be trusted to prescribe. And several patients had come, and one or two that were bent on being cured by the new doctor and no other awaited his convalescence. And now here were two men to be lodged and fed by one pregnant girl, and another mouth coming into the world.

But this last, though the most helpless of all, was their best friend. Nature was strong in Margaret Brandt, that same nature which makes the brutes, the birds and the insects, so cunning at providing food and shelter for their progeny yet to come. Stimulated by nature, she sat and brooded, and brooded, and thought and thought how to be beforehand with destitution. Ay, though she had still five gold pieces left, she saw starvation coming with inevitable foot.

She rose, bade Martin move Peter to another room, made her own very neat and clean, polished the glass globe and suspended it from the ceiling, dusted the crocodile and nailed him to the outside wall; and after duly instructing Martin, set him to play the lounging sentinel about the street door, and tell the crocodile-bitten that a great, and aged, and learned alchemist abode there, who in his moments of recreation would sometimes amuse himself by curing mortal diseases.

Patients soon came, were received by Margaret, and demanded to see the leech. That might not be. He was deep in his studies, searching for the grand elixir, and not princes could have speech of him. They must tell her their symptoms, and return in two hours. And, oh, mysterious powers! When they did return, the drug or draft was always ready for them. Sometimes, when it was a worshipful patient, she would carefully scan his face, and feeling both pulse and skin as well as hearing his story, would go softly with it to Peter's room, and there think and ask herself how her father, whose system she had long quietly observed, would have treated the case. Then she would write an illegible scrawl with a cabalistic letter and bring it down, reverentially, and show it the patient, and could he read that? Then it would be either "I am no reader" or, with admiration, "Nay mistress, naught can I make on't."

"Ay, but I can. 'Tis sovereign. Look on thyself as cured!" If she had the materials by her, and she was too good an economist not to favor somewhat those medicines she had in her own stock, she would sometimes let the patient see her compound it, often and anxiously consulting the sacred prescription lest great Science should suffer in her hands. And so she would send them away relieved of cash, but with their pockets full of medicine, and minds full of faith, and humbugged to their heart's content. And when they were gone, she would take down two little boxes Gerard had made her, and on one of these she had written *Today,* and on the other *Tomorrow,* and put the smaller coins into "Today," and the larger into "Tomorrow," along with such of her gold pieces as had survived the journey from Sevenbergen, and the expenses of housekeeping in a strange place. And so she met current expenses, and laid by for the rainy day she saw coming, and mixed drugs with simples and vice with virtue. On this last score her conscience pricked her sore, and after each day's comedy she knelt down and prayed God to forgive her for the sake of her child. But lo and behold, cure after cure was reported to her, so then her conscience began to harden.

Martin Wittenhaagen had of late been a dead weight on her hands. Like most men who have endured great hardships, he had stiffened rather suddenly. But though less supple, he was as strong as ever, and at his own pace could have carried the doctor herself round Rotterdam city. He carried her slops instead. In this new business he showed the qualities of a soldier: unreasoning obedience, punctuality, accuracy, dispatch, and drunkenness. He fell among "good fellows," the blackguards plied him with Schiedam, he babbled, he bragged.

Doctor Margaret had risen very high in his estimation. All this brandishing of a crocodile for a standard, and setting a dotard in ambush, and getting rid of slops, and taking good money in exchange, struck him not as science but something far superior, strategy. And he boasted in his cups and before a mixed company how "me and my General we are a-biting of the burghers."

When this revelation had had time to leaven the city, his General Doctor Margaret received a call from the constables. They took her, trembling and begging subordinate machines to forgive her, before the Burgomaster; and by his side stood real physicians, a terrible row, in long robes and square caps, accusing her of practicing unlawfully on the bodies of the Duke's lieges. At first she was too frightened to say a word. Novicelike, the very name of "law" paralyzed her. But being questioned closely, but not so harshly as if she had been ugly, she told the truth. She had long been her father's pupil, and had but followed his system, and she had cured many; "and it is not for myself in very deed, sirs, but I have two poor helpless honest men at home upon my hands, and how else can I keep them? Ah, good sirs, let a poor girl make her bread honestly. Ye hinder them not to make it idly and shamefully. And oh, sirs, ye are husbands, ye are fathers; ye cannot but see I have reason to work and provide as best I may." And ere this woman's appeal had left her lips, she would have given the world to recall it, and stood with one hand upon her heart and one before her face, hiding it but not the tears that trickled underneath. All which went to the wrong address. Perhaps a female bailiff might have yielded to such arguments, and bade her practice medicine and break law till such time as her child should be weaned, and no longer.

"What have we to do with that?" said the Burgomaster. "Save and except that if thou wilt pledge thyself to break the law no more, I will remit the imprisonment, and exact but the fine."

On this Doctor Margaret clasped her hands together and vowed most penitently never, never, never, to cure body or beast again; and being dismissed with the constables to pay the fine, she turned at the door and curtsied, poor soul, and thanked the gentlemen for their forbearance.

Toward evening she rose, and washed her face and did up her hair, and doggedly bade Martin take down the crocodile and put out a basket instead.

"I can get up linen better than they seem to do it in this street," said she, "and you must carry it in the basket."

Even while they were talking came a male for advice. Margaret told it the Mayor had interfered and forbidden her to sell drugs. "But," said she, "I will gladly iron and starch your linen for you, and—I will come and fetch it from your house."

"Are ye mad, young woman?" said the male. "I come for a leech, and ye proffer me a washerwoman." And it went out in dudgeon.

"There is a stupid creature," said Margaret sadly.

Presently came a female to tell the symptoms of her sick child. Margaret stopped it.

"We are forbidden by the bailiff to sell drugs. But I will gladly wash, iron, and starch your linen for you—and I will come and fetch it from your house."

"Oh, ay," said the female. "Well, I have some smocks and ruffs foul. Come for them, and when you *are* there, you can look at the boy." And it told her where it lived, and when its husband would be out.

An introduction is an introduction. And two or three patients, out of all those who came and were denied medicine, made Doctor Margaret their washerwoman. And so the brave girl, and the brave soldier, worked with a will, and kept the wolf from the door. More they could not do. They kept the weekly rent paid, and the pot boiling, but no more.

Something must be done to fill "Tomorrow's" box. She hawked her initial letters and her illuminated vellums all about the town. Printing had by this time dealt calligraphy in black-and-white a terrible blow in Holland and Germany. But some copies of the printed books were usually illuminated and lettered. The printers offered Margaret prices for work in these two kinds.

"I'll think on't," said she.

She took down her diurnal book, and calculated that the price of an hour's work on those arts would be about one fifth what she got for an hour at the tub and mangle. "I'll starve first," said she. "What, pay a craft and a mystery five times less than a handicraft!"

Martin, carrying the dry-clothes basket, got treated, and drunk. This time he babbled her whole story. The girls got hold of it and gibed her at the fountain.

All she had gone through was light to her, compared with the pins and bodkins her own sex drove into her heart whenever she came near the merry crew with her pitcher, and that was every day. These girls persisted that Margaret was deserted by her lover. And to be deserted was a crime. (They had not been deserted yet.) Not a word against the Gerard they had created out of their own heads. For his imaginary crime they fell foul of the supposed victim. Sometimes they affronted her to her face. Oftener they talked at her backward and forward with a subtle skill and a perseverance which, "oh, that they had bestowed on the arts!" as poor Aguecheek says.

Now Margaret was brave, and a coward; brave to battle difficulties and ill fortune, brave to shed her own blood for those she loved. Fortitude she had. But she had no true fighting courage. She was a powerful young woman, rather tall, full, and symmetrical, yet had one of those slips of girls slapped her face, the poor fool's hands would have dropped powerless, or gone to her own eyes instead of her adversary's. Nor was she even a match for so many tongues, and besides, what could she say? She knew nothing of these girls except that somehow they had found out her sorrows, and hated her; only, she thought to herself, they must be very happy, or they would not be so hard on her. So she took their taunts in silence, and all her struggle was not to let them see their power to make her writhe within. Here came in her fortitude, and she received their blows with well-feigned, icy hauteur. They slapped a statue.

But one day, when her spirits were weak, as happens at times to females in her condition, a dozen assailants followed suit so admirably that her whole sex seemed to the dispirited one to be against her, and she lost heart, and the tears began to run silently at each fresh stab. On this their triumph knew no bounds, and they followed her halfway home casting barbed speeches.

After that exposure of weakness the statue could be assumed no more. So then she would stand timidly aloof out of tongue-shot till her young tyrants' pitchers were all filled, and they gone, and then creep up with hers. And one day she waited so long that the fount had ceased to flow. So the next day she was obliged to face the phalanx, or her house go dry. She drew near slowly, but with the less tremor that she saw a man at the well talking to them. He would distract their attention, and besides, they would keep their foul tongues quiet if only to blind the male to their real character. This conjecture, though shrewd, was erroneous. They could not all flirt with that one man, so the outsiders indemnified themselves by talking at her the very moment she came up.

"Any news from foreign parts, Jacqueline?"

"None for me, Martha. My lad goes no farther from me than the town wall."

"I can't say as much," says a third.

"But if he goes t'Italy I have got another ready to take the fool's place."

"He'll not go thither, lass. They go not so far till they are sick of us that bide in Holland."

Surprise, and indignation, and the presence of a man, gave Margaret a moment's fighting courage. "Oh, flout me not, and show your ill nature before the very soldier. In heaven's name, what ill did I ever to ye, what harsh word cast back, for all you have flung on me, a desolate stranger in your cruel town, that ye flout me for my bereavement and my poor lad's most unwilling banishment? Hearts of flesh would surely pity us both, for that ye cast in my teeth these many days, ye brows of brass, ye bosoms of stone."

They stared at this novelty, resistance, and ere they could recover and make mincemeat of her, she put her pitcher quietly down and threw her coarse apron over her head, and stood there grieving, her short-lived spirit oozing fast. "Hallo!" cried the soldier. "Why, what is your ill?" She made no reply. But a little girl, who had long secretly hated the big ones, squeaked out: "They did flout her, they are aye flouting her. She may not come nigh the fountain for fear o' them, and 'tis a black shame."

"Who spoke to her? Not I, for one."

"Nor I. I would not bemean myself so far."

The man laughed heartily at this display of dignity. "Come, wife," said he, "never lower thy flag to such light skirmishers as these. Hast a tongue i' thy head as well as they."

"Alack, good soldier, I was not bred to bandy foul terms."

"Well, but hast a better arm than these. Why not take 'em by twos across thy knee and skelp 'em till they cry Meculpee?"

"Nay, I would not hurt their bodies, for all their cruel hearts."

"Then ye must e'en laugh at them, wife. What! a woman grown, and not see why mesdames give tongue? You are a buxom wife, they are a bundle of thread papers. You are fair and fresh, they have all the Dutch rim under their bright eyes that comes of dwelling in eternal swamps. There lies your crime. Come, gie me thy pitcher, and if they flout me, shalt see me scrub 'em all wi' my beard till they squeak holy mother." The pitcher was soon filled, and the soldier put it in Margaret's hand. She murmured, "Thank you kindly, brave soldier."

He patted her on the shoulder. "Come, courage, brave wife. The Divell is dead!" She let the heavy pitcher fall on his foot directly. He cursed horribly, and hopped in a circle, saying, "No, the Thief's alive and has broken my great toe."

The apron came down, and there was a lovely face all flushed with emotion, and two beaming eyes in front of him, and two hands held out clasped.

"Nay, nay, 'tis naught," said he, good-humoredly, mistaking.

"Denys?"

"Well?—But—Hallo! How know you my name is—"

"Denys of Burgundy!"

"Why, odsbodikins! I know you not, and you know me."

"By Gerard's letter. Crossbow! Beard! Handsome! The Divell is dead!"

"Sword of Goliah, this must be she! Red hair, violet eyes, lovely face. But I took ye for a married wife, seeing ye—"

"Tell me my name," said she quickly.

"Margaret Brandt."

"Gerard? Where is he? Is he in life? Is he well? Is he come? Why is he not here? Where have ye left him? Oh, tell me! Prithee, prithee, prithee, tell me!"

"Ay, ay, but not here. Oh, ye are all curiosity now, mesdames, eh? Lass, I have been three months afoot traveling all Holland to find ye, and here you are. Oh, be joyful!" And he flung his cap in the air and, seizing both her hands, kissed them ardently. "Ah, my pretty she-comrade, I have found thee at last. I knew I should. Shalt be flouted no more. I'll twist your necks at the first word, ye little trollops. And I have got fifteen gold angels left for thee, and our Gerard will soon be here. Shalt wet thy purple eyes no more."

But the fair eyes were wet even now, looking kindly and gratefully at the friend that had dropped among her foes as if from Heaven—Gerard's comrade. "Prithee come home with me, good kind Denys. I cannot speak of him before these." They went off together, followed by a chorus. "She has gotten a man. She has gotten a man at last. Hoo, hoo, hoo!"

Margaret quickened her steps, but Denys took down his crossbow and pretended to shoot them all dead. They fled quadrivious, shrieking.

CHAPTER XXVIII

It was a sweet yet bitter day for Margaret, since it brought her a true friend, and ill news; for now first she learned that Gerard was all alone in that strange land. She could not think with Denys that he would come home; indeed he would have arrived before this.

Denys was a balm. He called her his she-comrade, and was always cheering her up with his formula and hilarities, and she petted him and made much of him, and feebly hectored it over him as well as over Martin, and would not let him eat a single meal out of her house. And as it never' rains but it pours, other persons now solicited Margaret's friendship. She had written to Margaret Van Eyck a humble letter telling her she knew she was no longer the favorite she had been, and would keep her distance, but could not forget her benefactress's past kindness. She then told her briefly how many ways she had battled for a living, and in conclusion begged earnestly that her residence might not be betrayed, "least of all to his people. I do hate them, they drove him from me. And, even when he was gone, their hearts turned not to me as they would an if they had repented their cruelty to him."

The Van Eyck was perplexed. At last she made a confidante of Reicht. The secret ran through Reicht, as through a cylinder, to Catherine.

"Ay, and is she turned that bitter against us?" said that good woman. "She stole our son from us, and now she hates us for not running into her arms. Natheless it is a blessing she is alive and no farther away than Rotterdam."

The English Princess, now Countess Charolois, made a stately progress through the northern states of the Duchy, accompanied by her stepdaughter, the young heiress of Burgundy, Marie de Bourgogne. Then the old Duke, the most magnificent prince in Europe, put out his splendor. Troops of dazzling knights, and bevies of fair ladies gorgeously attired, attended the two Princesses; and minstrels, jongleurs, or storytellers, bards, musicians, actors, tumblers, followed in the train; and there were fencing, dancing, and joy in every town they shone on. Giles, a court favorite, sent a timely message to Tergou, inviting all his people to meet the pageant at Rotterdam.

They agreed to take a holiday for once in a way, and setting their married daughter to keep the shop, came to Rotterdam. But to two of them not the great folk, but little Giles, was the main attraction. They had been in Rotterdam some days when Denys met Catherine accidentally in the street, and after a warm greeting on both sides, bade her rejoice, for he had found the she-comrade, and crowed. But Catherine cooled him by showing him how much earlier he would have found her by staying quietly at Tergou than by vagabondizing it all over Holland.

"And being found, what the better are we? Her heart is set dead against us now."

"Oh, let that flea stick. Come you with me to her house."

No, she would not go where she was sure of an ill welcome. "Them that come unbidden sit unseated." No, let Denys be mediator and bring the parties to a good understanding. He undertook the office at once, and with great pomp and confidence. He trotted off to Margaret and said:

"She-comrade, I met this day a friend of thine."

"Thou didst look into the Rotter then, and see thyself."

"Nay, 'twas a female, and one that seeks thy regard. 'Twas Catherine, Gerard's mother."

"Oh, was it?" said Margaret. "Then you may tell her she comes too late. There was a time I longed and longed for her, but she held aloof in my hour of most need, so now we will be as we ha' been."

Denys tried to shake this resolution. He coaxed her, but she was bitter and sullen, and not to be coaxed. Then he scolded her well, at that she went into hysterics. He was frightened at this result of his eloquence and, being off his guard, allowed himself to be entrapped into a solemn promise never to recur to the subject. He went back to Catherine crestfallen and told her. She fired up and told the family how his overtures had been received. Then they fired up, it became a feud and burned fiercer every day. Little Kate alone made some excuses for Margaret.

The very next day another visitor came to Margaret, and found the military enslaved and degraded, Martin up to his elbows in soapsuds, and Denys ironing very clumsily, and Margaret plaiting ruffs, but with a mistress's eye on her raw levies. To these there entered an old man, venerable at first sight, but on nearer view keen and wizened.

"Ah!" cried Margaret. Then swiftly turned her back on him and hid her face with invincible repugnance. "Oh, that man, that man!"

"Nay, fear me not," said Ghysbrecht. "I come on a friend's errand. I bring ye a letter from foreign parts."

"Mock me not, old man." And she turned slowly round.

"Nay, see." And he held out an enormous letter. Margaret darted on it, and held it with trembling hands and glistening eyes. It was Gerard's handwriting.

"Oh, thank you, sir, bless you for this. I forgive you all the ill you ever wrought me." And she pressed the letter to her bosom with one hand and glided swiftly from the room with it.

As she did not come back, Ghysbrecht went away, but not without a scowl at Martin. Margaret was hours alone with her letter. When she came down again, she was a changed woman. Her eyes were wet, but calm, and all her bitterness and excitement charmed away.

"Denys," said she, softly, "I have got my orders. I am to read my lover's letter to his folk."

"Ye will never do that?"

"Ay, will I."

"I see there is something in the letter has softened ye toward them."

"Not a jot, Denys, not a jot. But an I hated them like poison I would not disobey my love. Denys, 'tis so sweet to obey, and sweetest of all to obey one who is far, far away and cannot enforce my duty, but must trust my love for my obedience. Ah, Gerard, my darling, at hand I might have slighted thy commands, misliking thy folk as I have cause to do; but now, didst bid me go into the raging sea and read thy sweet letter to the sharks, there I'd go. Therefore, Denys, tell his mother I have got a letter, and if she and hers would hear it, I am their servant. Let them say their hour, and I'll seat them as best I can and welcome them as best I may."

Denys went off to Catherine with his good news. He found the family at dinner, and told them there was a long letter from Gerard. Then in the midst of the joy this caused, he said:

"And her heart is softened, and she will read it to you herself. You are to choose your own time."

"What, does she think there are none can read but her?" asked Catherine. "Let her send the letter and we will read it."

"Nay, but, Mother," objected Little Kate, "mayhap she cannot bear to part it from her hand. She loves him dearly."

"What, thinks she we shall steal it?"

Cornelis suggested that she would fain wedge herself into the family by means of this letter. Denys cast a look of scorn on the speaker.

"There spoke a bad heart," said he. "*La camarade* hates you all like poison. Oh, mistake me not, dame; I defend her not, but so 'tis. Yet maugre her spleen, at a word from Gerard she proffers to read you his letter with her own pretty mouth, and hath a voice like honey—sure 'tis a fair proffer."

" 'Tis so, mine honest soldier," said the father of the family, "and merits a civil reply, therefore hold your whisht, ye that be women, and I shall answer her. Tell her I, his father, setting aside all past grudges, do for this grace thank her and, would she have double thanks, let her send my son's letter by thy faithful hand, the which will I read to his flesh and blood, and will then to her so surely and faithfully return, as I am Eli a Dierich a William a Luke, free burgher of Tergou, like my forebears, and, like them, a man of my word."

"Ay, and a man who is better than his word," cried Catherine, "the only one I ever did forgather."

"Hold thy peace, wife."

"Art a man of sense, Eli, a dirk, a *chose*, a *chose*,"[1] shouted Denys. "The she-comrade will be right glad to obey Gerard and yet not face you all, whom she hates as wormwood, saving your presence. Bless ye, the world hath changed, she is all submission today. 'Obedience is honey,' quoth she, and in sooth 'tis a sweetmeat she cannot but savor, eating so little on't. For what with her fair face and her mellow tongue; and what wi' flying in fits and terrifying us that be soldiers to death, an we thwart her; and what wi' chiding us one while, and petting us like lambs t'other, she hath made two of the crawlingest slaves ever you saw out of two honest swashbucklers. I be the ironing ruffian, t'other washes."

"What next?"

"What next? Why, whenever the brat is in the world I shall rock cradle, and t'other knave will wash tucker and bib. So, then, I'll go fetch the letter on the instant. Ye will let me bide and hear it read, will ye not?"

"Else our hearts were black as coal," said Catherine.

So Denys went for the letter. He came back crestfallen. "She will not let it out of her hand, neither to me nor you nor any he or she that lives."

"I knew she would not," said Cornelis.

"Whisht, whisht," said Eli, "and let Denys tell his story."

"'Nay,' said I, 'but be ruled by me.' 'Not I,' quoth she. 'Well, but,' quoth I, 'that same honey obedience ye spake of.' 'You are a fool,' says she. 'Obedience to Gerard is sweet, but obedience to any other body, who ever said that was sweet?'

"At last she seemed to soften a bit, and did give me a written paper for you, mademoiselle. Here 'tis."

"For me?" said Little Kate, coloring.

"Give that here!" said Eli, and he scanned the writing, and said almost in a whisper, "These be words from the letter. Hearken!

"'And, sweetheart, an if these lines should travel safe to thee, make thou trial of my people's hearts withal. Maybe they are somewhat turned toward me, being far away. If 'tis so, they will show it to thee, since now to me they may not. Read, then, this letter! But I do strictly forbid thee to let it from thy hand. And if they still hold aloof from thee, why then say naught, but let them think me dead. Obey me in this; for if thou dost disrespect my judgment and my will in this, thou lovest me not.'"

There was a silence, and Gerard's words copied by Margaret were handed round and inspected.

"Well," said Catherine, "that is another matter. But methinks 'tis for her to come to us, not we to her."

"Alas, Mother! What odds does that make?"

"Much," said Eli. "Tell her we are overmany to come to her, and bid her hither, the sooner the better."

[1] Anglice, a thing-em-bob. Author's note.

When Denys was gone, Eli owned it was a bitter pill to him. "When that lass shall cross my threshold, all the mischief and misery she hath made here will seem to come in a-doors in one heap. But what could I do, wife? We *must* hear the news of Gerard. I saw that in thine eyes, and felt it in my own heart. And she is backed by our undutiful but still beloved son, and so is she stronger than we, and brings our noses down to the grindstone, the sly, cruel jade! But never heed. We will hear the letter—and then let her go unblessed, as she came unwelcome."

"Make your mind easy," said Catherine. "She will not come at all." And a tone of regret was visible.

Shortly after, Richart, who had been hourly expected, arrived from Amsterdam, grave and dignified in his burgher's robe and gold chain, ruff, and furred cap, and was received not with affection only, but respect; for he had risen a step higher than his parents, and such steps were marked in medieval society almost as visibly as those in their staircases.

Admitted in due course to the family council, he showed plainly, though not discourteously, that his pride was deeply wounded by their having deigned to treat with Margaret Brandt. "I see the temptation," said he. "But which of us hath not at times to wish one way and do another?"

This threw a considerable chill over the old people. So Little Kate put in a word. "Vex not thyself, dear Richart. Mother says she will not come."

"All the better, sweetheart. I fear me if she do, I shall hie me back to Amsterdam."

Here Denys popped his head in at the door, and said, "She will be here at three on the great dial."

They all looked at one another in silence.

CHAPTER XXIX

"NAY, Richart," said Catherine at last, "for heaven's sake let not this one sorry wench set us all by the ears. Hath she not made ill blood enough already?"

"In very deed she hath. Fear me not, good Mother. Let her come and read the letter of the poor boy she hath by devilish arts bewitched, and then let her go. Give me your words to show her no countenance beyond decent and constrained civility—less we may not, being in our own house—and I will say no more." On this understanding they awaited the foe. She, for her part, prepared for the interview in a spirit little less hostile.

When Denys brought word they would not come to her, but would receive her, her lip curled, and she bade him observe how in them every feeling, however small, was larger than their love for Gerard.

"Well," said she, "I have not that excuse, so why mimic the pretty burgher's pride, the pride of all unlettered folk? I will go to them for Gerard's sake. Oh, how I loathe them!"

Thus poor good-natured Denys was bringing into one house the materials of an explosion.

Margaret made her toilet in the same spirit that a knight of her day dressed for battle—he to parry blows, and she to parry glances—glances of contempt at her poverty, or of irony at her extravagance. Her kirtle was of English cloth, dark blue, and her farthingale and hose of the same material, but a glossy roan, or claret-color. Not an inch of pretentious fur about her, but plain snowy linen wristbands, and curiously plaited linen from the bosom of the kirtle up to the commencement of the throat; it did not encircle her throat, but framed it, being square, not round. Her front hair still peeped in two waves, much after the fashion which Mary Queen of Scots revived a century later; but instead of the silver net, which would have ill become her present condition, the rest of her head was covered with a very small tight-fitting hood of dark-blue cloth hemmed with silver. Her shoes were red, but the roan petticoat and hose prepared the spectator's mind for the shock, and they set off the arched instep and shapely foot. Beauty knew its business then as now.

And with all this she kept her enemies waiting, though it was three by the dial. Meantime, they were all assembled, and waiting for her with a strange mixture of feelings. Mortification, curiosity, panting affection, aversion to her who came to gratify those feelings, yet another curiosity to see what she was like, and what there was in her to bewitch Gerard, and make so much mischief.

At last Denys came alone, and whispered, "The she-comrade is without."

"Fetch her in," said Eli. "Now whist, all of ye. None speak to her but I."

They all turned their eyes to the door in dead silence. A little muttering was heard outside, Denys's rough organ, and a woman's soft and mellow voice. Presently that stopped, and then the door opened slowly, and Margaret Brandt, dressed as I have described, and somewhat pale but calm and lovely, stood on the threshold looking straight before her. They all rose but Kate, and remained mute and staring.

"Be seated, mistress," said Eli, gravely, and motioned to a seat that had been set apart for her.

She inclined her head, and crossed the apartment, and in so doing her condition was very visible, not only in her shape, but in her languor.

She took her letter out of her bosom, and kissed it as if she had been alone, then disposed herself to read it with the air of one who knew she was there for that single purpose. She began to read her Gerard, their Gerard, to their eager ears in a mellow but clear voice, so soft, so earnest, so thrilling, her very soul seemed to cling about each precious sound. It was a voice as of a woman's bosom set speaking by Heaven itself.

"I do nothing doubt, my Margaret, that long ere this shall meet thy beloved eyes, Denys, my most dear friend, will have sought thee out, and told thee the manner of our unlooked-for and most tearful parting. Therefore I will e'en begin at that most doleful day. What befell him after, poor faithful soul, fain, fain would I hear, but may not. But I pray for him day and night next after thee, dearest. Friend more stanch and loving had not David in Jonathan than I in him. Be good to him for poor Gerard's sake."

At these words, which came quite unexpectedly to him, Denys leaned his head on Margaret's high chair, and groaned aloud. She turned quickly as she sat, and found his hand and pressed it.

"I went forward all dizzied, like one in an ill dream; and presently a gentleman came up with his servants, all on horseback, and had like to have rid o'er me. And he drew rein at the brow of the hill, and sent his armed men back to rob me. They robbed me civilly enough, and took my purse and the last copper, and rid gaily away. I wandered stupid on, a friendless pauper."

There was a general sigh, followed by an oath from Denys.

"Presently a strange dimness came o'er me, I lay down to sleep on the snow. 'Twas ill done, and with store of wolves hard by. Had I loved thee as thou dost deserve, I had shown more manhood. But oh, sweet love, the drowsiness that did crawl o'er me desolate, and benumb me, was more than nature. And so I slept, and but that God was better to us than I to thee or to myself, from that sleep I ne'er had waked, so all do say. I had slept an hour or two, as I supposed, but no more, when a hand did shake me rudely. I awoke to my troubles. And there stood a servant girl in her holiday suit. 'Are ye mad,' quoth she, in seeming choler, 'to sleep in snow, and under wolves' nosen? Art weary o' life, and not long weaned? Come now,' said she, more kindly, 'get up like a good lad.' So I did rise up.

"'Are ye rich, or are ye poor?' But I stared at her as one amazed. 'Why, 'tis easy of reply,' quoth she. 'Are ye rich, or are ye poor?' Then I gave a great, loud cry, that she did start back. 'Am I rich, or am I poor? Had ye asked me an hour agone, I had said I am rich. But now I am so poor as sure earth beareth on her bosom none poorer. An hour agone I was rich in a friend, rich in money, rich in hope and spirits of youth; but now the Bastard of Burgundy hath taken my friend and another gentleman my purse, and I can neither go forward to Rome nor back to her I left in Holland. I am poorest of the poor.' 'Alack!' said the wench. 'Natheless, an ye had been rich ye might ha' lain down again in the snow for any use I had for ye; and then I trow ye had soon fared out o' this world as bare as ye came into 't. But, being poor, you are our man, so come wi' me.' Then I went because she bade me, and because I recked not now whither I went. And she took me to a fine house hard by, and into a noble dining-hall hung with black, and there was set a table with many dishes, and but one plate and one chair. 'Fall to!' said she, in a whisper. 'What, alone?' said I. 'Alone? And which of us, think ye, would eat out of the same dish with ye? Are we robbers o' the dead?' Then she speered where I was born. 'At Tergou,' said I. Says she, 'And when a gentleman dies in that country, serve they not the dead man's dinner up as usual till he be in the ground, and set some poor man down to it?' I told her nay. She blushed for us then. 'Here they were better Christians.' So I behooved to sit down. But small was my heart for meat. Then this kind lass sat by me and poured me out wine. She made me eat of every dish. And she hearing me sigh, and seeing me like to choke at the food, took pity and bade me be of good cheer. I should sup and lie there that night. And she went to the hind, and he gave me a right good bed.

"They were all most kind to me next day, and the girl proffered me money from her small wage to help me toward Rhine."

"Oh, then he is coming home! He is coming home!" shouted Denys, interrupting the reader. She shook her head gently at him, by way of reproof.

"I beg pardon, all the company," said he stiffly.

" 'Twas a sore temptation; but, being a servant, my stomach rose against it. 'Nay, nay,' said I. She told me I was wrong. 'Twas pride out o' place; poor folk should help one another, or who on earth would? I said if I could do aught in return, 'twere well, but for a free gift, nay. I was overmuch beholden already. Should I write a letter for her? 'Nay, he is in the house at present,' said she. 'Should I draw her picture, and so earn my money?' 'What, can ye?' said she. I told her I could try, and her habit would well become a picture. So she was agog to be limned, and give it her lad. And I set her to stand in a good light, and soon made sketches two, whereof I send thee one, colored at odd hours. The other I did most hastily, and with little conscience daub, for which may Heaven forgive me, but time was short. They, poor things, knew no better, and were most proud and joyous; and, both kissing me after their country fashion—'twas the hind that was her sweetheart—they did bid me God speed, and I toward Rhine."

Margaret paused here, and gave Denys the colored drawing to hand round. It was eagerly examined by the females on account of the costume, which differed in some respects from that of a Dutch domestic. Margaret continued:

"But, oh, how I missed my Denys at every step! Often I sat down on the road and groaned. And in the afternoon it chanced that I did so set me down where two roads met, and with heavy head in hand, and heavy heart, did think of thee, my poor sweetheart, and of my lost friend, and of the little house at Tergou, where they all loved me once, though now it is turned to hate.

"And I did sigh loud, and often. And me sighing so, one came caroling like a bird a-down t'other road. 'Ay, chirp and chirp,' cried I, bitterly. 'Thou hast not lost sweetheart, and friend, thy father's hearth, thy mother's smile, and every penny in the world.' And at last he did so carol, and carol, I jumped up in ire to get away from his most jarring mirth. But ere I fled from it, I looked down the path to see what could make a man so light-hearted in this weary world, and lo! the songster was a humpbacked cripple, with a bloody bandage o'er his eye and both legs gone at the knee.

"And whenever he saw me, he left caroling and presently hobbled up and chanted, 'Charity, for love of Heaven, sweet master, charity,' with a whine as piteous as wind at keyhole. 'Alack, poor soul,' said I, 'charity is in my heart but not my purse. I am poor as thou.' Then he believed me none, and to melt me undid his sleeve and showed me a sore wound on his arm, and said he: 'Poor cripple though I be, I am like to lose this eye to boot, look else.' I saw and groaned for him, and to excuse myself let him wot how I have been robbed of my last copper. Thereat he left whining all in a moment and said, in a big manly voice: 'Then I'll e'en take a rest. Here, youngster, pull thou this strap. Nay, fear not!' I pulled, and down came a stout pair of legs out of his back, and half his hump had melted away, and the wound in his eye no deeper than the bandage."

"Oh!" ejaculated Margaret's hearers, in a body.

"Whereat, seeing me astounded, he laughed in my face, and told me I was not worth gulling, and offered me his protection. My face was prophetic, he said. 'Of what?' said I. 'Marry,' said he, 'that its owner will starve in this thievish land.' Travel teaches e'en the young wisdom. Time was I had turned and fled this impostor as a pestilence, but now I listened patiently to pick up crumbs of counsel. And well I did, for nature and his adventurous life had crammed the poor knave with shrewdness and knowledge of the homelier sort—a child was I beside him. When he had turned me inside out, said he, 'Didst well to leave France and make for Germany. But think not of Holland again. Nay, on to Augsburg and Nürnberg the Paradise of craftsmen; then to Venice, an thou wilt. But thou wilt never bide in Italy nor any other land, having once tasted the great German cities. Why, there is but one honest country in Europe, and that is Germany; and since thou art honest, and since I am a vagabond, Germany was made for us twain.'

"I bade him make that good. How might one country fit true men and knaves? 'Why, thou novice,' said he, 'because in an honest land are fewer knaves to bite the honest man, and many honest men for the knave to bite. I was in luck, being honest, to have fallen in with a friendly sharp. Be my pal,' said he. 'I go to Nürnberg, we will reach it with full pouches. I'll learn ye the *cul de bois*, and the *cul de jatte*, and how to maund, and chant, and patter, and to raise swellings, and paint sores and ulcers on thy body would take in the Divell.' I told him, shivering, I'd liever die than shame myself and my folk so."

Eli. "Good lad! good lad!"

"Why, what shame was it for such as I to turn beggar? Beggary was an ancient and most honorable mystery. What did holy monks, and bishops, and kings, when they would win Heaven's smile? Why, wash the feet of beggars, those favorites of the saints. 'The saints were no fools,' he told me. Then he did put out his foot. 'Look at that. That was washed by the greatest king alive, Louis of France, the last Holy Thursday that was. And the next day, Friday, clapped in the stocks by the warden of a petty hamlet.' So I told him my foot should walk between such high honor and such low disgrace, on the safe path of honesty, please God. Well, then, since I had not spirit to beg, he would indulge my perversity. I should work under him, he be the head, I the fingers. And with that he set himself up like a judge, on a heap of dust by the road's side, and questioned me strictly what I could do.

"I began to say I was strong and willing. 'Bah!' said he, 'so is an ox. Say, what canst do that Sir Ox cannot?' I could write, I had won a prize for it. 'Canst write as fast as the printers?' quo' he, jeering. 'What else?' I could paint. That was better. I was like to tear my hair to hear him say so, and me going to Rome to write. I could twang the psaltery a bit. That was well. Could I tell stories? Ay, by the score. 'Then,' said he, 'I hire you from this moment.' 'What to do?' said I. 'Nought crooked, Sir Candor,' says he. 'I will feed thee all the way and find thee work; and take half thine earnings, no more.' 'Agreed,' said I, and gave my hand on it.

" 'Now, servant,' said he, 'we will dine. But ye need not stand behind my chair, for two reasons: first I ha' got no chair, and next, good fellowship likes me better than state.' And out of his wallet he brought flesh, fowl, and pastry, a good dozen of spices lapped in flax paper, and wine fit for a king. Ne'er feasted I better than out of this beggar's wallet, now my master. When we had well eaten, I was for going on. 'But,' said he, 'servants should not drive their masters too hard, especially after feeding, for then the body is for repose, and the mind turns to contemplation,' and he lay on his back gazing calmly at the sky, and presently wondered whether there were any beggars up there. He forgot yesterday's grudge, and discoursed me freely of beggars, and gave me—who eftsoons thought a beggar was a beggar, and there an end—the names and qualities of full thirty sorts of masterful and crafty mendicants in France and Germany and England—his three provinces, for so the poor, proud knave yclept those kingdoms three, wherein his throne it was the stocks, I ween.

"We came to Strasburgh. And I looked down Rhine with longing heart. The stream how swift! It seemed running to clip Sevenbergen to its soft bosom. With but a piece of timber and an oar, I might drift at my ease to thee, sleeping yet gliding still. 'Twas a sore temptation. But the fear of an ill welcome from my folk, and of the neighbors' sneers, and the hope of coming back to thee victorious—not, as now I must, defeated and shamed, and thee with me—it did withhold me. And so, with many sighs, and often turning of the head to look on beloved Rhine, I turned sorrowful face and heavy heart toward Augsburg.

"The Germans are fonder of armorials than the French. So I found work every day. And whiles I wrought, my master would leave me, and doff his raiment and don his rags, and other infirmities, and cozen the world, which he did clepe it 'plucking of the goose.' This done, would meet me and demand half my earnings. Early in Germany we had a quarrel. I had seen him buy a skull of a jailer's wife, and mighty zealous a-polishing it. Thought I, 'How can he carry yon memento, and not repent, seeing where ends his way?' Presently I did catch him selling it to a woman for the head of Saint Barnabas, with a tale had cozened an Ebrew. So I snatched it out of their hands, and trundled it into the ditch. 'How, thou impious knave,' said I, 'wouldst sell for a saint the skull of some dead thief, thy brother?' He slunk away. But shallow she did crawl after the skull, and with apron reverently dust it for Barnabas—and it Barabbas—and so home with it. Then I to him, 'Take now thy psaltery, and part we here, for art a walking prison, a walking Hell.' But lo! my master fell on his knees and begged me for pity's sake not turn him off. What would become of him? He should be a true man by then we reached Nürnberg. 'Twas a long way to Nürnberg. Seeing him so humble, I said: 'Well, doff rags, and make thyself decent. 'Twill help me forget what thou art.' And he did so; and we sat down to our nonemete.

"I got armories to paint, so my master took the yellow jaundice and went begging through the town, and with his oily tongue and saffron-water face did fill his hat. Now in all the towns are certain licensed beggars, and one of these was an old favorite with the townsfolk, had his station at St. Martin's porch, the greatest church—a blind man, they called him Blind Hans. He saw my master drawing coppers on the other side of the street, and knew him by his tricks for an impostor, so sent and warned the constables, and I met my master in the constables' hands and going to his trial in the town hall. I followed and many more; and he was none abashed, neither by the pomp of justice nor memory of his misdeeds, but demanded his accuser like a trumpet. And Blind Hans's boy came forward, but was sifted narrowly by my master, and stammered, and faltered, and owned he had seen nothing, but only carried Blind Hans's tale to the chief constable. 'This is but hearsay,' said my master. 'Lo ye now, here standeth Misfortune backbit by Envy. But stand thou forth, blind Envy, and vent thine own lie.' And Blind Hans behooved to stand forth, sore against his will. Him did my master so press with questions, and so pinch and torture, asking him again and again how, being blind, he could see all that befell, and some that befell not, across a way; and why, an he could not see, he came there holding up his perjured hand, and maligning the misfortune, that at last he groaned aloud and would utter no word more. And an alderman said, 'In sooth, Hans, ye are to blame, hast cast more dirt of suspicion on thyself than on him.'

"But the burgomaster, a wondrous fat man, and methinks of his fat some had gotten into his head, checked him and said, 'Nay, Hans we know this many years and, be he blind or not, he hath passed for blind so long 'tis all one. Back to thy porch, good Hans, and let the strange varlet leave the town incontinent on pain of whipping.' Then my master winked to me, but there rose a civic officer in his gown of state and golden chain, a dignity with us lightly prized, and even shunned of some, but in Germany and France much courted, save by condemned malefactors; to wit, the hangman. And says he, 'An't please you, first let us see why he weareth his hair so thick and low.' And his man went and lifted Cul de Jatte's hair, and lo the upper gristle of both ears was gone. 'How is this, knave?' quoth the burgomaster. My master said, carelessly, he minded not precisely, his had been a life of misfortunes and losses. 'When a poor soul has lost use of his leg, noble sirs, these more trivial woes rest lightly in his memory.' But the hangman showed them the two cuts were made at one time, and by measurement. ''Tis no bungling soldier's work, my masters,' said he, ' 'tis ourn.' Then the burgomaster gave judgment:

" 'The present charge is not proven against thee, but an thou beest not guilty now, thou hast been at other times, witness thine ears. Wherefore I send thee to prison for one month, and to give a florin toward the new hall of the guilds now a-building, and to be whipt out of the town, and pay the hangman's fee for the same.' And all the aldermen approved, and my master was haled to prison with one look of anguish.

"I tried to get speech of him, but the jailer denied me. But lingering near the jail I heard a whistle, and there was Cul de Jatte at a narrow window twenty feet from earth. I went under, and he asked me what made I there. I told him I was loath to go forward and not bid him farewell. He seemed quite amazed, but soon his suspicious soul got the better. That was not all mine errand. I told him not all—the psaltery: 'Well, what of that?' 'Twas not mine, but his, I would pay him the price of it. 'Then throw me a rix dollar,' said he. I counted out my coins, and they came to a rix dollar and two batzen. I threw him up his money in three throws, and when he had got it all he said, softly, 'Bon Bec.' 'Master,' said I. Then the poor rogue was greatly moved. 'I thought ye had been mocking me,' said he. 'Oh, Bon Bec, Bon Bec, if I had found the world like thee at starting I had put my wit to better use, and I had not lain here.' Then he whimpered out, 'I gave not quite a rix dollar for the jingler,' and threw me back that he had gone to cheat me of, honest for once, and overlate. And so, with many sighs, bade me Godspeed. Thus did my master, after often baffling men's justice, fall by their injustice; for his lost ears proved not his guilt only, but of that guilt the bitter punishment. Natheless he was a parlous rogue. Yet he holp to make a man of me. Thanks to his good wit I went forward richer far with my psaltery and brush than with yon as good as stolen purse; for that must have run dry in time, like a big trough, but these a little fountain."

"One day I walked alone, and, sooth to say, lighthearted, for mine honest Denys sweetened the air on the way. The next day, passing a grand house, out came on prancing steeds a gentleman in brave attire and two servants; they overtook me. The gentleman bade me halt. I laughed in my sleeve, for a few batzen were all my store. He bade me doff my doublet and jerkin. Then I chuckled no more. 'Bethink you, my lord,' said I, ' 'tis winter. How may a poor fellow go bare and live?' So he told me I shot mine arrow wide of his thought, and off with his own gay jerkin, richly furred, and doublet to match, and held them forth to me. Then a servant let me know it was a penance. 'His lordship had had the ill luck to slay his cousin in their cups.'

"Down to my shoes he changed with me; and set me on his horse like a popinjay, and fared by my side in my worn weeds, with my psaltery on his back. And said he: 'Now, good youth, thou art Count Detstein, and I, late Count, thy Servant. Play thy part well, and help me save my bloodstained soul! Be haughty and choleric as any noble, and I will be as humble as I may.' I said I would do my best to play the noble. But what should I call him? He bade me call him naught but Servant. That would mortify him most, he wist. We rode on a long way in silence, for I was meditating this strange chance that from a beggar's servant had made me master to a Count, and also cudgeling my brains how best I might play the master without being run through the body all at one time like his cousin. For I mistrusted sore my spark's humility, your German nobles being, to my knowledge, proud as Lucifer and choleric as fire. As for the servants, they did slyly grin to one another to see their master so humbled—"

"*Ah! What is that?*"

A lump, as of lead, had just bounced against the door, and the latch was fumbled with unsuccessfully. Another bounce, and the door swung inward with Giles, arrayed in cloth of gold, sticking to it like a wasp. He landed on the floor and was embraced, but on learning what was going on, trumpeted that he would much liever hear of Gerard than gossip.

Sybrandt pointed to a diminutive chair. Giles showed his sense of this civility by tearing the said Sybrandt out of a very big one, and there ensconced himself, gorgeous and glowing. Sybrandt had to wedge himself into the one which was too small for the magnificent dwarf's soul, and Margaret resumed.

But as this part of the letter was occupied with notices of places, all which my reader probably knows and, if not, can find handled at large in a dozen well-known books, from Munster to Murray, I skip the topography, and hasten to that part where it occurred to him to throw his letter into a journal. The personal narrative that intervened may be thus condensed.

He spoke but little at first to his new companions, but listened to pick up their characters. Neither his noble Servant nor *his* servants could read or write, and as he often made entries in his tablets, he impressed them with some awe. One of his entries was *"Le peu que sont les hommes."* For he found the surly innkeepers licked the very ground before him now; nor did a soul suspect the hosier's son in the Count's feathers, nor the Count in the minstrel's weeds. This seems to have surprised him, for he enlarged on it with the naïveté and pomposity of youth. At one place, being humbly requested to present the inn with his armorial bearings, he consented loftily, but painted them himself, to mine host's wonder, who thought he lowered himself by handling brush. The true Count stood grinning by, and held the paint pot while the sham Count painted a shield with three red herrings rampant under a sort of Maltese cross made with two ell measures.

At first his plebeian servants were insolent. But this coming to the notice of his noble one, he forgot what he was doing penance for, and drew his sword to cut off their ears, heads included. But Gerard interposed and saved them, and rebuked the Count severely. And finally they all understood one another, and the superior mind obtained its natural influence. He played the barbarous noble of that day vilely. For his heart would not let him be either tyrannical or cold. Here were three human beings. He tried to make them all happier than he was, held them ravished with stories and songs, and set Herr Penitent & Company dancing with his whistle and psaltery. For his convenience he made them ride and tie, and thus pushed rapidly through the country, traveling generally fifteen leagues a day.

CHAPTER XXX

"JANUARY 3.—Yesterday between Nürnberg and Augsburg we parted company. I gave my lord, late Servant, back his brave clothes for mine, but his horse he made me keep, and five gold pieces, and said he was still my debtor. His penance it had been slight along of me, but profitable. But his best word was this: 'I see 'tis more noble to be loved than feared.' And then he did so praise me as I blush to put on paper; yet, poor fool, would fain thou couldst hear his words, but from some other pen than mine. And the servants did heartily grasp my hand, and wish me good luck. And riding apace, yet could I not reach Augsburg till the gates were closed. But it mattered little, for this Augsburg it is an enchanted city. For a small coin one took me a long way round to a famous postern called *Der Einlasse*. Here stood two guardians, like statues. To them I gave my name and business. They nodded me leave to knock, I knocked, and the iron gate opened with a great noise and hollow rattling of a chain. But no hand seen nor chain, and he who drew the hidden chain sits a butt's length from the gate; and I rode in, and the gate closed with a clang after me.

"I found myself in a great building with a bridge at my feet. This I rode over and presently came to a porter's lodge, where one asked me again my name and business, then rang a bell, and a great portcullis that barred the way began to rise, drawn by a wheel overhead, and no hand seen. Behind the portcullis was a thick oaken door studded with steel. It opened without hand, and I rode into a hall as dark as pitch. Trembling there a while, a door opened and showed me a smaller hall lighted. I rode into it: a tin goblet came down from the ceiling by a little chain: I put two batzen into it, and it went up again. Being gone, another thick door creaked and opened, and I rid through. It closed on me with a tremendous clang, and behold me in Augsburg city.

"The Burgomaster received me courteously and heard my story, then rebuked he the officers. 'Could ye not question him yourselves, or read in his face? This is to make our city stink in stranger's report.' Then he told me my curiosity was of a commendable sort: and seeing I was a craftsman and inquisitive, bade his clerk take me among the guilds. God bless the city where the very Burgomaster is cut of Solomon's cloth!

"*January 5.*—Dear Margaret, it is a noble city, and a kind mother to arts. Here they cut in wood and ivory, that 'tis like spiders' work, and paint on glass, and sing angelical harmonies. Writing of books is quite gone by; here be six printers. Yet was I offered a bountiful wage to write fairly a merchant's accounts, one Fugger, a grand and wealthy trader, and hath store of ships, yet his father was but a poor weaver. But here in commerce, her very garden, men swell like mushrooms. And he bought my horse of me, and abated me not a jot, which way of dealing is not known in Holland. But, oh, Margaret, the workmen of all the guilds are so kind and brotherly to one another, and to me. Here, methinks, I have found the true German mind, loyal, frank, and kindly, somewhat choleric withal, but naught revengeful.

"*January 10.*—This day started for Venice with a company of merchants, and among them him who had desired me for his scrivener; and, so we are now agreed, I to write at night the letters he shall dict, and other matters, he to feed and lodge me on the road. We be many and armed, and soldiers with us to boot, so fear not the thieves which men say lie on the borders of Italy. But an if I find the printing press at Venice, I trow I shall not go on to Rome, for man may not vie with iron.

"And, dearest, something tells me you and I shall end our days at Augsburg, whence going, I shall leave it all I can—my blessing.

"*January 18.*—In the midst of life we are in death. Oh! dear Margaret, I thought I had lost thee. Here I lie in pain and dole, and shall write thee that which read you it in a romance ye should cry 'most improbable!' And so still wondering that I am alive to write it, and thanking for it God and the saints, this is what befell thy Gerard. Yestreen I wearied of being shut up in litter, and of the mule's slow pace, and so went forward; and being, I know not why, strangely full of spirit and hope, as I have heard befall some men when on trouble's brink, seemed to tread on air, and soon outdistanced them all. Presently I came to two roads, and took the larger. I should have taken the smaller. After traveling a good half-hour I found my error and returned, and deeming my company had long passed by, pushed bravely on, but I could not overtake them; and small wonder, as you shall hear. Then I was anxious, and ran, but bare was the road of those I sought, and night came down and the wild beasts afoot, and I bemoaned my folly; also I was hungered. The moon rose clear and bright exceedingly, and presently, a little way off the road, I saw a tall windmill. 'Come,' said I, 'mayhap the miller will take ruth on me.'

"Near the mill was a haystack, and scattered about were store of little barrels, but lo, they were not flour barrels but tar barrels, one or two, and the rest of spirits, Brant vein and Schiedam. I knew them momently, having seen the like in Holland. I knocked at the mill door, but none answered. I lifted the latch and the door opened inward. I went in, and gladly, for the night was fine but cold, and a rime on the trees, which were a kind of lofty sycamores. There was a stove, but black. I lighted it with some of the hay and wood, for there was a great pile of wood outside, and, I know not how, I went to sleep. Not long had I slept, I trow, when hearing a noise I awoke, and there were a dozen men around me, with wild faces, and long black hair, and black sparkling eyes."

Catherine. "Oh, my poor boy! Those black-haired ones do still scare me to look on."

"I made my excuses in such Italian as I knew, and eking out by signs. They grinned. 'I had lost my company.' They grinned. I was a-hungered. Still they grinned, and spoke to one another in a tongue I knew not. At last one gave me a piece of bread and a tin mug of wine, as I thought, but it was spirits neat. I made a wry face, and asked for water. Then these wild men laughed a horrible laugh. I thought to fly but, looking toward the door, it was bolted with two enormous bolts of iron, and now first, as I ate my bread, I saw it was all guarded too, and ribbed with iron. My blood curdled within me, and yet I could not tell thee why; but hadst thou seen the faces, wild, stupid, and ruthless! I mumbled my bread, not to let them see I feared them, but oh, it cost me to swallow it and keep it in me. Then it whirled in my brain—was there no way to escape? Said I, 'They will not let me forth by the door. These be smugglers or robbers.' So I feigned drowsiness, and taking out two batzen said, 'Good men, for our Lady's grace let me lie on a bed and sleep, for I am faint with travel.' They nodded and grinned their horrible grin, and bade one light a lantern and lead me.

"He took me up a winding staircase, up, up, and I saw no windows, but the wooden walls were pierced like a barbican tower, and methinks for the same purpose, and through these slits I got glimpses of the sky, and thought, 'Shall I e'er see thee again?' He took me to the very top of the mill, and there was a room with a heap of straw in one corner, and many empty barrels, and by the wall a truckle bed. He pointed to it, and went downstairs heavily, taking the light, for in this room was a great window, and the moon came in bright. I looked out to see, and lo, it was so high that even the mill sails at their highest came not up to my window by some feet, but turned very slow and stately underneath, for wind there was scarce a breath. And the trees seemed silver filagree made by angel craftsmen. My hope of flight was gone.

"But now, those wild faces being out of sight, I smiled at my fears. What an if they were ill men, would it profit them to hurt me? Natheless, for caution against surprise, I would put the bed against the door. I went to move it, but could not. It was free at the head, but at the foot fast clamped with iron to the floor. So I flung my psaltery on the bed, but for myself made a layer of straw at the door, so as none could open on me unawares. And I laid my sword ready to my hand. And said my prayers for thee and me, and turned to sleep.

"Below they drank and made merry. And hearing this gave me confidence. Said I, 'Out of sight, out of mind. Another hour and the good Schiedam will make them forget that I am here.' And so I composed myself to sleep, and for some time could not for the boisterous mirth below. At last I dropped off. How long I slept I knew not; but I woke with a start. The noise had ceased below, and the sudden silence woke me. And scarce was I awake when sudden the truckle bed was gone with a loud clang, all but the feet, and the floor yawned, and I heard my psaltery fall and break to atoms deep, deep below the very floor of the mill. It had fallen into a well. And so had I done, lying where it lay."

Margaret shuddered and put her face in her hands. But speedily resumed.

"I lay stupefied at first. Then horror fell on me and I rose, but stood rooted there, shaking from head to foot. At last I found myself looking down into that fearsome gap, and my very hair did bristle as I peered. And then, I remember, I turned quite calm, and made up my mind to die sword in hand. For I saw no man must know this their bloody secret and live. And I said 'Poor Margaret!' And I took out of my bosom, where they lie ever, our marriage lines, and kissed them again and again. And I pinned them to my shirt again, that they might lie in one grave with me, if die I must. And I thought 'All our love and hopes to end thus!'"

Eli. "Whist all! Their marriage lines? Give her time! But no word. I can bear no chat. My poor lad!"

"Presently thinking, all in a whirl, of all that ever passed between us, and taking leave of all those pleasant hours, I called to mind how one day at

Sevenbergen thou taughtest me to make a rope of straw. Mindst thou? The moment memory brought that happy day back to me, I cried out very loud, 'Margaret gives me a chance for life even here.' I woke from my lethargy. I seized on the straw and twisted it eagerly, as thou didst teach me, but my fingers trembled and delayed the task. Whiles I wrought I heard a door open below. That was a terrible moment. Even as I twisted my rope I got to the window and looked down at the great arms of the mill coming slowly up, then passing, then turning less slowly down, as it seemed. And I thought 'They go not as when there is wind; yet, slow or fast, what man rid ever on such steed as these, and lived? Yet,' said I, 'better trust to them and God than to ill men.' And I prayed to Him whom even the wind obeyeth.

"Dear Margaret, I fastened my rope, and let myself gently down, and fixed my eye on that huge arm of the mill, which then was creeping up to me, and went to spring onto it. But my heart failed me at the pinch. And methought it was near enow. And it passed calm and awful by. I watched for another—they were three. And after a little while one crept up slower than the rest, methought. And I with my foot thrust myself in good time somewhat out from the wall and, crying aloud 'Margaret,' did grip with all my soul the woodwork of the sail, and that moment was swimming in the air."

Giles. "Well done! Well done!"

"Motion I felt little; but the stars seemed to go round the sky, and then the grass came up to me nearer and nearer, and when the hoary grass was quite close I was sent rolling along it as if hurled from a catapult, and got up breathless, and every point and tie about me broken. I rose, but fell down again in agony. I had but one leg I could stand on."

Catherine. "Eh, dear! His leg is broke, my boy's leg is broke!"

"And, e'en as I lay groaning, I heard a sound like thunder. It was the assassins running up the stairs. The crazy old mill shook under them. They must have found I had not fallen into their bloody trap, and were running to dispatch me. Margaret, I felt no fear, for I had now no hope. I could neither run nor hide, so wild the place, so bright the moon. I struggled up all agony and revenge, more like some wounded wild beast than your Gerard. Leaning on my sword hilt, I hobbled round; and swift as lightning, or vengeance, I heaped a great pile of their hay and wood at the mill door, then drove my dagger into a barrel of their smuggled spirits, and flung it on, then out with my tinder and lighted the pile. 'This will bring true men round my dead body,' said I. 'Aha,' I cried, 'think you I'll die alone, cowards, assassins, reckless fiends!' And at each word on went a barrel pierced.

"But, oh, Margaret! the fire fed by the spirits surprised me. It shot up and singed my very hair, it went roaring up the side of the mill, swift as falls the lightning; and I yelled and laughed in my torture and despair, and pierced more barrels, and the very tar barrels, and flung them on. The fire roared like a lion for its prey, and voices answered it inside from the top of the mill, and the feet came thundering down, and I stood as near that awful fire as I could with uplifted sword to slay and be slain. The bolt was drawn. A tar barrel caught fire. The door was opened.

"What followed? Not the men came out, but the fire rushed in at them like a living death, and the first I thought to fight with was blackened and crumpled on the floor like a leaf. One fearsome yell, and dumb forever. The feet ran up again, but fewer. I heard them hack with their swords a little way up, at the mill's wooden sides; but they had no time to hew their way out. The fire and reek were at their heels, and the smoke burst out at every loophole and oozed blue in the moonlight through each crevice. I hobbled back, racked with pain and fury. There were white faces up at my window. They saw me. They cursed me. I cursed them back and shook my naked sword. 'Come down the road I came!' I cried. 'But ye must come one by one, and, as ye come, ye die upon this steel.' Some cursed at that, but others wailed. For I had them all at deadly vantage. And doubtless with my smoke-grimed face and fiendish rage I looked a demon.

"And now there was a steady roar inside the mill. The flame was going up it as furnace up its chimney. The mill caught fire. Fire glimmered through it. Tongues of flame darted through each loophole and shot sparks and fiery flakes into the night. The fire gnawed through the mill in places, and shot forth showers of great flat sparks like flakes of fiery snow; and the sails caught fire one after another; and I became a man again and staggered away terror-stricken, leaning on my sword, from the sight of my revenge, and with great bodily pain crawled back to the road. And, dear Margaret, the rimy trees were now all like pyramids of golden filagree, and lace, cobweb-fine, in the red firelight. Oh, most beautiful!

"The next moment there was a loud crash. The mill fell in on its destroyer, and a million great sparks flew up, and the sails fell over the burning wreck, and at that a million more sparks flew up, and the ground was strewn with burning wood and men. I prayed God forgive me, and kneeling with my back to that fiery shambles, I saw lights on the road—a welcome sight. It was a company coming toward me, and scarce two furlongs off. I hobbled toward them. Ere I gone far I heard a swift step behind me. I turned. One had escaped—how escaped, who can divine? His sword shone in the moonlight. I feared him. Methought the ghost of all those dead sat on that glittering glaive. I put my other foot to the ground, maugre the anguish, and fled toward the torches, moaning with pain and shouting for aid.

"But what could I do? He gained on me. Behooved me turn and fight. Denys had taught me sword play in sport. I wheeled, our swords clashed. His clothes they smelled all singed. I cut swiftly upward with supple hand, and his dangled bleeding at the wrist, and his sword fell, it tinkled on the ground. I raised my sword to hew him should he stoop for't. He stood and cursed me. He drew his dagger with his left, I opposed my point and dared him with my eye to close. A great shout arose behind me from true men's throats. He started. He spat at me in his rage, then gnashed his teeth and fled blaspheming. I turned and saw torches close at hand. Lo, they fell to dancing up and down methought, and the next—moment—all—was—dark. I had—*ah!*"

Catherine. "Here, help! Water! Stand aloof, you that be men!"

Margaret had fainted away. When she recovered, her head was on Catherine's arm, and the honest half of the family she had invaded like a foe stood round her uttering rough homely words of encouragement, especially Giles, who roared at her that she was not to take on like that. "Gerard was alive and well, or he could not have writ this letter, the biggest mankind had seen as yet, and," as he thought, "the beautifulest, and most moving, and smallest writ."

"Ay, good Master Giles," sighed Margaret feebly, "he *was* alive. But how know I what hath since befallen him? Oh, why left he Holland to go among strangers fierce as lions? And why did I not drive him from me sooner than part him from his own flesh and blood? Forgive me, you that are his mother!"

"Read thou, Richart," said Eli. "Thine eyes be younger than mine."

Richart took the letter. "Well," said he, "such writing saw I never. A writeth with a needle's point, and clear to boot. Why is he not in my countinghouse at Amsterdam instead of vagabonding it out yonder?"

"When I came to myself I was seated in the litter, and my good merchant holding of my hand. I babbled I know not what, and then shuddered awhile in silence. He put a horn of wine to my lips."

Catherine. "Bless him! bless him!"

Eli. "Whist!"

"And I told him what had befallen. He would see my leg. It was sprained sore, and swelled at the ankle, and all my points were broken, as I could scarce keep up my hose, and I said, 'Sir, I shall be but a burden to you, I doubt, and can make you no harmony now—my poor psaltery it is broken.' And I did grieve over my broken music, companion of so many weary leagues. But he patted me on the cheek and bade me not fret; also he did put up my leg on a pillow, and tended me like a kind father.

"*January 14.*—I sit all day in the litter, for we are pushing forward with haste, and at night the good kind merchant sendeth me to bed, and will not let me work. Strange! Whene'er I fall in with men like fiends, then the next moment God still sendeth me some good man or woman, lest I should turn away from humankind. Oh, Margaret, how strangely mixed they be, and how old I am by what I was three months agone! And lo, if good Master Fugger hath not been and bought me a psaltery.

"*January 15.*—Safe at Venice. A place whose strange and passing beauty is well known to thee by report of our mariners. Dost mind too how Peter would oft fill our ears withal, we handed beneath the table, and he still discoursing of this sea-enthroned and peerless city, in shape a bow, and its great canal and palaces on piles, and its watery ways plied by scores of gilded boats; and that market place of nations, Saint Mark his place? And his statue with the peerless jewels in his eyes, and the lion at his gate? But I, lying at my window in pain, may see none of these beauties as yet, but only a street, fairly paced, which is dull, and houses with oiled paper and linen, in lieu of glass, which is rude; and the passers-by, their habits and their gestures, wherein they are superfluous.

"The Italians are a polished and subtle people. They judge a man not by his habits, but his speech and gesture. Here Sir Chough may by no means pass for falcon gentle, as did I in Germany, pranked in my noble servant's feathers. Wisest of all nations in their singular temperance of food and drink. Most foolish of all to search strangers coming into their borders, and stay them from bringing much money in. They should rather invite it, and, like other nations, let the traveler from taking of it out. Also here in Venice the dames turn their black hair yellow by the sun and art, to be wiser than Him who made them.

"Ye enter no Italian town without a bill of health, though now is no plague in Europe. This peevishness is for extortion's sake. The innkeepers cringe and fawn, and cheat, and, in country places, murder you. Yet will they give you clean sheets by paying therefor. Delicate in eating, and abhor from putting their hand in the plate; sooner they will apply a crust or what not. They do even tell of a Cardinal at Rome which armeth his guest's left hand with a little bifurcal dagger to hold the meat while his knife cutteth it. But methinks this, too, is to be wiser than Him who made the hand so supple and prehensile.

"*January 16.*—Sweetheart, I must be brief and tell thee but a part of that I have seen, for this day my journal ends. Tonight it sails for thee, and I, unhappy, not with it, but tomorrow, in another ship, to Rome."

"Eli," said Catherine, still sobbing a little, "tell me, for our Lady's sake, how our poor boy is to live at that nasty Rome. He is gone there to write, but here be his own words to prove writing avails naught; a had died o' hunger by the way but for paintbrush and psaltery. Welladay!"

"Well," said Eli, "he has got brush and music still. Besides, so many men, so many minds. Writing, thof it had no sale in other parts, may be merchandise at Rome."

"Father," said Little Kate, "have I your good leave to put in my word 'twixt Mother and you?"

"And welcome, little heart."

"Then, seems to me painting and music, close at hand, be stronger than writing, but being distant, naught to compare. For see what glamour written paper hath done here but now. Our Gerard, writing at Venice, hath verily put his hand into this room at Rotterdam, and turned all our hearts. Ay, dear dear Gerard, methinks thy spirit hath rid hither on these thy paper wings. And oh, dear Father, why not do as we should do were he here in the body?"

"Kate," said Eli, "fear not. Richart and I will give him glamour for glamour. We will write him a letter, and send it to Rome by a sure hand with money, and bid him home on the instant."

Cornelis and Sybrandt exchanged a gloomy look.

"Ah, good Father! And meantime?"

"Well, meantime?"

"Dear Father, dear Mother, what can we do to pleasure the absent but be kind to his poor lass, and her own trouble afore her?"

" 'Tis well!" said Eli. "But I am older than thou." Then he turned gravely to Margaret. "Wilt answer me a question, my pretty mistress?"

"If I may, sir," faltered Margaret.

"What are these marriage lines Gerard speaks of in the letter?"

"Our marriage lines, sir. His and mine. Know you not we are betrothed?"

"Before witnesses?"

"Ay, sure. My poor father and Martin Wittenhaagen."

"This is the first I ever heard of it. How came they in his hands? They should be in yours."

"Alas, sir, the more is my grief; but I ne'er doubted him, and he said it was a comfort to him to have them in his bosom."

"Y'are a very foolish lass."

"Indeed I was, sir. But trouble teaches the simple."

" 'Tis a good answer. Well, foolish or no, y'are honest. I had shown ye more respect at first but I thought y'had been his leman, and that is the truth."

"God forbid, sir! Denys, methinks 'tis time for us to go. Give me my letter, sir!"

"Bide ye, bide ye! Be not so hot, for a word! Natheless, wife, methinks her red cheek becomes her."

"Better than it did you to give it her, my man."

"Softly, wife, softly. I am not counted an unjust man, thof I be somewhat slow." Eli rose from his chair. "Wife," said he, solemnly, "you will set another chair at our table for every meal, also another plate and knife. They will be for Margaret and Peter. She will come when she likes, and stay away when she pleases. None may take her place at my left hand. Such as can welcome her are welcome to me. Such as cannot, I force them not to bide with me. The world is wide and free. Within my walls I am master, and my son's betrothed is welcome."

Catherine bustled out to prepare supper. Eli and Richart sat down and concocted a letter to bring Gerard home. Richart promised it should go by sea to Rome that very week. Sybrandt and Cornelis exchanged a gloomy wink, and stole out. Margaret, seeing Giles deep in meditation, for the dwarf's intelligence had taken giant strides, asked him to bring her the letter. "You have heard but half, good Master Giles," said she. "Shall I read you the rest?"

"I shall be much beholden to you," shouted the courtier.

She gave him her stool. Curiosity bowed his pride to sit on it, and Margaret murmured the first part of the letter into his ear very low, not to disturb Eli and Richart.

"Get him home on the instant!" roared Giles. "I'll make a man of him. I can do aught with the Duke."

"Hear the boy!" said Catherine, half comically, half proudly.

"We hear him," said Richart. "A mostly makes himself heard when a do speak."

CHAPTER XXXI

ABOUT two months before this scene in Eli's home, the natives of a little maritime place between Naples and Rome might be seen flocking to the sea beach, with eyes cast seaward at a ship that labored against a stiff gale blowing dead on the shore. At times she seemed likely to weather the danger, and then the spectators congratulated her aloud. At others the wind and sea drove her visibly nearer, and the lookers-on were not without a secret satisfaction they would not have owned even to themselves.

The mariners stumbled wildly about the deck, handling the ropes as each thought fit, and cursing and praying alternately. The passengers were huddled together round the mast, some sitting, some kneeling, some lying prostrate, and grasping the bulwarks as the vessel rolled and pitched in the mighty waves. One comely young man, whose ashy cheek but compressed lips showed how hard terror was battling in him with self-respect, stood a little apart, holding tight by a shroud and wincing at each sea. It was the ill-fated Gerard. Meantime prayers and vows rose from the trembling throng amidships, and, to hear them, it seemed there were almost as many gods about as men and women. The sailors, indeed, relied on a single goddess. They varied her titles only, calling on her as "Queen of Heaven," "Star of the Sea," "Mistress of the World," "Haven of Safety."

Suddenly, a more powerful gust than usual catching the sail at a disadvantage, the rotten shrouds gave way, and the sail was torn out with a loud crack and went down the wind smaller and smaller, blacker and blacker, and fluttered into the sea half a mile off, like a sheet of paper. And ere the helmsman could put the ship's head before the wind, a wave caught her on the quarter and drenched the poor wretches to the bone, and gave them a foretaste of chill death. Then one vowed aloud to turn Carthusian monk if Saint Thomas would save him. Another would go a pilgrim to Compostella, bareheaded, barefooted, with nothing but a coat of mail on his naked skin, if Saint James would save him. Others invoked Thomas, Dominic, Denys, and, above all, Catherine of Siena.

A Roman woman of the humbler class sat with her child at her half-bared breast, silent amid that wailing throng, her cheek ashy pale, her eye calm. And her lips moved at times in silent prayer, but she neither wept, nor lamented, nor bargained with the gods. Whenever the ship seemed really gone under their feet, and bearded men squeaked, she kissed her child, but that was all. And so she sat patient, and suckled him in death's jaws; for why should he lose any joy she could give him? Ay, there I do believe, sat Antiquity among those medievals. Sixteen hundred years had not tainted the old Roman blood in her veins, and the instinct of a race she had perhaps scarce heard of taught her to die with decent dignity.

A gigantic friar stood on the poop with feet apart, like the Colossus of Rhodes, not so much defying as ignoring the peril that surrounded him. He recited verses from the canticles with a loud, unwavering voice, and invited the passengers to confess to him. Some did so on their knees, and he heard them, and laid his hands on them, and absolved them as if he had been in a snug sacristy instead of a perishing ship. Gerard got nearer and nearer to him, by the instinct that takes the wavering to the side of the impregnable. And, in truth, the courage of heroes facing fleshly odds might have paled by the side of that gigantic friar, and his still more gigantic composure. Thus even here two were found who maintained the dignity of our race: a woman, tender, yet heroic, and a monk steeled by religion against mortal fears.

And now, the sail being gone, the sailors cut down the useless mast a foot above the board, and it fell with its remaining hamper over the ship's side. This seemed to relieve her a little. But now the hull, no longer impelled by canvas, could not keep ahead of the sea. It struck her again and again on the poop, and the tremendous blows seemed given by a rocky mountain, not by a liquid. The captain left the helm and came amidships pale as death.

"Lighten her!" he cried. "Fling all overboard, or we shall founder ere we strike, and lose the one little chance we have of life. She may, or may not, last half an hour; over that, impossible. She leaks like a sieve. Bustle, men, lighten her!"

The poor passengers seized on everything that was on deck and flung it overboard. And now the captain cried out: "See, there is a church in sight! Steer for that church, mate, and you, friends, pray to the saint, who'er he be."

So they steered for the church and prayed to the unknown god it was named after. A tremendous sea pooped them, broke the rudder and jammed it immovable, and flooded the deck. Then, wild with superstitious terror, some of them came round Gerard.

"Here is the cause of all," they cried. "He has never invoked a single saint. He is a heathen, here is a pagan aboard."

"Alas, good friends, say not so," said Gerard, his teeth chattering with cold and fear. "Rather call these heathens that lie a-praying to the sea. Friends, I do honor the saints—but I dare not pray to them now—there is no time—(oh!) what avail me Dominic, and Thomas and Catherine? Nearer God's throne than these Saint Peter sitteth; and, if I pray to him, it's odd, but I shall be drowned ere he has time to plead my cause with God. Oh, oh, oh, I must need go straight to Him that made the sea, and the saints, and me. Our Father which art in Heaven, save these poor souls and me that cry for the bare life! Oh, sweet Jesus, pitiful Jesus, that didst walk Gennesaret when Peter sank, and wept for Lazarus dead when the Apostles' eyes were dry, oh, save poor Gerard—for dear Margaret's sake!"

At this moment the sailors were seen preparing to desert the sinking ship in the little boat, which even at that epoch every ship carried. Then there was a rush of egotists, and thirty souls crowded into it. Remained behind three who were bewildered, and two who were paralyzed with terror. The paralyzed sat like heaps of wet rags, the bewildered ones ran to and fro, and saw the thirty egotists put off, but made no attempt to join them—only kept running to and fro, and wringing their hands.

Besides these, there was one on his knees praying over the wooden statue of the Virgin Mary, as large as life, which the sailors had reverently detached from the mast. It washed about the deck, as the water came slushing in from the sea, and pouring out at the scuppers; and this poor soul kept following it on his knees, with his hands clasped at it and the water playing with it.

The gigantic Dominican, having shriven the whole ship, stood calmly communing with his own spirit. And the Roman woman sat pale and patient, only drawing her child closer to her bosom as death came nearer. Gerard saw this and it awakened his manhood. "See, see!" he said. "They have ta'en the boat and left the poor woman and her child to perish." His heart soon set his wit working. "Wife, I'll save thee yet, please God."

And he ran to find a cask or a plank to float her. There was none. Then his eye fell on the wooden image of the Virgin. He caught it up in his arms, and heedless of a wail that issued from its worshiper, like a child robbed of its toy, ran aft with it. "Come, wife," he cried, "I'll lash thee and the child to this! 'Tis sore wormeaten, but 'twill serve."

She turned her great dark eyes on him and said a single word: "Thyself?"

But with wonderful magnanimity and tenderness.

"I am a man, and have no child to take care of."

"Ah!" said she, and his words seemed to animate her face with a desire to live. He lashed the image to her side. Then with the hope of life she lost something of her heroic calm—not much, her body trembled a little, but not her eye. The ship was now so low in the water that by using an oar as a lever he could slide her into the waves.

"Come," said he, "while yet there is time."

She turned her great Roman eyes, wet now, upon him. "Poor youth!— God forgive me!—My child!" And he launched her on the surge, and with his oar kept her from being battered against the ship. A heavy hand fell on him, a deep sonorous voice sounded in his ear:

" 'Tis well. Now come with me."

It was the gigantic friar. Gerard turned, and the friar took two strides and laid hold of the broken mast. Gerard did the same, obeying him instinctively. Between them, after a prodigious effort, they hoisted up the remainder of the mast and carried it off. "Fling it in," said the friar, "and follow it." They flung it in, but one of the bewildered passengers had run after them, and jumped first and got on one end. Gerard seized the other, the friar the middle. It was a terrible situation. The mast rose and plunged with each wave like a kicking horse, and the spray flogged their faces mercilessly, and blinded them, to help knock them off.

Presently was heard a long grating noise ahead. The ship had struck, and soon after, she being stationary now, they were hurled against her with tremendous force. Their companion's head struck against the upper part of the broken rudder with a horrible crack, and was smashed like a coconut by a sledge hammer. He sank directly, leaving no trace but a red stain on the water and a white clot on the jagged rudder, and a death cry ringing in their ears as they drifted clear under the lee of the black hull.

The friar uttered a short Latin prayer for the safety of his soul, and took his place composedly. One moment they saw nothing, and seemed down in a mere basin of watery hills: the next they caught glimpses of the shore speckled bright with people, who kept throwing up their arms with wild Italian gestures to encourage them, and the black boat driving bottom upward, and between it and them the woman rising and falling like themselves. She had come across a paddle, and was holding her child tight with her left arm and paddling gallantly with her right.

When they had tumbled along thus a long time, suddenly the friar said quietly: "I touched the ground."

"Impossible, Father," said Gerard. "We are more than a hundred yards from shore. Prithee, prithee, leave not our faithful mast."

"My son," said the friar, "you speak prudently. But know that I have business of Holy Church on hand, and may not waste time floating when I can walk in her service. There, I felt it with my toes again. See the benefit of wearing sandals, and not shoon. Again, and sandy. Thy stature is less than mine. Keep to the mast! I walk."

He left the mast accordingly and, extending his powerful arms, rushed through the water. Gerard soon followed him. At each overpowering wave the monk stood like a tower and, closing his mouth, threw his head back to encounter it, and was entirely lost under it awhile, then emerged and plowed lustily on. At last they came close to the shore; but the suction outward baffled all their attempts to land. Then the natives sent stout fishermen into the sea, holding by long spears in a triple chain, and so dragged them ashore.

The friar shook himself, bestowed a short paternal benediction on the natives, and went on to Rome, with eyes bent on earth, according to his rule, and without pausing. He did not even cast a glance back upon that sea which had so nearly engulfed him, but had no power to harm him without his Master's leave.

As Gerard stood by the sea watching, with horror and curiosity mixed, his late companions washed ashore, a hand was laid lightly on his shoulder. He turned. It was the Roman matron, burning with womanly gratitude. She took his hand gently and, raising it slowly to her lips, kissed it, but so nobly, she seemed to be conferring an honor on one deserving hand. Then, with face all beaming and moist eyes, she held her child up and made him kiss his preserver.

Gerard kissed the child—more than once. He was fond of children. But he said nothing. He was much moved, for she did not speak at all, except with her eyes and glowing cheeks and noble antique gesture, so large and stately. Perhaps she was right. Gratitude is not a thing of words. It was an ancient Roman matron thanking a modern from her heart of hearts.

Next day, toward afternoon, Gerard—twice as old as last year, thrice as learned in human ways, a boy no more, but a man who had shed blood in self-defense and grazed the grave by land and sea—reached the Eternal City.

CHAPTER XXXII

GERARD took a modest lodging on the west bank of the Tiber, and every day went forth in search of work, taking a specimen round to every shop he could hear of that executed such commissions.

They received him coldly. "We make our letter somewhat thinner than this," said one. "How dark your ink is," said another. But the main cry was, "What avails this? Scant is the Latin writ here now. Can ye not write Greek?"

"Ay, but not nigh so well as Latin."

"Then you shall never make your bread at Rome."

Gerard borrowed a beautiful Greek manuscript at a high price, and went home with a sad hole in his purse but none in his courage. In a fortnight he had made vast progress with the Greek character; so then, to lose no time, he used to work at it till noon and hunt customers the rest of the day.

When he carried round a better Greek specimen than any they possessed, the traders informed him that Greek and Latin were alike unsalable; the city was thronged with works from all Europe. He should have come last year. Gerard bought a psaltery.

His landlady, pleased with his looks and manners, used often to speak a kind word in passing. One day she made him dine with her, and somewhat to his surprise asked him what had dashed his spirits. He told her. She gave him her reading of the matter. "Those sly traders," she would be bound, "had writers in their pay for whose work they received a noble price and paid a sorry one. So no wonder they blow cold on you. Methinks you write too well. How know I that, say you? Marry—marry, because you lock not your door, like the churl Pietro, and women will be curious. Ay, ay, you write too well for *them*."

She then assured him that he should make his fortune in spite of the booksellers. "Seeing thee a stranger, they lie to thee without sense or discretion. Why, all the world knows that our great folk are bitten with the writing spider this many years, and pour out their money like water, and turn good land and houses into writ sheepskins to keep in a chest or a cupboard. Why, *I* can tell you two. There is His Eminence Cardinal Bassarion, and His Holiness the Pope himself. There be a pair could keep a score such as thee a-writing night and day. But I'll speak to Teresa; she hears the gossip of the court."

The next day she told him she had seen Teresa, and had heard of five more signors who were bitten with the writing spider. Gerard took down their names, and bought parchment, and busied himself for some days in preparing specimens. He left one, with his name and address, at each of these signors' doors, and hopefully awaited the result. There was none. Day after day passed and left him heartsick. Gerard saw ruin staring him in the face. He spent the afternoons picking up canzonets and mastering them. He laid in playing-cards to color, and struck off a meal per day. This last stroke of genius got him into fresh trouble. In these "*camere locande*" the landlady dressed all the meals, though the lodgers bought the provisions. So Gerard's hostess speedily detected him, and asked him if he was not ashamed of himself; by which brusque opening, having made him blush and look scared, she pacified herself all in a moment, and appealed to his good sense whether adversity was a thing to be overcome on an empty stomach.

"*Pazienza*, my lad! Times will mend. Meantime I will feed you for the love of heaven"—Italian for "gratis."

"Nay, hostess," said Gerard, "my purse is not yet quite void, and it would add to my trouble an if true folk should lose their due by me."

"Why, you are as mad as your neighbor Pietro, with his one bad picture."

"Why, how know you 'tis a bad picture?"

"Because nobody will buy it. There is one that hath no gift. He will have to don casque and glaive, and carry his panel for a shield."

Gerard pricked up his ears at this, so she told him more. Pietro had come from Florence with money in his purse and an unfinished picture, had taken her one unfurnished room, opposite Gerard's, and furnished it neatly. When his picture was finished, he received visitors and had offers for it. These, though in her opinion liberal ones, he had refused so disdainfully as to make enemies of his customers. Since then he had often taken it out with him to try and sell, but had always brought it back; and the last month she had seen one movable after another go out of his room, and now he wore but one suit, and lay at night on a great chest. She had found this out only by peeping through the keyhole, for he locked the door most vigilantly whenever he went out. "Is he afraid we shall steal his chest, or his picture that no soul in all Rome is weak enough to buy?"

"Nay, sweet hostess, see you not 'tis his poverty he would screen from view?"

"And the more fool he! Are all our hearts as ill as his? A might give us a trial first anyway."

"How you speak of him! Why, his case is mine, and your countryman to boot."

"Oh, we Sienese love strangers. His case yours? Nay, 'tis just the contrary. You are the comeliest youth ever lodged in this house—hair like gold. He is a dark, sour-visaged loon. Besides, you know how to take a woman on her better side, but not he. Natheless I wish he would not starve to death in my house, to get me a bad name. Anyway, one starveling is enough in any house. You are far from home, and it is for me, which am the mistress here, to number your meals—for me and the Dutch wife, your mother, that is far away. We two women shall settle that matter. Mind thou thine own business, being a man, and leave cooking and the like to us that are in the world for little else that I see but to roast fowls, and suckle men at starting, and sweep their grown-up cobwebs."

"Dear kind dame, in sooth you do often put me in mind of my mother that is far away."

"All the better. I'll put you more in mind of her before I have done with you." And the honest soul beamed with pleasure.

Gerard, not being an egotist, nor blinded by female partialities, saw his own grief in poor proud Pietro; and the more he thought of it, the more he resolved to share his humble means with that unlucky artist. Pietro's sympathy would repay him. He tried to waylay him, but without success.

One day he heard a groaning in the room. He knocked at the door, but received no answer. He knocked again. A surly voice bade him enter. He obeyed somewhat timidly, and entered a garret furnished with a chair, a picture, face to wall, an iron basin, an easel, and a long chest, on which was coiled a haggard young man with a wonderfully bright eye. Anything more like a coiled cobra ripe for striking the first comer was never seen.

"Good Signor Pietro," said Gerard, "forgive me that, weary of my own solitude, I intrude on yours; but I am your nighest neighbor in this house, and methinks your brother in fortune. I am an artist too."

"You are a painter? Welcome, signor. Sit down on my bed."

And Pietro jumped off and waved him into the vacant throne with a magnificent demonstration of courtesy. Gerard bowed, and smiled, but hesitated a little.

"I may not call myself a painter. I am a writer, a calligraph. I copy Greek and Latin manuscripts, when I can get them to copy."

"And you call that an artist?"

"Without offense to your superior merit, Signor Pietro."

"No offense, stranger, none. Only, meseemeth an artist is one who thinks and paints his thought. Now a calligraph but draws in black-and-white the thoughts of another."

" 'Tis well distinguished, signor. But then, a writer can write the thoughts of the great ancients, and matters of pure reason, such as no man may paint —ay, and the thoughts of God, which angels could not paint. But let that pass. I am a painter as well, but a sorry one."

"The better thy luck. They will buy thy work in Rome."

"But seeking to commend myself to one of thy eminence, I thought it well rather to call myself a capable writer than a scurvy painter."

At this moment a step was heard on the stair.

"Ah, 'tis the good dame!" cried Gerard. "What ho! hostess, I am here in conversation with Signor Pietro. I dare say he will let me have my humble dinner here."

The Italian bowed gravely. The landlady brought in Gerard's dinner, smoking and savory. She put the dish down on the bed with a face divested of all expression, and went. Gerard fell to. But ere he had eaten many mouthfuls he stopped, and said:

"I am an ill-mannered churl, Signor Pietro. I ne'er eat to my mind when I eat alone. For our Lady's sake put a spoon into this ragout with me. 'Tis not unsavory, I promise you."

Pietro fixed his glittering eye on him.

"What, good youth, thou a stranger, and offerest me thy dinner?"

"Why, see, there is more than one can eat."

"Well, I accept," said Pietro, and took the dish with some appearance of calmness, and flung the contents out of window. Then he turned trembling with mortification and ire, and said: "Let that teach thee to offer alms to an artist thou knowest not, Master Writer."

Gerard's face flushed with anger, and it cost him a bitter struggle not to box this high-souled creature's ears. And then to go and destroy good food! His mother's milk curdled in his veins with horror at such impiety. Finally, pity at Pietro's petulance and egotism, and a touch of respect for poverty-struck pride, prevailed. However, he said coldly:

"Likely what thou hast done might pass in a novel of thy countryman, Signor Boccaccio, but 'twas not honest."

"Make that good!" said the painter sullenly.

"I offered thee half my dinner, no more. But thou hast ta'en it all. Hadst a right to throw away thy share, but not mine. Pride is well, but justice is better."

Pietro stared, then reflected.

" 'Tis well. I took thee for a fool, so transparent was thine artifice. Forgive me! And prithee leave me! Thou seest how 'tis with me. The world hath soured me. I hate mankind. I was not always so. Once more, excuse that my discourtesy, and fare thee well!"

Gerard sighed and made for the door. But suddenly a thought struck him.

"Signor Pietro," said he, "we Dutchmen are hard bargainers. We are the lads *'een eij scheeren*,' that is, 'to shave an egg.' Therefore, I, for my lost dinner, do claim to feast mine eyes on your picture, whose face is toward the wall."

"Nay, nay," said the painter hastily, "ask me not that. I have already misconducted myself enough toward thee. I would not shed thy blood."

"Saints forbid! My blood?"

"Stranger," said Pietro sullenly, "irritated by repeated insults to my picture, which is my child, my heart, I did in a moment of rage make a solemn vow to drive my dagger into the next one that should flout it and the labor and love that I have given to it."

"What, are all to be slain that will not praise this picture?" And he looked at its back with curiosity.

"Nay, nay, if you would but look at it, and hold your parrot tongues. But you will be talking. So I have turned it to the wall forever. Would I were dead, and buried in it for my coffin!"

Gerard reflected.

"I accept the conditions. Show me the picture! I can but hold my peace."

Pietro went and turned its face, and put it in the best light the room afforded, and coiled himself again on his chest, with his eye and stiletto glittering. The picture represented the Virgin and Christ flying through the air in a sort of cloud of shadowy cherubic faces. Underneath was a landscape forty or fifty miles in extent, and a purple sky above.

Gerard stood and looked at it in silence. Then he stepped close and looked. Then he retired as far off as he could and looked, but said not a word. When he had been at this game half an hour, Pietro cried out querulously, and somewhat inconsistently:

"Well, have you not a word to say about it?"

Gerard started. "I cry your mercy, I forgot there were three of us here. Ay, I have much to say." And he drew his sword.

"Alas, alas!" cried Pietro, jumping in terror from his lair. "What wouldst thou?"

"Marry, defend myself against thy bodkin, signor, and at due odds, being, as aforesaid, a Dutchman. Therefore, hold aloof while I deliver judgment, or I will pin thee to the wall like a cockchafer."

"Oh, is that all!" said Pietro, greatly relieved. "I feared you were going to stab my poor picture with your sword, stabbed already by so many foul tongues."

Gerard "pursued criticism under difficulties." Put himself in a position of defense, with his sword's point covering Pietro and one eye glancing aside at the picture.

"First, signor, I would have you know that in the mixing of certain colors, and in the preparation of your oil, you Italians are far behind us Flemings. But let that flea stick. For as small as I am, I can show you certain secrets of the Van Eycks that you will put to marvelous profit in your next picture. Meantime I see in this one the great qualities of your nation. Verily, ye are *solis filii*. If we have color, you have imagination. Mother of Heaven, an he hath not flung his immortal soul upon the panel! One thing I go by is this. It makes other pictures I once admired seem drossy, earthborn things. The drapery here is somewhat short and stiff. Why not let it float freely, the figures being in air and motion?"

"I will! I will!" cried Pietro eagerly. "I will do anything for those who will but see what I *have* done."

"Humph! This landscape it enlightens me. Henceforth I scorn those little huddled landscapes that did erst content me. Here is Nature's very face: a spacious plain, each distance marked, and every tree, house, figure, field, and river smaller and less plain, by exquisite gradation, till vision itself melts into distance. Oh, beautiful! And the cunning rogue hath hung his celestial figure in air out of the way of his little world below. Here, floating saints beneath heaven's purple canopy. There, far down, earth and her busy hives. And they let you take this painted poetry, this blooming hymn, through the streets of Rome and bring it home unsold. But I tell thee in Ghent or Bruges, or even in Rotterdam, they would tear it out of thy hands. But 'tis a common saying that a stranger's eye sees clearest. Courage, Pietro Vanucci! I reverence thee, and though myself a scurvy painter, do forgive thee for being a great one. Forgive thee? I thank God for thee and such rare men as thou art, and bow the knee to thee in just homage. Thy picture is immortal, and thou, that hast but a chest to sit on, art a king in thy most royal art. *Viva, il maestro! Viva!*"

At this unexpected burst the painter, with all the abandon of his nation, flung himself on Gerard's neck. "They said it was a maniac's dream," he sobbed.

"Maniacs themselves! No, idiots!" shouted Gerard.

"Generous stranger, I will hate men no more, since the world hath such as thee! I was a viper to fling thy poor dinner away, a wretch, a monster."

"Well, monster, wilt be gentle now, and sup with me?"

"Ah, that I will! Whither goest thou?"

"To order supper on the instant. We will have the picture for third man."

"I will invite it whiles thou art gone. My poor picture, child of my heart."

"Ah, master, 'twill look on many a supper after the worms have eaten you and me."

"I hope so," said Pietro.

CHAPTER XXXIII

ABOUT a week after this the two friends sat working together, but not in the same spirit. Pietro dashed fitfully at his, and did wonders in a few minutes and then did nothing, except abuse it; then presently resumed it in a fury, to lay it down with a groan. Through all which kept calmly working, calmly smiling, the canny Dutchman.

To be plain, Gerard, who never had a friend he did not master, had put his Onagra in harness. The friends were painting playing-cards to boil the pot. When done, the indignant master took up his picture to make his daily tour in search of a customer. Gerard begged him to take the cards as well, and try and sell them. He looked all the rattlesnake, but eventually embraced Gerard in the Italian fashion, and took them, after first drying the last finished ones in the sun, which was now powerful in that happy clime.

Gerard, left alone, executed a Greek letter or two, and then mended a little rent in his hose. His landlady found him thus employed, and inquired ironically whether there were no women in the house.

"When you have done that," said she, "come and talk to Teresa, my friend I spoke to thee of, that hath a husband not good for much which brags his acquaintance with the great."

Gerard went down, and who should Teresa be but the Roman matron.

"Ah, madama," said he, "is it you? The good dame told me not that. And the little fair-haired boy, is he well? Is he none the worse for his voyage in that strange boat?"

"He is well," said the matron.

"Why, what are you two talking about?" said the landlady, staring at them both in turn, "and why tremble you so, *Teresa mia?*"

"He saved my child's life," said Teresa, making an effort to compose herself.

"What, my lodger? And he never told me a word of that. Art not ashamed to look me in the face?"

"Alas, speak not harshly to him!" said the matron. She then turned to her friend and poured out a glowing description of Gerard's conduct, during which Gerard stood blushing like a girl, and scarce recognizing his own performance, gratitude painted it so fair.

"And to think thou shouldst ask me to serve thy lodger, of whom I knew naught but that he had thy good word, oh, Fiammina, and that was enough for me. Dear youth, in serving thee I serve myself."

Then ensued an eager description by the two women of what had been done, and what should be done, to penetrate the thick wall of fees, commissions, and chicanery which stood between the patrons of art and an unknown artist in the Eternal City. Teresa smiled sadly at Gerard's simplicity in leaving specimens of his skill at the doors of the great.

"What!" said she. "Without promising the servants a share—without even feeing them, to let the signors see thy merchandise! As well have flung it into Tiber."

"Welladay!" sighed Gerard. "Then how is an artist to find a patron? For artists are poor, not rich."

"By going to some city nobler and not so greedy as this," said Teresa. "*La corte Romana non vuol' pecora senza lana.*"[1]

She fell into thought, and said she would come again tomorrow. The landlady felicitated Gerard. "Teresa has got something in her head," said she.

Teresa was scarce gone when Pietro returned with his picture, looking black as thunder. Gerard exchanged a glance with the landlady and followed him up stairs to console him.

"What, have they let thee bring home thy masterpiece?"

"As heretofore."

"More fools they, then."

"That is not the worst."

"Why, what is the matter?"

"They have bought the cards!" yelled Pietro, and hammered the air furiously right and left.

[1]"The Roman court does not want sheep without wool."

"All the better," said Gerard cheerfully.

"They flew at me for them. They were enraptured with them. They tried to conceal their longing for them, but could not. I saw, I feigned, I pillaged, curse the boobies."

And he flung down a dozen small silver coins on the floor and jumped on them, and danced on them with basilisk eyes, and then kicked them assiduously, and sent them spinning and flying and running all abroad. Down went Gerard on his knees and followed the maltreated innocents directly, and transferred them tenderly to his purse.

"Shouldst rather smile at their ignorance, and put it to profit," said he.

"And so I will," said Pietro, with concentrated indignation. "The brutes! We will paint a pack a day. We will set the whole city gambling and ruining itself while we live like princes on its vices and stupidity. There was one of the queens, though, I had fain have kept back. 'Twas you limned her, brother. She had lovely red-brown hair and sapphire eyes, and above all, soul."

"Pietro," said Gerard, softly, "I painted that one from my heart."

The quick-witted Italian nodded, and his eyes twinkled.

"You love her so well, yet leave her."

"Pietro, it is because I love her so dear that I have wandered all this dreary road."

This interesting colloquy was interrupted by the landlady crying from below, "Come down, you are wanted!" He went down, and there was Teresa again.

"Come with me, Ser Gerard."

Gerard walked silently beside Teresa, wondering in his own mind, after the manner of artists, what she was going to do with him, instead of asking her. So at last she told him of her own accord. A friend had informed her of a working goldsmith's wife who wanted a writer. "Her shop is hard by. You will not have far to go." Accordingly they soon arrived at the goldsmith's wife.

"Madama," said Teresa, "Leonora tells me you want a writer. I have brought you a beautiful one. He saved my child at sea. Prithee look on him with favor."

The goldsmith's wife complied in one sense. She fixed her eyes on Gerard's comely face, and could hardly take them off again. But her reply was unsatisfactory. "Nay, I have no use for a writer. Ah, I mind now, it is my gossip, Claelia, the sausage-maker, wants one. She told me, and I told Leonora."

Teresa made a courteous speech and withdrew. Claelia lived at some distance, and when they reached her house she was out. Teresa said calmly, "I will await her return," and sat so still, and dignified, and statuesque that Gerard was beginning furtively to draw her when Claelia returned.

"Madama, I hear from the goldsmith's wife, the excellent Olympia, that you need a writer." Here she took Gerard by the hand and led him forward. "I have brought you a beautiful one. He saved my child from the cruel waves. For our Lady's sake look with favor on him."

"My good dame, my fair Ser," said Claelia, "I have no use for a writer. But now you remind me, it was my friend Appia Claudia asked me for one but the other day. She is a tailor, lives in the Via Lepida."

Teresa retired calmly.

"Madama," said Gerard, "this is likely to be a tedious business for you."

Teresa opened her eyes.

"What was ever done without a little patience?" She added mildly, "We will knock at every door at Rome but you shall have justice."

"But, madama, I think we are dogged. I noticed a man that follows us, sometimes afar, sometimes close."

"I have seen it," said Teresa coldly, but her cheek colored faintly. "It is my poor Lodovico."

She stopped and turned, and beckoned with her finger. A figure approached them somewhat unwillingly. When he came up, she gazed him full in the face, and he looked sheepish. "*Lodovico mio*," said she, "know this young Ser, of whom I have so often spoken to thee. Know him and love him, for he it was who saved thy wife and child."

At these last words, Lodovico, who had been bowing and grinning artificially, suddenly changed to an expression of heartfelt gratitude, and embraced Gerard warmly. Yet somehow there was something in the man's original manner, and his having followed his wife by stealth, that made Gerard uncomfortable under this caress. However, he said, "We shall have your company, Ser Lodovico?"

"No, signor," replied Lodovico. "I go not on that side Tiber."

"*Addio*, then," said Teresa significantly.

"When shall you return home, *Teresa mia?*"

"When I have done mine errand, Lodovico."

To be brief, Appia Claudia was merciful, and did not send them over Tiber again, but only a hundred yards down the street to Lucretia, who kept the glove shop. She it was wanted a writer, but what for Appia Claudia could not conceive. Lucretia was a merry little dame, who received them heartily enough, and told them she wanted no writer, kept all her accounts in her head. "It was for my confessor, Father Colonna. He is mad after them."

"I have heard of his Excellency," said Teresa.

"Who has not?"

"But, good dame, he is a friar, he has made vow of poverty. I cannot let the young man write and not be paid. He saved my child at sea."

"Did he now?" And Lucretia cast an approving look on Gerard. "Well, make your mind easy, a Colonna never wants for money. The good Father has only to say the word and the princes of his race will pour a thousand crowns into his lap. His wench Onesta mostly looks in here for a chat when she goes an errand."

"This is the man for thee, my friend," said Teresa.

"All you have to do," continued Lucretia, "is to go to his lodgings (my boy shall show them you), and tell Onesta you came from me, and you are a writer, and she will take you up to him. If you put a piece of silver in the wench's hand, 'twill do you no harm. That stands to reason."

"I have silver," said Teresa, warmly.

"But stay," said Lucretia, "mind one thing. What the young man sayeth he can do, that he must be able to do, or let him shun the good friar like poison. He is a very wild beast against all bunglers. Why, 'twas but t'other day one brought him an ill-carved crucifix. Says he: 'Is this how you present "Salvator Mundi" who died for you in mortal agony? And you go and grudge him careful work. This slovenly gimcrack a crucifix? But that it *is* a crucifix of some sort, and I am a holy man, I'd dust your jacket with your crucifix,' says he. Onesta heard every word through the key-hole, so mind."

"Have no fears, madama," said Teresa, loftily. "I will answer for his ability; he saved my child."

Gerard was not subtle enough to appreciate this conclusion, and was so far from sharing Teresa's confidence that he begged a respite. He would rather not go to the friar today. Would not tomorrow do as well?

"Here is a coward for ye," said Lucretia.

"No, he is not a coward," said Teresa, firing up. "He is modest."

"I am afraid of this highborn, fastidious friar," said Gerard. "Consider, he has seen the handiwork of all the writers in Italy, dear dame Teresa. If you would but let me prepare a better piece of work than yet I have done, and then tomorrow I will face him with it."

"I consent," said Teresa.

They walked home together. Not far from his own lodging was a shop that sold vellum. There was a beautiful white skin in the window. Gerard looked at it wistfully, but he knew he could not pay for it, so he went on rather hastily. However, he soon made up his mind where to get vellum and, parting with Teresa at his own door, ran hastily upstairs and took the bond he had brought all the way from Sevenbergen, and laid it with a sigh on the table. He then prepared with his chemicals to erase the old writing. But as this was his last chance of reading it, he now overcame his deadly repugnance to bad writing, and proceeded to decipher the deed in spite of its detestable contractions. It appeared by this deed that Ghysbrecht van Swieten was to advance some money to Floris Brandt on a piece of land, and was to repay himself out of the rent.

On this Gerard felt it would be imprudent and improper to destroy the deed. On the contrary, he vowed to decipher every word, at his leisure. He went downstairs determined to buy a small piece of vellum with his half of the card money. At the bottom of the stairs he found the landlady and Teresa talking. At sight of him the former cried: "Here he is. You are caught, *donna mia*. See what she has bought you!" And whipped out from under her apron the very skin of vellum Gerard had longed for.

"Why, dame! Why, Donna Teresa!" And he was speechless with pleasure and astonishment. "Dear Donna Teresa, there is not a skin in all Rome like it. How ever came you to hit on this one? 'Tis glamour."

"Alas, dear boy, did not thine eye rest on it with desire? And didst thou not sigh in turning away from it? And was it for Teresa to let thee want the thing after that?"

"What sagacity! What goodness, madama! Oh, dame, I never thought I should possess this. What did you pay for it?"

"I forget. *Addio*, Fiammina. *Addio*, Ser Gerard. Be happy, be prosperous, as you are good." And the Roman matron glided away while Gerard was hesitating and thinking how to offer to pay so stately a creature for her purchase.

The next day in the afternoon he went to Lucretia, and her boy took him to Fra Colonna's lodgings. He announced his business and feed Onesta, and she took him up to the friar. Gerard entered with a beating heart. The room, a large one, was strewed and heaped with objects of art, antiquity, and learning, lying about in rich profusion, and confusion. Manuscripts, pictures, carvings in wood and ivory, musical instruments; and in this glorious chaos sat the friar poring intently over an Arabian manuscript. He looked up a little peevishly at the interruption. Onesta whispered in his ear.

"Very well," said he. "Let him be seated. Stay, young man, show me how you write!" And he threw Gerard a piece of paper and pointed to an inkhorn.

"So please you, Reverend Father," said Gerard, "my hand, it trembleth too much at this moment, but last night I wrote a vellum page of Greek, and the Latin version by its side, to show the various character."

"Show it me!"

Gerard brought the work to him in fear and trembling; then stood, heartsick, awaiting his verdict. When it came it staggered him. For the verdict was a Dominican falling on his neck.

CHAPTER XXXIV

BORN without controversial bile in so zealous an epoch, Francesco Colonna, a young nobleman of Florence, lived for the arts. At twenty he turned Dominican friar. His object was quiet study. He retired from idle company, and faction fights, the humming and the stinging of the human hive, to Saint Dominic and the Nine Muses. An eager student of languages, pictures, statues, chronology, coins, and monumental inscriptions. These last loosened his faith in popular histories.

He traveled many years in the East, and returned laden with spoils: master of several choice MSS., and versed in Greek and Latin, Hebrew and Syriac. He found his country had not stood still. Other lettered princes besides Cosmo had sprung up. Alfonso King of Naples, Nicolas d'Este, Lionel d'Este, and so on. Above all, his old friend Thomas of Sarzana had been made Pope, and had lent a mighty impulse to letters, had accumulated five thousand MSS. in the library of the Vatican, and had set Poggio to translate Diodorus Siculus and Xenophon's *Cyropaedia*, Laurentius Valla to translate Herodotus and Thucydides, Theodore Gaza, Theophrastus; George of Trebizond, Eusebius, and certain treatises of Plato, and so on, and so on.

The monk found Plato and Aristotle under armistice, but Poggio and Valla at loggerheads over verbs and nouns, and on fire with *odium philologicum*. All this was heaven, and he settled down in his native land, his life a rosy dream. None so happy as the versatile, provided they have not their bread to make by it. And Fra Colonna was Versatility. He knew seven or eight languages, and a little mathematics; could write a bit, paint a bit, model a bit, sing a bit, strum a bit; and could relish superior excellence in all these branches. For this last trait he deserved to be as happy as he was. For, gauge the intellects of your acquaintances, and you will find but few whose minds are neither deaf, nor blind, nor dead to some great art or science,

"And wisdom at one entrance quite shut out."

And such of them as are conceited as well as stupid, shall even parade, instead of blushing for, the holes in their intellects. A zealot in art, the friar was a skeptic in religion.

Fra Colonna was charmed with his new artist, and, having the run of half the palaces in Rome, sounded his praises so that he was soon called upon to resign him. He told Gerard what great princes wanted him. "But I am so happy with you, Father," objected Gerard. "Fiddlestick about being happy with me," said Fra Colonna. "You must not be happy, you must be a man of the world; the grand lesson I impress on the young is be a man of the world. Now these Montesini can pay you three times as much as I can, and they shall too—by Jupiter."

And the friar clapped a terrific price on Gerard's pen. It was acceded to without a murmur. Much higher prices were going for *copying* than *authorship* ever obtained for centuries under the printing press. Gerard had three hundred crowns for Aristotle's treatise on rhetoric.

The great are mighty sweet upon all their pets, while the fancy lasts, and in the rage for Greek MSS. the handsome writer soon became a pet, and nobles of both sexes caressed him like a lap dog. It would have turned a vain fellow's head, but the canny Dutchman saw the steel hand beneath the velvet glove, and did not presume. Nevertheless it was a proud day for him when he found himself seated with Fra Colonna at the table of his present employer, Cardinal Bessarion. They were about a mile from the top of that table, but, never mind, there they were.

But greater honor was in store. One day the Cardinal sent for him, and after praising the beauty of his work took him in his coach to the Vatican, and up a private stair to a luxurious little room with a great oriel window. Here were inkstands, sloping frames for writing on, and all the instruments of art. The Cardinal whispered a courtier, and presently the Pope's private secretary appeared with a glorious grimy old MS. of Plutarch's *Lives*. And soon Gerard was seated alone copying it, awestruck, yet half-delighted at the thought that his Holiness would handle his work and read it. The papal inkstands were all glorious externally, but within the ink was vile. But Gerard carried ever good ink, homemade, in a dirty little inkhorn. He prayed on his knees for a firm and skillful hand, and set to work.

Who so happy now as Gerard? His art was honored, and fabulous prices paid for it; in a year or two he should return by sea to Holland, with good store of money, and set up with his beloved Margaret in Bruges, or Antwerp, or dear Augsburg, and end their days in peace, and love, and healthy, happy labor. His heart never strayed an instant from her.

In his prosperity he did not forget poor Pictro. He took the Fra Colonna to see his picture. The friar inspected it severely and closely, fell on the artist's neck, and carried the picture to one of the Colonnas, who gave a noble price for it. Pietro descended to the first floor; and lived like a gentleman.

But Gerard remained in his garret. To increase his expenses would have been to postpone his return to Margaret. Luxury had no charms for the singlehearted one, when opposed to love.

One afternoon when Gerard had finished his day's work, a fine lackey came and demanded his attendance at the Palace Cesarini. He went, and was ushered into a noble apartment; there was a girl seated in it, working on a tapestry. She rose and left the room, and said she would let her mistress know.

A good hour did Gerard cool his heels in that great room, and at last he began to fret. "These nobles think nothing of a poor fellow's time." However, just as he was making up his mind to slip out and go about his business, the door opened, and a superb beauty entered the room followed by two maids. It was the young Princess of the House of Cesarini. She came in talking rather loudly and haughtily to her dependents, but at sight of Gerard lowered her voice to a very feminine tone, and said, "Are you the writer, messer?"

"I am, signora."

" 'Tis well." She then seated herself, Gerard and her maids remaining standing.

"What is your name, good youth?"

"Gerard, signora."

"Gerard? Body of Bacchus! Is that the name of a human creature?"

"It is a Dutch name, signora. I was born at Tergou, in Holland."

"A harsh name, girls, for so well-favored a youth. What say you?" The maids assented warmly.

"What did I send for him for?" inquired the lady, with lofty languor. "Ah, I remember. Be seated, Ser Gerardo, and write me a letter to Ercole Orsini, my lover—at least he says so."

Gerard seated himself, took out paper and ink, and looked up to the Princess for instructions.

She, seated on a much higher chair, almost a throne, looked down at him with eyes equally inquiring.

"Well, Gerardo."

"I am ready, your Excellence."

"Write, then."

"I but await the words."

"And who, think you, is to provide *them?*"

"Who but your Grace, whose letter it is to be."

"Gramercy! What, you writers, find you not the words? What avails your art without the words? I doubt you are an impostor, Gerardo."

"Nay, signora, I am none. I might make shift to put your Highness's speech into grammar, as well as writing. But I cannot interpret your silence. Therefore speak what is in your heart, and I will empaper it before your eyes."

"But there is nothing in my heart. And sometimes I think I have got no heart."

"What is in your mind, then?"

"But there is nothing in my mind, nor my head neither."

"Then why write at all?"

"Why, indeed? That is the first word of sense either you or I have
spoken, Gerardo. Pestilence seize him! Why writeth he not first? Then I
could say nay to this, and ay to that, withouten headache. Also, is it a
lady's part to say the first word?"

"No, signora, the last."

"It is well spoken, Gerardo. Ha, ha! Shalt have a gold piece for thy wit.
Give me my purse!" And she paid him for the article on the nail *à la moyen
âge*. Money never yet chilled zeal. Gerard, after getting a gold piece so
cheap, felt bound to pull her out of her difficulty, if the wit of man might
achieve it. "Signorina," said he, "these things are only hard because folk
attempt too much, are artificial and labor phrases. Do but figure to yourself the signor you love—"

"I love him not."

"Well, then, the signor you love not—seated at this table, and dict to
me just what you would say to him."

"Well, if he sat there I should say, 'Go away.'"

Gerard, who was flourishing his pen by way of preparation, laid it down
with a groan.

"And when he was gone," said Floretta, "your Highness would say,
'Come back.'"

"Like enough, wench. Now silence all, and let me think. He pestered
me to write, and I promised, so mine honor is engaged. What lie shall I
tell the Gerardo to tell the fool?"

And she turned her head away from them and fell into deep thought,
with her noble chin resting on her white hand, half-clenched. She was so
lovely and statuesque, and looked so inspired with thoughts celestial as
she sat thus, impregnating herself with mendacity, that Gerard forgot
all except art, and proceeded eagerly to transfer that exquisite profile to
paper. He had very nearly finished when the fair statue turned brusquely
round and looked at him.

"Nay, signora," said he, a little peevishly, "for heaven's sake change not
your posture, 'twas perfect. See, you are nearly finished."

All eyes were instantly on the work, and all tongues active. "How like!
and done in a minute. Nay, methinks her Highness's chin is not quite
so—"

"Oh, a touch will make that right."

"What a pity 'tis not colored. I'm all for colors. Hang black-and-white!
And her Highness hath such a lovely skin. Take away her skin, and half
her beauty is lost."

"Peace. Can you color, Ser Gerardo?"

"Ay, signorina. I am a poor hand at oils—there shines my friend Pietro—
but in this small way I can tint you to the life, if you have time to waste on
such vanity."

"Call you this vanity? And for time, it hangs on me like lead. Send for your colors now—quick—this moment—for love of all the saints."

"Nay, signorina, I must prepare them. I could come at the same time tomorrow."

"So be it. And you, Floretta, see that he be admitted at all hours. Alack! Leave my head! Leave my head!"

"Forgive me, signorina, I thought to prepare it at home to receive the colors. But I will leave it. And now let us dispatch the letter."

"What letter?"

"To the Signor Orsini."

"And shall I waste my *time* on such *vanity* as writing letters—and to that empty creature, to whom I am as indifferent as the moon? Nay, not indifferent, for I have just discovered my real sentiments. I hate him and despise him. Girls, I here forbid you once for all to mention that signor's name to me again, else I'll whip you till the blood comes. You know how I can lay on when I'm roused."

"We do. We do."

"Then provoke me not to it." And her eye flashed daggers, and she turned to Gerard all instantaneous honey. "*Addio, il Gerar-do.*" And Gerard bowed himself out of this velvet tiger's den.

He came next day and colored her; and next he was set to make a portrait of her on a large scale; and then a full-length figure; and he was obliged to set apart two hours in the afternoon for drawing and painting this Princess, whose beauty and vanity were prodigious, and candidates for a portrait of her numerous. Here the thriving Gerard found a new and fruitful source of income. Margaret seemed nearer and nearer.

CHAPTER XXXV

The Princess Claelia ordered a full-length portrait of herself. Gerard advised her to employ his friend Pietro Vanucci. But she declined.

"'Twill be time to put a slight on the Gerardo when his work discontents me."

Then Gerard, who knew he was an excellent draftsman, but not so good a colorist, begged her to stand to him as a Roman statue. He showed her how closely he could mimic marble on paper. She consented at first, but demurred when this enthusiast explained to her that she must wear the tunic, toga, and sandals of the ancients.

"Why, I had as lieve be presented in my smock," said she, with medieval frankness.

"Alack, signorina," said Gerard, "you have surely never noted the ancient habit—so free, so ample, so simple, yet so noble, and most becoming your Highness, to whom Heaven hath given the Roman features, and eke a shapely arm and hand, hid in modern guise."

"What, can you flatter like the rest, Gerardo? Well, give me time to think on't. Come o' Saturday, and then I will say ay or nay."

The respite thus gained was passed in making the tunic and toga, and so on and trying them on in her chamber, to see whether they suited her style of beauty well enough to compensate their being a thousand years out of date.

Gerard, hurrying along to this interview, was suddenly arrested and rooted to earth at a shop window. His quick eye had discerned in that window a copy of Lactantius, lying open. "That is fairly writ, anyway," thought he. He eyed it a moment more with all his eyes. It was not written at all. It was printed. Gerard groaned. "I am sped. Mine enemy is at the door. The press is in Rome."

He went into the shop and, affecting nonchalance, inquired how long the printing press had been in Rome. The man said he believed there was no such thing in the city. "Oh, the Lactantius, that was printed on the top of the Apennines."

"What, did the printing press fall down there out o' the moon?"

"Nay, messer," said the trader, laughing, "it shot up there out of Germany. See the title page!"

Gerard took the Lactantius eagerly, and saw the following:

Operâ et impensis Sweynheim et Pannartz
Alumnorum Joannis Fust.
Impressum Subiacis. A.D. 1465.

"Will ye buy, messer? See how fair and even be the letters. Few are left can write like that, and scarce a quarter of the price."

"I would fain have it," said Gerard, sadly, "but my heart will not let me. Know that I am a calligraph, and these disciples of Fust run after me round the world a-taking the bread out of my mouth. But I wish them no ill. Heaven forbid!" And he hurried from the shop.

"Dear Margaret," said he to himself, "we must lose no time, we must make our hay while shines the sun. One month more and an avalanche of printer's type shall roll down on Rome from those Apennines, and lay us waste that writers be."

And he almost ran to the Princess Claelia. He was ushered into an apartment new to him. It was not very large, but most luxurious. A fountain played in the center, and the floor was covered with the skins of panthers, dressed with the hair so that no footfall could be heard. The room was an antechamber to the Princess's boudoir, for on one side there was no door, but an ample curtain of gorgeous tapestry. Here Gerard was left alone till he became quite uneasy, and doubted whether the maid had not shown him to the wrong place.

These doubts were agreeably dissipated. A light step came swiftly behind the curtain. It parted in the middle, and there stood a figure the heathens might have worshiped. It was not quite Venus, nor quite Minerva, but between the two—nobler than Venus, more womanly than Jupiter's daughter. Toga, tunic, sandals—nothing was modern. And as for beauty, that is of all times. Gerard started up, and all the artist in him flushed with pleasure.

"Oh!" he cried, innocently, and gazed in rapture.

This added the last charm to his model. A light blush tinted her cheeks, and her eyes brightened, and her mouth smiled with delicious complacency at this genuine tribute to her charms. When they had looked at one another so some time, and she saw Gerard's eloquence was confined to ejaculating and gazing, she spoke.

"Well, Gerardo, thou seest I have made myself an antique monster for thee."

"A monster? I doubt Fra Colonna would fall down and adore your Highness, seeing you so habited."

"Nay, I care not to be adored by an old man. I would liever be loved by a young one—of my own choosing."

Gerard took out his pencils, arranged his canvas, which he had covered with stout paper, and set to work; and so absorbed was he that he had no mercy on his model. At last, after near an hour in one posture, "Gerardo," said she, faintly, "I can stand so no more, even for thee."

"Sit down and rest awhile, signora."

"I thank thee," said she, and sinking into a chair turned pale and sighed.

Gerard was alarmed, and saw also he had been inconsiderate. He took water from the fountain and was about to throw it in her face, but she put up a white hand deprecatingly. "Nay, hold it to my brow with thine hand. Prithee, do not fling it at me!"

Gerard timidly and hesitating applied his wet hand to her brow.

"Ah," she sighed, "that is reviving! Again."

He applied it again. She thanked him, and asked him to ring a little hand bell on the table. He did so, and a maid came, and was sent to Floretta with orders to bring a large fan. Floretta speedily came with the fan.

She no sooner came near the Princess than that lady's highbred nostrils suddenly expanded like a blood horse's. "Wretch!" said she, and rising up with a sudden return to vigor, seized Floretta with her left hand, twisted it in her hair, and with the right hand boxed her ears severely three times.

Floretta screamed and blubbered, but obtained no mercy. The antique toga left quite disengaged a bare arm that now seemed as powerful as it was beautiful. It rose and fell like the piston of a modern steam engine, and heavy slaps resounded one after another on Floretta's shoulders. The last one drove her sobbing and screaming through the curtain, and there she was heard crying bitterly for some time after.

"Saints of heaven," cried Gerard, "what is amiss? What hath she done?"

"She knows right well. 'Tis not the first time. The nasty toad! I'll learn her to come to me stinking of the musk cat."

"Alas! signora, 'twas a small fault, methinks."

"A small fault? Nay, 'twas a foul fault." She added with an amazing sudden descent to humility and sweetness, "Are you wroth with me for beating her, Gerar-do?"

"Signora, it ill becomes me to school you, but methinks such as Heaven appoints to govern others should govern themselves."

"That is true, Gerardo. How wise you are, to be so young." She then called the other maid, and gave her a little purse. "Take that to Floretta, and tell her 'the Gerardo' hath interceded for her; and so I must needs forgive her. There, Gerardo."

Gerard colored all over at the compliment, but not knowing how to turn a phrase equal to the occasion, asked her if he should resume her picture.

"Not yet. Beating that hussy hath somewhat breathed me. I'll sit awhile, and you shall talk to me. I know you can talk, an it pleases you, as rarely as you draw."

"That were easily done."

"Do it then, Gerardo."

Gerard was taken aback.

"But, signora, I know not what to say. This is sudden."

"Say your real mind. Say you wish you were anywhere but here."

"Nay, signora, that would not be sooth. I wish one thing, though."

"Ay, and what is that?" said she gently.

"I wish I could have drawn you as you were beating that poor lass. You were awful, yet lovely. Oh, what a subject for a Pythoness!"

"Alas, he thinks but of his art! And why keep such a coil about my beauty, Gerardo? You are far fairer than I am. You are more like Apollo than I to Venus. Also, you have lovely hair, and lovely eyes—but you know not what to do with them."

"Ay, do I. To draw you, signora."

"Ah, yes, you can see my features with them, but you cannot see what any Roman gallant had seen long ago in your place. Yet sure you must have noted how welcome you are to me, Gerardo?"

"I can see your Highness is always passing kind to me, a poor stranger like me."

"No, I am not, Gerardo. I have often been cold to you, rude sometimes; and you are so simple you see not the cause. Alas, I feared for my own heart! I feared to be your slave, I who have hitherto made slaves. Ah,

Gerardo, I am unhappy. Ever since you came here I have lived upon your visits. The day you are to come I am bright. The other days I am listless, and wish them fled. You are not like the Roman gallants. You make me hate them. You are ten times braver to my eye; and you are wise and scholarly, and never flatter and lie. I scorn a man that lies. Gerar-do. Teach me thy magic, teach me to make thee as happy by my side as I am still by thine."

As she poured out these strange words, the Princess's mellow voice sank almost to a whisper, and trembled with half-suppressed passion, and her white hand stole timidly yet earnestly down Gerard's arm till it rested like a soft bird upon his wrist, and as ready to fly away at a word.

Destitute of vanity and experience, wrapped up in his Margaret and his art, Gerard had not seen this revelation coming, though it had come by regular and visible gradations. He blushed all over. His innocent admiration of the regal beauty that besieged him did not for a moment displace the absent Margaret's image. Yet it was regal beauty, and wooing with a grace and tenderness he had never even figured in imagination. How to check her without wounding her? He blushed and trembled.

The siren saw, and encouraged him. "Poor Gerardo," she murmured, "fear not. None shall ever harm thee under my wing. Wilt not speak to me, *Gerar-do mio?*" "Signora!" muttered Gerard, deprecatingly.

At this moment his eye, lowered in his confusion, fell on the shapely white arm and delicate hand that curled round his elbow like a tender vine, and it flashed across him how he had just seen that lovely limb employed on Floretta. He trembled and blushed.

"Alas!" said the Princess. "I scare him. Am I then so very terrible? Is it my Roman robe? I'll doff it, and habit me as when thou first camest to me. Mindest thou? 'Twas to write a letter to yon barren knight Ercole d'Orsini. Shall I tell thee? 'Twas the sight of thee, and thy pretty ways, and thy wise words, made me hate him on the instant. I liked the fool well enough before, or wist I liked him. Tell me now how many times hast thou been here since then. Ah, thou knowest not—lovest me not, I doubt, as I love thee. Eighteen times, Gerardo. And each time dearer to me. The day thou comest not 'tis night, not day, to Claelia. Alas, I speak for both! Cruel boy, am I not worth a word? Hast every day a princess at thy feet? Nay, prithee, prithee, speak to me, Gerar-do."

"Signora," faltered Gerard, "what can I say that were not better left unsaid? Oh, evil day that ever I came here!"

"Ah, say not so. 'Twas the brightest day ever shone on me, or indeed on thee. I'll make thee confess so much ere long, ungrateful one."

"Your Highness," began Gerard in a low, pleading voice.

"Call me Claelia, Gerar-do."

"Signora, I am too young and too little wise to know how I ought to speak to you so as not to seem blind nor yet ungrateful. But this I know, I were both naught and ungrateful, and the worst foe e'er you had, did I take advantage of this mad fancy. Sure some ill spirit hath had leave to afflict you withal. For 'tis all unnatural that a princess adorned with every grace should abase her affections on a churl."

The Princess withdrew her hand slowly from Gerard's wrist. Yet as it passed lightly over his arm it seemed to linger a moment at parting.

"You fear the daggers of my kinsmen," said she, half sadly, half contemptuously.

"No more than I fear the bodkins of your women," said Gerard, haughtily. "But I fear God and the saints, and my own conscience."

"The truth, Gerardo, the truth! Hypocrisy sits awkwardly on thee. Princesses, while they are young, are not despised for love of God, but of some other woman. Tell me whom thou lovest, and if she is worthy thee I will forgive thee."

"No she in Italy, upon my soul."

"Ah, there is one somewhere, then! Where? Where?"

"In Holland, my native country."

"Ah! Marie de Bourgoyne is fair, they say. Yet she is but a child."

"Princess, she I love is not noble. She is as I am. Nor is she so fair as thou. Yet is she fair, and linked to my heart forever by her virtues, and by all the dangers and griefs we have borne together, and for one another. Forgive me, but I would not wrong my Margaret for all the highest dames in Italy."

The slighted beauty started to her feet and stood opposite him, as beautiful, but far more terrible, than when she slapped Floretta, for then her cheeks were red but now they were pale, and her eyes full of concentrated fury.

"This to my face, unmannered wretch!" she cried. "Was I born to be insulted, as well as scorned, by such as thou? Beware! We nobles brook no rivals. Bethink thee whether is better, the love of a Cesarini, or her hate; for after all I have said and done to thee, it must be love or hate between us and to the death. Choose now!"

He looked up at her with wonder and awe as she stood towering over him in her Roman toga, offering this strange alternative. He seemed to have affronted a goddess of antiquity—he, a poor puny mortal. He sighed deeply, but spoke not. Perhaps something in his deep and patient sigh touched a tender chord in that ungoverned creature; or perhaps the time had come for one passion to ebb and another to flow. The Princess sank languidly into a seat, and the tears began to steal rapidly down her cheeks.

"Alas! alas!" said Gerard. "Weep not, sweet lady. Your tears they do accuse me, and I am like to weep for company. My kind patron, be yourself! You will live to see how much better a friend I was to you than I seemed."

"I see it now, Gerardo," said the Princess. "Friend is the word—the only word can ever pass between us twain. I was mad. Any other man had ta'en advantage of my folly. You must teach me to be your friend and nothing more."

Gerard hailed this proposition with joy, and told her out of Cicero how godlike a thing was friendship, and how much better and rarer and more lasting than love. To prove to her he was capable of it, he even told her about Denys and himself. She listened with her eyes half-shut, watching his words to fathom his character and learn his weak point. At last, she addressed him calmly thus:

"Leave me now, Gerardo, and come as usual tomorrow. You will find your lesson well bestowed." She held out her hand to him. He kissed it, and went away pondering deeply this strange interview, and wondering whether he had done prudently or not.

The next day he was received with marked distance, and the Princess stood before him literally like a statue, and after a very short sitting, excused herself and dismissed him. Gerard felt the chilling difference, but said to himself, "She is wise." So she was in her way.

The next day he found the Princess waiting for him surrounded by young nobles flattering her to the skies. She and they treated him like a dog that could do one little trick they could not. The cavaliers in particular criticized his work with a mass of ignorance and insolence combined that made his cheeks burn. The Princess watched his face demurely with half-closed eyes, at each sting the insects gave him: And when they had fled, had her doors closed against every one of them for their pains.

The next day Gerard found her alone, cold, and silent. After standing to him so some time, she said, "You treated my company with less respect than became you."

"Did I, signora?"

"Did you? You fired up at the comments they did you the honor to make on your work."

"Nay, I said naught," observed Gerard.

"Oh, high looks speak as plain as high words. Your cheeks were red as blood."

"I was nettled a moment at seeing so much ignorance and ill-nature together."

"Now it is me, their hostess, you affront."

"Forgive me, signora, and acquit me of design. It would ill become me to affront the kindest patron and friend I have in Rome—but one."

"How humble we are all of a sudden! In sooth, Ser Gerardo, you are a capital feigner. You can insult or truckle at will."

"Truckle? To whom?"

"To me, for one, to one whom you affronted for a baseborn girl like yourself, but whose patronage you claim all the same."

Gerard rose, and put his hand to his heart. "These are biting words, signora. Have I really deserved them?"

"Oh, what are words to an adventurer like you? Cold steel is all you fear."

"I am no swashbuckler, yet I have met steel with steel, and methinks I had rather face your kinsmen's swords than your cruel tongue, lady. Why do you use me so?"

"Gerar-do, for no good reason but because I am wayward, and shrewish, and curst, and because everybody admires me but you."

"I admire you too, signora. Your friends may flatter you more, but believe me they have not the eye to see half your charms. Their babble yesterday showed me that. None admire you more truly, or wish you better, than the poor artist who might not be your lover, but hoped to be your friend. But no, I see that may not be between one so high as you and one so low as I."

"Ay, but it shall, Gerardo!" said the Princess, eagerly. "I will not be so curst. Tell me now where abides thy Margaret, and I will give thee a present for her, and on that you and I will be friends."

"She is the daughter of a physician called Peter, and they bide at Sevenbergen—ah me, shall I e'er see it again?"

"'Tis well. Now go." And she dismissed him somewhat abruptly.

Poor Gerard. He began to wade in deep waters when he encountered this Italian Princess. He resolved to go no more when once he had finished her likeness. Indeed he now regretted having undertaken so long and laborious a task. This resolution was shaken for a moment by his next reception, which was all gentleness and kindness. After standing to him some time in her toga, she said she was fatigued, and wanted his assistance in another way. Would he teach her to draw a little? He sat down beside her, and taught her to make easy lines. He found her wonderfully apt. He said so.

"I had a teacher before thee, Gerar-do. Ay, and one as handsome as thyself." She then went to a drawer and brought out several heads drawn with a complete ignorance of the art, but with great patience and natural talent. They were all heads of Gerard, and full of spirit, and really not unlike. One was his very image.

"There," said she. "Now thou seest who was my teacher."

"Not I, signora."

"What, know you not who teaches us women to do all things? 'Tis love, Gerar-do. Love made me draw because thou drawest, Gerar-do. Love prints thine image in my bosom. My fingers touch the pen, and love supplies the want of art, and lo! thy beloved features lie upon the paper."

Gerard opened his eyes with astonishment at this return to an interdicted topic. "Oh, signora, you promised me to be friends and nothing more."

She laughed in his face. "How simple you are! Who believes a woman promising nonsense, impossibilities? Friendship, foolish boy—who ever built that temple on red ashes? Nay, Gerardo," she added gloomily, "between thee and me it must be love or hate."

"Which you will, signora," said Gerard, firmly. "But for me I will neither love nor hate you, but with your permission I will leave you." And he rose abruptly.

She rose too pale as death, and said: "Ere thou leavest me so, know thy fate. Outside that door are armed men who wait to slay thee at a word from me."

"But you will not speak that word, signora."

"That word I will speak. Nay, more, I shall noise it abroad it was for proffering brutal love to me thou wert slain, and I will send a special messenger to Sevenbergen, a cunning messenger, well taught his lesson. Thy Margaret shall know thee dead, and think thee faithless. Now, go to thy grave—a dog's. For a man thou art not."

Gerard turned pale, and stood dumb-stricken. "God have mercy on us both!"

"Nay, have thou mercy on her, and on thyself. She will never know in Holland what thou dost in Rome, unless I be driven to tell her my tale. Come, yield thee, *Gerar-do mio*. What will it cost thee to say thou lovest me? I ask thee but to feign it handsomely. Thou art young. Die not for the poor pleasure of denying a lady what—the shadow of a heart. Who will shed a tear for thee? I tell thee men will laugh, not weep, over thy tombstone—ah!" She ended in a little scream, for Gerard threw himself in a moment at her feet and poured out in one torrent of eloquence the story of his love and Margaret's. How he had been imprisoned, hunted with bloodhounds for her, driven to exile for her; how she now pined at home. How he had walked through Europe, environed by perils, torn by savage brutes, attacked by furious men with sword and ax and trap, robbed, shipwrecked for her.

The Princess trembled, and tried to get away from him. But he held her robe, he clung to her, he made her hear his pitiful story and Margaret's. He caught her hand, and clasped it between both his, and his tears fell fast on her hand as he implored her to think on all the woes of the true lovers she would part; and what but remorse, swift and lasting, could come of so deep a love betrayed, and so false a love feigned, with mutual hatred lurking at the bottom.

In such moments none ever resisted Gerard. The Princess, after in vain trying to get away from him, for she felt his power over her, began to waver, and sigh, and her bosom to rise and fall tumultuously, and her fiery eyes to fill.

"You conquer me," she sobbed. "You, or my better angel. Leave Rome!"

"I will, I will."

"If you breathe a word of my folly, it will be your last."

"Think not so poorly of me. You are my benefactress once more. Is it for me to slander you?"

"Go! I will send you the means. I know myself. If you cross my path again, I shall kill you. *Addio*. My heart is broken."

She touched her bell. "Floretta," she said, in a choked voice, "take him safe out of the house through my chamber and by the side postern."

He turned at the door. She was leaning with one hand on a chair, crying, with averted head. Then he thought only of her kindness, and ran back and kissed her robe. She never moved. Once clear of the house he darted home, thanking Heaven for his escape, soul and body.

"Landlady," said he, "there is one would pick a quarrel with me. What is to be done?"

"Strike him first, and at vantage! Get behind him, and then draw."

"Alas, I lack your Italian courage. To be serious, 'tis a noble."

"Oh, holy saints, that is another matter! Change thy lodging awhile, and keep snug, and alter the fashion of thy habits."

She then took him to her own niece, who let lodgings at some little distance, and installed him there. He had little to do now, and no Princess to draw, so he set himself resolutely to read that deed of Floris Brandt, from which he had hitherto been driven by the abominably bad writing. He mastered it, and saw at once that the loan on this land must have been paid over and over again by the rents, and that Ghysbrecht was keeping Peter Brandt out of his own.

"Fool, not to have read this before!" he cried. He hired a horse and rode down to the nearest port. A vessel was to sail for Amsterdam in four days. He took a passage; and paid a small sum to secure it.

"The land is too full of cutthroats for me," said he, "and 'tis lovely fair weather for the sea. Our Dutch skippers are not shipwrecked like these bungling Italians."

When he returned home, there sat his old landlady with her eyes sparkling.

"You are in luck, my young master," said she. "All the fish run to your net this day, methinks. See what a lackey hath brought to our house. This bill and this bag."

Gerard broke the seals, and found it full of silver crowns. The letter contained a mere slip of paper with this line, cut out of some MS.—"*La lingua non ha osso, ma fa rompere il dosso.*"[1]

[1] The tongue has no bone, but it can break a back.

"Fear me not!" said Gerard, aloud. "I'll keep mine between my teeth."

"What is that?"

"Oh, nothing. Am I not happy, dame? I am going back to my sweetheart with money in one pocket and land in the other." And he fell to dancing around her.

"Well," said she, "I trow nothing could make you happier."

"Nothing, except to be there."

"Well, that is a pity, for I thought to make you a little happier with a letter from Holland."

"A letter? For me? Where? How? Who brought it? Oh, dame!"

"A stranger, a painter, with a reddish face and an outlandish name—Anselmin, I trow."

"Hans Memling? A friend of mine. God bless him!"

"Ay, that is it, Anselmin. He could scarce speak a word, but a had the wit to name thee; and a puts the letter down, and a nods and smiles, and I nods and smiles, and gives him a pint o'wine, and it went down him like a spoonful."

"That is Hans, honest Hans. Oh, dame, I am in luck today—but I deserve it. For, I care not if I tell you, I have just overcome a great temptation for dear Margaret's sake."

"Who is she?"

"Nay, I'd have my tongue cut out sooner than betray her, but oh, it *was* a temptation. Gratitude pushing me wrong, Beauty almost divine pulling me wrong: curses, reproaches, and, hardest of all to resist, gentle tears from eyes used to command. Sure some saint helped me, Anthony belike. But my reward is come."

"Ay, is it, lad, and no farther off than my pocket. Come out, Gerard's reward." And she brought a letter out of her capacious pocket.

Gerard threw his arm around her neck and hugged her. "My best friend," said he, "my second mother, I'll read it to you."

"Ay, do, do."

"Alas, it is not from Margaret! This is not her hand." And he turned it about.

"Alack, but may be her bill is within. The lasses are aye for gliding in their bills under cover of another hand."

"True. Whose hand is this? Sure I have seen it. I trow 'tis my dear friend the Demoiselle Van Eyck. Oh, then Margaret's bill *will* be inside." He tore it open. "Nay, 'tis all in one writing. 'Gerard, my well beloved son,'—she never called me that before that I mind—'this letter brings thee heavy news from one would liever send thee joyful tidings. Know that Margaret Brandt died in these arms on Thursday sennight last.' What does the doting old woman mean by that? 'The last word on her lips was "Gerard." She said, "Tell him I prayed for him at my last hour, and bid him pray for me." She died very comfortable, and I saw her laid in the earth, for her father was useless, as you shall know. So no more at present from her that is with sorrowing heart thy loving friend and servant,   'MARGARET VAN EYCK.'

"Ay, that is her signature, sure enough. Now what d'ye think of that, dame?" cried Gerard with a grating laugh. "There is a pretty letter to send to a poor fellow so far from home. But it is Reicht Heynes I blame for humoring the old woman and letting her do it. As for the old woman herself, she dotes, she has lost her head, she is fourscore. Oh, my heart, I'm choking! For all that, she ought to be locked up, or her hands tied. Say this had come to a fool, say I was idiot enough to believe this, know ye what I should do? Run to the top of the highest church tower in Rome and fling myself off it, cursing Heaven. Woman! Woman! What are you doing?" And he seized her rudely by the shoulder. "What are ye weeping for?" he cried in a voice all unlike his own, and loud and hoarse as a raven. "Would ye scald me to death with your tears? She believes it. She believes it. Ah, ah, ah, ah, ah, ah! —Then there is no God."

The poor woman sighed and rocked herself. "And must I be the one to bring it thee all smiling and smirking? I could kill myself for't. Death spares none," she sobbed. "Death spares none."

Gerard staggered against the window sill. "But He is master of death," he groaned. "Or they have taught me a lie. I begin to fear there is no God, and the saints are but dead bones, and Hell is master of the world. My pretty Margaret, my sweet, my loving Margaret. The best daughter, the truest lover! The pride of Holland! The darling of the world! It is a lie. Where is this caitiff Hans? I'll hunt him round the town. I'll cram his murdering falsehood down his throat."

And he seized his hat and ran furiously about the streets for hours. Toward sunset he came back white as a ghost. He had not found Memling, but his poor mind had had time to realize the woman's simple words, that death spares none. He crept into the house bent, and feeble as an old man, and refused all food. Nor would he speak, but sat, white, with great staring eyes, muttering at intervals, "There is no God."

Alarmed both on his account and her own (for he looked a desperate maniac), his landlady ran for her aunt. The good dame came, and the two women, braver together, sat one on each side of him and tried to soothe him with kind and consoling voices. But he heeded them no more than the chairs they sat on. Then the younger held a crucifix out before him, to aid her. "Maria, Mother of Heaven, comfort him," they sighed. But he sat glaring, deaf to all external sounds.

Presently, without any warning, he jumped up, struck the crucifix rudely out of his way with a curse, and made a headlong dash at the door. The poor women shrieked. But ere he reached the door, something seemed to them to draw him up straight by his hair, and twirl him round like a top. He whirled twice around with arms extended, then fell like a dead log upon the floor, with blood trickling from his nostrils and ears.

CHAPTER XXXVI

GERARD returned to consciousness and to despair. On the second day he was raving with fever on the brain. On a table hard by lay his rich auburn hair, long as a woman's. The deadlier symptoms succeeded one another rapidly. On the fifth day his leech retired and gave him up. On the sunset of that same day he fell into a deep sleep. Some said he would wake only to die. But an old gossip, whose opinion carried weight (she had been a professional nurse), declared that his youth might save him yet could he sleep twelve hours. On this his old landlady cleared the room and watched him alone. She vowed a wax candle to the Virgin for every hour he should sleep.

He slept twelve hours. The good soul rejoiced, and thanked the Virgin on her knees.

He slept twenty-four hours. His kind nurse began to doubt. At the thirtieth hour she sent for the woman of art. "Thirty hours! Shall we wake him?"

The other inspected him closely for some time.

"His breath is even, his hand moist. I know there be learned leeches would wake him, to look at his tongue, and be none the wiser; but we that be women should have the sense to let *bon* Nature alone. When did sleep ever harm the racked brain or the torn heart?"

When he had been forty-eight hours asleep, it got wind, and they had much ado to keep the curious out. But they admitted only Fra Colonna and his friend the gigantic Fra Jerome. These two relieved the women, and sat silent, the former eying his young friend with tears in his eyes. The latter with beads in his hand looked as calmly on him as he had on the sea when Gerard and he encountered it hand to hand.

At last, I think it was about the sixtieth hour of this strange sleep, the landlady touched Fra Colonna with her elbow. He looked. Gerard had opened his eyes as gently as if he had been but dozing. He stared. He drew himself up a little in bed. He put his hand to his head, and found his hair was gone.

He noticed his friend Colonna, and smiled with pleasure. But in the middle of smiling his face stopped, and was convulsed in a moment with anguish unspeakable, and he uttered a loud cry, and turned his face to the wall. His good landlady wept at this. She had known what it is to awake bereaved.

Fra Jerome recited canticles, and prayers from his breviary. Gerard rolled himself in the bedclothes. Fra Colonna went to him, and, whimpering, reminded him that all was not lost. The divine Muses were immortal. He must transfer his affection to them; they would never betray him nor fail him, like creatures of clay. The good, simple Father then hurried away, for he was overcome by his emotion. Fra Jerome remained behind.

"Young man," said he, "the Muses exist but in the brains of pagans and visionaries. The Church alone gives repose to the heart on earth, and happiness to the soul hereafter. Hath earth deceived thee, hath passion broken thy heart after tearing it, the Church opens her arms. Consecrate thy gifts to her! The Church is peace of mind."

He spoke these words solemnly at the door, and was gone as soon as they were uttered.

"The Church!" cried Gerard, rising furiously and shaking his fist after the friar. "Malediction on the Church! But for the Church I should not lie broken here, and she lie cold, cold, cold, in Holland. Oh, my Margaret! Oh, my darling, my darling! And I must run from thee the few months thou hadst to live. Cruel, cruel! The monsters, they let her die. Death comes not without some signs. These the blind, selfish wretches saw not, or recked not; but I had seen them, I that love her. Oh, had I been there, I had saved her, I had saved her. Idiot, idiot, to leave her for a moment!"

He wept bitterly a long time. Then, suddenly bursting into rage again, he cried vehemently:

"The Church! For whose sake I was driven from her—my malison be on the Church, and the hypocrites that name it to my broken heart! Accursed be the world! Ghysbrecht lives, Margaret dies. Thieves, murderers, harlots, live forever. Only angels die. Curse life! Curse death, and whosoever made them what they are!"

The friar did not hear these mad and wicked words, but only the yell of rage with which they were flung after him. It was as well. For if he had heard them, he would have had his late shipmate burned in the Forum with as little hesitation as he would have roasted a kid.

His old landlady, who had accompanied Fra Colonna down the stair, heard the raised voice, and returned in some anxiety. She found Gerard putting on his clothes, and crying. She remonstrated.

"What avails my lying here?" said he gloomily. "Can I find here that which I seek?"

"Saints preserve us! Is he distraught again? What seek ye?"

"Oblivion."

"Oblivion, my little heart? Oh, but y' are young to talk so."

"Young or old, what else have I to live for?"

He put on his best clothes. The good dame remonstrated. "My pretty Gerard, know that it is Tuesday, not Sunday."

"Oh, Tuesday is it? I thought it had been Saturday."

"Nay, thou has slept long. Thou never wearest thy brave clothes on working days. Consider."

"What I did when she lived, I did. Now I shall do whatever erst I did not. The past is the past. There lies my hair, and with it my way of life. I have served one Master as well as I could. You see my reward. Now I'll serve another, and give him a fair trial too."

"Alas," sighed the woman, turning pale, "what mean these dark words? And what new master is this whose service thou wouldst try?"

"*Satan.*"

And with this horrible declaration on his lips the miserable creature walked out with his cap and feather set jauntily on one side, and feeble limbs, and a sinister face pale as ashes, and all drawn down as if by age.

A dark cloud fell on a noble mind. His pure and unrivaled love for Margaret had been his polar star. It was quenched, and he drifted on the gloomy sea of no hope. Nor was he a prey to despair alone, but to exasperation at all his self-denial, fortitude, perils, virtue, wasted and worse than wasted; for it kept burning and stinging him that had he stayed lazily, selfishly, at home, he should have saved his Margaret's life.

These two poisons, raging together in his young blood, maddened and demoralized him. He rushed fiercely into pleasure. And in those days, even more than now, pleasure was vice. Wine, women, gambling—whatever could procure him an hour's excitement and a moment's oblivion. He plunged into these things as men tired of life have rushed among the enemy's bullets. The large sums he had put by for Margaret gave him ample means for debauchery, and he was soon the leader of those loose companions he had hitherto kept at a distance.

His heart deteriorated along with his morals. He sulked with his old landlady for thrusting gentle advice and warning on him; and finally removed to another part of the town, to be clear of remonstrance and reminiscences. When he had carried this game on some time, his hand became less steady, and he could no longer write to satisfy himself. Moreover, his patience declined as the habits of pleasure grew on him. So he gave up that art, and took likenesses in colors.

But this he neglected whenever the idle rakes, his companions, came for him. And so he dived in foul waters, seeking that sorry oyster shell, Oblivion. Enough—the man was not born to do things by halves. And he was not vicious by halves.

His humble female friends often gossiped about him. His old landlady told Teresa he was going to the bad, and prayed her to try and find out where he was. Teresa told her husband Lodovico his sad story, and bade him look about and see if he could discover the young man's present abode. "Shouldst remember his face, *Lodovico mio?*"

"Teresa, a man in my way of life never forgets a face, least of all a benefactor's. But thou knowest I seldom go abroad by daylight."

Teresa sighed. "And how long is it to be so, Lodovico?"

"Till some cavalier passes his sword through me. They will not let a poor fellow like me take to any honest trade."

Pietro Vanucci was one of those who bear prosperity worse than adversity. Having been ignominiously ejected for late hours by their old landlady, and meeting Gerard in the street, he greeted him warmly and soon after took up his quarters in the same house. He brought with him a lad called Andrea, who ground his colors, and was his pupil and also his model, being a youth of rare beauty, and as sharp as a needle.

Pietro had not quite forgotten old times, and professed a warm friendship for Gerard. Gerard, in whom all warmth of sentiment seemed extinct, submitted coldly to the other's friendship. And a fine acquaintance it was. This Pietro was not only a libertine, but half a misanthrope, and an open infidel. And so they ran in couples, with mighty little in common. Oh, rare phenomenon!

One day when Gerard had undermined his health, and taken the bloom off his beauty, and run through most of his money, Vanucci got up a gay party to mount the Tiber in a boat drawn by buffaloes. Lorenzo de' Medici had imported these creatures into Florence about three years before. But they were new in Rome, and nothing would content this beggar on horseback, Vanucci, but being drawn by the brutes up the Tiber.

Each libertine was to bring a lady, and she must be handsome, or he be fined. But the one that should contribute the loveliest was to be crowned with laurel, and voted a public benefactor. They got a splendid galley, and twelve buffaloes. And all the libertines and their female accomplices assembled by degrees at the place of embarkation. But no Gerard. They waited for him some time, at first patiently, then impatiently. Vanucci excused him.

"I heard him say he had forgotten to provide himself with a farthingale. Comrades, the good lad is hunting for a beauty fit to take rank among these peerless dames. Consider the difficulty, ladies, and be patient!"

At last Gerard was seen at some distance with a female in his hand.

"She is long enough," said one of her sex, criticizing her from afar.

"Gemini, what step she takes!" said another. "Oh, it is wise to hurry into good company!" was Pietro's excuse.

But when the pair came up, satire was choked. Gerard's companion was a peerless beauty; she extinguished the boatload as stars the rising sun. Tall, but not too tall, and straight as a dart, yet supple as a young panther. Her face a perfect oval, her forehead white, her cheeks a rich olive with the eloquent blood mantling below; and her glorious eyes fringed with long thick silken eyelashes that seemed made to sweep up sensitive hearts by the half-dozen. Saucy red lips, and teeth of the whitest ivory.

The women were visibly depressed by this wretched sight, the men in ecstasies—they received her with loud shouts and waving of caps, and one enthusiast even went down on his knees upon the boat's gunwale, and hailed her of origin divine. But his *chère amie* pulling his hair for it—and the goddess giving him a little kick, cotemporaneously—he lay supine, and the peerless creature frisked over his body without deigning him a look, and took her seat at the prow. Pietro Vanucci sat in a sort of collapse, glaring at her, and gaping with his mouth open like a dying codfish. The drover spoke to the buffaloes, the ropes tightened, and they moved upstream.

At this moment a galley drifting slowly down stream got entangled for an instant in their ropes: for, the river turning suddenly, they had shot out into the stream, and this galley came between them and the bank. In it a lady of great beauty was seated under a canopy with gallants and dependents standing behind her. Gerard looked up at the interruption. It was the Princess Claelia. He colored and withdrew his hand from Marcia's head.

Two of the females had been for some time past putting their heads together and casting glances at Marcia. One of them now addressed her.

"Signorina, do you love almonds?"

The speaker had a lapful of them.

"Yes, I love them, when I can get them," said Marcia, pettishly, and eying the fruit with ill-concealed desire, "but yours is not the hand to give me any, I trow."

"You are much mistook," said the other. "Here, catch!"

And suddenly threw a double handful into Marcia's lap. Marcia brought her knees together by an irresistible instinct.

"Aha, you are caught, my lad," cried she of the nuts. "'Tis a man, or a boy. A woman still parteth her knees to catch the nuts the surer in her apron; but a man closeth his for fear they shall fall between his hose. Confess now, didst never wear farthingale ere today?"

"Give me another handful, sweetheart, and I'll tell thee."

"There! I said he was too handsome for a woman."

"Ser Gerard, they have found me out," observed the epicene, calmly cracking an almond. The libertines vowed it was impossible, and all glared at the goddess like a battery. But Vanucci struck in, and reminded the gaping gazers of a recent controversy, in which they had, with a unanimity not often found among dunces, laughed Gerard and him to scorn for saying that men were as beautiful as women in a true artist's eye.

"Where are ye now? This is my boy Andrea. And you have all been down on your knees to him."

"The little impostor! Duck him!"

"What for, signors?" cried Andrea in dismay, and lost his rich carnation. But the females collected round him, and vowed nobody should harm a hair of his head.

But one there was who was still among these butterflies but no longer of them. The sight of the Princess Claelia had torn open his wound. Scarce three months ago he had declined the love of that peerless creature, a love illicit and insane, but at least refined. How much lower had he fallen now!

How happy he must have been, when the blandishments of Claelia, that might have melted an anchorite, could not tempt him from the path of loyalty! Now what was he? He had blushed at her seeing him in such company. Yet it was his daily company. He hung over the boat in moody silence. And from that hour another phase of his misery began, and grew up on him.

Some wretched fools try to drown care in drink. The fumes of intoxication vanish; the inevitable care remains, and must be faced at last—with an aching head, a disordered stomach, and spirits artificially depressed. Gerard's conduct had been of a piece with these maniacs'. To survive his terrible blow he needed all his forces—his virtue, his health, his habits of labor, and the calm sleep that is labor's satellite; above all, his piety. Yet all these balms to wounded hearts he flung away, and trusted to moral intoxication. Its brief fumes fled; the bereaved heart lay still heavy as lead within his bosom; but now the dark vulture Remorse sat upon it rending it.

Broken health, means wasted, innocence fled, Margaret parted from him by another gulf wider than the grave! The hot fit of despair passed away. The cold fit of despair came on. Then this miserable young man spurned his gay companions, and all the world. He wandered alone. He drank wine alone to stupefy himself, and paralyze a moment the dark foes to man that preyed upon his soul. He wandered alone amid the temples of old Rome, and lay stony-eyed, woebegone, among their ruins, worse wrecked than they.

Last of all came the climax, to which solitude, that gloomy yet fascinating foe of minds diseased, pushes the hopeless. He wandered alone at night by dark streams, and eyed them, and eyed them with decreasing repugnance. There glided peace, perhaps annihilation. What else was left him?

Where was Teresa? Where his hearty, kind, old landlady? They would see with their homely but swift intelligence; they would see and save. No, they knew not where he was, or whither he was gliding. And is there no mortal eye upon the poor wretch, and the dark road he is going? Yes, one eye there is upon him, watching his every movement, following him abroad, tracking him home. And that eye is the eye of an enemy. An enemy to the death.

CHAPTER XXXVII

In an apartment richly furnished, the floor covered with striped and spotted skins of animals, a lady sat with her arms extended before her and her hands half-clenched. The agitation of her face corresponded with this attitude. She was pale and red by turns, and her foot restless. Presently the curtain was drawn by a domestic. The lady's brow flushed. The maid said, in an awe-struck whisper, "Altezza, the man is here."

The lady bade her admit him, and snatched up a little black mask and put it on; and in a moment her color was gone, and the contrast between her black mask and her marble cheeks was strange and fearful. A man entered bowing and scraping. It was such a figure as crowds seem made of—short hair, roundish head, plain but decent clothes, features neither comely nor forbidding. Nothing to remark in him but a singularly restless eye. After a profusion of bows he stood opposite the lady, and awaited her pleasure.

"They have told you for what you are wanted."

"Yes, signora."

"Did those who spoke to you agree as to what you are to receive?"

"Yes, signora. 'Tis the full price, and purchases the greater vendetta—unless of your benevolence you choose to content yourself with the lesser."

"I understand you not," said the lady.

"Ah, this is the signora's first. The lesser vendetta, lady, is the death of the body only. We watch our man come out of a church, or take him in an innocent hour, and so deal with him. In the greater vendetta we watch him and catch him hot from some unrepented sin, and so slay his soul as well as his body. But this vendetta is not so run upon now as it was a few years ago."

"Man, silence me his tongue, and let his treasonable heart beat no more. But his soul I have no feud with."

"So be it, signora. He who spoke to me knew not the man, nor his name, nor his abode. From whom shall I learn these?"

"From myself."

At this the man, with the first symptoms of anxiety he had shown, entreated her to be cautious and particular in this part of the business.

"Fear me not," said she. "Listen. It is a young man, tall of stature, and auburn hair, and dark-blue eyes, and an honest face would deceive a saint. He lives in the Via Claudia, at the corner house, the glover's. In that house there lodge but three males: he, and a painter short of stature and dark-visaged, and a young, slim boy. He that hath betrayed me is a stranger, fair, and taller than thou art."

The bravo listened with all his ears. "It is enough," said he. "Stay, signora, haunteth he any secret place where I may deal with him?"

"My spy doth report me he hath of late frequented the banks of Tiber after dusk, doubtless to meet his light-o'-love, who calls me her rival. Even there slay him! And let my rival come and find him, the smooth, heartless, insolent traitor."

"Be calm, signora. He will betray no more ladies."

"I know not that. He weareth a sword, and can use it. He is young and resolute."

"Neither will avail him."

"Are ye so sure of your hand? What are your weapons?"

The bravo showed her a steel gauntlet. "We strike with such force we needs must guard our hand. This is our mallet." He then undid his doublet and gave her a glimpse of a coat of mail beneath, and finally laid his glittering stiletto on the table with a flourish. The lady shuddered at first, but presently took it up in her white hand and tried its point against her finger.

"Beware, madam," said the bravo.

"What, is it poisoned?"

"Saints forbid! We steal no lives. We take them with steel point, not drugs. But 'tis newly ground, and I feared for the signora's white skin."

"His skin is as white as mine," said she, with a sudden gleam of pity. It lasted but a moment. "But his heart is black as soot. Say, do I not well to remove a traitor that slanders me?"

"The signora will settle that with her confessor. I am but a tool in noble hands, like my stiletto."

The Princess appeared not to hear the speaker. "Oh, how I could have loved him—to the death, as now I hate him. Fool, he will learn to trifle with princes, to spurn them and fawn on them and prefer the scum of the town to them, and make them a byword." She looked up. "Why loiter'st thou here? Haste thee, revenge me."

"It is customary to pay half the price beforehand, signora."

"Ah, I forgot, thy revenge is bought. Here is more than half." And she pushed a bag across the table to him. "When the blow is struck, come for the rest."

"You will soon see me again, signora."

And he retired bowing and scraping. The Princess, burning with jealousy, mortified pride, and dread of exposure (for till she knew Gerard no public stain had fallen on her), sat where he left her, masked, with her arms straight out before her, and the nails of her clenched hand nipping the table. So sat the fabled sphynx: so sits a tigress. Yet there crept a chill upon her now that the assassin was gone. And moody misgivings heaved within her, precursors of vain remorse. Gerard and Margaret were before their age. *This* was your true medieval. Proud, amorous, vindictive, generous, foolish, cunning, impulsive, unprincipled—and ignorant as dirt.

Power is the curse of such a creature. Forced to do her own crimes, the weakness of her nerves would have balanced the violence of her passions, and her bark been worse than her bite. But power gives a feeble, furious, woman male instruments. And the effect is as terrible as the combination is unnatural.

In this instance it whetted an assassin's dagger for a poor forlorn wretch just meditating suicide.

CHAPTER XXXVIII

IT HAPPENED, two days after the scene I have endeavored to describe, that Gerard, wandering through one of the meanest streets of Rome, was overtaken by a thunderstorm, and entered a low hostelry. He called for wine and, the rain continuing, soon drank himself into a half-stupid condition, and dozed with his head on his hands and his hands upon the table. In course of time the room began to fill and the noise of the rude guests to wake him. Then it was he became conscious of two figures near him conversing in a low voice.

One was a pardoner. The other, by his dress, clean but modest, might have passed for a decent tradesman; but the way he had slouched his hat over his brows so as to hide all his face except his beard showed he was one of those who shun the eye of honest men, and of the law. The pair were driving a bargain in the sin market. And by an arrangement not uncommon at that date, the crime to be forgiven was yet to be committed—under the celestial contract.

He of the slouched hat was complaining of the price pardons had reached. "If they go up any higher we poor fellows shall be shut out of Heaven altogether." The pardoner denied the charge flatly. "Indulgences were never cheaper to good husbandmen." The other inquired "who were they?" "Why such as sin by the market, like reasonable creatures. But if your will be so perverse as go and pick out a crime the Pope hath set his face against, blame yourself, not me."

Then, to prove that crime of one sort or another was within the means of all but the very scum of society, he read out the scale from a written parchment. It was a curious list, but not one that could be printed in this book. And to mutilate it would be to misrepresent it. It is to be found in any great library. Suffice it to say that murder of a layman was much cheaper than many crimes my lay readers would deem light by comparison. This told, and by a little trifling concession on each side, the bargain was closed, the money handed over, and the aspirant to Heaven's favor forgiven beforehand for removing a layman. The price for disposing of a clerk bore no proportion. The word "assassination" was never once uttered by either merchant.

All this buzzed in Gerard's ear. But he never lifted his head from the table, only listened stupidly. However, when the parties rose and separated, he half raised his head and eyed with a scowl the retiring figure of the purchaser.

"If Margaret was alive," muttered he, "I'd take thee by the throat and throttle thee, thou cowardly stabber. But she is dead, dead, dead. Die all the world—'tis naught to me, so that I die among the first."

When he got home, there was a man in a slouched hat walking briskly to and fro on the opposite side of the way.

"Why, there is that cur again," thought Gerard.

But in his state of mind the circumstance made no impression whatever on him.

Two nights after this Pietro Vanucci and Andrea sat waiting supper for Gerard. The former grew peevish. It was past nine o'clock. At last he sent Andrea to Gerard's room on the desperate chance of his having come in unobserved. Andrea shrugged his shoulders and went. He returned without Gerard, but with a slip of paper. Andrea could not read, as scholars in his day and charity boys in ours understand the art, but he had a quick eye, and had learned how the words Pietro Vanucci looked on paper.

"That is for you, I trow," said he, proud of his intelligence.

Pietro snatched it, and read it to Andrea, with his satirical comments.

"'Dear Pietro, dear Andrea, life is too great a burden.'

"So 'tis, my lad; but that is no reason for being abroad at suppertime. Supper is not a burden.

"'Wear my habits!'

"Said the poplar to the juniper bush.

"'And thou, Andrea, mine amethyst ring, and me in both your hearts, a month or two.'

"Why, Andrea?

"'For my body, ere this ye read, it will lie in Tiber. Trouble not to look for it. 'Tis not worth the pains. Oh, unhappy day that it was born, oh, happy night that rids me of it!

"'Adieu, adieu!

"'The brokenhearted Gerard.'"

"Here is a sorry jest of the peevish rogue," said Pietro. But his pale cheek and chattering teeth belied his words. Andrea filled the house with his cries.

"Oh, miserable day! Oh, calamity of calamities! Gerard, my friend, my sweet patron! Help! Help! He is killing himself! Oh, good people, help me save him!"

And after alarming all the house he ran into the street, bareheaded, imploring all good Christians to help him save his friend. A number of persons soon collected. But poor Andrea could not animate their sluggishness. Go down to the river? No. It was not their business. What part of the river? It was a wild-goose chase. It was not lucky to go down to the river after sunset. Too many ghosts walked those banks all night.

A lackey, however, who had been standing some time opposite the house said he would go with Andrea, and this turned three or four of the younger ones. The little band took the way to the river. The lackey questioned Andrea. Andrea, sobbing, told him about the letter, and Gerard's moody ways of late. That lackey was a spy of the Princess Claelia.

Their Italian tongues went fast till they neared the Tiber. But the moment they felt the air from the river, and the smell of the stream in the calm spring night, they were dead silent. The moon shone calm and clear in a cloudless sky. Their feet sounded loud and ominous. Their tongues were hushed.

Presently, hurrying round a corner, they met a man. He stopped irresolute at sight of them. The man was bareheaded, and his dripping hair glistened in the moonlight; and at the next step they saw his clothes were drenched with water.

"Here he is!" cried one of the young men, unacquainted with Gerard's face and figure.

The stranger turned instantly and fled. They ran after him might and main, Andrea leading, and the Princess's lackey next. Andrea gained on him, but in a moment he twisted up a narrow alley. Andrea shot by, unable to check himself, and the pursuers soon found themselves in a labyrinth in which it was vain to pursue a quick-footed fugitive who knew every inch of it, and could now only be followed by the ear.

They returned to their companions, and found them standing on the spot where the man had stood, and utterly confounded. For Pietro had assured them that the fugitive had neither the features nor the stature of Gerard.

"Are ye verily sure?" said they. "He had been in the river. Why, in the saints' names, fled he at our approach?"

Then said Vanucci: "Friends, methinks this has naught to do with him we seek. What shall we do, Andrea?"

Here the lackey put in his word. "Let us track him to the water's side, to make sure. See, he hath come dripping all the way."

This advice was approved, and with very little difficulty they tracked the man's course. But soon they encountered a new enigma. They had gone scarcely fifty yards ere the drops turned away from the river, and took them to the gate of a large gloomy building. It was a monastery. They stood irresolute before it, and gazed at the dark pile. It seemed to them to hide some horrible mystery. But presently Andrea gave a shout.

"Here be the drops again," cried he. "And this road leadeth to the river."

They resumed the chase, and soon it became clear the drops were now leading them home. The tracks became wetter and wetter, and took them to the Tiber's edge. And there on the bank a bucketful appeared to have been discharged from the stream.

At first they shouted, and thought they had made a discovery, but reflection showed them it amounted to nothing. Certainly a man had been in the water, and had got out of it in safety; but that man was not Gerard. One said he knew a fisherman hard by that had nets and drags. They found the fisher and paid him liberally to sink nets in the river below the place, and to drag it above and below, and promised him gold should he find the body. Then they ran vainly up and down the river, which flowed so calm and voiceless, holding this and a thousand more strange secrets. Suddenly Andrea, with a cry of hope, ran back to the house. He returned in less than half an hour.

"No." He groaned, and wrung his hands.

"What is the hour?" asked the lackey.

"Four hours past midnight."

"My pretty lad," said the lackey, solemnly, "say a mass for thy friend's soul, for he is not among living men."

The morning broke. Worn out with fatigue, Andrea and Pietro went home, heartsick. The days rolled on, mute as the Tiber as to Gerard's fate.

It would indeed have been strange if with such barren data as they possessed those men could have read the handwriting on the river's bank. For there on that spot an event had just occurred which, take it altogether, was perhaps without a parallel in the history of mankind, and may remain so to the end of time. But it shall be told in a very few words, partly by me, partly by an actor in the scene.

Gerard, then, after writing his brief adieu to Pietro and Andrea, had stolen down to the river at nightfall. He had taken his measures with a dogged resolution not uncommon in those who are bent on self-destruction. He filled his pockets with all the silver and copper he possessed, that he might sink the surer, and, so provided, hurried to a part of the stream that he had seen was little frequented.

There are some, especially women, who look about to make sure there is somebody at hand. But this resolute wretch looked about him to make sure there was nobody. And, to his annoyance, he observed a single figure leaning against the corner of an alley. So he affected to stroll carelessly away, but returned to the spot. Lo, the same figure emerged from a side street and loitered about.

"Can he be watching me? Can he know what I am here for?" thought Gerard. "Impossible."

He went briskly off, walked along a street or two, made a detour, and came back. The man had vanished. But, lo, on Gerard looking all round, to make sure, there he was a few yards behind, apparently fastening his shoe. Gerard saw he was watched, and at this moment observed in the moonlight a steel gauntlet in his sentinel's hand. Then he knew it was an assassin. Strange to say, it never occurred to him that his was the life aimed at. To be sure, he was not aware he had an enemy in the world.

He turned and walked up to the bravo. "My good friend," said he eagerly, "sell me thine arm! A single stroke! See, here is all I have," and he forced his money into the bravo's hands. "Oh, prithee, prithee, do one good deed, and rid me of my hateful life!" And even while speaking he undid his doublet, and bared his bosom. The man stared in his face.

"Why do ye hesitate?" shrieked Gerard. "Have ye no bowels? Is it so much pains to lift your arm and fall it? Is it because I am poor, and can't give ye gold? Useless wretch, canst only strike a man behind, not look one in the face. There, then, do but turn thy head and hold thy tongue!"

And with a snarl of contempt he ran from him, and flung himself into the water.

"Margaret!"

At the heavy plunge of his body in the stream the bravo seemed to recover from a stupor. He ran to the bank, and with a strange cry the assassin plunged in after the self-destroyer.

CHAPTER XXXIX

A WOMAN has her own troubles, as a man has his. And we male writers seldom do more than indicate the griefs of the other sex. The intelligence of the female reader must come to our aid, and fill up our cold outlines. So have I indicated, rather than described, what Margaret Brandt went through up to that eventful day when she entered Eli's house an enemy, read her sweetheart's letter, and remained a friend.

And now a woman's greatest trial drew near, and Gerard far away. She availed herself but little of Eli's sudden favor. For this reserve she had always a plausible reason ready, and never hinted at the true one, which was this— there were two men in that house at sight of whom she shuddered with instinctive antipathy and dread. She had read wickedness and hatred in their faces, and mysterious signals of secret intelligence. She preferred to receive Catherine and her daughter at home. The former went to see her every day, and was wrapped up in the expected event.

Catherine was one of those females whose office is to multiply and rear the multiplied, who when at last they consent to leave off pelting one out of every room in the house with babies, hover about the fair scourges that are still in full swing, and do so cluck they seem to multiply by proxy. It was in this spirit she entreated Eli to let her stay at Rotterdam while he went back to Tergou.

"The poor lass hath not a soul about her that knows anything about anything. What avail a pair o' soldiers? Why, that sort o' cattle should be putten out o' doors the first, at such a time."

Need I say that this was a great comfort to Margaret? Poor soul, she was full of anxiety as the time drew near. She should die, and Gerard away. But things balance themselves. Her poverty, and her father's helplessness, which had cost her such a struggle, stood her in good stead now. Adversity's iron hand had forced her to battle the lassitude that overpowers the rich of her sex, and to be forever on her feet, working. She kept this up to the last by Catherine's advice.

And so it was that one fine evening just at sunset, she lay weak as water, but safe, with a little face by her side, and the heaven of maternity opening on her.

"Why dost weep, sweetheart? All of a sudden?"

"He is not here to see it."

"Ah, well, lass, he will be here ere 'tis weaned. Meantime, God hath been as good to thee as to e'er a woman born. And do but bethink thee it might have been a girl. Didn't my very own Kate threaten me with one? And here we have got the bonniest boy in Holland, and a rare heavy one, the saints be praised for't."

"Ay, Mother, I am but a sorry, ungrateful wretch to weep. If only Gerard were here to see it! 'Tis strange, I bore him well enow to be away from me in my sorrow; but oh, it doth seem so hard he should not share my joy. Prithee, prithee, come to me, Gerard, dear, dear, Gerard!" And she stretched out her feeble arms.

Catherine bustled about, but avoided Margaret's eyes; for she could not restrain her own tears at hearing her own absent child thus earnestly addressed. Presently, turning round, she found Margaret looking at her with a singular expression.

"Heard you naught?"

"No, my lamb. What?"

"I did cry on Gerard but now."

"Ay, ay, sure I heard that."

"Well, he answered me."

"Tush, girl, say not that."

"Mother, as sure as I lie here with his boy by my side, his voice came back to me—'Margaret!' So. Yet methought 'twas not his *happy* voice. But that might be the distance. All voices go off sad-like at a distance. Why art not happy, sweetheart, and I so happy this night? Mother, I seem never to have felt a pain or known a care." And her sweet eyes turned and gloated on the little face in silence.

That very night Gerard flung himself into the Tiber. And, that very hour she heard him speak her name, he cried aloud in death's jaws and despair's.

"Margaret!"

Account for it those who can. I cannot.

CHAPTER XL

IN THE guest chamber of a Dominican convent lay a single stranger, exhausted by successive and violent fits of nausea, which had at last subsided, leaving him almost as weak as Margaret lay that night in Holland. A huge wood fire burned on the hearth, and beside it hung the patient's clothes. A gigantic friar sat by his bedside reading pious collects aloud from his breviary. The patient at times eyed him, and seemed to listen: at others, closed his eyes and moaned.

The monk knelt down with his face touching the ground and prayed for him, then rose and bade him farewell. "Day breaks," said he. "I must prepare for matins."

"Good Father Jerome, before you go, how came I hither?"

"By the hand of Heaven. You flung away God's gift. He bestowed it on you again. Think on it! Hast tried the world, and found its gall. Now try the Church! The Church is peace. *Pax vobiscum.*"

He was gone. Gerard lay back, meditating and wondering, till, weak and wearied, he fell into a doze. When he awoke again he found a new nurse seated beside him. It was a layman, with an eye as small and restless as Friar Jerome's was calm and majestic. The man inquired earnestly how he felt.

"Very, very weak. Where have I seen you before, messer?"

"None the worse for my gauntlet?" inquired the other with considerable anxiety. "I was fain to strike you withal, or both you and I should be at the bottom of Tiber."

Gerard stared at him. "What, 'twas you saved me? How?"

"Well, signor, I was by the banks of Tiber on—on—an errand, no matter what. You came to me and begged hard for a dagger stroke. But ere I could oblige you, ay, even as you spoke to me, I knew you for the signor that saved my wife and child upon the sea."

"It *is* Teresa's husband. And an assassin?!!?"

"At your service. Well, Ser Gerard, the next thing was, you flung yourself into Tiber, and bade me hold aloof."

"I remember that."

"Had it been any but you, believe me I had obeyed you, and not wagged a finger. Men are my foes. They may all hang on one rope or drown in one river for me. But when thou, sinking in Tiber, didst cry 'Margaret!'——"

"Ah!"

"My heart it cried 'Teresa!' How could I go home and look her in the face did I let thee die, and by the very death thou savedst her from? So in I went, and luckily for us both I swim like a duck. You, seeing me near, and being bent on destruction, tried to grip me, and so end us both. But I swam round thee, and (receive my excuses) so buffeted thee on the nape of the neck with my steel glove that thou lost sense, and I with much ado, the stream being strong, did draw thy body to land, but insensible and full of water. Then I took thee on my back and made for my own home. 'Teresa will nurse him, and be pleased with me,' thought I. But hard by this monastery, a holy friar, the biggest e'er I saw, met us and asked the matter. So I told him. He looked hard at thee. 'I know the face,' quoth he. ' 'Tis one Gerard, a fair youth from Holland.' 'The same,' quo' I. Then said his Reverence, 'He hath friends among our brethren. Leave him with us! Charity, it is our office.'

"Also he told me they of the convent had better means to tend thee than I had. And that was true enow. So I just bargained to be let in to see thee once a day, and here thou art."

And the miscreant cast a strange look of affection and interest upon Gerard. Gerard did not respond to it. He felt as if a snake were in the room. He closed his eyes.

"Ah, thou wouldst sleep," said the miscreant eagerly. "I go."

And he retired on tiptoe with a promise to come every day. Gerard lay with his eyes closed—not asleep, but deeply pondering. Saved from death by an assassin! Was not this the finger of Heaven? Of that Heaven he had insulted, cursed, and defied. He shuddered at his blasphemies. He tried to pray. He found he could utter prayers. But he could not pray.

"I am doomed eternally," he cried, "doomed, doomed!"

The organ of the convent church burst on his ear in rich and solemn harmony. Then rose the voices of the choir chanting a full service. Among them was one that seemed to hover above the others, and tower toward Heaven, a sweet boy's voice, full, pure, angelic. He closed his eyes and listened. The days of his own boyhood flowed back upon him in those sweet, pious harmonies. No earthly dross there, no foul, fierce passions, rending and corrupting the soul. Peace, peace, sweet, balmy peace.

"Ay," he sighed, "the Church is peace of mind. Till I left her bosom I ne'er knew sorrow, nor sin."

And the poor torn, worn creature wept. And even as he wept, there beamed on him the sweet and reverend face of one he had never thought to see again. It was the face of Father Anselm. The good Father had only reached the convent the night before last. Gerard recognized him in a moment, and cried to him: "Oh, Father Anselm, you cured my wounded body in Juliers. Now cure my hurt soul in Rome! Alas, you cannot."

Anselm sat down by the bedside, and putting a gentle hand on his head, first calmed him with a soothing word or two. He then (for he had learned how Gerard came there) spoke to him kindly but solemnly, and made him feel his crime, and urged him to repentance, and gratitude to that Divine Power which had thwarted his will to save his soul.

"Come, my son," said he, "first purge thy bosom of its load."

"Ah, Father," said Gerard, "in Juliers I could. Then I was innocent, but now, impious monster that I am, I dare not confess to you."

"Why not, my son? Thinkest thou I have not sinned against Heaven in my time, and deeply—oh, how deeply! Come, poor laden soul, pour forth thy grief, pour forth thy faults, hold back naught! Lie not oppressed and crushed by hidden sins."

And soon Gerard was at Father Anselm's knees confessing his every sin with sighs and groans of penitence.

"Thy sins are great," said Anselm. "Thy temptation also was great, terribly great. I must consult our good prior."

The good Anselm kissed his brow, and left him to consult the superior as to his penance. And, lo! Gerard could pray now. And he prayed with all his heart.

The phase through which this remarkable mind now passed may be summed in a word—Penitence. He turned with terror and aversion from the world, and begged passionately to remain in the convent. To him, convent-nurtured, it was like a bird returning wounded, wearied, to its gentle nest. He passed his novitiate in prayer, and mortification, and pious reading, and meditation.

The Princess Claelia's spy went home and told her that Gerard was certainly dead, the manner of his death unknown at present. She seemed literally stunned. When, after a long time, she found breath to speak at all, it was to bemoan her lot, cursed with such ready tools.

"So soon," she sighed. "See how swift these monsters are to do ill deeds. They come to us in our hot blood, and first tempt us with their venal daggers, then enact the mortal deeds we ne'er had thought on but for them."

Ere many hours had passed, her pity for Gerard and hatred of his murderer had risen to fever heat, which with this fool was blood heat.

"Poor soul! I cannot call thee back to life. But he shall never live that traitorously slew thee."

And she put armed men in ambush, and kept them on guard all day, ready, when Lodovico should come for his money, to fall on him in a certain antechamber and hack him to pieces.

"Strike at his head," said she, "for he weareth a privy coat of mail, and if he goes hence alive your own heads shall answer it."

And so she sat weeping her victim, and pulling the strings of machines to shed the blood of a second for having been her machine to kill the first.

One of the novice Gerard's self-imposed penances was to receive Lodovico kindly, feeling secretly as to a slimy serpent.

Never was self-denial better bestowed, and, like most rational penances, it soon became no penance at all. At first the pride and complacency with which the assassin gazed on the one life he had saved was perhaps as ludicrous as pathetic, but it is a great thing to open a good door in a heart. One good thing follows another through the aperture. Finding it so sweet to save life, the miscreant went on to be averse to taking it; and from that to remorse; and from remorse to something very like penitence. And here Teresa co-operated by threatening, not for the first time, to leave him unless he would consent to lead an honest life. The good Fathers of the convent lent their aid, and Lodovico and Teresa were sent by sea to Leghorn, where Teresa had friends, and the assassin settled down and became a porter. He found it miserably dull work at first—and said so.

But methinks this dull life of plodding labor was better for him than the brief excitement of being hewn in pieces by the Princess Claelia's myrmidons. His exile saved the unconscious penitent from that fate, and the Princess, balked of her revenge, took to brooding, and fell into a profound melancholy, dismissed her confessor, and took a new one with a great reputation for piety, to whom she confided what she called her griefs. The new confessor was no other than Fra Jerome. She could not have fallen into better hands.

He heard her grimly out. Then took her and shook the delusions out of her as roughly as if she had been a kitchenmaid. For, to do this hard monk justice, on the path of duty he feared the anger of princes as little as he did the sea. He showed her in a few words, all thunder and lightning, that she was the criminal of criminals.

"Thou art the devil, that with thy money hath tempted one man to slay his fellow, and then, blinded with self-love, instead of blaming and punishing thyself, art thirsting for more blood of guilty men—but not so guilty as thou."

At first she resisted, and told him she was not used to be taken to task by her confessors. But he overpowered her, and so threatened her with the Church's curse here and hereafter, and so tore the scales off her eyes, and thundered at her, and crushed her, that she sank down and groveled with remorse and terror at the feet of the gigantic Boanerges.

"Oh, holy Father, have pity on a poor weak woman, and help me save my guilty soul. I was benighted for want of ghostly counsel like thine, good Father. I waken as from a dream."

"Doff thy jewels," said Fra Jerome, sternly.

"I will. I will."

"Doff thy silk and velvet, and, in humbler garb than wears thy meanest servant, wend thou instant to Loretto."

"I will," said the Princess, faintly.

"No shoes, but a bare sandal."

"No, Father."

"Wash the feet of pilgrims both going and coming, and to such of them as be holy friars tell thy sin, and abide their admonition."

"Oh, holy Father, let me wear my mask."

"Humph!"

"Oh, mercy! Bethink thee! My features are known through Italy."

"Ay, beauty is a curse to most of ye. Well, thou mayst mask thine eyes, no more."

On this concession she seized his hand and was about to kiss it, but he snatched it rudely from her.

"What would ye do? That hand handled the Eucharist but an hour agone. Is it fit for such as thou to touch it?"

"Ah, no. But oh, go not without giving your penitent daughter your blessing."

"Time enow to ask it when you come back from Loretto."

Thus that marvelous occurrence by Tiber's banks left its mark on all the actors, as prodigies are said to do. The assassin, softened by saving the life he was paid to take, turned from the stiletto to the porter's knot. The Princess went barefoot to Loretto, weeping her crime and washing the feet of baseborn men.

And Gerard, carried from the Tiber into that convent a suicide, now passed for a young saint within its walls. Loving but experienced eyes were on him. Upon a shorter probation than usual he was admitted to priests' orders. And soon after took the monastic vows, and became a friar of Saint Dominic. Dying to the world, the monk parted with the very name by which he had lived in it, and so broke the last link of association with earthly feelings. Here Gerard ended, and Brother Clement began.

"As is the race of leaves so is that of man." And a great man budded unnoticed in a tailor's house at Rotterdam this year, and a large man dropped to earth with great éclat.

Philip Duke of Burgundy, Earl of Holland, etc., etc., lay sick at Bruges. The Duke's complaint, nameless then, is now diphtheria. It is, and was, a very weakening malady, and the Duke was old, and he died.

Philip the Good left thirty-one children, of whom one, somehow or another, was legitimate, and reigned in his stead.

The good Duke's body was carried into Burgundy, and laid in a noble mausoleum of black marble at Dijon. Holland rang with his death; and little dreamed that anything as famous was born in her territory that year. That judgment has been long reversed. Men gaze at the tailor's house where the great birth of the fifteenth century took place. In what house the good Duke died "no one knows and no one cares," as the song says. And why? Dukes Philip the Good come and go, and leave mankind not a halfpenny wiser, nor better, nor other, than they found it. But when, once in three hundred years, such a child is born to the world as Margaret's son, lo! a human torch lighted by fire from Heaven, and "*fiat lux*" thunders from pole to pole.

The Dominicans, or preaching friars, once the most powerful order in Europe, were now on the wane. Their rivals and bitter enemies, the Franciscans, were overpowering them throughout Europe, even in England, a rich and religious country where, under the name of the Black Friars, they had once been paramount.

Therefore the sagacious men who watched and directed the interests of the order were never so anxious to incorporate able and zealous sons, and send them forth to win back the world. The zeal and accomplishments of Clement, especially his rare mastery of language (for he spoke Latin, Italian, French, High and Low Dutch) soon transpired, and he was destined to travel and preach in England, corresponding with the Roman center. But Jerome, who had the superior's ear, obstructed this design.

"Clement," said he, "has the milk of the world still in his veins, its feelings, its weaknesses. Let not his newborn zeal and his humility tempt us to forgo our ancient wisdom. Try him first, and temper him, lest one day we find ourselves leaning on a reed for a staff."

"It is well advised," said the Prior. "Take him in hand thyself."

Jerome took Clement to many deathbeds. And then into noisome dungeons —places where the darkness was appalling, and the stench loathsome, pestilential, and men looking like wild beasts lay coiled in rags and filth and despair. It tried his body hard, but the soul collected all its powers to comfort such poor wretches there as were not past comfort. And Clement shone in that trial. Jerome reported that Clement's spirit was willing, but his flesh was weak.

"Good!" said Anselm. "His flesh is weak, but his spirit is willing."

It was announced to Clement that he was to go to England immediately with brother Jerome.

Clement folded his hands on his breast, and bowed his head in calm submission.

CHAPTER XLI

A CATHERINE is not an unmixed good in a strange house. The governing power is strong in her. She has scarce crossed the threshold ere the utensils seem to brighten, the hearth to sweep itself, the windows to let in more light, and the soul of an enormous cricket to animate the dwelling-place. But this cricket is a busybody. And that is a tremendous character. It has no discrimination. It sets everything to rights, and everybody. Now many things are the better for being set to rights. But everything is not. Everything is the one thing that won't stand being set to rights—except in that calm and cool retreat, the grave.

Catherine altered the position of every chair and table in Margaret's house, and perhaps for the better. But she must go farther and upset the live furniture. When Margaret's time was close at hand, Catherine treacherously invited the aid of Denys and Martin; and, on the poor simple-minded fellows asking her earnestly what service they could be, she told them they might make themselves comparatively useful by going for a little walk. So far, so good. But she intimated further that should the promenade extend into the middle of next week, all the better. This was not ingratiating.

The subsequent conduct of the strong under the yoke of the weak might have propitiated a she-bear with three cubs, one sickly. They generally slipped out of the house at daybreak, and stole in like thieves at night. And if by any chance they were at home, they went about like cats on a wall tipped with broken glass, and wearing awe-struck visages, and a general air of subjugation and depression.

But all would not do. Their very presence was ill-timed, and jarred upon Catherine's nerves. The breastplate is no armor against a female tongue: and Catherine ran infinite pins and needles of speech into them. In a word, when Margaret came downstairs, she found the kitchen swept of heroes.

Martin, old and stiff, had retreated no farther than the street, and with the honors of war; for he had carried off his baggage, a stool, and sat on it in the air. Margaret saw he was out in the sun, but was not aware he was a fixture in that luminary. She asked for Denys. "Good, kind Denys, he will be right pleased to see me about again."

Catherine, wiping a bowl with now superfluous vigor, told her Denys was gone to his friends in Burgundy. "And high time. Hasn't been a-nigh them this three years, by all accounts."

"What, gone without bidding me farewell?" said Margaret, opening two tender eyes like full-blown violets.

Catherine reddened. For this new view of the matter set her conscience pricking her. But she gave a little toss, and said, "Oh, you were asleep at the time, and I would not have you wakened."

"Poor Denys," said Margaret, and the dew gathered visibly on the open violets.

Catherine saw out of the corner of her eye, and without taking a bit of open notice, slipped off and lavished hospitality and tenderness on the surviving depopulator. It was sudden, and Martin old and stiff in more ways than one.

"No, thank you, dame. I have got used to out o' doors. And I love not changing and changing. I meddle wi' nobody here, and nobody meddles wi' me."

"Oh, you nasty, cross old wretch!" screamed Catherine, passing in a moment from treacle to sharpest vinegar. And she flounced back into the house.

On calm reflection she had a little cry. Then she half-reconciled herself to her conduct by vowing to be so kind Margaret should never miss her plagues of soldiers. But, feeling still a little uneasy, she dispersed all regrets by a process at once simple and sovereign. She took and washed the child. From head to foot she washed him in tepid water: and heroes, and their wrongs, became as dust in an ocean—of soap and water.

While this celestial ceremony proceeded, Margaret could not keep quiet. She hovered round the fortunate performer. She must have an apparent hand in it, if not a real. She put her finger into the water—to pave the way for her boy, I suppose; for she could not have deceived herself so far as to think Catherine would allow her to settle the temperature. During the ablution she knelt down opposite the little Gerard, and prattled to him with amazing fluency.

"I wish you could wash out *that*," said she, fixing her eyes on the little boy's hand.

"What?"

"What, have you not noticed? On his little finger."

Granny looked, and there was a little brown mole.

"Eh, but this is wonderful!" she cried. "Nature, my lass, y' are strong, and meddlesome to boot. Hast noticed such a mark on someone else? Tell the truth, girl!"

"What, on *him*? Nay, Mother, not I."

"Well, then, he has, and on the very spot. And you never noticed that much. But, dear heart, I forgot, you ha'n't known him from child to man as I have. I have had him hundreds o' times on my knees, the same as this, and washed him from top to toe in lukewarm water." And she swelled with conscious superiority, and Margaret looked meekly up to her as a woman beyond competition.

The new Pope favored the Dominican order. The convent received a message from the Vatican requiring a capable friar to teach at the University of Basle. Now Clement was the very monk for this—well versed in languages, and in his worldly days had attended the lectures of Guarini the Younger. His visit to England was therefore postponed, though not resigned, and meantime he was sent to Basle. But not being wanted there for three months, he was to preach on the road.

He passed out of the northern gate with his eyes lowered, and the whole man wrapped in pious contemplation. Oh, if we could paint a mind and its story, what a walking fresco was this barefooted friar! Hopeful, happy love, bereavement, despair, impiety, vice, suicide, remorse, religious despondency, penitence, death to the world, resignation. And all in twelve short months.

And now the traveler was on foot again. But all was changed: no perilous adventures now. The very thieves and robbers bowed to the ground before him, and instead of robbing him, forced stolen money on him, and begged his prayers.

The first Sunday of Clement's journey was marked by this: He prayed for the soul of Margaret. He had never done so before. Not that her eternal welfare was not dearer to him than anything on earth. It was his humility. The terrible impieties that burst from him on the news of her death horrified him who had uttered them. For a long time during his novitiate he was oppressed with religious despair. He thought he must have committed that sin against the Holy Spirit which dooms the soul forever. By degrees that dark cloud cleared away, but deep self-abasement remained. He felt his own salvation insecure, and moreover thought it would be mocking Heaven should he, the deeply stained, pray for a soul so innocent, comparatively, as Margaret's. So he used to coax good Anselm and another kindly monk to pray for her. They did not refuse, nor do it by halves. In general the good old monks (and there were good, bad, and indifferent in every convent) had a pure and tender affection for their younger brethren, which, in truth, was not of this world.

Clement then, having preached on Sunday morning in a small Italian town, and being mightily carried onward, was greatly encouraged, and that day a balmy sense of God's forgiveness and love descended on him. And he prayed for the welfare of Margaret's soul. And from that hour this became his daily habit, and the one purified tie that by memory connected his heart with earth. For his family were to him as if they had never been. The Church would not share with earth. Nor could even the Church cure the great love without annihilating the smaller ones.

During most of this journey Clement rarely felt any spring of life within him but when he was in the pulpit. The other exceptions were, when he happened to relieve some fellow creature.

He found a mob haling a decently dressed man along, who struggled and vociferated, but in a strange language. This person had walked into their town erect and sprightly, waving a mulberry branch over his head. Thereupon the natives first gazed stupidly, not believing their eyes, then pounced on him and dragged him before the podestá.

Clement went with them, but on the way drew quietly near the prisoner and spoke to him in Italian—no answer. In French, German, Dutch—no assets. Then the man tried Clement in tolerable Latin, but with a sharpish accent. He said he was an Englishman and, oppressed with the heat of Italy, had taken a bough off the nearest tree, to save his head. "In my country anybody is welcome to what grows on the highway. Confound the fools, I am ready to pay for it. But here is all Italy up in arms about a twig and a handful of leaves."

The pigheaded podestá would have sent the dogged islander to prison, but Clement mediated, and with some difficulty made the prisoner comprehend that silkworms, and by consequence mulberry leaves, were sacred, being under the wing of the sovereign, and his source of income; and urged on the podestá that ignorance of his mulberry laws was natural in a distant country, where the very tree perhaps was unknown. The opinionative islander turned the still vibrating scale by pulling out a long purse and repeating his original theory, that the whole question was mercantile. The podestá snuffed the gold, fined him a ducat for the Duke, about the value of the whole tree, and pouched the coin.

The Englishman shook off his ire the moment he was liberated, and laughed heartily at the whole thing, but was very grateful to Clement. "You are too good for this hole of a country, Father," said he. "Come to England! That is the only place in the world. I am a Kentish squire, and educated at Cambridge University. My name it is Rolfe, my place Betshanger. The man and the house are both at your service. Come over and stay till Domesday."

"I will visit thee some day, my son," said Clement, "but not to weary thy hospitality. But, alas! how shall I learn your English tongue? No book have I."

"I would give you my book of hours, Father. 'Tis in English and Latin, cheek by jowl. But then what would become of my poor soul, wanting my 'hours' in a strange land? Stay, you are a holy man, and I am an honest one, let us make a bargain—you to pray for me every day for two months, and I to give you my book of hours. Here it is. What say you to that?" And his eyes sparkled, and he was all on fire with mercantility.

Clement smiled gently at this trait, and quietly detached a MS. from his girdle, and showed him that it was in Latin and Italian.

"See, my son," said he, "Heaven hath foreseen our several needs, and given us the means to satisfy them. Let us change books, and, my dear son, I will give thee my poor prayers and welcome, not sell them thee. I love not religious bargains."

The islander was delighted. "So shall I learn the Italian tongue without risk to my eternal weal. Near is my purse, but nearer is my soul."

At a town in Tuscany the holy friar had a sudden and strange rencontre with the past. He fell in with one of those motley assemblages of patricians and plebeians, piety and profligacy, "a company of pilgrims." They were in an immense barn belonging to the inn. Clement, dusty and wearied, and no lover of idle gossip, sat in a corner studying the Englishman's hours, and making them out as much by his own Dutch as by the Latin version.

Presently a servant brought a bucket half-full of water and put it down at his feet. A female servant followed with two towels. And then a woman came forward and, crossing herself, knelt down without a word at the bucketside, removed her sleeves entirely, and motioned to him to put his feet into the water. It was some lady of rank doing penance. She wore a mask scarce an inch broad, but effectual. Moreover, she handled the friar's feet more delicately than those do who are born to such offices.

These penances were not uncommon, and Clement, though he had little faith in this form of contrition, received the services of the incognita as a matter of course. But presently she sighed deeply and, with her heartfelt sigh and her head bent low over her menial office, she seemed so bowed with penitence that he pitied her and said, calmly but gently, "Can I aught for your soul's weal, my daughter?"

She shook her head with a faint sob. "Naught, holy Father, naught, only to hear the sin of her who is most unworthy to touch thy holy feet. 'Tis part of my penance to tell sinless men how vile I am."

"Speak, my daughter."

"Father," said the lady, bending lower and lower, "these hands of mine look white, but they are stained with blood—the blood of the man I loved. Alas, you withdraw your foot! Ah, me! What shall I do? All holy things shrink from me."

"*Culpa mea! Culpa mea!*" said Clement eagerly. "My daughter, it was an unworthy movement of earthly weakness, for which *I* shall do penance. Judge not the Church by her feebler servants. Not her foot, but her bosom, is offered to thee, repenting truly. Take courage, then, and purge thy conscience of his load."

On this the lady, in a trembling whisper, and hurriedly, and cringing a little, as if she feared the Church would strike her bodily for what she had done, made this confession.

"He was a stranger, and baseborn, but beautiful as spring and wise beyond his years. I loved him. I had not the prudence to conceal my love. Nobles courted me. I ne'er thought one of humble birth could reject me. I showed him my heart—oh, shame of my sex! He drew back, yet he admired me—but innocently. He loved another, and he was constant. I resorted to a woman's wiles. They availed not. I borrowed the wickedness of men, and threatened his life, and to tell his truelover he died false to her. Ah, you shrink, your foot trembles. Am I not a monster? Then he wept and prayed to me for mercy. Then my good angel helped me, I bade him leave Rome. Gerard, Gerard, why did you not obey me?

"I thought he was gone. But two months after this I met him. Never shall I forget it. I was descending the Tiber in my galley when he came up it with a gay company, and at his side a woman beautiful as an angel, but bold and bad. That woman claimed me aloud for her rival. Traitor and hypocrite, he had exposed me to her, and to all the loose tongues in Rome. In terror and revenge I hired—a bravo. When he was gone on his bloody errand, I wavered too late. The dagger I had hired struck. He never came back to his lodgings. He was dead.

"His poor body is not found, or I should kiss its wounds and slay myself upon it. All around his very name seems silent as the grave, to which this murderous hand has sent him." Clement's eyes were drawn by her movement. He recognized her shapely arm, and soft white hand. "And, oh, he was so young to die! A poor thoughtless boy that had fallen a victim to that bad woman's arts, and she had made him tell her everything. Monster of cruelty, what penance can avail me? Oh, holy Father, what shall I do?"

Clement's lips moved in prayer, but he was silent. He could not see his duty clear. Then she took his feet and began to dry them. She rested his foot upon her soft arm, and pressed it with the towel so gently she seemed incapable of hurting a fly. Yet her lips had just told another story, and a true one.

While Clement was still praying for wisdom, a tear fell upon his foot. It decided him. "My daughter," said he, "I myself have been a great sinner."

"You, Father?"

"I, quite as great a sinner as thou, though not in the same way. The Devil has gins and snares, as well as traps. But penitence softened my impious heart, and then gratitude remolded it. Therefore, seeing you penitent, I hope you can be grateful to Him who has been more merciful to you than you have to your fellow creature. Daughter, the Church sends you comfort."

"Comfort to me? Ah, never! Unless it can raise my victim from the dead."

"Take this crucifix in thy hand, fix thine eyes on it, and listen to me," was all the reply.

"Yes, Father, but let me thoroughly dry your feet first. 'Tis ill sitting in wet feet, and you are the holiest man of all whose feet I have washed. I know it by your voice."

"Woman, I am not. As for my feet, they can wait their turn. Obey thou me!"

"Yes, Father," said the lady, humbly. But with a woman's evasive pertinacity she wreathed one towel swiftly round the foot she was drying, and placed his other foot on the dry napkin, then obeyed his command. And as she bowed over the crucifix, the low, solemn tones of the friar fell upon her ear, and his words soon made her whole body quiver with various emotions, in quick succession.

"My daughter, he you murdered—in intent—was one Gerard, a Hollander. He loved a creature as man should love none but their Redeemer and his Church. Heaven chastised him. A letter came to Rome. She was dead."

"Poor Gerard! Poor Margaret!" moaned the penitent.

Clement's voice faltered at this a moment. But soon, by a strong effort, he recovered all his calmness.

"His feeble nature yielded, body and soul, to the blow. He was stricken down with fever. He revived only to rebel against Heaven. He said, 'There is no God.'"

"Poor, poor Gerard!"

"Poor Gerard? Thou feeble, foolish woman! Nay, wicked, impious Gerard. He plunged into vice, and soiled his eternal jewel. Those you met him with were his daily companions. But know, rash creature, that the seeming woman you took to be his leman was but a boy, dressed in woman's habits to flout the others, a fair boy called Andrea. What that Andrea said to thee I know not, but be sure neither he, *nor any layman*, knows thy folly. This Gerard, rebel against Heaven, was no traitor to thee, unworthy."

The lady moaned like one in bodily agony, and the crucifix began to tremble in her trembling hands.

"Courage!" said Clement. "Comfort is at hand. From crime he fell into despair and, bent on destroying his soul, he stood one night by Tiber resolved on suicide. He saw one watching him. It was a bravo."

"Holy saints!"

"He begged the bravo to dispatch him. He offered him all his money to slay him body and soul. The bravo would not. Then this desperate sinner, not softened even by that refusal, flung himself into Tiber."

"Ah!"

"And the assassin saved his life. Thou hadst chosen for the task Lodovico, husband of Teresa, whom this Gerard had saved at sea, her and her infant child."

"He lives! He lives! He lives! I am faint."

The friar took the crucifix from her hands, fearing it might fall. A shower of tears relieved her. The friar gave her time, then continued, calmly: "Ay, he lives, thanks to thee and thy wickedness, guided to his eternal good by an almighty and all-merciful hand. Thou art his greatest earthly benefactor."

"Where is he? Where? Where?"

"What is that to thee?"

"Only to see him alive. To beg him on my knees forgive me. I swear to you I will never presume again to— How could I? He knows all. Oh, shame! Father, *does* he know?"

"All."

"Then never will I meet his eye, I should sink into the earth. But I would repair my crime. I would watch his life unseen. He shall rise in the world whence I so nearly thrust him, poor soul. The Caesare, my family, are all-powerful in Rome, and I am near their head."

"My daughter," said Clement, coldly, "he you call Gerard needs nothing man can do for him. Saved by a miracle from double death, he has left the world, and taken refuge from sin and folly in the bosom of the Church."

"A priest?"

"A priest, and a friar."

"A friar? Then you are not his confessor? Yet you know all. That gentle voice!"

She raised her head slowly, and peered at him through her mask. The next moment she uttered a faint shriek, and lay with her brow upon his bare feet.

Clement sighed. He began to doubt whether he had taken the wisest course with a creature so passionate. But young as he was, he had already learned many lessons of ecclesiastical wisdom. For one thing he had been taught to pause: that is, in certain difficulties neither to do nor say anything until the matter should clear itself a little. He therefore held his peace and prayed for wisdom.

All he did was gently to withdraw his foot. But his penitent flung her arms round it with a piteous cry, and held convulsively, and wept over it. And now the agony of shame, as well as penitence, she was in showed itself by the bright red that crept over her very throat as she lay quivering at his feet.

"My daughter," said Clement gently, "take courage. Torment thyself no more about this Gerard, who is not. As for me, I am Brother Clement, whom Heaven hath sent to thee this day to comfort thee, and help thee save thy soul. Thou hast made me thy confessor. I claim, then, thine obedience."

"Oh, yes," sobbed the penitent.

"Leave this pilgrimage, and instant return to Rome. Penitence abroad is little worth. There where we live lie the temptations we must defeat, or perish, not fly in search of others more showy, but less lethal. Easy to wash the feet of strangers, masked ourselves. Hard to be merely meek and charitable with those about us."

"I'll never, never, lay finger on her again."

"Nay, I speak not of servants only, but of dependents, kinsmen, friends. This be thy penance—the last thing at night, and the first thing after matins, call to mind thy sin and God His goodness, and so be humble, and gentle to the faults of those around thee. The world it courts the rich, but seek thou the poor. Not beggars, these for the most are neither honest nor truly poor. But rather find out those who blush to seek thee, yet need thee sore. Giving to them shalt lend to Heaven. Marry a good son of the Church."

"Me? I will never marry."

"Thou wilt marry within the year. I do entreat and command thee to marry one that feareth God. For thou art very clay. Mated ill, thou shalt be naught. But wedding a worthy husband, thou mayest, *Dei gratiâ*, live a pious Princess, ay, and die a saint."

"I?"

"Thou."

He then desired her to rise and go about the good work he had set her. She rose to her knees and, removing her mask, cast an eloquent look upon him, then lowered her eyes meekly.

"I will obey you as I would an angel. How happy I am, yet unhappy; for oh, my heart tells me I shall never look on you again. I will not go till I have dried your feet."

"It needs not. I have excused thee this bootless penance."

" 'Tis no penance to me. Ah, you do not forgive me if you will not let me dry your poor feet."

"So be it, then," said Clement, resignedly.

But these weak creatures, that gravitate toward the small, as heavenly bodies toward the great, have yet their own flashes of angelic intelligence. When the Princess had dried the friar's feet, she looked at him with tears in her beautiful eyes, and murmured with singular tenderness and goodness:

"I will have masses said for her soul. May I?" she added timidly.

This brought a faint blush into the monk's cheek, and moistened his cold blue eye. It came so suddenly from one he was just rating so low.

"It is a gracious thought," he said. "Do as thou wilt. Often such acts fall back on the doer like blessed dew. I am thy confessor, not hers. Thine is the soul I must now do my all to save, or woe be to my own. My daughter, my dear daughter, I see good and ill angels fighting for thy soul this day, ay, this moment. Oh, fight thou on thine own side! Doth thou remember all I bade thee?"

"Remember!" said the Princess. "Sweet saint, each syllable of thine is graved in my heart."

"But one word more then. Pray much to Christ, and little to his saints."

"I will."

"And that is the best word I have light to say to thee. So part we on it. Thou to the place becomes thee best, thy father's house, I to my holy mother's work."

"Adieu," faltered the Princess. "Adieu, thou that I have loved too well, hated too ill, known and revered too late. Forgiving angel adieu—forever."

The monk caught her words, though but faltered in a sigh.

"Forever?" he cried aloud with sudden ardor. "Christians live 'forever,' and love 'forever,' but they never part 'forever.' They part, as part the earth and sun, to meet more brightly in a little while. You and I part here for life. And what is our life? One line in the great story of the Church, whose son and daughter we are, one handful in the sand of time, one drop in the ocean of 'forever.' Adieu—for the little moment called 'a life!' We part in trouble, we shall meet in peace. We part creatures of clay, we shall meet immortal spirits. We part in a world of sin and sorrow, we shall meet where all is purity and love divine, where no ill passions are, but Christ is, and His saints around Him clad in white. There, in the turning of an hourglass, in the breaking of a bubble, in the passing of a cloud, she, and thou, and I shall meet again, and sit at the feet of angels and archangels, Apostles and saints, and beam like them with joy unspeakable, in the light of the shadow of God upon his throne, *forever—and ever—and ever.*"

And so they parted. The monk erect, his eyes turned heavenward and glowing with the sacred fire of zeal, the Princess slowly retiring and turning more than once to cast a lingering glance of awe and tender regret on that inspired figure.

She went home subdued, and purified. Clement, in due course, reached Basle and entered on his duties, teaching in the university and preaching in the town and neighborhood. He led a life that can be comprised in two words: deep study, and mortification. At Basle he advanced in holy zeal and knowledge. The brethren of his order began to see in him a descendant of the saints and martyrs.

CHAPTER XLII

WHEN little Gerard was nearly three months old, a messenger came hot from Tergou for Catherine.

"Now just you go back," said she, "and tell them I can't come and I won't. They have got Kate." So he departed, and Catherine continued her sentence: "There, child, I *must* go, they are all at sixes and sevens. This is the third time of asking, and tomorrow my man would come himself and take me home by the ear, with a flea in't." She then recapitulated her experiences of infants, and instructed Margaret what to do in each coming emergency, and pressed money upon her. Margaret declined it with thanks. Catherine insisted, and turned angry. Margaret made excuses, all so reasonable that Catherine rejected them with calm contempt, to her mind they lacked femininity. "Come, out with your heart," said she, "and you and me parting, and mayhap shall never see one another's face again."

"Oh, Mother, say not so!"

"Alack, girl, I have seen it so often, 'twill come into my mind now at each parting. When I was your age, I never had such a thought. Nay, we were all to live forever then—so out wi' it."

"Well then, Mother—I would rather not have told you—your Cornelis must say to me, 'So you are come to share with us, eh, mistress?' Those were his words. I told him I would be very sorry."

"Beshrew his ill tongue! What signifies it? He will never know."

"Most likely he would sooner or later. But, whether or no, I will take no grudge bounty from any family—unless I saw my child starving, and then Heaven only knows what I might do. Nay, Mother, give me but thy love—I do prize that above silver, and they grudge me not that, by all I can find—for not a stiver of money will I take out of your house."

"You are a foolish lass. Why, were it me, I'd take it just to spite him."

"No, you would not. You and I are apples off one tree."

Catherine yielded with a good grace; and when the actual parting came, embraces and tears burst forth on both sides. When she was gone the child cried a good deal, and all attempts to pacify him failing, Margaret suspected a pin and, searching between his clothes and his skin, found a gold angel incommoding his backbone.

"There now, Gerard," said she to the babe, "I *thought* Granny gave in rather *sudden.*"

She took the coin and wrapped it in a piece of linen and laid it at the bottom of her box, bidding the infant observe she could be at times as resolute as Granny herself.

Catherine told Eli of Margaret's foolish pride, and how she had baffled it. Eli said Margaret was right, and she was wrong. Catherine tossed her head. Eli pondered.

Margaret was not without domestic anxieties. She had still two men to feed, and could not work so hard as she had done. She had enough to do to keep the house—and the child, and cook for them all. But she had a little money laid by, and she used to tell her child his father would be home to help them before it was spent. And with these bright hopes, and that treasury of bliss, her boy, she spent some happy months.

Time wore on, and no Gerard came; and, stranger still, no news of him. Then her mind was disquieted, and, contrary to her nature, which was practical, she was often lost in sad reverie, and sighed in silence. And while her heart was troubled, her money was melting. And so it was that one day she found the cupboard empty, and looked in her dependents' faces; and at the sight of them her bosom was all pity; and she appealed to the baby whether she could let Grandfather and poor old Martin want a meal, and went and took out Catherine's angel. As she unfolded the linen a tear of gentle mortification fell on it.

She sent Martin out to change it. While he was gone a Frenchman came with one of the dealers in illuminated work who had offered her so poor a price. He told her he was employed by his sovereign to collect masterpieces for her book of hours. Then she showed him the two best things she had; and he was charmed with one of them—the flowers and raspberries and creeping things which Margaret Van Eyck had shaded. He offered her an unheard-of price. "Nay, flout not my need, good stranger," said she. "Three mouths there be in this house, and none to fill them but me." Curious arithmetic! Left out No. 1.

"I flout thee not, fair mistress. My Princess charged me strictly, 'Seek the best craftsmen, but I will no hard bargains. Make them content with me, and me with them.'"

The next minute Margaret was on her knees kissing little Gerard in the cradle, and showering four gold pieces on him again and again, and relating the whole occurrence to him in very broken Dutch.

"And oh, what a good princess, wasn't she? We will pray for her, won't we, my lambkin, when we are old enough?"

Martin came in furious. "They will not change it. I trow they think I stole it."

"I am beholden to thee," said Margaret hastily, and almost snatched it from Martin, and wrapped it up again, and restored it to its hiding-place.

Ere these unexpected funds were spent, she got to her ironing and starching again. In the midst of which Martin sickened and died after an illness of nine days. Nearly all of her money went to bury him decently. He was gone, and there was an empty chair by her fireside. For he had preferred the hearth to the sun as soon as the busybody was gone.

Margaret would not allow anybody to sit in this chair now. Yet whenever she let her eye dwell too long on it, vacant, it was sure to cost her a tear. And now there was nobody to carry her linen home. To do it herself she must leave little Gerard in charge of a neighbor. But she dared not trust such a treasure to mortal, and besides, she could not bear him out of her sight for hours and hours. So she set inquiries on foot for a boy to carry her basket on Saturday and Monday.

A plump, fresh-colored youth called Luke Peterson, who looked fifteen but was eighteen, came in, and blushing, and twiddling his bonnet, asked her if a man would not serve her turn as well as a boy.

Before he spoke she was saying to herself, "This boy will just do."

But she took the cue, and said, "Nay, but a man will maybe seek more than I can well pay."

"Not I," said Luke, warmly. "Why, Mistress Margaret, I am your neighbor, and I do very well at the coopering. I can carry your basket for you before or after my day's work, and welcome. You have no need to pay *me* anything. 'Tisn't as if we were strangers, ye know."

"Why, Master Luke, I know your face, for that matter, but I cannot call to mind that ever a word passed between us."

"Oh, yes, you did, Mistress Margaret. What, have you forgotten? One day you were trying to carry your baby and eke your pitcher full o' water, and, quo' I, 'Give me the baby to carry.' 'Nay,' says you, 'I'll give you the pitcher, and keep the bairn myself.' And I carried the pitcher home, and you took it from me at this door, and you said to me, 'I am muckle obliged to you, young man,' with such a sweet voice, not like the folk in this street speak to a body."

"I do mind now, Master Luke, and methinks it was the least I could say."

"Well, Mistress Margaret, if you will say as much every time I carry your basket, I care not how often I bear it, nor how far."

"Nay, nay," said Margaret, coloring faintly. "I would not put upon good nature. You are young, Master Luke, and kindly. Say I give you your supper on Saturday night, when you bring the linen home, and your dawn mete o' Monday. Would that make us anyway even?"

"As you please, only say not I sought a couple o' diets, I, for such a trifle as yon."

With chubby-faced Luke's timely assistance, and the health and strength which Heaven gave this poor young woman, to balance her many ills, the house went pretty smoothly awhile. But the heart became more and more troubled by Gerard's long and now most mysterious silence.

And then that mental torture, suspense, began to tear her heavy heart with his hot pinchers, till she cried often and vehemently, "Oh, that I could know the worst." While she was in this state, one day she heard a heavy step mount the stair. She started and trembled. "That is no step that I know. Ill tidings!" The door opened and an unexpected visitor, Eli, came in, looking grave and kind. Margaret eyed him in silence, and with increasing agitation.

"Girl," said he, "the skipper is come back."

"One word," gasped Margaret. "Is he alive?"

"Surely, I hope so. No one has seen him dead."

"Then they must have seen him alive."

"No, girl, neither dead nor alive hath he been seen this many months in Rome. My daughter Kate thinks he is gone to some other city. She bade me tell you her thought."

"Ay, like enough," said Margaret, gloomily, "like enough. My poor babe!"

The old man in a faintest voice asked her for a morsel to eat. He had come fasting. The poor thing pitied him with the surface of her agitated mind, and cooked a meal for him, trembling, and scarce knowing what she was about.

Ere he went he laid his hand upon her head, and said: "Be he alive, or be he dead, I look on thee as my daughter. Can I do naught for thee this day? Bethink thee now."

"Ay, old man. Pray for him, and for me!"

Eli sighed, and went sadly and heavily down the stairs. She listened half-stupidly to his retiring footsteps till they ceased. Then she sank moaning down by the cradle, and drew little Gerard tight to her bosom. "Oh, my poor fatherless boy, my fatherless boy!"

Not long after this, as the little family at Tergou sat at dinner, Luke Peterson burst in on them, covered with dust.

"Good people, Mistress Catherine is wanted instantly at Rotterdam."

"My name is Catherine, young man. Kate, it will be Margaret."

"Ay, dame, she said to me, 'Good Luke, hie thee to Tergou, and ask for Eli the hosier, and pray his wife Catherine to come to me, for God His love.' I didn't wait for daylight."

"Holy saints! He has come home, Kate. Nay, she would sure have said so. What on earth can it be?" And she heaped conjecture on conjecture.

"Mayhap the young man can tell us," hazarded Kate, timidly.

"That I can," said Luke. "Why, her babe is a-dying. And she was so wrapped up in it!"

Catherine started up: "What is his trouble?"

"Nay, I know not. But it has been peaking and pining worse and worse this while."

A furtive glance of satisfaction passed between Cornelis and Sybrandt. Luckily for them, Catherine did not see it. Her face was turned toward her husband. "Now, Eli," cried she, furiously, "if you say a word against it, you and I shall quarrel, after all these years."

"Who gainsays thee, foolish woman? Quarrel with your own shadow while I go borrow Peter's mule for ye."

"Bless thee, my good man! Bless thee! Didst never yet fail me at a pinch. Now eat your dinners who can while I go and make ready."

She took Luke back with her in the cart, and, on the way, questioned and cross-questioned him, severely and seductively by turns, till she had turned his mind inside out, what there was of it. Margaret met her at the door, pale and agitated, and threw her arms round her neck, and looked imploringly in her face.

"Come, he is alive, thank God," said Catherine, after scanning her eagerly.

She looked at the failing child, and then at the poor hollow-eyed mother, alternately. "Lucky you sent for me," said she. "The child is poisoned."

"Poisoned! By whom?"

"By you. You have been fretting."

"Nay, indeed, Mother. How can I help fretting?"

"Don't tell me, Margaret. A nursing mother has no business to fret. She must turn her mind away from her grief to the comfort that lies in her lap. Know you not that the child pines if the mother vexes herself? This comes of your reading and writing. Those idle crafts befit a man, but they keep all useful knowledge out of a woman. The child must be weaned."

"Oh, you cruel woman!" cried Margaret, vehemently; "I am sorry I sent for you. Would you rob me of the only bit of comfort I have in the world? A-nursing my Gerard, I forget I am the most unhappy creature beneath the sun."

"That you do not," was the retort, "or he would not be the way he is."

"Mother!" said Margaret, imploringly.

" 'Tis hard," replied Catherine, relenting. "But bethink thee, would it not be harder to look down and see his lovely wee face a-looking up at you out of a little coffin?"

"Oh, Jesu!"

"And how could you face your other troubles with your heart aye full, and your lap empty?"

"Oh, Mother, I consent to anything. Only save my boy."

"That is a good lass. Trust to me! I do stand by, and see clearer than thou."

Unfortunately there was another consent to be gained, the babe's, and he was more refractory than his mother.

"There," said Margaret, trying to affect regret at his misbehavior, "he loves me too well."

But Catherine was a match for them both. As she came along she had observed a healthy young woman sitting outside her own door with an infant hard by. She went and told her the case, and would she nurse the pining child for the nonce, till she had matters ready to wean him? The young woman consented with a smile, and popped her child into the cradle and came into Margaret's house. She dropped a curtsy, and Catherine put the child into her hands. She examined, and pitied it, and purred over it, and proceeded to nurse it just as if it had been her own. Margaret, who had been paralyzed at her assurance, cast a rueful look at Catherine, and burst out crying.

The visitor looked up. "What is to do? Wife, ye told me not the mother was unwilling."

"She is not, she is only a fool. Never heed her—and you, Margaret, I am ashamed of you."

"You are a cruel, hardhearted woman," sobbed Margaret.

"Them as take in hand to guide the weak need be hardish. And you will excuse me, but you are not my flesh and blood, and your boy is." After giving this blunt speech time to sink, she added: "Come now, she is robbing her own to save yours, and you can think of nothing better than bursting out a-blubbering in the woman's face. Out, fie, for shame!"

"Nay, wife," said the nurse. "Thank heaven, I have enough for my own and for hers to boot. And prithee wyte not on her! Maybe the troubles o' life ha' soured her own milk."

"And her heart into the bargain," said the remorseless Catherine.

Margaret looked her full in the face; and down went her eyes.

"I know I ought to be very grateful to you," sobbed Margaret to the nurse, then turned her head and leaned away over the chair, not to witness the intolerable sight of another nursing her Gerard, and Gerard drawing no distinction between this new mother and her the banished one.

The nurse replied: "You are very welcome, my poor woman. And so are you, Mistress Catherine, which are my townswoman, and know it not."

"What, are ye from Tergou? All the better. But I cannot call your face to mind."

"Oh, you know not me—my husband and me, we are very humble folk by you. But true Eli and his wife are known of all the town, and respected. So I am at your call, dame, and at yours, wife, and yours, my pretty poppet, night or day."

"There's a woman of the right old sort," said Catherine, as the door closed upon her.

"I *hate* her. I *hate* her. I *hate* her," said Margaret, with wonderful fervor. Catherine only laughed at this outburst.

"That is right," said she, "better say it, as set sly and think it. It is very natural after all. Come, here is your bundle o' comfort. Take and hate that—if ye can." And she put the child in her lap.

"No, no," said Margaret, turning her head half away from him. She could not for her life turn the other half. "He is not my child now, he is hers. I know not why she left him here, for my part. It was very good of her not to take him to her house, cradle and all—oh, oh, oh, oh, oh, oh, oh, oh!

"Ah, well, one comfort, *he* is not dead. This gives me light. Some other woman has got him away from me—like father, like son, oh, oh, oh, oh, oh!"

Catherine was sorry for her, and let her cry in peace. And after that, when she wanted Joan's aid, she used to take Gerard out to give him a little fresh air. Margaret never objected, nor expressed the least incredulity, but on their return was always in tears.

This connivance was short-lived. She was now altogether as eager to wean little Gerard. It was done, and he recovered health and vigor, and another trouble fell upon him directly: teething. But here Catherine's experience was invaluable, and now, in the midst of her grief and anxiety about the father, Margaret had moments of bliss, watching the son's tiny teeth come through. "Teeth, mother? I call them not teeth, but pearls of pearls." And each pearl that peeped and sparkled on his red gums was to her the greatest feat Nature had ever achieved.

Catherine gossiped with Joan and learned that she was the wife of Jorian Ketel of Tergou, who had been servant to Ghysbrecht van Swieten, but fallen out of favor, and come back to Rotterdam, his native place. His friends had got him the place of sexton to the parish, and what with that and carpentering, he did pretty well.

Catherine told Joan in return whose child it was she had nursed, and all about Margaret and Gerard, and the deep anxiety his silence had plunged them in. "Ay," said Joan, "the world is full of trouble." One day she said to Catherine: "It's my belief my man knows more about your Gerard than anybody in these parts; but he has got to be closer than ever of late. Drop in some day just afore sunset, and set him talking. And, for our Lady's sake, say not I set you on. The only hiding he ever gave me was for babbling his business, and I do not want another. Gramercy! I married a man for the comfort of the thing, not to be hided."

Catherine dropped in. Jorian was ready enough to tell her how he had befriended her son and perhaps saved his life. But this was no news to Catherine, and the moment she began to cross-question him as to whether he could guess why her lost boy neither came nor wrote, he cast a grim look at his wife, who received it with a calm air of stolid candor and innocent unconsciousness, and his answers became short and sullen. "What should he know more than another?" and so on. He added, after a pause, "Think you the Burgomaster takes such as me into his secrets?"

"Oh, then the Burgomaster knows something?" said Catherine sharply.

"Likely. Who else should?"

"I'll ask him."

"I would."

"And tell him you say he knows."

"That is right, dame. Go make him mine enemy. That is what a poor fellow always gets if he says a word to you women." And Jorian from that moment shrank in and became impenetrable as a hedgehog, and almost as prickly.

His conduct caused both the poor women agonies of mind, alarm, and irritated curiosity. Ghysbrecht was for some cause Gerard's mortal enemy, had stopped his marriage, imprisoned him, hunted him. And here was his late servant, who when off his guard had hinted that this enemy had the clue to Gerard's silence. After sifting Jorian's every word and look, all remained dark and mysterious. Then Catherine told Margaret to go herself to him. "You are young, you are fair. You will maybe get more out of him than I could."

The conjecture was a reasonable one. Margaret went with her child in her arms and tapped timidly at Jorian's door just before sunset. "Come in," said a sturdy voice. She entered, and there sat Jorian by the fireside. At sight of her he rose, snorted, and burst out of the house. "Is that for me, wife?" inquired Margaret, turning very red.

"You must excuse him," replied Joan, rather coldly. "He lays it to your door that he is a poor man instead of a rich one. It is something about a piece of parchment. There was one missing, and he got naught from the Burgomaster all along of that one."

"Alas, Gerard took it!"

"Likely. But my man says you should not have let him—you were pledged to him to keep them all safe. And, sooth to say, I blame not my Jorian for being wroth. 'Tis hard for a poor man to be so near fortune and lose it by those he has befriended. However, I tell *him* another story. Says I, 'Folk that are out o' trouble, like you and me, didn't ought to be too hard on folk that are in trouble, and she has plenty.' "

Margaret came to a resolution which she did not confide even to Catherine. After six weeks' stay that good woman returned home. On the child's birthday, which occurred soon after, Margaret did no work, but put on her Sunday clothes, and took her boy in her arms and went to the church and prayed there long and fervently for Gerard's safe return.

That same day and hour Father Clement celebrated a mass and prayed for Margaret's departed soul in the minster church at Basle.

CHAPTER XLIII

SOME blackguard or other, I think it was Sybrandt, said, "A lie is not like a blow with a curtal ax." True, for we can predict in some degree the consequences of a stroke with any material weapon. But a lie has no bounds at all. The nature of the thing is to ramify beyond human calculation. Often in the everyday world a lie has cost a life, or laid waste two or three. And so, in this story, what tremendous consequences of that one heartless falsehood!

Yet the tellers reaped little from it. The brothers, who invented it merely to have one claimant the less for their father's property, saw little Gerard take their brother's place in their mother's heart. Nay, more, one day Eli openly proclaimed that, Gerard being lost, and probably dead, he had provided by will for little Gerard, and also for Margaret, his poor son's widow. At this the look that passed between the black sheep was a caution to traitors. Cornelis had it on his lips to say Gerard was most likely alive. But he saw his mother looking at him, and checked himself in time.

Ghysbrecht van Swieten, the other partner in that lie, was now a failing man. He saw the period fast approaching when all his wealth would drop from his body, and his misdeeds cling to his soul. Too intelligent to deceive himself entirely, he had never been free from gusts of remorse. In taking Gerard's letter to Margaret he had compounded. "I cannot give up land and money," said his giant avarice. "I will cause her no unnecessary pain," said his dwarf conscience.

So, after first tampering with the seal, and finding there was not a syllable about the deed, he took it to her with his own hand, and made a merit of it to himself—a set-off, and on a scale not uncommon where the self-accuser is the judge.

The birth of Margaret's child surprised and shocked him, and put his treacherous act in a new light. Should his letter take effect, he should cause the dishonor of her who was the daughter of one friend, the granddaughter of another, and whose land he was keeping from her too. These thoughts, preying on him at that period of life when the strength of body decays and the memory of old friends revives, filled him with gloomy horrors. Yet he was afraid to confess. For the curé was an honest man, and would have made him disgorge. And with him avarice was an ingrained habit, penitence only a sentiment.

Matters were thus when one day, returning from the town hall to his own house, he found a woman waiting for him in the vestibule, with a child in her arms. She was veiled, and so, concluding she had something to be ashamed of, he addressed her magisterially. On this she let down her veil and looked him full in the face. It was Margaret Brandt. Her sudden appearance and manner startled him, and he could not conceal his confusion.

"Where is my Gerard?" cried she, her bosom heaving. "Is he alive?"

"For aught I know," stammered Ghysbrecht. "I hope so, for your sake. Prithee come into this room. The servants!"

"Not a step," said Margaret, and she took him by the shoulder and held him with all the energy of an excited woman. "You know the secret of that which is breaking my heart. Why does not my Gerard come, nor send a line this many months? Answer me, or all the town is like to hear me, let alone thy servants. My misery is too great to be sported with."

In vain he persisted he knew nothing about Gerard. She told him those who had sent her to him told her another tale. "You do know why he neither comes nor sends," said she, firmly.

At this Ghysbrecht turned paler and paler, but he summoned all his dignity, and said, "Would you believe those two knaves against a man of worship?"

"What two knaves?" said she, keenly.

He stammered, "Said ye not—? There, I am a poor old broken man whose memory is shaken. And you come here, and confuse me so, I know not what I say."

"Ay, sir, your memory *is* shaken, or sure you would not be my enemy. My father saved you from the plague when none other would come a-nigh you, and was ever your friend. My Grandfather Floris helped you in your early poverty, and loved you, man and boy. Three generations of us you have seen, and here is the fourth of us. This is your old friend Peter's grandchild, and your old friend Floris his great-grandchild. Look down on his innocent face, and think of theirs!"

"Woman, you torture me," sighed Ghysbrecht, and sank upon a bench. But she saw her advantage, and knelt before him, and put the boy on his knees. "This fatherless babe is poor Margaret Brandt's, that never did you ill, and comes of a race that loved you. Nay, look at his face. 'Twill melt thee more than any word of mine. Saints of heaven, what can a poor desolate girl and her babe have done to wipe out all memory of thine own young days, when you wert guiltless as he is that now looks up in thy face and implores thee to give him back his father?"

And with her arms under the child she held him up higher and higher, smiling under the old man's eyes. He cast a wild look of anguish on the child, and another on the kneeling mother, and started up shrieking, "Avaunt, ye pair of adders!"

The stung soul gave the old limbs a momentary vigor, and he walked rapidly, wringing his hands and clutching at his white hair. "Forget those days? I forget all else. Oh, woman, woman, sleeping or waking I see but the faces of the dead, I hear but the voices of the dead, and I shall soon be among the dead. There, there, what is done is done. I am in Hell. I am in Hell."

And unnatural force ended in prostration. He staggered, and but for Margaret would have fallen. With her one disengaged arm she supported him as well as she could, and cried for help. A couple of servants came running, and carried him away in a state bordering on syncope. The last Margaret saw of him was his old furrowed face, white and helpless as his hair that hung down over the servant's elbow.

"Heaven forgive me," she said. "I doubt I have killed the poor old man."

Then this attempt to penetrate the torturing mystery left it as dark or darker than before. For when she came to ponder every word, her suspicion was confirmed that Ghysbrecht did know something about Gerard. "And who were the two knaves he thought had done a good deed, and told me? Oh, my Gerard, my poor deserted babe, you and I are wading in deep waters!"

The visit to Tergou took more money than she could well afford, and a customer ran away in her debt. She was once more compelled to unfold Catherine's angel. But, strange to say, as she came downstairs with it in her hand she found some loose silver on the table, with a written line—

For Gerard His Wife

She fell with a cry of surprise on the writing: and soon it rose into a cry of joy.

"He is alive! He sends me this by some friendly hand."

She kissed the writing again and again, and put it in her bosom.

Time rolled on, and no news of Gerard. And about every two months a small sum in silver found its way into the house. Sometimes it lay on the table. Once it was flung in through the bedroom window in a purse. Once it was at the bottom of Luke's basket. He had stopped at the public house to talk to a friend. The giver or his agent was never detected. Catherine disowned it. Margaret Van Eyck swore she had no hand in it. So did Eli. And Margaret, whenever it came, used to say to little Gerard, "Oh, my poor deserted child, you and I are wading in deep waters!"

She applied at least half this modest but useful supply to dressing the little Gerard beyond his station in life. "If it does come from Gerard, he shall see his boy neat." All the mothers in the street began to sneer, especially such as had brats out at elbows.

The months rolled on, and dead sickness of heart succeeded to these keener torments. She returned to her first thought: Gerard must be dead. She should never see her boy's father again, nor her marriage lines. This last grief, which had been somewhat allayed by Eli and Catherine recognizing her betrothal, now revived in full force. Others would not look so favorably on her story. And often she moaned over her boy's illegitimacy. "Is it not enough for us to be bereaved? Must we be dishonored too? Oh, that we had ne'er been born!"

A change took place in Peter Brandt. His mind, clouded for nearly two years, seemed now to be clearing; he had intervals of intelligence, and then he and Margaret used to talk of Gerard till he wandered again. But one day, returning after an absence of some hours, Margaret found him conversing with Catherine in a way he had never done since his paralytic stroke. "Eh, girl, why must you be out?" said she. "But indeed I have told him all, and we have been a-crying together over thy troubles."

Margaret stood silent, looking joyfully from one to the other. Peter smiled on her, and said, "Come, let me bless thee."

She knelt at his feet, and he blessed her most eloquently. He told her she had been all her life the lovingest, truest, and most obedient daughter Heaven ever sent to a poor old widowed man. "May thy son be to thee what thou hast been to me!"

After this he dozed. Then the females whispered together, and Catherine said: "All our talk e'en now was of Gerard. It lies heavy on his mind. His poor head must often have listened to us when it seemed quite dark. Margaret, he is a very understanding man, he thought of many things. 'He may be in prison,' says he, 'or forced to go fighting for some king, or sent to Constantinople to copy books there, or gone into the Church after all. He had a bent that way.'"

"Ah, Mother," whispered Margaret, in reply, "he doth but deceive himself as we do."

Ere she could finish the sentence, a strange interruption occurred.

A loud voice cried out, "*I see him. I see him.*" And the old man with dilating eyes seemed to be looking right through the wall of the house.

"*In a boat, on a great river, coming this way.* Sore disfigured, but I knew him. Gone, gone! All dark." And he sank back, and asked feebly where was Margaret.

"Dear Father, I am by thy side. Oh, Mother, Mother, what is this?"

"I cannot see thee, and but a moment agone I saw all round the world. Ay, ay. Well, I am ready. Is this thy hand? Bless thee, my child, bless thee! Weep not! The tree is ripe."

The old physician read the signs aright. These calm words were his last. The next moment he drooped his head and gently, placidly, drifted away from earth, like an infant sinking to rest. The torch had flashed up before going out.

She who had wept for poor old Martin was not likely to bear this blow so stoically as the death of the old is apt to be borne. In vain Catherine tried to console her with commonplaces, in vain told her it was a happy release for him, and that, as he himself had said, the tree was ripe. But her worst failure was when she urged that there were now but two mouths to feed, and one care the less.

"Such cares are all the joys I have," said Margaret. "They fill my desolate heart, which now seems void as well as waste. Oh, empty chair, my bosom it aches to see thee! Poor old man, how could I love him by halves, I that did use to sit and look at him and think 'But for me thou wouldst die of hunger.' He, so wise, so learned erst, was got to be helpless as my own sweet babe, and I loved him as if he had been my child instead of my father. Oh, empty chair! Oh, empty heart! Welladay, welladay!"

And the pious tears would not be denied. Then Catherine held her peace, and hung her head. And one day she made this confession: "I speak to thee out o' my head, and not out o' my bosom; thou dost well to be deaf to me. Were I in thy place, I should mourn the old man all one as thou dost."

Then Margaret embraced her, and this bit of true sympathy did her a little good. The commonplaces did none.

CHAPTER XLIV

BROTHER CLEMENT had taught and preached in Basle more than a twelve-month when one day Jerome stood before him, dusty, with a triumphant glance in his eye.

"Give the glory to God, Brother Clement. Thou canst now wend to England with me."

"I am ready, Brother Jerome and, expecting thee these many months, have in the intervals of teaching and devotion studied the English tongue somewhat closely."

" 'Twas well thought of," said Jerome. He then told him he had but delayed till he could obtain extraordinary powers from the Pope to collect money for the Church's use in England, and to hear confession in all the secular monasteries. "So now gird up thy loins and let us go forth and deal a good blow for the Church, and against the Franciscans."

The two friars went preaching down the Rhine, for England. In the larger places they both preached. At the smaller they often divided, and took different sides of the river, and met again at some appointed spot. Both were able orators, but in different styles. Jerome's was noble and impressive, but a little contracted in religious topics, and a trifle monotonous in delivery compared with Clement's, though in truth not so compared with most preachers.

Clement's was full of variety, and often remarkably colloquial. In its general flow tender and gently winning, it curled round the reason and the heart. But it always rose with the rising thought, and so at times Clement soared as far above Jerome as his level speaking was below him. Indeed, in these noble heats he was all that we have read of inspired prophet or heathen orator. Clement used secretly to try and learn the recent events and the besetting sin of each town he was to preach in.

But Jerome the unbending scorned to go out of his way for any people's vices. At one great town some leagues from the Rhine, they mounted the same pulpit in turn. Jerome preached against vanity in dress, a favorite theme of his. He was eloquent and satirical, and the people listened with complacency. It was a vice that they were little given to.

Clement preached against drunkenness. It was a besetting sin, and sacred from preaching in these parts, for the clergy themselves were infected with it, and popular prejudice protected it. Clement dealt it merciless blows out of Holy Writ and worldly experience. This discourse caused quite an uproar. The hearers formed knots. The men were indignant, so the women flattered them, and took their part openly against the preacher. A married man had a right to a drop—he needed it, working for all the family.

Jerome thought this sermon too earthly. "Drunkenness is not heresy, Clement, that a whole sermon should be preached against it." As they went on he found to his surprise that Clement's sermons sank into his hearers deeper than his own, made them listen, think, cry, and sometimes even amend their ways. "He hath the art of sinking to their peg," thought Jerome. "Yet he can soar high enough at times."

Upon the whole, it puzzled Jerome, who had a secret sense of superiority to his tenderer brother. And after about two hundred miles of it, it got to displease him as well as puzzle him. But he tried to check this sentiment as petty and unworthy. "Souls differ like locks," said he, "and preachers must differ like keys, or the fewer doors should the Church open for God to pass in. And, certes, this novice hath the key to these Northern souls, being himself a Northern man."

And so they came slowly down the Rhine, sometimes drifting a few miles on the stream, but in general walking by the banks preaching, and teaching, and confessing sinners in the towns and villages, and they reached the town of Düsseldorf.

There was the little quay where Gerard and Denys had taken boat up the Rhine. The friars landed on it. There were the streets, there was the Silver Lion. Nothing had changed but he, who walked through it barefoot, with his heart calm and cold, his hands across his breast and his eyes bent meekly on the ground, a true son of Dominic and Holy Church.

CHAPTER XLV

"ELI," said Catherine, "answer me one question like a man, and I'll ask no more today. What is wormwood?"

Eli looked a little helpless at this sudden demand upon his faculties, but soon recovered enough to say it was something that tasted main bitter.

"That is a fair answer, my man, but not the one I look for."

"Then answer it yourself."

"And shall. Wormwood is—to have two in the house a-doing naught but waiting for thy shoes and mine." Eli groaned. The shaft struck home.

"Methinks waiting for their best friend's coffin, that and nothing to do, are enow to make them worse than Nature meant. Why not set them up somewhere, to give 'em a chance?"

Eli said he was willing, but afraid they would drink and gamble their very shelves away.

"Nay," said Catherine. "Dost take me for a simpleton? Of course I mean to watch them at starting, and drive them wi' a loose rein, as the saying is."

"Where did you think of? Not here, to divide our own custom."

"Not likely. I say Rotterdam, against the world. Then I could start them."

Oh, self-deception! The true motive of all this was to get near little Gerard. After many discussions, and eager promises of amendment on these terms from Cornelis and Sybrandt, Catherine went to Rotterdam shopping, and took Kate with her. They soon found one, and in a good street, but it was sadly out of order. However, they got it cheaper for that, and instantly set about brushing it up, fitting proper shelves for the business, and making the dwelling-house habitable.

Luke Peterson was always asking Margaret what he could do for her. The answer used to be in a sad tone, "Nothing, Luke, nothing."

"What, you that are so clever, can you think of nothing for me to do for you?"

"Nothing, Luke, nothing."

But one day, as if tired with his importuning, she turned on him and said with a look and accent I should in vain try to convey:

"Find me my boy's father!"

"Mistress, they all say he is dead."

"Not so. They feed me still with hopes."

"Ay, to your face, but behind your back they all say he is dead."

At this revelation Margaret's tears began to flow.

Luke whimpered for company. He had the body of a man, but the heart of a girl.

"Prithee, weep not so, sweet mistress," said he. "I'd bring him back to life an I could rather than see thee weep so sore."

Margaret said she thought she was weeping because they were so double-tongued with her. She recovered herself, and laying her hand on his shoulder, said solemnly:

"Luke, he is not dead. Dying men are known to have a strange sight. And listen, Luke! My poor father, when he was a-dying, and I, simple fool, was so happy, thinking he was going to get well altogether, he said to Mother and me—he was sitting in that very chair where you are now, and Mother was as might be here, and I was yonder making a sleeve—said he, 'I see him! I see him!' Just so. Not like a failing man at all, but all o' fire. 'Sore disfigured—on a great river—coming this way.'

"Ah, Luke, if you were a woman, and had the feeling for me you think you have, you would pity me, and find him for me. Take a thought! The father of my child!"

"Alack, I would if I knew how," said Luke. "But how can I? Let me think, for my mind cannot gallop like thine. On a great river? Well, the Maas is a great river." He pondered on. "Coming this way? Then if 'twas the Maas, he would have been here by this time, so 'tis not the Maas. The Rhine is a great river, greater than the Maas, and very long. I think it will be the Rhine."

"And so do I, Luke, for Denys bade him come down the Rhine. But even if it is, he may turn off before he comes a-nigh his birthplace."

"Let me think again," said Luke. "I cannot gallop."

The result of this meditation was this. He knew a station about sixty miles up the Rhine where all the public boats put in; and he would go to that station and try and cut the truant off. To be sure, he did not even know him by sight, but as each boat came in he would mingle with the passengers, and ask if one Gerard was there. "And, mistress, if you were to give me a bit of a letter to him; for, with us being strangers, mayhap a won't believe a word I say."

"Good, kind, thoughtful Luke, I will. But give me till suppertime to get it writ."

At supper she put a letter into his hand with a blush. It was a long letter tied round with silk after the fashion of the day, and sealed over the knot. Luke weighed it in his hand, with a shade of discontent, and said to her very gravely:

"Tomorrow, at peep of day, I start. But, hold, I have no money. My mother, she takes care of all mine, and I ne'er see it again."

Then Margaret took out Catherine's gold angel, which had escaped so often, and gave it to Luke, and he set out on his mad errand. It did not however seem so mad to him as to us. It was a superstitious age, and Luke acted on the dying man's dream, or vision, or illusion, or whatever it was, much as we should act on respectable information.

CHAPTER XLVI

THE two friars reached Holland from the south just twelve hours after Luke started up the Rhine. Thus, wild-goose chase or not, the parties were nearing each other, and rapidly too. For Jerome, unable to preach in Low Dutch, now began to push on toward the coast, anxious to get to England as soon as possible. And, having the stream with them, the friars would in point of fact have missed Luke by passing him in full stream below his station but for the incident which I am about to relate.

About twenty miles above the station Luke was making for, Clement landed to preach in a large village, and toward the end of his sermon he noticed a gray nun weeping. He spoke to her kindly, and asked her what was her grief.

"Nay," said she, " 'tis not for myself flow these tears, 'tis for my lost friend. Thy words reminded me of what she was, and what she is, poor wretch. But you are a Dominican, and I am a Franciscan nun."

"It matters little, my Sister, if we are both Christians and if I can aid thee in aught."

The nun looked in his face, and said: "These are strange words, but methinks they are good, and thy lips are oh, most eloquent. I will tell thee our grief."

She then let him know that a young nun, the darling of the convent and her bosom friend, had been lured away from her vows, and after various gradations of sin, was actually living in a small inn as chambermaid, in reality as a decoy, and was known to be selling her favors to the wealthier customers. She added:

"Anywhere else we might by kindly violence force her away from perdition. But this innkeeper was the servant of the fierce baron on the height there, and hath his ear still, and he would burn our convent to the ground were we to take her by force."

"Moreover, souls will not be saved by brute force," said Clement.

While they were talking Jerome came up, and Clement persuaded him to lie at the convent that night. But when in the morning Clement told him he had had a long talk with the abbess, and that she was very sad, and he had promised her to try and win back her nun, Jerome objected, and said it was not their business, and was a waste of time. Clement, however, was no longer a mere pupil. He stood firm, and at last they agreed that Jerome should go forward and secure their passage in the next ship for England, and Clement be allowed time to make his well-meant but idle experiment.

About ten o'clock that day, a figure in a horseman's cloak, and great boots to match, and a large flapping felt hat, stood like a statue near the auberge where was the apostate nun, Mary. The friar thus disguised was at that moment truly wretched. These ardent natures undertake wonders, but are dashed when they come hand to hand with the sickening difficulties. But then, as their hearts are steel, though their nerves are anything but iron, they turn not back, but panting and dispirited, struggle on to the last.

Clement hesitated long at the door, prayed for help and wisdom, and at last entered the inn and sat down faint at heart, and with his body in a cold perspiration. But outside he was another man. He called lustily for a cup of wine. It was brought him by the landlord. He paid for it with money the convent had supplied him, and made a show of drinking it.

"Landlord," said he, "I hear there is a fair chambermaid in thine house."

. "Ay, stranger, the buxomest in Holland. But she gives not her company to all comers, only to good customers."

Friar Clement dangled a massive gold chain in the landlord's sight. He laughed, and shouted: "Here, Janet, here is a lover for thee would bind thee in chains of gold, and a tall lad into the bargain, I promise thee!"

"Then I am in double luck," said a female voice. "Send him hither."

Clement rose, shuddered, and passed into the room where Janet was seated playing with a piece of work, and laying it down every minute to sing a mutilated fragment of a song. For in her mode of life she had not the patience to carry anything out. After a few words of greeting, the disguised visitor asked her if they could not be more private somewhere.

"Why not?" said she. And she rose and smiled, and went tripping before him. He followed, groaning inwardly, and sore perplexed.

"There," said she. "Have no fear! Nobody ever comes here but such as pay for the privilege."

Clement looked round the room, and prayed silently for wisdom. Then he went softly and closed the window shutters carefully.

"What on earth is that for?" said Janet in some uneasiness.

"Sweetheart," whispered the visitor, with a mysterious air, "it is that God may not see us."

"Madman," said Janet, "think you a wooden shutter can keep out His eye?"

"Nay, I know not. Perchance He has too much on hand to notice *us*. But I would not the saints and angels should see us. Would you?"

"My poor soul, I hope not to escape their sight! The only way is not to think of them, for if you do, it poisons your cup. For two pins I'd run and leave thee. Art pleasant company, in sooth."

"After all, girl, so that men see us not, what signify God and the saints seeing us? Feel this chain! 'Tis virgin gold. I shall cut two of these heavy links off for thee."

"Ah, now thy discourse is to the point!" And she handled the chain greedily. "Why, 'tis as massy as the chain round the Virgin's neck at the conv—" She did not finish the word.

"Whisht, whisht, whisht! 'Tis *it*. And thou shalt have thy share. But betray me not."

"Monster!" cried Janet, drawing back from him with repugnance. "What, rob the Blessed Virgin of her chain, and give it to an—"

"You are none," cried Clement, exultingly, "or you had not recked for that.—Mary!"

"Ah, ah, ah!"

"Thy patron saint, whose chain this is, sends me to greet thee."

She ran screaming to the window and began to undo the shutters. Her fingers trembled, and Clement had time to debarrass himself of his boots and his hat before the light streamed in upon him. He then let his cloak quietly fall, and stood before her, a Dominican friar, calm and majestic as a statue, and held his crucifix towering over her with a loving, sad, and solemn look that somehow relieved her of the physical part of fear, but crushed her with religious terror and remorse. She crouched and cowered against the wall.

"Mary," said he, gently, "one word! Are you happy?"

"As happy as I shall be in Hell."

"And they are not happy at the convent. They weep for you."

"For me?"

"Day and night, above all the Sister Ursula."

"Poor Ursula!" And the strayed nun began to weep herself at the thought of her friend.

"The angels weep still more. Wilt not dry all their tears in earth and Heaven, and save thyself?"

"Ah, would I could! But it is too late."

"Satan avaunt!" cried the monk sternly. " 'Tis thy favorite temptation. And thou, Mary, listen not to the enemy of man, belying God, and whispering despair. I who come to save thee have been a far greater sinner than thou. Come, Mary, sin, thou seest, is not so sweet e'en in this world as holiness, and eternity is at the door."

"How can they ever receive me again?"

"'Tis their worthiness thou doubtest now. But in truth they pine for thee. 'Twas in pity of their tears that I, a Dominican, undertook this task, and broke the rule of my order by entering an inn, and broke it again by donning these lay vestments. But all is well done, and quit for a light penance, if thou will let us rescue thy soul from this den of wolves and bring thee back to thy vows."

The nun gazed at him with tears in her eyes. "And thou a Dominican hast done this for a daughter of Saint Francis! Why, the Franciscans and Dominicans hate one another."

"Ay, my daughter, but Francis and Dominic love one another."

The recreant nun seemed struck and affected by this answer. Clement now reminded her how shocked she had been that the Virgin should be robbed of her chain. "But see now," said he, "the convent and the Virgin too think ten times more of their poor nun than of golden chains; for they freely trusted their chain to me a stranger, that peradventure the sight of it might touch their lost Mary and remind her of their love."

Finally he showed her with such terrible simplicity the end of her present course, and on the other hand so revived her dormant memories and better feelings, that she kneeled sobbing at his feet and owned she had never known happiness nor peace since she betrayed her vows, and said she would go back if he would go with her, but alone she dared not, could not—even if she reached the gate she could never enter. How could she face the Abbess and the Sisters? He told her he would go with her as joyfully as the shepherd bears a strayed lamb to the fold. But when he urged her to go at once, up sprung a crop of those prodigiously petty difficulties that entangle her sex, like silken nets, liker iron cobwebs. He quietly swept them aside.

"But how can I walk beside thee in this habit?"

"I have brought the gown and cowl of thy holy order. Hide thy bravery with them. And leave thy shoes as I leave these," pointing to his horseman's boots.

She collected her jewels and ornaments.

"What are these for?" inquired Clement.

"To present to the convent, Father."

"Their source is too impure."

"But," objected the penitent, "it would be a sin to leave them here. They can be sold to feed the poor."

"Mary, fix thine eye on this crucifix, and trample those devilish baubles beneath thy feet."

She hesitated, but soon threw them down and trampled on them.

"Now open the window and fling them out on that dunghill. 'Tis well done. So pass the wages of sin from thy hands, its glittering yoke from thy neck, its pollution from thy soul. Away, daughter of Saint Francis, we tarry in this vile place too long."

She followed him. But they were not clear yet. At first the landlord was so astounded at seeing a black friar and a gray nun pass through his kitchen from the inside that he gaped, and muttered, "Why, what mummery is this?" But he soon comprehended the matter, and whipped in between the fugitives and the door. "What ho! Reuben! Carl! Gavin! Here is a false friar spiriting away our Janet."

The men came running in with threatening looks. The friar rushed at them crucifix in hand. "Forbear," he cried, in a stentorian voice. "She is a holy nun returning to her vows. The hand that touches her cowl or her robe to stay her, it shall wither, his body shall lie unburied, cursed by Rome, and his soul shall roast in eternal fire." They shrank back as if a flame had met them. "And thou—miserable panderer!—"

He did not end the sentence in words, but seized the man by the neck and, strong as a lion in his moments of hot excitement, whirled him furiously from the door and sent him all across the room, pitching headforemost onto the stone floor, then tore the door open and carried the screaming nun out into the road. "Hush! poor trembler," he gasped, "they dare not molest thee on the highroad. Away!"

The landlord lay terrified, half-stunned, and bleeding, and Mary, though she often looked back apprehensively, saw no more of him.

On the road he bade her observe his impetuosity.

"Hitherto," said he, "we have spoken of thy faults. Now for mine. My choler is ungovernable, furious. It is by the grace of God I am not a murderer. I repent the next moment, but a moment too late is all too late. Mary, had the churls laid finger on thee, I should have scattered their brains with my crucifix. Oh, I know myself, go to, and tremble at myself. There lurketh a wild beast beneath this black gown of mine."

"Alas, Father," said Mary, "were you other than you are I had been lost. To take me from that place needed a man wary as a fox, yet bold as a lion."

Clement reflected. "Thus much is certain: God chooseth well His fleshly instruments, and with imperfect hearts doeth His perfect work. Glory be to God!"

When they were near the convent Mary suddenly stopped, and seized the friar's arm, and began to cry. He looked at her kindly, and told her she had nothing to fear. It would be the happiest day she had ever spent. He then made her sit down and compose herself till he should return. He entered the convent, and desired to see the Abbess.

"My Sister, give the glory to God—Mary is at the gate."

The astonishment and delight of the Abbess were unbounded. She yielded at once to Clement's earnest request that the road of penitence might be smoothed at first to this unstable wanderer, and, after some opposition, she entered heartily into his views as to her actual reception. To give time for their little preparations Clement went slowly back, and seating himself by Mary soothed her, and heard her confession.

"The Abbess has granted me that you shall propose your own penance."

"It shall be none the lighter," said she.

"I trow not," said he, "but that is future. Today is given to joy alone."

He then led her round the building to the Abbess's postern. As they went they heard musical instruments and singing.

" 'Tis a feast day," said Mary, "and I come to mar it."

"Hardly," said Clement, smiling, "seeing that you are the queen of the fête."

"I, Father? What mean you?"

"What, Mary, have you never heard that there is more joy in Heaven over one sinner that repenteth than over ninety-nine just persons which need no repentance? Now this convent is not Heaven, nor the nuns angels, yet are there among them some angelic spirits, and these sing and exult at thy return. And here methinks comes one of them, for I see her hand trembles at the keyhole."

The postern was flung open, and in a moment Sister Ursula clung sobbing and kissing round her friend's neck. The Abbess followed more sedately, but little less moved.

Clement bade them farewell. They entreated him to stay, but he told them with much regret he could not. He had already tried his good Brother Jerome's patience, and must hasten to the river, and perhaps sail for England tomorrow.

So Mary returned to the fold, and Clement strode briskly on toward the Rhine, and England. This was the man for whom Margaret's boy lay in wait with her letter.

CHAPTER XLVII

AND that letter was one of those simple, touching appeals only her sex can write to those who have used them cruelly, and they love them. She began by telling him of the birth of the little boy, and the comfort he had been to her in all the distress of mind his long and strange silence had caused her. She described the little Gerard minutely, not forgetting the mole on his little finger. "Know you anyone that hath the like on his?

If you only saw him, you could not choose but be proud of him. All the mothers in the street do envy me; but I the wives, for thou comest not to us. My own Gerard, some say thou art dead. But if thou wert dead, how could I be alive? Others say that thou, whom I love so truly, art false. But this will I believe from no lips but thine. My father loved thee well; and as he lay a-dying he thought he saw thee on a great river, with thy face turned toward thy Margaret, but sore disfigured. Is't so, perchance? Have cruel men scarred thy sweet face? Or hast thou lost one of thy precious limbs? Why, then thou hast the more need of me, and I shall love thee not worse—alas, thinkest thou a woman's love is light as a man's?—but better."

The letter continued in this strain, and concluded without a word of reproach or doubt as to his faith and affection. Not that she was free from most distressing doubts; but they were not certainties, and to show them might turn the scale and frighten him away from her with fear of being scolded.

Luke mingled with the passengers of two boats, and could hear nothing of Gerard Eliassoen. Nor did this surprise him. He was more surprised when, at the third attempt, a Black Friar said to him, somewhat severely, "And what would you with him you call Gerard Eliassoen?"

"Why, Father, if he is alive I have got a letter for him."

"Humph!" said Jerome. "I am sorry for it. However, the flesh is weak. Well, my son, he you seek will be here by the next boat, or the next boat after. And if he chooses to answer to that name—After all, I am not the keeper of his conscience."

"Good Father, one plain word, for heaven's sake. This Gerard Eliassoen of Tergou—is he alive?"

"Humph! Why, certes, he that went by that name is alive."

"Well, then, that is settled," said Luke, dryly.

Writing an earnest letter seldom leaves the mind in statu quo. Margaret, in hers, vented her energy and her faith in her dying father's vision, or illusion; and when this was done, and Luke gone, she wondered at her credulity. She was found in this state by a stanch friend she had lately made: Joan Ketel. This good woman came in radiant with an idea.

"Margaret, I know the cure for thine ill—the hermit of Gouda, a wondrous holy man. Why, he can tell what is coming, when he is in the mood."

"Ay, I have heard of him," said Margaret hopelessly. Joan with some difficulty persuaded her to walk out as far as Gouda, and consult the hermit. They took some butter and eggs in a basket, and went to his cave.

What had made the pair such fast friends? Jorian some six weeks ago fell ill of a bowel disease. It began with raging pain, and when this went off, leaving him weak, an awkward symptom succeeded—nothing, either liquid or solid, would stay in his stomach a minute. The doctor said: "He must die if this goes on many hours. Therefore boil thou now a chicken with a golden angel in the water, and let him sup that!" Alas! Gilt chicken broth shared the fate of the humbler viands, its predecessors. Then the curé steeped the thumb of Saint Sergius in beef broth. Same result.

Then Joan ran weeping to Margaret to borrow some linen to make his shroud. "Let me see him," said Margaret. She came in and felt his pulse. "Ah!" said she, "I doubt they have not gone to the root. Open the window! Art stifling him; now change all his linen."

"Alack, woman, what for? Why foul more linen for a dying man?" objected the medieval wife.

"Do as thou art bid," said Margaret dully, and left the room.

Joan somehow found herself doing as she was bid. Margaret returned with her apron full of a flowering herb. She made a decoction, and took it to the bedside, and before giving it to the patient, took a spoonful herself, and smacked her lips hypocritically. "That is fair," said he with a feeble attempt at humor. "Why, 'tis sweet, and now 'tis bitter." She engaged him in conversation as soon as he had taken it. This bitter-sweet stayed by him. Seeing which, she built on it as cards are built—mixed a very little Schiedam in the third spoonful, and a little beaten yolk of egg in the seventh. And so with the patience of her sex, she coaxed his body out of death's grasp; and finally Nature, being patted on the back instead of kicked under the bed, set Jorian Ketel on his legs again. But the doctress made them both swear never to tell a soul her guilty deed. "They would put me in prison, away from my child." The simple that saved Jorian was called sweet feverfew. She gathered it in his own garden. Her eagle eye had seen it growing out of the window.

Margaret and Joan, then, reached the hermit's cave, and placed their present on the little platform. Margaret then applied her mouth to the aperture made for that purpose, and said: "Holy hermit, we bring thee butter and eggs of the best. And I, a poor deserted girl, wife yet not wife, and mother of the sweetest babe, come to pray thee tell me whether he is quick or dead, true to his vows or false."

A faint voice issued from the cave: "Trouble me not with the things of earth, but send me a holy friar. I am dying."

"Alas!" cried Margaret. "Is it e'en so, poor soul? Then let us in to help thee."

"Saints forbid! Thine is a woman's voice. Send me a holy friar!"

They went back as they came. Joan could not help saying, "Are women imps o' darkness then, that they must not come a-nigh a dying bed?" But Margaret was too deeply dejected to say anything. Joan applied rough consolation. But she was not listened to till she said:

"And Jorian will speak out ere long. He is just on the boil. He is very grateful to thee, believe it."

"Seeing is believing," replied Margaret with quiet bitterness.

"Not but what he thinks you might have saved him with something more out o' the common than yon. 'A man of my inches to be cured wi' feverfew,' says he. 'Why, if there is a sorry herb,' says he. 'Why, I was thinking o' pulling all mine up,' says he. I up and told him remedies were none the better for being far-fetched; you and feverfew cured him when the grand medicines came up faster than they went down. So says I, 'You may go down on your four bones to feverfew.' But indeed, he is grateful at bottom. You are all his thought and all his chat. But he sees Gerard's folk coming around ye, and good friends, and he said only last night—"

"Well?"

"He made me vow not to tell ye."

"Prithee, tell me."

"Well, he said: 'An' if I tell what little I know, it won't bring him back, and it will set them all by the ears. I wish I had more headpiece,' said he, 'I am sore perplexed. But least said is soonest mended.' Yon is his favorite word, he comes back to't from a mile off."

Margaret shook her head. "Ay, we are wading in deep waters, my poor babe and me."

It was Saturday night—and no Luke.

CHAPTER XLVIII

BROTHER CLEMENT, directed by the nuns, avoided a bend in the river, and striding lustily forward, reached a station some miles nearer the coast than that where Luke lay in wait for Gerard Eliassoen. And the next morning he started early, and was in Rotterdam at noon. He made at once for the port, not to keep Jerome waiting. He observed several monks of his Order on the quay. He went to them, but Jerome was not amongst them. He asked one of them whether Jerome had arrived. "Surely, Brother," was the reply.

"Prithee, where is he?"

"Where? Why, there!" said the monk, pointing to a ship in full sail. And Clement now noticed that all the monks were looking seaward.

"What, gone without me! Oh, Jerome! Jerome!" cried he in a voice of anguish. Several of the friars turned round and stared.

"You must be Brother Clement," said one of them at length, and on this they kissed him and greeted him with brotherly warmth, and gave him a letter Jerome had charged them with for him. It was a hasty scrawl.

The writer told him coldly a ship was about to sail for England, and he was loath to lose time. He (Clement) might follow if he pleased, but he would do much better to stay behind and preach to his own countryfolk. "Give the glory to God, Brother. You have a wonderful power over Dutch hearts, but you are no match for those haughty islanders—you are too tender.

"Know thou that on the way I met one who asked me for thee under the name thou didst bear in the world. Be on thy guard! Let not the world catch thee again by any silken net. And remember, solitude, fasting, and prayer are the sword, spear, and shield of the soul. Farewell."

Clement was deeply shocked and mortified at this contemptuous desertion, and this cold-blooded missive. He promised the good monks to sleep at the convent, and to preach wherever the Prior should appoint (for Jerome had raised him to the skies as a preacher), and then withdrew abruptly, for he was cut to the quick, and wanted to be alone. He asked himself, was there some incurable fault in him, repulsive to so true a son of Dominic? Or was Jerome himself devoid of that Christian Love which Saint Paul had placed above faith itself? Shipwrecked with him, and saved on the same fragment of the wreck—his pupil, his penitent, his son in the Church—and now for four hundred miles his fellow traveler in Christ—and to be shaken off like dirt the first opportunity, with harsh and cold disdain. "Why, worldly hearts are no colder nor less trusty than this," said he. "The only one that ever really loved me lies in a grave hard by. Fly me, fly to England, man born without a heart! I will go and pray over a grave at Sevenbergen."

Three hours later he passed Peter's cottage. A troop of noisy children were playing about the door, and the house had been repaired, and a new outhouse added. He turned his head hastily away, not to disturb a picture his memory treasured, and went to the churchyard. He sought among the tombstones for Margaret's. He could not find it. He could not believe they had begrudged her a tombstone, so searched the churchyard all over again.

"Oh, poverty! Stern poverty! Poor soul, thou wert like me, no one was left that loved thee when Gerard was gone."

He went into the church, and after kissing the steps, prayed long and earnestly for the soul of her whose resting-place he could not find. Coming out of the church he saw a very old man looking over the little churchyard gate. He went toward him, and asked him did he live in the place.

"Fourscore and twelve years, man and boy. And I come here every day of late, holy Father, to take a peep. This is where I look to bide ere long."

"My son, can you tell me where Margaret lies?"

"Margaret? There's a-many Margarets here."

"Margaret Brandt. She was daughter to a learned physician."

"As if I don't know that," said the old man, pettishly. "But she doesn't lie here. Bless you, they left this a longful while ago. Gone in a moment, and the house empty. What, is she dead? Margaret a Peter dead? Now only think on't. Like enow, like enow. They great towns do terribly disagree wi' countryfolk."

"What great towns, my son?"

"Well, 'twas Rotterdam they went to from here, so I heard tell, or was it Amsterdam? Nay, I trow 'twas Rotterdam. And gone there to die!" Clement sighed.

" 'Twas not in her face now, that I saw. And I can mostly tell. Alack, there was a blooming young flower to be cut off so soon, and an old weed like me left standing still. Well, well, she was a May rose yon. Dear heart, what a winsome smile she had, and—"

"God bless thee, my son," said Clement, "farewell!" and he hurried away.

He reached the convent at sunset, and watched and prayed in the chapel for Jerome, and Margaret, till it was long past midnight and his soul had recovered its cold calm.

The next day, Sunday, after mass, was a bustling day at Catherine's house in the Hoog Straet. The shop was now quite ready, and Cornelis and Sybrandt were to open it next day. Their names were above the door; also their sign, a white lamb sucking a gilt sheep. Eli had come, and brought them some more goods from his store to give them a good start. The hearts of the parents glowed at what they were doing, and the pair themselves walked in the garden together, and agreed they were sick of their old life, and it was more pleasant to make money than waste it; they vowed to stick to business like wax. Their mother's quick and ever watchful ear overheard this resolution through an open window and she told Eli. The family supper was to include Margaret and her boy, and be a kind of inaugural feast, at which good trade advice was to flow from the elders, and good wine to be drunk to the success of the converts to commerce from agriculture in its unremunerative form—wild oats. So Margaret had come over to help her mother-in-law, and also to shake off her own deep languor, and both their faces were as red as the fire. Presently in came Joan with a salad from Jorian's garden.

"He cut it for you, Margaret. You are all his chat, I shall be jealous. I told him you were to feast today. But oh, lass, what a sermon in the new kerk! Preaching? I never heard it till this day."

"Would I had been there, then," said Margaret, "for I am dried up for want of dew from Heaven."

"Why, he preacheth again this afternoon. But mayhap you are wanted here."

"Not she," said Catherine. "Come, away ye go, if y' are minded."

"Indeed," said Margaret, "methinks I should not be such a damper at table if I could come to't warm from a good sermon."

"Then you must be brisk," observed Joan. "See, the folk are wending that way, and as I live, there goes the holy friar. Oh bless us and save us, Margaret, the hermit! We forgot." And this active woman bounded out of the house and ran across the road and stopped the friar. She returned as quickly. "There, I was bent on seeing him nigh hand."

"What said he to thee?"

"Says he, 'My daughter, I will go to him ere sunset, God willing.' The sweetest voice. But oh, my mistresses, what thin cheeks for a young man, and great eyes—not far from your color, Margaret."

"I have a great mind to go hear him," said Margaret. "But my cap is not very clean, and they will all be there in their snow-white mutches."

"There, take my handkerchief out of the basket," said Catherine. "You cannot have the child, I want him for my poor Kate. It is one of her ill days."

Margaret replied by taking the boy upstairs. She found Kate in bed.

"How art thou, sweetheart? Nay, I need not ask. Thou art in sore pain, thou smilest so. See, I have brought thee one thou lovest."

"Two, by my way of counting," said Kate, with an angelic smile. She had a spasm at that moment would have made some of us roar like bulls.

"What, in your lap?" said Margaret, answering a gesture of the suffering girl. "Nay, he is too heavy, and thou in such pain."

"I love him too dear to feel his weight," was the reply.

Margaret took this opportunity and made her toilet. "I am for the kerk," said she, "to hear a beautiful preacher." Kate sighed. "And a minute ago, Kate, I was all agog to go—that is the way with me this month past, up and down, up and down, like the waves of the Zuyder Zee. I'd as lieve stay aside thee—say the word!"

"Nay," said Kate, "prithee go, and bring me back every word. Welladay that I cannot go myself." And the tears stood in the patient's eyes. This decided Margaret, and she kissed Kate, looked under her lashes at the boy, and heaved a little sigh.

"I trow I must not," said she. "I never could kiss him a little, and my father was dead against waking a child by day or night. When 'tis thy pleasure to wake, speak thy Aunt Kate the two new words thou hast gotten." And she went out, looking lovingly over her shoulder, and shut the door inaudibly.

"Joan, you will lend me a hand, and peel these?" said Catherine.

"That I will, dame." And the cooking proceeded with silent vigor.

"Now, Joan, them which help me cook and serve the meat, they help me eat it—that's a rule."

"There's worse laws in Holland than that. Your will is my pleasure, mistress, for my Jorian hath got his supper i' the air. He is digging today, by good luck."

Margaret came down.

"Eh, woman, yon is an ugly trade. There, she has just washed her face and gi'en her hair a turn, and now who is like her? Rotterdam, that for you!" And Catherine snapped her fingers at the capital. "Give us a buss, hussy! Now mind, Eli won't wait supper for the Duke. Wherefore, loiter not after your kerk is over."

Joan and she both followed her to the door, and stood at it watching her a good way down the street. For among homely housewives going out o' doors is half an incident. Catherine commented on the launch. "There, Joan, it is almost to me as if I had just started my own daughter for kerk, and stood a-looking after—the which I've done it many's and many's the times. Joan, lass, she won't hear a word against our Gerard; and, be he alive, he has used her cruel; that is why my bowels yearn for the poor wench."

CHAPTER XLIX

THE sermon had begun when Margaret entered the great church of St. Laurens. It was a huge edifice, far from completed. Churches were not built in a year. The side aisles were roofed, but not the mid-aisle nor the chancel; the pillars and arches were pretty perfect, and some of them whitewashed. But only one window in the whole church was glazed; the rest were at present great jagged openings in the outer walls.

But today all these uncouth imperfections made the church beautiful. It was a glorious summer afternoon, and the sunshine came broken into marvelous forms through those irregular openings, and played bewitching pranks upon so many broken surfaces. It streamed through the gaping walls, and clove the dark cool side aisles with rivers of glory, and dazzled and glowed on the white pillars beyond.

And nearly the whole central aisle was checkered with light and shade in broken outlines. The shades seeming cooler and more soothing than ever shade was, and the light like patches of amber diamond, animated with heavenly fire. And above, from west to east the blue sky vaulted the lofty aisle, and seemed quite close.

The sunny caps of the women made a sea of white contrasting exquisitely with that vivid vault of blue. For the mid-aisle, huge as it was, was crammed, yet quite still. The words and the mellow, gentle, earnest voice of the preacher held them mute.

Margaret stood spellbound at the beauty, the devotion, "the great calm." She got behind a pillar in the north aisle; and there, though she could hardly catch a word, a sweet devotional languor crept over her at the loveliness of the place and the preacher's musical voice; and balmy oil seemed to trickle over the waves in her heart and smooth them. So she leaned against the pillar with eyes half-closed, and all seemed soft and dreamy. She felt it good to be there.

Presently she saw a lady leave an excellent place opposite, to get out of the sun, which was indeed pouring on her head from the window. Margaret went round softly but swiftly, and was fortunate enough to get the place. She was now beside a pillar of the south aisle, and not above fifty feet from the preacher. She was at his side, a little behind him, but could hear every word.

Her attention however was soon distracted by the shadow of a man's head and shoulders bobbing up and down so drolly she had some ado to keep from smiling. Yet it was nothing essentially droll. It was the sexton digging. She found that out in a moment by looking behind her through the window, to whence the shadow came.

Now as she was looking at Jorian Ketel digging, suddenly a tone of the preacher's voice fell upon her ear and her mind so distinctly, it seemed literally to strike her, and make her vibrate inside and out. Her hand went to her bosom, so strange and sudden was the thrill. Then she turned round and looked at the preacher. His back was turned and nothing visible but his tonsure. She sighed. That tonsure, being all she saw, contradicted the tone effectually.

Yet she now leaned a little forward with downcast eyes, hoping for that accent again. It did not come. But the whole voice grew strangely upon her. It rose and fell as the preacher warmed, and it seemed to waken faint echoes of a thousand happy memories. She would not look to dispel the melancholy pleasure this voice gave her.

Presently, in the middle of an eloquent period, the preacher stopped. She almost sighed; a soothing music had ended. Could the sermon be ended already? No. She looked around, the people did not move. A good many faces seemed now to turn her way. She looked behind her sharply. There was nothing there. Startled countenances near her now eyed the preacher. She followed their looks, and there in the pulpit was a face of a staring corpse. The friar's eyes, naturally large and made larger by the thinness of his cheeks, were dilated to supernatural size, and glaring, her way, out of a bloodless face.

She cringed and turned fearfully round; for she thought there *must* be some terrible thing near her. No, there was nothing; she was the outside figure of the listening crowd.

At this moment the church fell into commotion. Figures got up all over the building, and craned forward. Agitated faces by hundreds gazed from the friar to Margaret, and from Margaret to the friar. The turning to and fro of so many caps made a loud rustle. Then came shrieks of nervous women, and buzzing of men; and Margaret, seeing so many eyes leveled at her, shrank terrified behind the pillar, with one scared, hurried glance at the preacher.

Momentary as that glance was, it caught in that stricken face an expression that made her shiver. She turned faint and sat down on a heap of chips the workmen had left, and buried her face in her hands. The sermon went on again. She heard the sound of it, but not the sense. She tried to think, but her mind was in a whirl. Thought would fix itself in no shape but this: that on that prodigy-stricken face she had seen a look stamped. And the recollection of that look now made her quiver from head to foot. For that look was *"recognition."*

The sermon, after wavering some time, ended in a strain of exalted, nay, feverish, eloquence that went far to make the crowd forget the preacher's strange pause and ghastly glare.

Margaret mingled hastily with the crowd, and went out of the church with them. They went their ways home. But she turned at the door and went into the churchyard, to Peter's grave. Poor as she was, she had given him a slab and a headstone. She sat down on the slab and kissed it. Then threw her apron over her head that no one might distinguish her by her hair.

"Father," she said, "thou hast often heard me say I am wading in deep waters, but now I begin to think God only knows the bottom of them. I'll follow that friar round the world, but I'll see him at arm's length. And he shall tell me why he looked toward me like a dead man wakened—and not a soul behind me. Oh, Father, you often praised me here. Speak a word for me *there.* For I am wading in deep waters."

Her father's tomb commanded a side view of the church door. And on that tomb she sat, with her face covered, waylaying the holy preacher.

The cool church, checkered with sunbeams and crowned with heavenly purple, soothed and charmed Father Clement, as it did Margaret; and more, it carried his mind direct to the Creator of all good and pure delights. Then his eye fell on the great aisle crammed with his countryfolk—a thousand snowy caps, filigreed with gold. Many a hundred leagues he had traveled, but seen nothing like them, except snow. In the morning he had thundered, but this sweet afternoon seemed out of tune with threats. His bowels yearned over that multitude, and he must tell them of God's love. Poor souls, they heard almost as little of it from the pulpit then a-days as the heathen used. He told them the glad tidings of salvation. The people hung upon his gentle, earnest tongue.

He was not one of those preachers who keep gyrating in the pulpit like the weathercock on the steeple. He moved the hearts of others more than his own body. But on the other hand he did not entirely neglect those who were in bad places. And presently, warm with this theme, that none of all that multitude might miss the joyful tidings of Christ's love, he turned him toward the south aisle.

And there, in a stream of sunshine from the window, was the radiant face of Margaret Brandt. He gazed at it without emotion. It just benumbed him, soul and body. But soon the words died in his throat, and he trembled as he glared at it. There, with her auburn hair bathed in sunbeams, and glittering like the gloriola of a saint, and her face glowing doubly, with its own beauty and the sunshine it was set in—stood his dead love. She was leaning very lightly against a white column. She was listening with tender, downcast lashes. He had seen her listen so to him a hundred times. There was no change in *her*. This was the blooming Margaret he had left, only a shade riper and more lovely. He stared at her with monstrous eyes and bloodless cheeks.

The people died out of his sight. He heard, as in a dream, a rustling and rising all over the church, but could not take his prodigy-stricken eyes off that face, all life, and bloom, and beauty, and that wondrous auburn hair glistening gloriously in the sun. He gazed, thinking she must vanish. She remained. All in a moment she was looking at him, full. Her own violet eyes! !

At this he was beside himself, and his lips parted to shriek out her name, when she turned her head swiftly, and soon after vanished, but not without one more glance, which, though rapid as lightning, encountered his, and left her crouching and quivering with her mind in a whirl, and him panting and gripping the pulpit convulsively. For this glance of hers, though not recognition, was the startled inquiring, nameless, indescribable look that precedes recognition. He made a mighty effort, and muttered something nobody could understand, then feebly resumed his discourse, and stammered and babbled on a while, till by degrees, forcing himself, now she was out of sight, to look on it as a vision from the other world, he rose into a state of unnatural excitement, and concluded in a style of eloquence that electrified the simple, for it bordered on rhapsody.

The sermon ended, he sat down on the pulpit stool, terribly shaken. But presently an idea very characteristic of the time took possession of him. He had sought her grave at Sevenbergen in vain. She had now been permitted to appear to him, and show him that she was buried *here*—probably hard by that very pillar where her spirit had showed itself to him. This idea once adopted soon settled on his mind with all the certainty of a fact. And he felt he had only to speak to the sexton (whom to his great disgust he had seen working during the sermon) to learn the spot where she was laid.

The church was now quite empty. He came down from the pulpit and stepped through an aperture in the south wall onto the grass, and went up to the sexton. He knew him in a moment. But Jorian never suspected the poor lad whose life he had saved in this holy friar. The loss of his shapely beard had wonderfully altered the outline of his face. This had changed him even more than his tonsure, his short hair sprinkled with premature gray, and his cheeks thinned and paled by fasts and vigils.

"My son," said Friar Clement, softly, "if you keep any memory of those whom you lay in the earth, prithee tell me, is any Christian buried inside the church, near one of the pillars?"

"Nay, Father," said Jorian, "here in the churchyard lie buried all that buried be. Why?"

"No matter. Prithee tell me then where lieth Margaret Brandt."

"Margaret Brandt?" And Jorian stared stupidly at the speaker.

"She died about three years ago, and was buried here."

"Oh, that is another matter," said Jorian. "That was before my time; the vicar could tell you, likely, if so be she was a gentlewoman, or at least rich enough to pay him his fee."

"Alas, my son, she was poor (and paid a heavy penalty for it), but born of decent folk. Her father, Peter, was a learned physician. She came hither from Sevenbergen—to die."

When Clement had uttered these words his head sunk upon his breast, and he seemed to have no power nor wish to question Jorian more. I doubt even if he knew where he was. He was lost in the past. Jorian put down his spade, and standing upright in the grave, set his arms akimbo and said sulkily:

"Are you making a fool of me, holy sir, or has some wag been making a fool of you?"

And having relieved his mind thus, he proceeded to dig again, with a certain vigor that showed his somewhat irritable temper was ruffled. Clement gazed at him with a puzzled but gently reproachful eye; for the tone was rude, and the words unintelligible. Good-natured, though crusty, Jorian had not thrown up three spadesful ere he became ashamed of it himself.

"Why, what a base churl am I to speak thus to thee, holy Father, and thou standing there looking at me like a lamb. Aha! I have it. 'Tis Peter Brandt's grave you would fain see, not Margaret's. He does lie here, hard by the west door. There, I'll show you." And he laid down his spade, and put on his doublet and jerkin to go with the friar.

He did not know there was anybody sitting on Peter's tomb. Still less that she was watching for this holy friar.

CHAPTER L

WHILE Jorian was putting on his doublet and jerkin to go to Peter's tomb, his tongue was not idle.

"They used to call him a magician out Sevenbergen way. And they do say he gave 'em a touch of his trade at parting, told 'em he saw Margaret's lad a-coming down Rhine in brave clothes and store o' money, but his face scarred by foreign glaive, and not altogether so many arms and legs as a went away wi'. But, dear heart, naught came on't. Margaret is still wearying for her lad, and Peter, he lies as quiet as his neighbors. Not but what she hath put a stone slab over him, to keep him where he is, as you shall see."

He put both hands on the edge of the grave and was about to raise himself out of it, but the friar laid a trembling hand on his shoulder, and said in a strange whisper:

"How long since died Peter Brandt?"

"About two months. Why?"

"And his daughter buried him, say you?"

"Nay, I buried him, but she paid the fee and reared the stone. Why?"

"Then—but he had but one daughter, Margaret?"

"No more, leastways, that he owned to."

"Then you think Margaret is—is alive?"

"Think? Why I should be dead else. Riddle me that."

"Alas, how can I? You love her!"

"No more than reason, being a married man and father of four more sturdy knaves like myself. Nay, the answer is, she saved my life scarce six weeks agone. Now had she been dead she couldn't ha' kept me alive. Bless your heart, I couldn't keep a thing on my stomach, nor doctors couldn't make me. My Joan says ' 'Tis time to buy thee a shroud.' 'I dare say, so 'tis,' says I, 'but try and borrow one first.' In comes my lady, this Margaret, which she died three years ago, by your way on't, opens the windows, makes 'em shift me where I lay, and cures me in the twinkling of a bedpost. But wi' what? There pinches the shoe—with the scurviest herb, and out of my own garden, too, with sweet feverfew. A herb, quotha, 'tis a weed; leastways it was a weed till it cured me; but now whene'er I pass my bunch I doff bonnet, and, says I, 'My service t'ye.' Why, how now, Father, you look wondrous pale, and now you are red, and now you are white. Why, what is the matter? What in heaven's name is the matter?"

"The surprise—the joy—the wonder—the fear," gasped Clement.

"Why, what is it to thee? Art thou of kin to Margaret Brandt?"

"Nay, but I knew one that loved her well, so well her death nigh killed him, body and soul. And yet thou sayest she lives. And I believe thee."

Jorian stared, and after a considerable silence said very gravely: "Father, you have asked me many questions, and I have answered them truly. Now for our Lady's sake answer me but two. Did you in very sooth know one who loved this poor lass? Where?"

Clement was on the point of revealing himself, but he remembered Jerome's letter, and shrank from being called by the name he had borne in the world.

"I knew him in Italy," said he.

"If you knew him, you can tell me his name," said Jorian, cautiously.

"His name was Gerard Eliassoen."

"Oh, but this is strange! Stay, what made thee say Margaret Brandt was dead?"

"I was with Gerard when a letter came from Margaret Van Eyck. The letter told him she he loved was dead and buried. Let me sit down, for my strength fails me. Foul play! Foul play!"

"Father," said Jorian, "I thank Heaven for sending thee to me. Ay, sit ye down, ye do look like a ghost—ye fast overmuch to be strong. My mind misgives me. Methinks I hold the clue to this riddle, and if I do, there be two knaves in this town whose heads I would fain batter to pieces as I do this mold." And he clenched his teeth and raised his long spade above his head, and brought it furiously down upon the heap several times. "Foul play? You never said a truer word i' your life; and if you know where Gerard is now, lose no time, but show him the trap they have laid for him. Mine is but a dull head, but whiles the slow hound puzzles out the scent—go to. And I do think you and I ha' got hold of two ends o' one stick, and a main foul one."

Jorian then, after some of those useless preliminaries men of his class always deal in, came to the point of his story. He had been employed by the Burgomaster of Tergou to repair the floor of an upper room in his house, and when it was almost done, coming suddenly to fetch away his tools, curiosity had been excited by some loud words below, and he had lain down on his stomach and heard the Burgomaster talking about a letter which Cornelis and Sybrandt were minded to convey into the place of one that a certain Hans Memling was taking to Gerard. "And it seems their will was good, but their stomach was small; so to give them courage the old man showed them a drawer full of silver, and if they did the trick they should each put a hand in, and have all the silver they could hold in't. Well, Father," continued Jorian, "I thought not much on't at the time, except for the bargain itself. *That* kept me awake mostly all night. Think on't! Next morning at peep of day who should I see but my masters Cornelis and Sybrandt come out of their house each with a black eye. 'Oho,' says I, 'what yon Hans hath put his mark on ye. Well now, I hope that is all you have got for your pains.' Didn't they make for the Burgomaster's house? I to my hiding-place."

At this part of Jorian's revelation the monk's nostril dilated, and his restless eye showed the suspense he was in.

"Well, Father," continued Jorian, "the Burgomaster brought them into that same room. He had a letter in his hand, but I am no scholar. However, I have got as many eyes in my head as the Pope hath, and I saw the drawer opened, and those two knaves put in each a hand and draw it out full. And, saints in glory, how they tried to hold more, and more, and more o' yon stuff! And Sybrandt, he had daubed his hand in something sticky—I think 'twas glue—and he made shift to carry one or two pieces away a-sticking to the back of his hand, he, he, he! 'Tis a sin to laugh. So you see luck was on the wrong side as usual. They had done the trick, but how they did it, that, methinks, will never be known till Doomsday. Go to, they left their immortal jewels in yon drawer.

"Well, they got a handful of silver for them; the Devil had the worst o' yon bargain. There, Father, that is off my mind. Often I longed to tell it someone, but I durst not to the women, or Margaret would not have had a friend left in the world; for those two black-hearted villains are the favorites. 'Tis always so. Have not the old folk just taken a brave new shop for them in this very town, in the Hoog Straet? There may you see their sign, a gilt sheep and a lambkin; a brace of wolves sucking their dam would be nigher the mark. And there the whole family feast this day. Oh, 'tis a fine world! What, not a word, holy Father? You sit there like stone, and have not even a curse to bestow on them, the stony-hearted miscreants. What, was it not enough the poor lad was all alone in a strange land? Must his own flesh and blood go and lie away the one blessing his enemies had left him?

"And then think of her pining and pining all these years, and sitting at the window looking a-down the street for Gerard! And so constant, so tender, and true. My wife says she is sure no woman ever loved a man truer than she loves the lad those villains have parted from her; and the day never passes but she weeps salt tears for him. And when I think that but for those two greedy lying knaves, yon winsome lad, whose life I saved, might be by her side this day the happiest he in Holland; and the sweet lass, that saved my life, might be sitting with her cheek upon her sweetheart's shoulder, the happiest she in Holland in place of the saddest—oh, I thirst for their blood, the nasty, sneaking, lying, cogging, cowardly, heartless, bowelless—how now?!"

The monk started wildly up, livid with fury and despair, and rushed headlong from the place with both hands clenched and raised on high. So terrible was this inarticulate burst of fury that Jorian's puny ire died out at sight of it, and he stood looking dismayed after the human tempest he had launched.

While thus absorbed he felt his arm grasped by a small, tremulous hand. It was Margaret Brandt. He started. Her coming there just then seemed so strange. She had waited long on Peter's tombstone, but the friar did not come. So she went into the church to see if he was there still. She could not find him.

Presently, going up the south aisle, the gigantic shadow of a friar came rapidly along the floor and part of a pillar, and seemed to pass through her. She was near screaming, but in a moment remembered Jorian's shadow had come in so from the churchyard, and tried to clamber out the nearest way. She did so, but with some difficulty, and by that time Clement was just disappearing down the street. Yet so expressive at times is the body as well as the face, she could see he was greatly agitated. Jorian and she looked at one another, and at the wild figure of the distant friar.

"Well?" said she to Jorian, trembling.

"Well," said he, "you startled me. How come you here, of all people?"

"Is this a time for idle chat? What said he to you? He has been speaking to you. Deny it not."

"Girl, as I stand here, he asked me whereabout you were buried in this churchyard."

"Ah?"

"I told him nowhere, thank heaven. You were alive and saving other folk from the churchyard."

"Well?"

"Well, the long and the short is, he knew thy Gerard in Italy, and a letter came saying you were dead, and it broke thy poor lad's heart. Let me see, who was the letter written by? Oh, by the Demoiselle Van Eyck. That was *his* way of it. But I up and told him nay, 'twas neither demoiselle nor dame that penned yon lie, but Ghysbrecht van Swieten, and those foul knaves Cornelis and Sybrandt. These changed the true letter for one of their own. I told him as how I saw the whole villainy done, through a chink, and now if I have not been and told you!"

"Oh, cruel, cruel! But he lives. The fear of fears is gone. Thank God!"

"Ay, lass, and as for thine enemies, I have given them a dig. For yon friar is friendly to Gerard, and he is gone to Eli's house, methinks. For I told him where to find Gerard's enemies and thine, and wow, but he will give them their lesson! If ever a man was mad with rage, it's yon. He turned black and white, and parted like a stone from a sling. Girl, there was thunder in his eye and silence on his lips. Made me cold, a did."

"Oh, Jorian, what have you done?" cried Margaret. "Quick, quick! Help me thither, for the power is gone all out of my body. You know him not as I do. Oh, if you had seen the blow he gave Ghysbrecht, and heard the frightful crash! Come, save him from worse mischief. The water is deep enow, but not bloody yet. Come!"

Her accents were so full of agony that Jorian sprang out of the grave and came with her, huddling on his jerkin as he went. But as they hurried along, he asked her what on earth she meant. "I talk of this friar, and you answer me of Gerard."

"Man, see you not, *this* is Gerard!"

"This, Gerard? What mean ye?"

"I mean, yon friar is my boy's father. I have waited for him long, Jorian. Well, he is come to me at last. And thank God for it. Oh, my poor child! Quicker, Jorian, quicker!"

"Why, thou art mad as he. Stay! By Saint Bavon, yon *was* Gerard's face.

'Twas naught like it, yet somehow—'twas it. Come on! Come on! Let me see the end of this."

"The end? How many of us will live to see that?"

They hurried along in breathless silence, till they reached Hoog Straet. Then Jorian tried to reassure her.

"You are making your own trouble," said he. "Who says he has gone thither? More likely to the convent to weep and pray, poor soul. Oh, cursed, cursed villains!"

"Did you tell him where those villains bide?"

"Ay, that I did."

"Then quicker, oh, Jorian, quicker! I see the house. Thank God and all the saints, I shall be in time to calm him. I know what I'll say to him, Heaven forgive me! Poor Catherine, 'tis of her I think. She has been a mother to me."

The shop was a corner house with two doors: one in the main street, for customers, and a house door round the corner. Margaret and Jorian were now within twenty yards of the shop when they heard a roar inside, like as of some wild animal, and the friar burst out, white and raging, and went tearing down the street. Margaret screamed, and sank fainting on Jorian's arm. Jorian shouted after him:

"Stay, madman, know thy friends."

But he was deaf, and went headlong, shaking his clenched fists high, high, in the air.

"Help me in, good Jorian," moaned Margaret, turning suddenly calm. "Let me know the worst, and die."

He supported her trembling limbs into the house. It seemed unnaturally still; not a sound. Jorian's own heart beat fast. A door was before him, unlatched. He pushed it softly with his left hand, and Margaret and he stood on the threshold.

It was suppertime. Eli's family were collected round the board, Margaret only was missing. To Catherine's surprise Eli said he would wait a bit for her.

"Why, I told her you would not wait for the Duke."

"She is not the Duke. She is a poor, good lass that hath waited not minutes, but years, for a graceless son of mine. You can put the meat on the board all the same. Then we can fall to without further loss o' time when she does come."

The smoking dishes smelt so savory that Eli gave way. "She will come if we begin," said he. "They always do. Come, sit ye down, Mistress Joan, y' are not here for a slave, I trow, but a guest. There, I heard a quick step—off covers, and fall to."

The covers were withdrawn, and the knives brandished. Then burst into the room not the expected Margaret, but a Dominican friar, livid with rage. He was at the table in a moment, in front of Cornelis and Sybrandt, threw his tall body over the narrow table, and, with two hands hovering above their shrinking heads like eagles over a quarry, he cursed them by name, soul and body, in this world and the next. It was an age eloquent in curses, and this curse was so full, so minute, so blighting, blasting, withering, and tremendous, that I am afraid to put all the words on paper:

"Cursed be the lips," he shrieked, "which spoke the lie that Margaret was dead! May they rot before the grave, and kiss the white-hot iron in Hell thereafter. Doubly cursed be the hands that changed those letters, and be they struck off by the hangman's knife, and handle hellfire forever. Thrice accursed be the cruel hearts that did conceive that damned lie, to part true love forever. May they sicken and wither on earth joyless, loveless, hopeless, and wither to dust before their time, and burn in eternal fire."

He cursed the meat at their mouths, and every atom of their bodies, from their hair to the soles of their feet. Then, turning from the cowering, shuddering pair, who had almost hid themselves beneath the table, he tore a letter out of his bosom and flung it down before his father.

"Read that, thou hard old man that didst imprison thy son, read, and see what monsters thou hast brought into the world. The memory of my wrongs, and hers, dwell with you all forever! I will meet you again at the Judgment Day. On earth ye will never see me more."

And in a moment, as he had come so he was gone, leaving them stiff, and cold, and white as statues round the smoking board. And this was the sight that greeted Margaret's eyes and Jorian's—pale figures of men and women petrified around the untasted food, as Eastern poets feigned. Margaret glanced her eye round, and gasped out: "Oh, joy! All here, no blood hath been shed. Oh, you cruel, cruel men! I thank God he hath not slain you."

At sight of her Catherine gave an eloquent scream, then turned her head away. But Eli, who had just cast his eye over the false letter and begun to understand it all, seeing the other victim come in at that very moment with *her* wrongs reflected in her sweet, pale face, started to his feet in a transport of rage, and shouted, "Stand clear, and let me get at the traitors! I'll hang for them." And in a moment he whipped out his short sword and fell upon them.

"Fly!" screamed Margaret. "Fly!"

They slipped howling under the table, and crawled out the other side. But, ere they could get to the door, the furious old man ran round and intercepted them. Catherine only screamed and wrung her hands, and blood would certainly have flowed but Margaret and Jorian seized the fiery old man's arms, and held them with all their might whilst the pair got clear of the house. Then they let him go, and he went vainly raging after them out into the street. They were a furlong off, running like hares. He hacked down the board on which their names were written, and brought it indoors, and flung it into the chimney place.

Catherine was sitting rocking herself, with her apron over her head. Joan had run to her husband. Margaret had her arms round Catherine's neck, and, pale and panting, was yet making efforts to comfort her. But it was not to be done.

"Oh, my poor children!" she cried. "Oh, miserable mother! 'Tis a mercy Kate was ill upstairs. There, I have lived to thank God for that!" she cried, with a fresh burst of sobs. "It would have killed her. He had better have stayed in Italy, as come home to curse his own flesh and blood, and set us all by the ears."

"Oh, hold your chat, woman," cried Eli, angrily. "You are still on the side of the ill-doer. You are cheap served, your weakness made the rogues what they are. I was for correcting them in their youth—for sore ills, sharp remedies—but you still sided with their faults, and undermined me, and baffled wise severity. And you, Margaret, leave comforting her that ought rather to comfort you, for what is her hurt to yours? But she never had a grain of justice under her skin, and never will. So come thou to me, that am thy father from this hour."

This was a command, so she kissed Catherine, and went tottering to him, and he put her on a chair beside him, and she laid her feeble head on his honest breast. But not a tear—it was too deep for that.

"Poor lamb," said he. After awhile: "Come, good folks," said true Eli, in a broken voice, to Jorian and Joan, "we are in a little trouble, as you see, but that is no reason you should starve. For our Lady's sake, fall to, and add not to my grief the reputation of a churl. What the dickens!" added he, with a sudden ghastly attempt at stoutheartedness, "the more knaves I have the luck to get shut of, the more my need of true men and women to help me clear the dish, and cheer mine eye with honest faces about me where else were gaps. Fall to, I do entreat ye."

Catherine, sobbing, backed his request. Poor, simple, antique, hospitable souls! Jorian, whose appetite, especially since his illness, was very keen, was for acting on this hospitable invitation, but Joan whispered a word in his ear, and he instantly drew back.

"Nay, I'll touch no meat that Holy Church hath cursed."

"In sooth, I forgot," said Eli, apologetically. "My son, who was reared at my table, hath cursed my victuals. That seems strange. Well, what God wills, man must bow to."

The supper was flung out into the yard. Jorian took his wife home, and heavy sadness reigned in Eli's house that night. Meantime, where was Clement? Lying at full length upon the floor of the convent church, with his lips upon the lowest step of the altar, in an indescribable state of terror, misery, penitence, and self-abasement, through all which struggled gleams of joy that Margaret was alive.

Night fell and found him lying there weeping, and praying, and morning would have found him there too, but he suddenly remembered that, absorbed in his own wrongs and Margaret's, he had committed another sin besides intemperate rage. He had neglected a dying man.

He rose instantly, groaning at his accumulated wickedness, and set-out to repair the omission. The weather had changed. It was raining hard, and when he got clear of the town, he heard the wolves baying; they were on foot. But Clement was himself again, or nearly. He thought little of danger or discomfort, having a shameful omission of religious duty to repair. He went stoutly forward through rain and darkness.

And, as he went, he often beat his breast, and cried, "*Mea culpa! Mea culpa!*"

CHAPTER LI

WHAT that sensitive mind, and tender conscience, and loving heart, and religious soul went through even in a few hours, under a situation so sudden and tremendous, is perhaps beyond the power of words to paint.

After spending the night with the dying hermit in giving and receiving holy consolations, he set out not for Rotterdam, but for Tergou. He went there to confront his fatal enemy the Burgomaster, and by means of that parchment, whose history was itself a romance, to make him disgorge, and give Margaret her own.

Heated and dusty, he stopped at the fountain, and there began to eat his black bread and drink of the water. But in the middle of his frugal meal a female servant came running and begged him to come and shrive her dying master. He returned the bread to his wallet, and followed her without a word. She took him—to the Stadthouse. He drew back with a little shudder when he saw her go in. But he almost instantly recovered himself, and followed her into the house, and up the stairs. And there in bed, propped up by pillows, lay his deadly enemy, looking already like a corpse.

Clement eyed him a moment from the door, and thought of all—the tower, the wood, the letter. Then he said in a low voice, "*Pax vobiscum!*" He trembled a little while he said it.

The sick man welcomed him as eagerly as his weak state permitted. "Thank heaven, thou art come in time to absolve me from my sins, Father, and pray for my soul, thou and thy brethren."

"My son," said Clement, "before absolution cometh confession. In which act there must be no reservation, as thou valuest thy soul's weal. Bethink thee, therefore, wherein thou hast most offended God and the Church while I offer up a prayer for wisdom to direct thee."

Clement then knelt and prayed, and when he rose from his knees, he said to Ghysbrecht, with apparent calmness, "My son, confess thy sins."

"Ah, Father," said the sick man, "they are many and great."

"Great then be thy penitence, my son, so shalt thou find God's mercy great."

Ghysbrecht put his hands together and began to confess with every appearance of contrition. He owned he had eaten meat in mid-Lent. He had often absented himself from mass on the Lord's Day, and saints' days, and had trifled with other religious observances, which he enumerated with scrupulous fidelity. When he had done, the friar said, quietly:

" 'Tis well, my son. These be faults. Now to thy crimes. Thou hadst done better to begin with them."

"Why, Father, what crimes lie to my account if these be none?"

"Am I confessing to thee, or thou to me?" said Clement somewhat severely.

"Forgive me, Father! Why, surely, I to you. But I know not what you call crimes."

"The seven deadly sins, art thou clear of them?"

"Heaven forfend I should be guilty of them. I know them not by name."

"Many do them all that cannot name them. Begin with that one which leads to lying, theft, and murder."

"I am quit of that one anyway. How call you it?"

"*Avarice*, my son."

"Avarice? Oh, as to that, I have been a saving man all my day, but I have kept a good table, and not altogether forgotten the poor. But, alas, I am a great sinner! Mayhap the next will catch me. What is the next?"

"We have not yet done with this one. Bethink thee, the Church is not to be trifled with."

"Alas, am I in a condition to trifle with her now? Avarice? Avarice?" He looked puzzled and innocent.

"Hast thou ever robbed the fatherless?" inquired the friar.

"Me? Robbed the fatherless?" gasped Ghysbrecht. "Not that I mind."

"Once more, my son, I am forced to tell thee thou art trifling with the Church. Miserable man! Another evasion and I leave thee, and fiends will straightway gather round thy bed, and tear thee down to the bottomless pit."

"Oh, leave me not! Leave me not!" shrieked the terrified old man. "The Church knows all. I *must* have robbed the fatherless. I will confess. Who shall I begin with? My memory for names is shaken."

The defense was skillful, but in this case failed.

"Hast thou forgotten Floris Brandt?" said Clement stonily.

The sick man reared himself in bed in a pitiable state of terror.

"How knew you that?" said he.

"The Church knows many things," said Clement, coldly, "and by many ways that are dark to thee. Miserable impenitent, you called her to your side hoping to deceive her. You said 'I will not confess to the curé, but to some friar who knows not my misdeeds. So will I cheat the Church on my deathbed, and die as I have lived.' But God, kinder to thee than thou art to thyself, sent to thee one whom thou couldst not deceive. He has tried thee; he was patient with thee, and warned thee not to trifle with Holy Church, but all is in vain. Thou canst not confess, for thou art impenitent as a stone. Die, then, as thou hast lived. Methinks I see the fiends crowding round the bed for their prey. They wait but for me to go. And I go."

He turned his back, but Ghysbrecht, in extremity of terror, caught him by the frock. "Oh, holy man, mercy! Stay. I will confess all, all. I robbed my friend Floris. Alas, would it had ended there, for he lost little by me, but I kept the land from Peter his son, and from Margaret, Peter's daughter. Yet I was always going to give it back, but I couldn't, I couldn't."

"Avarice, my son, avarice. Happy for thee 'tis not too late."

"No. I will leave it her by will. She will not have long to wait for it now— not above a month or two at farthest."

"For which month's possession thou wouldst damn thy soul forever. Thou fool!"

The sick man groaned, and prayed the friar to be reasonable. The friar firmly, but gently and persuasively, persisted, and with infinite patience detached the dying man's grip from another's property. There were times when his patience was tried, and he was on the point of thrusting his hand into his bosom and producing the deed, which he had brought for that purpose. But after yesterday's outbreak he was on his guard against choler, and, to conclude, he conquered his impatience, he conquered a personal repugnance to the man so strong as to make his own flesh creep all the time he was struggling with this miser for his soul. And at last, without a word about the deed, he won him to make full and prompt restitution.

How the restitution was made will be briefly related elsewhere, also certain curious effects produced upon Ghysbrecht by it, and when and on what terms Ghysbrecht and Clement parted.

As soon as he was quite sure Margaret had her own, and was a rich woman—

He disappeared.

CHAPTER LII

IT was the day after that terrible scene. The little house in the Hoog Straet was like a grave, and none more listless and dejected than Catherine, so busy and sprightly by nature. After dinner, her eyes red with weeping, she went to the convent to try and soften Gerard, and lay the first stone at least of a reconciliation. It was some time before she could make the porter understand whom she was seeking. Eventually she learned he had left late last night and was not expected back. She went sighing with the news to Margaret. She found her sitting idle, like one with whom life had lost its savor. She had her boy clasped so tight in her arms as if he was all she had left, and she feared someone would take him too. Catherine begged her to come to the Hoog Straet.

"What for?" sighed Margaret. "You cannot but say to yourselves, 'She is the cause of all.' "

"Nay, nay," said Catherine, "we are not so ill-hearted, and Eli is so fond on you. You will maybe soften him."

"Oh, if you think I can do any good, I'll come," said Margaret, with a weary sigh.

They found Eli and a carpenter putting up another name in place of Cornelis's and Sybrandt's and what should that name be but Margaret Brandt's? With all her affection for Margaret, this went through poor Catherine like a knife.

"The bane of one is another's meat," said he.

"Can he make me spend the money unjustly?" replied Margaret coldly.

"You are a good soul," said Catherine. "Ay, so best, sith he is the strongest."

The next day Giles dropped in, and Catherine told the story all in favor of the black sheep, and invited his pity for them, anathematized by their brother and turned on the wide world by their father. But Giles's prejudices ran the other way. He heard her out, and told her bluntly the knaves had got off cheap; they deserved to be hanged at Margaret's door into the bargain, and, dismissing them with contempt, crowed with delight at the return of his favorite.

"I'll show him," said he, "what 'tis to have a brother at court with a heart to serve a friend, and a head to point the way."

"Bless thee, Giles," murmured Margaret, softly.

"Thou wast ever his stanch friend, dear Giles," said Little Kate, "but alack I know not what thou canst do for him now."

Giles had left them, and all was sad and silent again when a well-dressed man opened the door softly and asked was Margaret Brandt here.

"D'ye hear, lass? You are wanted," said Catherine briskly. In her the gossip was indestructible.

"Well, Mother," said Margaret listlessly, "and here I am."

A shuffling of feet was heard at the door, and a colorless, feeble, old man was assisted into the room. It was Ghysbrecht van Swieten. At sight of him Catherine shrieked and threw her apron over her head and Margaret shuddered violently and turned her head swiftly away not to see him. A feeble voice issued from the strange visitor's lips,

"Good people, a dying man hath come to ask your forgiveness."

"Come to look on your work, you mean," said Catherine, taking down her apron and bursting out sobbing. "There, there, she is fainting. Look to her, Eli, quick!"

"Nay," said Margaret, in a feeble voice, "the sight of him gave me a turn, that is all. Prithee let him say his say, and go, for he is the murderer of me and mine."

"Alas," said Ghysbrecht, "I am too feeble to say it standing, and no one biddeth me sit down."

Eli, who had followed him into the house, interfered here, and said half-sullenly, half-apologetically, "Well, Burgomaster, 'tis not our wont to leave a visitor standing whiles we sit. But, man, man, you have wrought us too much ill." And the honest fellow's voice began to shake with anger he fought hard to contain, because it was his own house.

Then Ghysbrecht found an advocate in one who seldom spoke in vain in that family.

It was Little Kate. "Father, Mother," said she, "my duty to you, but this is not well. Death squares all accounts. And see you not death in his face? I shall not live long, good friends, and his time is shorter than mine."

Eli made haste and set a chair for their dying enemy with his own hands. Ghysbrecht's attendants put him into it. "Go fetch the boxes," said he. They brought in two boxes, and then retired, leaving their master alone in the family he had so cruelly injured.

Every eye was now bent on him except Margaret's. He undid the boxes with unsteady fingers, and brought out of one the title deeds of a property at Tergou.

"This land and these houses belonged to Floris Brandt, and do belong to thee of right, his granddaughter. These I did usurp for a debt long since defrayed with interest. These I now restore their rightful owner with penitent tears. In this other box are three hundred and forty golden angels, being the rent and fines I have received from that land more than Floris Brandt's debt to me. I have kept compt, still meaning to be just one day, but avarice withheld me. Pray, good people, against temptation! I was not born dishonest, yet you see."

"Well, to be sure!" cried Catherine. "And you the Burgomaster! Hast whipt good store of thieves in thy day. However," said she, on second thought, " 'tis better late than never. What, Margaret? Art deaf? The good man hath brought thee back thine own. Art a rich woman. Alack, what a mountain o' gold!"

"Bid him keep land and gold and give me back my Gerard, that he stole from me with his treason," said Margaret, with her head still averted.

"Alas," said Ghysbrecht, "would I could! What I can I have done. Is it naught? It cost me a sore struggle, and I rose from my last bed to do it myself, lest some mischance should come between her and her rights."

"Old man," said Margaret, "since thou, whose idol is pelf, hast done this, God and His saints will, as I hope, forgive thee. As for me, I am neither saint nor angel, but only a poor woman whose heart thou hast broken. Speak to him, Kate, for I am like the dead."

Kate meditated a little while, and then her soft silvery voice fell like a soothing melody upon the air.

"My poor sister hath a sorrow that riches cannot heal. Give her time, Ghysbrecht. 'Tis not in nature she should forgive thee all. Her boy is fatherless, and she is neither maid, wife, nor widow, and the blow fell but two days syne that laid her heart a-bleeding."

A single heavy sob from Margaret was the comment to these words.

"Therefore, give her time! And ere thou diest, she will forgive thee all, ay, even to pleasure me, that haply shall not be long behind thee, Ghysbrecht. Meantime, we, whose wounds be sore but not so deep as hers, do pardon thee, a penitent and a dying man, and I, for one, will pray for thee from this hour. Go in peace!"

Their little oracle had spoken, it was enough. Eli even invited him to break a manchet and drink a stoup of wine to give him heart for his journey. But Ghysbrecht declined, and said what he had done was a cordial to him.

"Man seeth but a little way before him, neighbor. This land I clung so to it was a bed of nettles to me all the time. 'Tis gone, and I feel happier and livelier-like for the loss on't."

He called his men and they lifted him into the litter. When he was gone Catherine gloated over the money. She had never seen so much together, and was almost angry with Margaret, for "sitting out there like an image." And she dilated on the advantages of money. And she teased Margaret till at last she prevailed on her to come and look at it.

"Better let her be, Mother," said Kate. "How can she relish gold, with a heart in her bosom liker lead?" But Catherine persisted.

The result was, Margaret looked down at all her wealth with wondering eyes. Then suddenly wrung her hands and cried with piercing anguish, "*Too late! Too late!*"

And shook off her leaden despondency only to go into strong hysterics over the wealth that came too late to be shared with him she loved. A little of this gold, a portion of this land, a year or two ago when it was as much her own as now, and Gerard would have never left her side for Italy or any other place. Too late! Too late!

Not many days after this came the news that Margaret Van Eyck was dead and buried. By a will she had made a year before, she left all her property, after her funeral expenses and certain presents to Reicht Heynes, to her dear daughter Margaret Brandt, requesting her to keep Reicht as long as unmarried. By this will Margaret inherited a furnished house, and pictures and sketches that in the present day would be a fortune. Among the pictures was one she valued more than a gallery of others. It represented "A Betrothal." The solemnity of the ceremony was marked in the grave face of the man and the demure complacency of the woman. She was painted almost entirely by Margaret Van Eyck, but the rest of the picture by Jan. The accessories were exquisitely finished, and remain a marvel of skill to this day. Margaret Brandt sent word to Reicht to stay in the house till such time as she could find the heart to put foot in it, and miss the face and voice that used to meet her there, and to take special care of the picture "in the little cubboard"—meaning the diptych.

For some days Margaret dreaded, almost as much as she desired, the coming interview with Gerard. She said to herself, "I wonder not he keeps away a while, for so should I." However, he would hear he was a father, and the desire to see their boy would overcome everything. "And," said the poor girl to herself, "if so be that meeting does not kill me, I feel I shall be better after it than I am now."

But when day after day went by and he was not heard of, a freezing suspicion began to crawl and creep toward her mind. What if his absence was intentional? What if he had gone to some cold-blooded monks his fellows, and they had told him never to see her more? The convent had ere this shown itself as merciless to truelovers as the grave itself.

At this thought the very life seemed to die out of her. And now for the first time deep indignation mingled at times with her grief and apprehension. "Can he have ever loved me? To run from me and his boy without a word!"

While her mind was in this state, Giles came roaring: "I've hit the clout! *Our Gerard is Vicar of Gouda.*"

A very brief sketch of the dwarf's court life will suffice to prepare the reader for his own account of this feat. Some months before he went to court his intelligence had budded. He himself dated the change from a certain eighth of June when, swinging by one hand along with the week's washing on a tight rope in the drying-ground, something went crack inside his head, and lo! intellectual powers unchained. At court his shrewdness and bluntness of speech, coupled with his gigantic voice and his small stature, made him a power. Without the last item I fear they would have conducted him to that unpopular gymnasium, the gallows. The young Duchess of Burgundy, and Marie, the heiress apparent, both petted him, as great ladies have petted dwarfs in all ages.

Finding Margaret unable to believe the good news, and skeptical as to the affairs of Holy Church being administered by dwarfs, he narrated as follows:

"When the Princess sent for me to her bedroom as of custom, to keep her out of languor, I came not mirthful nor full of country dicts, as is my wont, but dull as lead.

" 'Why, what aileth thee?' quo' she. 'Art sick?' 'At heart,' quo' I. 'Alas, he is in love,' quo' she. Whereat five brazen hussies, which they call them maids of honor, did giggle loud. 'Not so mad as that,' said I, 'seeing what I see at court of womenfolk.'

" 'There, ladies,' quo' the Princess, 'best let him a be. 'Tis a liberal mannikin, and still giveth more than he taketh of saucy words.'

" 'In all sadness,' quo' she, 'what is the matter?'

"I told her I was meditating, and what perplexed me was that other folk could now and then keep their word, but princes never.

" 'Heydey,' says she, 'thy shafts fly high this morn.' I told her, 'Ay, for they hit the truth.'

"She said I was as keen as keen, but it became not me to put riddles to her, nor her to answer them. 'Stand aloof a bit, mesdames,' said she, 'and thou speak without fear,' for she saw I was in sad earnest.

"I began to quake a bit, for mind ye, she can doff freedom and don dignity quicker than she can slip out of her dressing-gown into kirtle of state. But I made my voice so soft as honey (wherefore smilest?), and I said, 'Madam, one evening, a matter of five years agone, as ye sat with your mother, the Countess of Charolois, who is now in Heaven, worse luck, you wi' your lute and she wi' her tapestry, or the like, do ye mind there came in to ye a fair youth—with a letter from a painter body, one Margaret Van Eyck?'

"She said she thought she did. 'Was it not a tall youth, exceedingly comely?'

" 'Ay, madam,' said I. 'He was my brother.'

" 'Your brother?' said she, and did eye me like all over. (What dost smile at?)

"So I told her all that passed between her and Gerard, and how she was for giving him a bishopric, but the good Countess said, 'Gently, Marie! He is too young,' and with that they did both promise him a living. 'Yet,' said I, 'he hath been a priest a long while, and no living. Hence my bile.'

" 'Alas!' said she, ' 'tis not by my goodwill. For all this thou hast said is sooth, and more, I do remember, my dear mother said to me, "See thou to it if I be not here." ' So then she cried out, 'Ay, dear Mother, no word of thine shall ever fall to the ground.'

"I seeing her so ripe, said quickly, 'Madam, the Vicar of Gouda died last week.' (For when ye seek favors of the great, behooves ye know the very thing ye aim at.)

" 'Then thy brother is Vicar of Gouda,' quo' she, 'so sure as I am heiress of Burgundy and the Netherlands. Nay, thank me not, good Giles,' quo' she, 'but my good mother. And I do thank thee for giving of me somewhat to do for her memory.' And doesn't she fall a-weeping for her mother? And doesn't that set me off a-sniveling for my good brother that I love so dear, and to think that a poor little elf like me could yet speak in the ear of princes, and make my beautiful brother Vicar of Gouda. Eh, lass, it is a bonny place, and a bonny manse, and hawthorn in every bush at springtide, and dog roses and eglantine in every summer hedge. I know what the poor fool affects, leave that to me."

The dwarf began his narrative strutting to and fro before Margaret, but he ended it in her arms. For she could not contain herself, but caught him and embraced him warmly. "Oh, Giles," she said, blushing, and kissing him, "I cannot keep my hands off thee, thy body it is so little and thy heart so great. Thou art his true friend. Bless thee! Bless thee! Bless thee! Now we shall see him again. We have not set eyes on him since that terrible day."

"Gramercy, but that is strange," said Giles. "Maybe he is ashamed of having cursed those two vagabones, being our own flesh and blood, worse luck."

"Think you that is why he hides?" said Margaret eagerly.

"Ay, if he is hiding at all. However, I'll cry him by bellman."

"Nay, that might much offend him."

"What care I? Is Gouda to go vicarless, and the manse in nettles?"

And to Margaret's secret satisfaction, Giles had the new Vicar cried in Rotterdam and the neighboring towns. He easily persuaded Margaret that in a day or two Gerard would be sure to hear, and come to his benefice. She went to look at his manse, and thought how comfortable it might be made for him, and how dearly she should love to do it.

But the days rolled on, and Gerard came neither to Rotterdam nor Gouda. Giles was mortified, Margaret indignant, and very wretched. She said to herself, "Thinking me dead, he comes home, and now, because I am alive, he goes back to Italy, for that is where he has gone."

Joan advised her to consult the hermit of Gouda.

"Why, sure he is dead by this time."

"Yon one, belike. But the cave is never long void. Gouda ne'er wants a hermit."

But Margaret declined to go again to Gouda on such an errand. "What can he know, shut up in a cave? Less than I, belike. Gerard hath gone back t' Italy. He hates me for not being dead."

Presently a Tergovian came in with a word from Catherine that Ghysbrecht van Swieten had seen Gerard later than anyone else. On this Margaret determined to go and see the house and goods that had been left her, and take Reicht Heynes home to Rotterdam. And, as may be supposed, her steps took her first to Ghysbrecht's house. She found him in his garden, seated in a chair with wheels. He greeted her with a feeble voice, but cordially, and when she asked him whether it was true he had seen Gerard since the fifth of August, he replied:

"Gerard no more, but Friar Clement. Ay, I saw him, and blessed be the day he entered my house."

He then related in his own words his interview with Clement. He told her, moreover, that the friar had afterward acknowledged he came to Tergou with the missing deed in his bosom on purpose to make him disgorge her land, but that finding him disposed toward penitence, he had gone to work the other way.

"Was not this a saint, who came to right thee, but must needs save his enemy's soul in the doing it?"

To her question whether he had recognized him, he said:

"I ne'er suspected such a thing. 'Twas only when he had been three days with me that he revealed himself. Listen while I speak my shame and his praise. I said to him 'The land is gone home, and my stomach feels lighter; but there is another fault that clingeth to me still.' Then told I him of the letter I had writ at request of his brethren, I whose place it was to check them. Said I, 'Yon letter was writ to part truelovers, and, the Devil aiding, it hath done the foul work. Land and houses I can give back, but yon mischief is done forever.' 'Nay,' quoth he, 'not forever, but for life. Repent it then while thou livest.' 'I shall,' said I, 'but how can God forgive it? I would not,' said I, 'were I He.'

" 'Yet will He certainly forgive it,' quoth he, 'for He is ten times more forgiving than I am, and I forgive thee.' I stared at him, and then he said softly, but quavering-like: 'Ghysbrecht, look at me closer. I am Gerard the son of Eli.' And I looked, and looked, and at last, lo! it was Gerard. Verily I had fallen at his feet with shame and contrition, but he would not suffer me. That became not mine years and his, for a particular fault. 'I say not I forgive thee without a struggle,' said he, 'not being a saint. But these three days thou hast spent in penitence, I have worn under thy roof in prayer, and I do forgive thee.' Those were his very words."

Margaret's tears began to flow, for it was in a broken and contrite voice the old man told her this unexpected trait in her Gerard. He continued:

"And even with that he bade me farewell. 'My work here is done now,' said he. I had not the heart to stay him, for, let him forgive me ever so, the sight of me must be wormwood to him. He left me in peace, and may a dying man's blessing wait on him, go where he will! Oh, girl, when I think of his wrongs, and thine, and how he hath avenged himself by saving this stained soul of mine, my heart is broken with remorse, and these old eyes shed tears by night and day."

"Ghysbrecht," said Margaret, weeping, "since he hath forgiven thee, I forgive thee too. What is done is done, and thou hast let me know this day that which I had walked the world to hear. But oh, Burgomaster, thou art an understanding man—now help a poor woman which hath forgiven thee her misery." She then told him all that had befallen. "And," said she, "they will not keep the living for him forever. He bids fair to lose that, as well as break all our hearts."

"Call my servant!" cried the Burgomaster with sudden vigor.

He sent him for a table and writing materials, and dictated letters to the burgomasters in all the principal towns in Holland, and one to a Prussian authority, his friend. His clerk and Margaret wrote them, and he signed them.

"There," said he, "the matter shall be dispatched throughout Holland by trusty couriers, and as far as Basle in Switzerland. And fear not but we will soon have the Vicar of Gouda to his village."

She went home animated with fresh hopes, and accusing herself of ingratitude to Gerard. "I value my wealth now," said she. She also made a resolution never to blame his conduct till she should hear from his own lips his reasons.

Not long after her return from Tergou, a fresh disaster befell. Catherine, I must premise, had secret interviews with the black sheep, the very day after they were expelled. Cornelis followed her to Tergou, and lived there on secret contribution; but Sybrandt chose to remain in Rotterdam. Ere Catherine left, she asked Margaret to lend her two gold angels. "For," said she, "all mine are spent." Margaret was delighted to lend them or give them, but the words were scarce out of her mouth ere she caught a look of regret and distress on Kate's face, and she saw directly whither her money was going. She gave Catherine the money, and went and shut herself up with her boy. Now this money was to last Sybrandt till his mother could make some good excuse for visiting Rotterdam again, and then she would bring the idle dog some of her own industrious scrapings.

But Sybrandt, having gold in his pocket, thought it inexhaustible, and, being now under no shadow of restraint, led the life of a complete sot until one afternoon, in a drunken frolic, he climbed on the roof of the stable at the inn he was carousing in, and proceeded to walk along it, a feat he had performed many times when sober. But now his unsteady brain made his legs unsteady, and he rolled down the roof and fell with a loud thwack onto a horizontal paling, where he hung a moment in a semicircle, then toppled over and lay silent on the ground, amid roars of laughter from his boon companions.

When they came to pick him up he could not stand, but fell down giggling at each attempt. On this they went staggering and roaring down the street with him, and carried him, at great risk of another fall, to the shop in the Hoog Straet. For he had babbled his own shame all over the place.

As soon as he saw Margaret he hiccupped out, "Here is the doctor that cures all hurts, a bonny lass." He also bade her observe he bore her no malice, for he was paying her a visit sore against his will. "Wherefore, prithee send away these drunkards; and let you and me have t'other glass, to drown all unkindness."

All this time Margaret was pale and red by turns at sight of her enemy and at his insolence. But one of the men whispered what had happened, and a streaky something in Sybrandt's face arrested her attention.

"And he cannot stand up, say you?"

"A couldn't just now. Try, comrade! Be a man now!"

"I am a better man than thou," roared Sybrandt. "I'll stand up and fight ye all for a crown."

He started to his feet, and instantly rolled into his attendant's arms with a piteous groan. He then began to curse his boon companions, and declare they had stolen away his legs. He could feel nothing below the waist.

"Alas, poor wretch!" said Margaret. She turned very gravely to the men, and said: "Leave him here. And if you have brought him to this, go on your knees, for you have spoiled him for life. He will never walk again. His back is broken."

The drunken man caught these words, and the foolish look of intoxication fled, and a glare of anguish took its place. "The curse," he groaned, "the curse!"

Margaret and Reicht Heynes carried him carefully and laid him on the softest bed.

"I must do as *he* would do," whispered Margaret. "He was kind to Ghysbrecht."

Her opinion was verified. Sybrandt's spine was fatally injured, and he lay groaning and helpless, fed and tended by her he had so deeply injured. The news was sent to Tergou; and Catherine came over. It was a terrible blow to her. Moreover she accused herself as the cause. "Oh, false wife, oh, weak mother," she cried. "I am rightly punished for my treason to my poor Eli." She sat for hours at a time by his bedside rocking herself in silence, and was never quite herself again, and the first gray hairs began to come in her poor head from that hour.

As for Sybrandt, all his cry was now for Gerard. He used to whine to Margaret like a suffering hound: "Oh, sweet Margaret, oh, bonny Margaret, for our Lady's sake find Gerard, and bid him take his curse off me. Thou art gentle, thou art good, thou wilt entreat for me, and he will refuse thee naught." Catherine shared his belief that Gerard could cure him, and joined her entreaties to his. Margaret hardly needed this. The Burgomaster and his agents having failed, she employed her own, and spent money like water.

The months rolled on, and Sybrandt improved in spirit but not in body, he was Margaret's pensioner for life. And a long-expected sorrow fell upon poor Catherine, and left her still more bowed down; and she lost her fine hearty bustling way, and never went about the house singing now; and her nerves were shaken, and she lived in dread of some terrible misfortune falling on Cornelis. The curse was laid on him as well as Sybrandt. She prayed Eli, if she had been a faithful partner all these years, to take Cornelis into his house again, and let her live awhile at Rotterdam.

"I have good daughters here," said she, "but Margaret is so tender, and thoughtful, and the little Gerard, he is my joy. He grows liker his father every day, and his prattle cheers my heavy heart, and I do love children."

And Eli, sturdy but kindly, consented sorrowfully.

And the people of Gouda petitioned the Duke for a vicar, a real Vicar. "Ours cometh never nigh us," said they, "this six months past. Our children they die unchristened, and our folk unburied, except by some chance comer." Giles's influence baffled this just complaint once, but a second petition was prepared, and he gave Margaret little hope that the present position could be maintained a single day. So then Margaret went sorrowfully to the pretty manse to see it for the last time, ere it should pass forever into a stranger's hands.

"I think he would have been happy here," she said, and turned heartsick away.

On their return, Reicht Heynes proposed to her to go and consult the hermit.

"What?" said Margaret. "Joan has been at you. She is the one for hermits. I'll go, if 'tis but to show thee they know no more than we do." And they went to the cave.

It was an excavation partly natural, partly artificial, in a bank of rock overgrown by brambles. There was a rough stone door on hinges, and a little window high up, and two apertures, through one of which the people announced their gifts to the hermit and put questions of all sorts to him; and when he chose to answer, his voice came dissonant and monstrous out at another small aperture.

On the face of the rock this line was cut—

Felix qui in Domino nirus ab orbe fugit.

Margaret observed to her companion that this was new since she was here last.

"Ay," said Reicht, "like enough," and looked up at it with awe. Writing even on paper she thought no trifle, but on rock!

She whispered: " 'Tis a far holier hermit than the last; he used to come in the town now and then, but this one ne'er shows his face to mortal man."

"And that is holiness?"

"Ay, sure."

"Then what a saint a dormouse must be!"

"Out, fie, mistress! Would ye even a beast to a man?"

"Come, Reicht," said Margaret, "my poor father taught me overmuch. So I will e'en sit here, and look at the manse once more. Go thou forward and question thy solitary, and tell me whether ye get naught or nonsense out of him, for 'twill be one."

As Reicht drew near the cave, a number of birds flew out of it. She gave a little scream, and pointed to the cave to show Margaret they had come thence. On this Margaret felt sure there was no human being in the cave, and gave the matter no further attention. She fell into a deep reverie while looking at the little manse. She was startled from it by Reicht's hand upon her shoulder, and a faint voice, saying, "Let us go home."

"You got no answer at all, Reicht," said Margaret, calmly.

"No, Margaret," said Reicht, despondently. And they returned home.

Perhaps after all Margaret had nourished some faint secret hope in her heart, though her reason had rejected it, for she certainly went home more dejectedly. Just as they entered Rotterdam, Reicht said: "Stay! Oh, Margaret, I am ill at deceit, but 'tis death to utter ill news to thee, I love thee so dear."

"Speak out, sweetheart," said Margaret. "I have gone through so much I am almost past feeling any fresh trouble."

"Margaret, the hermit did speak to me."

"What, a hermit there? Among all those birds?"

"Ay, and doth not that show him a holy man?"

"I' God's name, what said he to thee, Reicht?"

"Alas! Margaret, I told him thy story, and I prayed him for our Lady's sake, tell me where thy Gerard is. And I waited long for an answer, and presently a voice came like a trumpet. 'Pray for the soul of Gerard, the son of Eli!'"

"Ah!"

"Oh, woe is me that I have this to tell thee, sweet Margaret! Bethink thee thou hast thy boy to live for yet."

"Let me get home," said Margaret, faintly.

Passing down the Brede Kirk Straet they saw Joan at the door.

Reicht said to her, "Eh, woman, she has been to your hermit, and heard no good news."

"Come in," said Joan, eager for a gossip.

Margaret would not go in. But she sat down disconsolate on the lowest step but one of the little external staircase that led into Joan's house, and let the other two gossip their fill at the top of it.

"Oh," said Joan, "what yon hermit says is sure to be sooth. He is that holy, I am told, that the very birds consort with him."

"What does that prove?" said Margaret, deprecatingly. "I have seen my Gerard tame the birds in winter till they would eat from his hand."

A look of pity at this parallel passed between the other two. But they were both too fond of her to say what they thought. Joan proceeded to relate all the marvelous tales she had heard of this hermit's sanctity. How he never came out but at night, and prayed among the wolves, and they never molested him; and how he bade the people not bring him so much food to pamper his body, but to bring him candles.

"The candles are to burn before his saint," whispered Reicht, solemnly.

"Ay, lass, and to read his holy books wi'. A neighbor o' mine saw his hand come out and the birds sat thereon and pecked crumbs. She went for to kiss it, but the holy man whippit it away in a trice. They can't abide a woman to touch 'em, or even look at 'em, saints can't."

"What like was his hand, wife? Did you ask her?"

"What is my tongue for, else? Why, dear heart, all one as ourn; by the same token a had a thumb and four fingers."

"Look ye there now."

"But a deal whiter nor yourn and mine."

"Ay, ay."

"And main skinny."

"Alas."

"What could ye expect? Why a live upon air, and prayer, and candles."

"Ah, well," continued Joan, "poor thing, I whiles think 'tis best for her to know the worst. And now she hath gotten a voice from Heaven, or almost as good, and behooves her pray for his soul. One thing, she is not so poor now as she was, and never fell riches to a better hand. And she is only come into her own for that matter, so she can pay the priest to say masses for him, and that is a great comfort."

In the midst of their gossip Margaret, in whose ears it was all buzzing, though she seemed lost in thought, got softly up and crept away with her eyes on the ground, and her brows bent.

"She hath forgotten I am with her," said Reicht Heynes ruefully.

She had her gossip out with Joan, and then went home. She found Margaret seated cutting out a pelisse of gray cloth, and a cape to match. Little Gerard was standing at her side, inside her left arm, eying the work and making it more difficult by wriggling about, and fingering the arm with which she held the cloth steady; to all which she submitted with imperturbable patience and complacency.

"Ot's that, mammy?"

"A pelisse, my pet."

"Ot's a p'lisse?"

"A great frock. And this is the cape to't."

"Ot's it for?"

"To keep his body from the cold, and the cape is for his shoulders, or to go over his head like the countryfolk. 'Tis for a hermit."

"Ot's a 'ermit?"

"A holy man that lives in a cave all by himself."

"In de dark?"

"Ay, whiles."

"Oh."

In the morning Reicht was sent to the hermit with the pelisse, and a pound of thick candles. As she was going out of the door, Margaret said to her,

"Said you whose son Gerard was?"

"Nay, not I."

"Think, girl! How could he call him Gerard, son of Eli, if you had not told him?"

Reicht persisted she had never mentioned him but as plain Gerard. But Margaret told her flatly she did not believe her, at which Reicht was affronted, and went out with a little toss of her head. However, she determined to question the hermit again, and did not doubt he would be more liberal in his communication when he saw his nice new pelisse and the candles.

She had not been gone long when Giles came in with ill news. The living of Gouda would be kept vacant no longer. Margaret was greatly distressed at this. "Oh, Giles," said she, "ask for another month. They will give thee another month maybe."

He returned in an hour to tell her he could not get a month. "They have given me a week," said he. "And what is a week?"

"Drowning bodies catch at strawen," was her reply. "A week? A little week?"

Reicht came back from her errand out of spirits. Her oracle had declined all further communications. So at least its obstinate silence might fairly be interpreted.

The next day Margaret put Reicht in charge of the shop, and disappeared all day. So the next day, and so the next. Nor would she tell anyone where she had been. Perhaps she was ashamed. The fact is she spent all those days on one little spot of ground. When they thought her dreaming, she was applying to every word that fell from Joan and Reicht the whole powers of a far acuter mind than either of them possessed.

She went to work on a scale that never occurred to either of them. She was determined to see the hermit, and question him face to face, not through a wall. She found that by making a circuit she could get above the cave and look down without being seen by the solitary. But when she came to do it, she found an impenetrable mass of brambles. After tearing her clothes and her hands and feet, so that she was soon covered with blood, the resolute, patient girl took out her scissors and steadily snipped and cut till she made a narrow path through the enemy. But so slow was the work that she had to leave it half-done. The next day she had her scissors fresh-ground, and brought a sharp knife as well; and gently, silently, cut her way through to the roof of the cave.

There she made an ambush of some of the cut brambles, so that the passers-by might not see her, and crouched with watchful eye till the hermit should come out. She heard him move underneath her. But he never left his cell. She began to think it was true that he only came out at night. The next day she came early, and brought a jerkin she was making for little Gerard, and there she sat all day working and watching with dogged patience.

At four o'clock the birds began to feed, and a great many of the smaller kinds came fluttering round the cave, and one or two went in. But most of them, taking a preliminary seat on the bushes, suddenly discovered Margaret, and went off with an agitated flirt of their little wings. And although they sailed about in the air they would not enter the cave. Presently, to encourage them, the hermit, all unconscious of the cause of their tremors, put out a thin white hand with a few crumbs in it. Margaret laid down her work softly, and gliding her body forward like a snake, looked down at it from above. It was but a few feet from her. It was as the woman described it, a thin, white hand.

Presently the other hand came out with a piece of bread, and the two hands together broke it and scattered the crumbs. But that other hand had hardly been out two seconds ere the violet eyes that were watching above dilated, and the gentle bosom heaved and the whole frame quivered like a leaf in the wind. What her swift eye had seen I leave the reader to guess. She suppressed the scream that rose to her lips, but the effort cost her dear. Soon the left hand of the hermit began to swim indistinctly before her gloating eyes, and with a deep sigh her head drooped, and she lay like a broken lily.

She was in a deep swoon, to which perhaps her long fast today and the agitation and sleeplessness of many preceding days contributed. And there lay beauty, intelligence, and constancy, pale and silent. And little that hermit guessed who was so near him. The little birds hopped on her now, and one nearly entangled his little feet in her rich auburn hair.

She came back to her troubles. The sun was set. She was very cold. She cried a little, but I think it was partly from the remains of physical weakness. And then she went home, praying God and the saints to enlighten her and teach her what to do for the best.

When she got home she was pale and hysterical, and would say nothing in answer to all their questions but her favorite word—"We are wading in deep waters."

The night seemed to have done wonders for her. She came to Catherine, who was sitting sighing by the fireside, and kissed and said, "Mother, what would you like best in the world?"

"Eh, dear," replied Catherine, despondently, "I know naught that would make me smile now. I have parted from too many that were dear to me. Gerard lost again as soon as found. Kate in Heaven, and Sybrandt down for life."

"Poor Mother! Mother dear, Gouda manse is to be furnished and cleaned and made ready all in a hurry. See, here be ten gold angels. Make them go far, good Mother, for I have ta'en over many already from my boy for a set of useless loons that were aye going to find him for me."

Catherine and Reicht stared at her a moment in silence, and then out burst a flood of questions, to none of which would she give a reply. "Nay," said she, "I have lain on my bed, and thought, and thought, and thought whiles you were all sleeping, and methinks I have got a clue to all. I love you, dear Mother, but I'll trust no woman's tongue. If I fail this time, I'll have none to blame but Margaret Brandt."

A resolute woman is a very resolute thing. And there was a deep, dogged determination in Margaret's voice and brow that at once convinced Catherine it would be idle to put any more questions at that time. She and Reicht lost themselves in conjectures, and Catherine whispered Reicht, "Bide quiet, then 'twill leak out,"—a shrewd piece of advice founded on general observation.

Within an hour Catherine was on the road to Gouda in a cart with two stout girls to help her, and quite a siege artillery of mops, and pails, and brushes. She came back with heightened color and something of the old sparkle in her eye, and kissed Margaret with a silent warmth that spoke volumes, and at five in the morning was off again to Gouda.

That night as Reicht was in her first sleep a hand gently pressed her shoulder, and she awoke and was going to scream.

"Whisht," said Margaret, and put her finger to her lips.

She then whispered, "Rise softly, don thy habits, and come with me!"

When she came down, Margaret begged her to loose Dragon and bring him along. Now Dragon was a great mastiff who had guarded Margaret Van Eyck and Reicht, two lone women, for some years, and was devotedly attached to the latter.

Margaret and Reicht went out with Dragon walking majestically behind them. They came back long after midnight and retired to rest. Catherine never knew. Margaret read her friends. She saw the sturdy faithful Frisian could hold her tongue, and Catherine could not. Yet I am not sure she would have trusted even Reicht had her nerve equaled her spirit. But with all her daring and resolution, she was a tender, timid woman, a little afraid of the dark, very afraid of being alone in it, and desperately afraid of wolves. Now Dragon could kill a wolf in a brace of shakes, but then Dragon would not go with her, but only with Reicht. So altogether she made one confidante.

The next night they made another moonlight reconnaissance, and with some result. Not the next night (it rained that night and extinguished their courage), but the next after, they took with them a companion, the last in the world Reicht Heynes would have thought of, yet she gave her warm approval as soon as she was told he was to go with them.

Imagine how these stealthy assailants trembled and panted when the moment of action came. Imagine, if you can, the tumult in Margaret's breast, the thrilling hopes, chasing and chased by sickening fears; the strange, and perhaps unparalleled mixture of tender familiarity and distant awe with which a lovely, and high-spirited, but tender adoring woman, wife in the eye of the law, and no wife in the eye of the Church, trembling, blushing paling, glowing, shivering, stole at night, noiseless as the dew, upon the hermit of Gouda.

And the stars above seemed never so bright and calm.

CHAPTER LIII

Yes, the hermit of Gouda was the vicar of Gouda, and knew it not, so absolute was his seclusion.

My reader is aware that the moment the frenzy of his passion passed, he was seized with remorse for having been betrayed into it. But perhaps only those who have risen as high in religious spirit as he had, and suddenly fallen, can realize the terror at himself that took possession of him. He felt like one whom self-confidence had betrayed to the very edge of a precipice. "Ah, good Jerome," he cried, "how much better you knew me than I knew myself! How bitter yet wholesome was your admonition!"

Accustomed to search his own heart, he saw at once that the true cause of his fury was Margaret. "I love her better than God," said he, despairingly, "better than the Church. From such a love what can spring to me, or to her?" He shuddered at the thought. "Let the strong battle temptation; 'tis for the weak to flee. And who is weaker than I have shown myself? What is my penitence, my religion? A pack of cards built by degrees into a fair-seeming structure, and lo! one breath of earthly love and it lies in the dust. I must begin again, and on a surer foundation." He resolved to leave Holland at once, and spend years of his life in some distant convent before returning to it. By that time the temptations of earthly passion would be doubly baffled; an older, and a better, monk, he should be more master of his earthly affections, and Margaret, seeing herself abandoned, would marry, and love another.

The very anguish this last thought cost him showed the self-searcher and self-denier that he was on the path of religious duty.

But in leaving her for his immortal good and hers, he was not to neglect her temporal weal. Indeed, the sweet thought he could make her comfort-able for life, and rich in this world's goods, which she was not bound to despise, sustained him in the bitter struggle it cost him to turn his back on her without one kind word or look. "Oh, what will she think of me?" he groaned. "Shall I not seem to her of all creatures the most heartless, inhu-man? But so best—ay, better she should hate me, miserable that I am. Heaven is merciful, and giveth my broken heart this comfort: I can make that villain restore her own, and she shall never lose another truelover by poverty. Another? Ah me, ah me! God and the saints to mine aid!"

How he fared on this errand has been related. But first, as you may perhaps remember, he went at night to shrive the hermit of Gouda. He found him dying, and never left him till he had closed his eyes and buried him beneath the floor of the little oratory attached to his cell. It was the peaceful end of a stormy life. The hermit had been a soldier, and even now carried a steel corselet next his skin, saying he was now Christ's soldier as he had been Satan's. When Clement had shriven him and prayed by him, he, in his turn, sought counsel of one who was dying in so pious a frame. The hermit advised him to be his successor in this peaceful re-treat. His had been a hard fight against the world, the flesh, and the Devil, and he had never thoroughly baffled them till he retired into the citadel of solitude.

These words and the hermit's pious and peaceful death, which speedily followed, and set as it were the seal of immortal truth on them, made a deep impression upon Clement. Nor in his case had they any prejudice to combat. The solitary recluse was still profoundly revered in the Church, whether immured as an anchorite, or anchoress, in some cave or cell be-longing to a monastery, or hidden in the more savage but laxer seclusion of the independent hermitage. And Clement knew more about the hermits of the Church than most divines at his time of life. He had read much thereon at the monastery near Tergou, had devoured their lives with won-der and delight in the manuscripts of the Vatican, and conversed earnestly about them with the mendicant friars of several nations.

Thus, though in those days he never thought to be a recluse, the road was paved, so to speak, and when the dying hermit of Gouda blessed the citadel of solitude, where he had fought the good fight and won it, and invited him to take up the breastplate of faith that now fell off his own shrunken body, Clement said within himself: "Heaven itself led my foot hither to this end." It struck him, too, as no small coincidence that his patron, Saint Bavon, was a hermit, and an austere one.

As soon as he was reconciled to Ghysbrecht van Swieten, he went eagerly to his new abode, praying Heaven it might not have been already occupied in these three days. The fear was not vain. These famous dens never wanted a human tenant long. He found the rude stone door ajar, then he made sure he was too late. He opened the door and went softly in. No, the cell was vacant, and there were the hermit's great ivory crucifix, his pens, ink, seeds, and memento mori, a skull; his cilice of hair, and another of bristles; his well-worn sheepskin pelisse and hood, his hammer, chisel, and psaltery, and so on. Men and women had passed that way, but none had ventured to intrude, far less to steal. Faith and simplicity had guarded that keyless door more securely than the houses of the laity were defended by their gates like a modern jail and thick iron bars at every window, and the gentry by moat, bastion, chevaux-de-frise, and portcullis.

As soon as Clement was fairly in the cell, there was a loud flap and a flutter, and down came a great brown owl from a corner, and whirled out of the window, driving the air cold on Clement's face. He started and shuddered. Was this seeming owl something diabolical, trying to deter him from his soul's good? On second thoughts, might it not be some good spirit the hermit had employed to keep the cell for him, perhaps the hermit himself? Finally he concluded that it was just an owl, and that he would try and make friends with it.

He knelt down and inaugurated his new life with prayer.

Clement had not only an earthly passion to quell, the power of which made him tremble for his eternal weal, but he had a penance to do for having given way to ire, his besetting sin, and cursed his own brothers.

He looked round this roomy cell furnished with so many comforts, and compared it with the pictures in his mind of the hideous place, a desert in a desert, where holy Jerome, hermit and the Plutarch of hermits, had wrestled with sickness, temptation, and despair four mortal years; and with the inaccessible and thorny niche, a hole in a precipice, where the boy hermit Benedict buried himself and lived three years on the pittance the good monk Romanus could spare him from his scanty commons, and subdivided that mouthful with his friend, a raven; and the hollow tree of his patron Saint Bavon, and the earthly purgatory at Fribourg, where lived a nameless saint in a horrid cavern, his eyes chilled with perpetual gloom and his ears stunned with an eternal waterfall. These and scores more of the dismal dens in which true hermits had worn out their wasted bodies on the rock, and the rock under their sleeping bodies, and their praying knees, all came into his mind, and he said to himself: "This sweet retreat is for safety of the soul, but what for penance? Jesu aid me against faults to come, and for the fault I rue, face of man I will not see for a twelvemonth and a day." He had famous precedents in his eye even for this last and unusual severity. In fact the original hermit of this very cell was clearly under the same vow. Hence the two apertures through which he was spoken to, and replied.

Adopting, in other respects, the uniform rule of hermits and anchorites, he divided his day into the seven offices, ignoring the petty accidents of light and dark, creations both of Him to whom he prayed so unceasingly. He learned the psalter by heart, and in all the intervals of devotion not occupied by broken slumbers, he worked hard with his hands. No article of the hermit's rule was more strict or more ancient than this. And here his self-imposed penance embarrassed him, for what work could he do without being seen that should benefit his neighbors? For the hermit was to labor *for himself* in those cases only where his subsistence depended on it. Now Clement's modest needs were amply supplied by the villagers.

On moonlight nights he would steal out like a thief and dig some poor man's garden on the outskirts of the village. He made baskets and dropped them slyly at humble doors. And since he could do nothing for the bodies of those who passed by his cell in daytime, he went out in the dead of the night with his hammer and his chisel and carved moral and religious sentences all down the road upon the sandstone rocks. "Who knows?" said he, "often a chance shaft striketh home. Oh, sore heart, comfort thou the poor and bereaved with holy words of solace in their native tongue: Also he remembered the learned Colonna had told him of the written mountains in the east where kings had inscribed their victories. "What," said Clement, "are they so wise, those Eastern monarchs, to engrave their warlike glory upon the rock, making a blood bubble endure so long as earth, and shall I leave the rocks about me silent on the King of Glory, at whose word they were, and at whose breath they shall be dust? Nay, but these stones shall speak to weary wayfarers of eternal peace, and of the Lamb, whose frail and afflicted yet happy servant worketh them among."

Now at this time the inspired words that have consoled the poor and the afflicted for so many ages, were not yet printed in Dutch, so that these sentences of gold from the holy Evangelists came like fresh oracles from Heaven, or like the dew on parched flowers, and the poor hermit's written rocks softened a heart or two, and sent the heavy laden singing on their way.[1]

These holy oracles that seemed to spring up around him like magic; his prudent answers through his window to such as sought ghostly counsel; and above all, his invisibility, soon gained him a prodigious reputation. This was not diminished by the medical advice they now and then extorted from him, sore against his will, by tears and entreaties; for if the patients got well, they gave the holy hermit the credit, and if not, they laid all the blame on the Devil. I think he killed nobody, for his remedies were "womanish and weak." Sage, and wormwood, sion, hyssop, borage,

[1]It requires nowadays a strong effort of the imagination to realize the effect on poor people who had never seen them before, of such sentences as this: "Blessed are the poor . . ."

spikenard, dog's-tongue, our Lady's mantle, feverfew, and faith, and all in small quantities except the last.

Then his abstinence, sure sign of a saint. The eggs and milk they brought him at first he refused with horror. Know ye not the hermit's rule is bread, or herbs, and water? Eggs, they are birds in disguise; for when the bird dieth, then the egg rotteth. As for milk, it is little better than white blood. And when they brought him too much bread he refused it. Then they used to press it on him. "Nay, holy Father, give the overplus to the poor."

"You who go among the poor can do that better. Is bread a thing to fling haphazard from a hermit's window?" And to those who persisted after this: "To live on charity, yet play Sir Bountiful, is to lie with the right hand. Giving another's to the poor, I should beguile them of their thanks, and cheat thee, the true giver. Thus do thieves, whose boast it is they bleed the rich into the lap of the poor."

This great reputation of sanctity was all external. Inside the cell was a man who held the hermit of Gouda as cheap as dirt.

"Ah," said he, "I cannot deceive myself, I cannot deceive God's animals. See the little birds, how coy they be! I feed and feed them and long for their friendship, yet will they never come within, nor take my hand by lighting on't. For why? No Paul, no Benedict, no Hugh of Lincoln, no Columbia, no Guthlac bides in this cell. Hunted doe flieth not hither, for here is no Fructuosus, nor Aventine, nor Albert of. Suabia, nor e'en a pretty squirrel cometh from the wood hard by for the acorns I have hoarded, for here abideth no Columban. The very owl that was here hath fled. They are not to be deceived; I have a Pope's word for that, Heaven rest his soul."

Clement had one advantage over her whose image in his heart he was bent on destroying. He had suffered and survived the pang of bereavement, and the mind cannot quite repeat such anguish. Then he had built up a habit of looking on her as dead. After that strange scene in the church and churchyard of St. Laurens, that habit might be compared to a structure riven by a thunderbolt. It was shattered, but stones enough stood to found a similar habit on, to look on her as dead *to him*.

And by severe subdivision of his time and thoughts, by unceasing prayers, and manual labor, he did, in about three months, succeed in benumbing the earthly half of his heart. But, lo! within a day or two of this first symptom of mental peace returning slowly, there descended upon his mind a horrible despondency. Words cannot utter it, for words never yet painted a likeness of despair. Voices seemed to whisper in his ear, "Kill thyself, kill! Kill! Kill!"

And he longed to obey the voices, for life was intolerable. He wrestled with his dark enemy with prayers and tears; he prayed God but to vary his temptation. "Oh, let mine enemy have power to scourge me with red-hot whips, to tear me leagues and leagues over rugged places by the hair of my head, as he has served many a holy hermit that yet baffled him at last; to fly on me like a raging lion; to gnaw me with a serpent's fangs—any pain, any terror, but this horrible gloom of the soul that shuts me from all light of Thee and of the saints."

And now a freezing thought crossed him. What if the triumphs of the powers of darkness over Christian souls in desert places had been suppressed, and only their defeats recorded, or at least in full; for dark hints were scattered about antiquity that now first began to grin at him with terrible meaning.

The darkened recluse now cast his despairing eyes over antiquity to see what weapons the Christian arsenal contained that might befriend him. The greatest of all was prayer. Alas, it was a part of his malady to be unable to pray with true fervor. The very system of mechanical supplication he had for months carried out so severely by rule had rather checked than fostered his power of originating true prayer. He prayed louder than ever, but the heart hung back cold and gloomy, and let the words go up alone.

"Poor wingless prayers," he cried, "you will not get halfway to Heaven!"

A fiend of this complexion had been driven out of King Saul by music. Clement took up the hermit's psaltery, and with much trouble mended the strings and tuned it. No, he could not play it. His soul was so out of tune. The sounds jarred on it, and made him almost mad.

"Ah, wretched me!" he cried. "Saul had a saint to play to him. He was not alone with the spirits of darkness; but here is no sweet bard of Israel to play to me. I, lonely, with crushed heart, on which a black fiend sitteth mountain high, must make the music to uplift that heart to Heaven. It may not be." And he groveled on the earth weeping and tearing his hair.

One day as he lay there sighing and groaning, prayerless, tuneless, hopeless, a thought flashed into his mind. What he had done for the poor and the wayfarer, he would do for himself. He would fill his den of despair with the name of God and the magic words of Holy Writ, and the pious, prayerful, consolations of the Church.

Then, like Christian at Apollyon's feet, he reached his hand suddenly out and caught not his sword, for he had none, but peaceful labor's humbler weapon, his chisel, and worked with it as if his soul depended on his arm. He begged his visitors for candle ends, and rancid oil.

"Anything is good enough for *me*," he said, "if 'twill but burn." So at night the cave glowed afar off like a blacksmith's forge, through the window and the gaping chinks of the rude stone door, and the rustics beholding crossed themselves and suspected deviltries, and within, the holy talismans one after another came upon the walls, and the sparks and the chips flew day and night, night and day, as the soldier of solitude and of the

Church plied, with sighs and groans, his bloodless weapon, between work-ing and fighting.

Kyrie Eleeison
Christe Eleeison

Τον Σαταναν συντριψον ὑπο τουζ ποδας ἡμων.[1]

Sursum corda[2]

Deus refugium nostrum et virtus[3]

Agnus Dei, qui tollis peccata mundi, miserere mihi.[4]

Sancta Trinitas unus Deus, miserere nobis.[5]

Ab infestationibus Daemonum, a ventura ira, a damnatione perpetua
                                              Libera nos Domine.[6]

Deus, qui miro ordine Angelorum ministeria, etc. (the whole collect).[7]

Quem quaerimus adjutorem nisi te Domine, qui pro peccatis nostris juste irascaris?[8]

Sancte Deus, Sancte fortis, Sancte et misericors Salvator, amarae morti ne tradas nos.

And underneath the great crucifix, which was fastened to the wall, he graved this from Augustine:

O anima Christiana, respice vulnera patientis, sanguinem morientis, pre-tium redemptionis.—Haec quanta sint cogitate, et in statera mentis vestrae appendite, ut totus vobis figatur in corde, qui pro vobis totus firus est in cruce. Nam, si passio Christi ad memorium revocetur, nihil est tam durum quod non aequo animo toleretur.

[1] Beat down Satan under our feet.
[2] Up, hearts!
[3] Oh, God our refuge and strength.
[4] Oh, Lamb of God, that takest away the sins of the world, have mercy upon me!
[5] Oh, Holy Trinity, one God, have mercy upon us!
[6] From the assaults of demons—from the wrath to come—from everlasting damna-tion—Deliver us, O Lord!
[7] See the English collect Saint Michael and All Angels.
[8] Of whom may we seek succor but of thee, O Lord, who for our sins art justly displeased (and that torrent of prayer, the following verse).

Which may be thus rendered:—

O Christian soul, look on the wounds of the suffering One, the blood of the dying One, the price paid for our redemption! These things, oh, think how great they be, and weigh them in the balance of thy mind: that He may be wholly nailed to thy heart who for thee was all nailed unto the cross. For do but call to mind the sufferings of Christ, and there is naught on earth too hard to endure with composure.

Soothed a little a very little by the sweet and pious words he was raising all round him, and weighed down with watching and working night and day, Clement one morning sank prostrate with fatigue, and a deep sleep overpowered him for many hours.

Awaking quietly, he heard a little cheep. He opened his eyes, and, lo! upon his breviary, which was on a lone stool near his feet, ruffling all his feathers with a single pull and smoothing them as suddenly, and cocking his bill this way and that with a vast display of cunning purely imaginary, perched a robin redbreast.

Clement held his breath. He half closed his eyes lest they should frighten the airy guest. Down came robin on the floor. When there he went through his pantomime of astuteness; and then, pim, pim, pim, with three stiff little hops, like a ball of worsted on vertical wires, he was on the hermit's bare foot. On this eminence he swelled, and contracted again, with ebb and flow of feathers; but Clement lost this, for he quite closed his eyes and scarce drew his breath in fear of frightening and losing his visitor. He was content to feel the minute claw on his foot. He could but just feel it, and that by help of knowing it was there. Presently a little flirt with two little wings, and the feathered busybody was on the breviary again.

Then Clement determined to try and feed this pretty little fidget without frightening it away. But it was very difficult. He had a piece of bread within reach, but how get at it? I think he was five minutes creeping his hand up to that bread, and when there he must not move his arm. He slyly got a crumb between a finger and thumb and shot it as boys do marbles, keeping the hand quite still. Cock robin saw it fall near him, and did sagacity, but moved not.

When another followed, and then another, he popped down and caught up one of the crumbs, but, not quite understanding this mystery, fled with it, for more security, to an eminence—to wit, the hermit's knee. And so the game proceeded till a much larger fragment than usual rolled along.

Here was a prize. Cock robin pounced on it, bore it aloft, and fled so swiftly into the world with it, the cave resounded with the buffeted air.

"Now, bless thee, sweet bird," sighed the stricken solitary. "Thy wings are music, and thou a feathered ray camest to light my darkened soul."

And from that to his orisons; and then to his tools with a little bit of courage; and this was his day's work:

Veni Creator Spiritus
Mentes tuorum visita
Imple superna gratia
Quae tu creasti pectora

Accende lumen sensibus
Infunde amorem condibus
Infirma nostri corporis
Virtute firmans perpetim.

And so the days rolled on, and the weather got colder and Clement's heart got warmer, and despondency was rolling away, and by-and-by, somehow or another, it was gone. He had outlived it. It had come like a cloud, and it went like one.

And presently all was reversed; his cell seemed illuminated with joy. His work pleased him, his prayers were full of unction, his psalms of praise. Hosts of little birds followed their crimson leader, and flying from snow and a parish full of Cains, made friends one after another with Abel, fast friends. And one keen frosty night as he sang the praises of God to his tuneful psaltery and his hollow cave rang forth the holy psalmody upon the night as if that cave itself was Tubal's sounding shell, or David's harp, he heard a clear whine, not unmelodious. It became louder, and less in tune. He peeped through the chinks of his rude door, and there sat a great red wolf moaning melodiously with his nose high in the air.

Clement was rejoiced. "My sins are going," he cried, "and the creatures of God are owning me, one after another." And in a burst of enthusiasm he struck up the laud:

"Praise Him all ye creatures of His!
"Let everything that hath breath praise the Lord."
And all the time he sang the wolf bayed at intervals.

But above all he seemed now to be drawing nearer to that celestial intercourse which was the sign and the bliss of the true hermit; for he had dreams about the saints and angels, so vivid they were more like visions. He saw bright figures clad in woven snow. They bent on him eyes lovelier than those of the antelopes he had seen at Rome, and fanned him with broad wings hued like the rainbow, and their gentle voices bade him speed upon his course.

He had not long enjoyed this felicity when his dreams began to take another and a strange complexion. He wandered with Fra Colonna over the relics of antique nations, and the friar was lame and had a staff, and this staff he waved over the mighty ruins, and were they Egyptian, Greek, or Roman, straightway the temples and palaces, whose wrecks they were, rose again like an exhalation, and were thronged with the famous dead.

And one night that the wizard Colonna had transcended himself, he pointed with his stick, and there was a swallowing-up of many great ancient cities, and the pair stood on a vast sandy plain with a huge crimson sun sinking to rest. There were great palm trees, and there were bulrush hives, scarce a man's height, dotted all about to the sandy horizon, and the crimson sun.

"These are the anchorites of the Theban desert," said Colonna, calmly. "Followers not of Christ and his Apostles, and the great Fathers, but of the Greek pupils of the Egyptian pupils of the Brahmans and Gymnosophists."

And Clement thought that he burned to go and embrace the holy men and tell them his troubles, and seek their advice. But he was tied by the feet somehow, and could not move, and the crimson sun sank, and it got dusk, and the hives scarce visible. And Colonna's figure became shadowy and shapeless, but his eyes glowed ten times brighter, and this thing all eyes spoke and said: "Nay, let them be, a pack of fools! See how dismal it all is." Then with a sudden sprightliness, "But I hear one of them has a manuscript of Petronius, on papyrus. I go to buy it. Farewell forever, forever, forever."

And it was pitch-dark, and a light came at Clement's back like a gentle stroke, a glorious roseate light. It warmed as well as brightened. It loosened his feet from the ground. He turned round, and there, her face irradiated with sunshine and her hair glittering like the gloriola of a saint, was Margaret Brandt. She blushed and smiled and cast a look of ineffable tenderness on him. "Gerard," she murmured, "be whose thou wilt by day, but at night be mine!" Even as she spoke, the agitation of seeing her so suddenly awakened him, and he found himself lying trembling from head to foot. That radiant figure and mellow voice seemed to have struck his nightly keynote.

Awake he could pray, and praise, and worship God; he was master of his thoughts. But if he closed his eyes in sleep, Margaret, or Satan in her shape, beset him, a seeming angel of light. He might dream of a thousand different things, wide as the poles asunder; ere he woke the imperial figure was sure to come and extinguish all the rest in a moment, for she came glowing with two beauties never before united, an angel's radiance and a woman's blushes. Angels cannot blush. So he knew it was a fiend.

He was alarmed, but not so much surprised as at the demon's last artifice. From Anthony to Nicholas of the Rock scarce a hermit that had not been thus beset, sometimes with gay voluptuous visions, sometimes with lovely phantoms, warm, tangible, and womanly without, demons within, nor always baffled even by the saints. Witness that "angel form with a devil's heart" that came hanging its lovely head, like a bruised flower, to Saint Macarius, with a feigned tale, and wept, and wept, and wept, and beguiled him first of his tears and then of half his virtue.

But with the examples of Satanic power and craft had come down copious records of the hermits' triumphs and the weapons by which they had conquered. The body must be tamed. This had been their watchword for twelve hundred years. It was a tremendous warcry, for they called the earthly affections, as well as appetites, body, and crushed the whole heart through the suffering and mortified flesh.

Clement then said to himself that the great enemy of man had retired but to spring with more effect, and had allowed him a few days of true purity and joy only to put him off his guard against the soft blandishments he was pouring over the soul that had survived the buffeting of his black wings. He applied himself to tame the body. He shortened his sleep, lengthened his prayers, and increased his severe temperance to abstinence. Hitherto, following the ordinary rule, he had eaten only at sunset. Now he ate but once in forty-eight hours, drinking a little water every day. On this the visions became more distinct.

Then he flew to a famous antidote; to "the grand febrifuge" of anchorites—cold water. He found the deepest part of the stream that ran by his cell; it rose not far off at a holy well, and clearing the bottom of the large stones made a hole where he could stand in water to the chin and, fortified by so many examples, he sprang from his rude bed upon the next diabolical assault and entered the icy water. It made him gasp and almost shriek with the cold. It froze his marrow. "I shall die," he cried. "I shall die, but better this than fire eternal."

And the next day he was so stiff in all his joints he could not move, and he seemed one great ache. And even in sleep he felt that his very bones were like so many raging teeth, till the phantom he dreaded came and gave one pitying smile, and all the pain was gone.

Then, feeling that to go into the icy water again, enfeebled by fasts as he was, might perhaps carry the guilt of suicide, he scourged himself till the blood ran, and so lay down smarting. And when exhaustion began to blunt the smart down to a throb, that moment the present was away, and the past came smiling back. He sat with Margaret at the Duke's feast, the minstrels played divinely, and the purple fountains gushed. Youth and love reigned in each heart and perfumed the very air.

Then the scene shifted and they stood at the altar together, man and wife. And no interruption this time, and they wandered hand in hand, and told each other their horrible dreams. As for him, he had dreamed she was dead, and he was a monk; and really the dream had been so vivid and so full of particulars that only his eyesight could even now convince him it was only a dream, and they were really one.

And this new keynote once struck, every tune ran upon it. Awake he was Clement the hermit, risen from unearthly visions of the night as dangerous as they were sweet. Asleep he was Gerard Eliassoen, the happy husband of the loveliest and best and truest girl in Holland—all the happier that he had been for some time the sport of hideous dreams in which he had lost her.

His constant fasts, coupled with other austerities, and the deep mental anxiety of a man fighting with a supernatural foe, had now reduced him nearly to a skeleton; but still on those aching bones hung flesh unsubdued, quivering with an earthly passion. So, however, he thought, or why had ill spirits such power over him? His opinion was confirmed when one day he detected himself sinking to sleep actually with a feeling of complacency, because now Margaret would come and he should feel no more pain, and the unreal would be real, and the real unreal, for an hour.

On this he rose hastily with a cry of dismay, and stripping to the skin, climbed up to the brambles above his cave and flung himself on them, and rolled on them writhing with the pain. Then he came into his den a mass of gore, and lay moaning for hours till, out of sheer exhaustion, he fell into a deep and dreamless sleep. He awoke to bodily pain and mental exultation; he had broken the fatal spell. Yes, it was broken. Another and another day passed, and her image molested him no more. But he caught himself sighing at his victory.

The birds got tamer and tamer, they perched upon his hand. Two of them let him gild their little claws. Eating but once in two days, he had more to give them.

His tranquillity was not to last long. A woman's voice came in from the outside, told him his own story in a very few words, and asked him to tell her where Gerard was to be found. He was so astounded he could only say, with an instinct of self-defense, "Pray for the soul of Gerard, the son of Eli!" meaning that he was dead to the world. And he sat wondering.

When the woman was gone, he determined, after an inward battle, to risk being seen, and he peeped after her to see who it could be; but he took so many precautions, and she ran so quickly back to her friend, that the road was clear.

"Satan!" said he directly.

And that night back came his visions of earthly love and happiness so vividly he could count every auburn hair in Margaret's head, and see the pupils of her eyes. Then he began to despair, and said: "I must leave this country. Here I am bound fast in memory's chain," and began to dread his cell. He said, "A breath from Hell hath infected it, and robbed even these holy words of their virtue." And unconsciously imitating Saint Jerome, a victim of earthly hallucinations as overpowering, and coarser, he took his warmest covering out into the wood hard by, and there flung down under ᵃ tree that torn and wrinkled leather bag of bones which a little ago might have served a sculptor for Apollo.

His sleep was dreamless. He awoke nearly frozen, but warm with joy within. "I shall yet be a true hermit, *Dei gratiâ*," said he. The next day some good soul left on his little platform a new lamb's-wool pelisse and cape, warm, soft, and ample. He had a moment's misgiving on account of its delicious softness and warmth, but that passed. It was the right skin, and a mark that Heaven approved his present course. It restored warmth to his bones after he came in from his short rest.

And now, at one moment he saw victory before him if he could but live to it; at another, he said to himself, " 'Tis but another lull, be on thy guard, Clement."

And this thought agitated his nerves and kept him in continual awe. He was like a soldier within the enemy's lines.

One night, a beautiful clear frosty night, he came back to his cell after a short rest. The stars were wonderful. Heaven seemed a thousand times larger as well as brighter than earth, and to look with a thousand eyes instead of one.

"Oh, wonderful," he cried, "that there should be men who do crimes by night, and others scarce less mad who live for this little world, and not for that great and glorious one which nightly, to all eyes not blinded by custom, reveals its glowing glories. Thank God I am a hermit."

And in this mood he came to his cell door. He paused at it; it was closed.

"Why, methought I left it open," said he. "The wind. There is not a breath of wind. What means this?"

He stood with his hand upon the rugged door. He looked through one of the great chinks, for it was much smaller in places than the aperture it pretended to close, and saw his little oil wick burning just where he had left it.

"How is it with me," he sighed, "when I start and tremble at nothing? Either I did shut it, or the Fiend hath shut it after me to disturb my happy soul. *Retro Sathanas!*"

And he entered his cave rapidly, and began with somewhat nervous expedition to light one of his largest tapers. While he was lighting it, there was a soft sigh in the cave. He started and dropped the candle just as it was lighting, and it went out. He stooped for it hurriedly and lighted it, listening intently. When it was lighted, he shaded it with his hand from behind, and threw the faint light all round the cell. In the farthest corner the outline of the wall seemed broken. He took a step toward the place with his heart beating. The candle at the same time getting brighter, he saw it was the figure of a woman. Another step with his knees knocking together.

It was Margaret Brandt.

CHAPTER LIV

Her attitude was one to excite pity rather than terror in eyes not blinded by a preconceived notion. Her bosom was fluttering like a bird and the red and white coming and going in her cheeks, and she had her hand against the wall by the instinct of timid things, she trembled so; and the marvelous mixed gaze of love and pious awe and pity and tender memories those purple eyes cast on the emaciated and glaring hermit was an event in nature.

"Aha!" he cried. "Thou art come at last in flesh and blood, come to me as thou camest to holy Anthony. But I am ware of thee, I thought thy wiles were not exhausted. I am armed." With this he snatched up his small crucifix and held it out at her, astonished, and the candle in the other hand, both crucifix and candle shaking violently, "*Exorcizo te.*"

"Ah, no!" cried she, piteously, and put out two pretty deprecating palms. "Alas, work me no ill! It is Margaret."

"Liar!" shouted the hermit. "Margaret was fair, but not so supernatural fair as thou. Thou didst shrink at that sacred name, thou subtle hypocrite. *In nomine Dei exorcizo vos.*"

"Ah, Jesu!" gasped Margaret, in extremity of terror, "Curse me not! I will go home. I thought *I* might come. For very manhood be-Latin me not! Oh, Gerard, is it thus you and I meet after all, after all?"

And she cowered almost to her knees, and sobbed with superstitious fear, and wounded affection. Impregnated as he was with Satanophobia, he might perhaps have doubted still whether this distressed creature, all woman and nature, was not all art and fiend. But her spontaneous appeal to that sacred name dissolved his chimera, and let him see with his eyes, and hear with his ears.

He uttered a cry of self-reproach, and tried to raise her; but what with fasts, what with the overpowering emotion of a long solitude so broken, he could not. "What," he gasped shaking over her, "and is it thou? And have I met thee with hard words? Alas!" And they were both choked with emotion, and could not speak for a while.

"I heed it not much," said Margaret bravely, struggling with her tears. "You took me for another, for a devil, oh, oh, oh, oh, oh!"

"Forgive me, sweet soul!" And as soon as he could speak more than a word at a time, he said, "I have been much beset by the Evil One since I came here."

Margaret looked round with a shudder. "Like enow. Then oh, take my hand, and let me lead thee from this foul place."

He gazed at her with astonishment.

"What, desert my cell, and go into the world again? Is it for that thou hast come to me?" said he sadly and reproachfully.

"Ay, Gerard. I am come to take thee to thy pretty vicarage. Art Vicar of Gouda, thanks to Heaven and thy good brother Giles, and Mother and I have made it so neat for thee, Gerard. 'Tis well enow in winter, I promise thee. But bide a bit till the hawthorn bloom, and anon thy walls put on their kirtle of brave roses and sweet woodbine. Have we forgotten thee, and the foolish things thou lovest? And, dear Gerard, thy mother is waiting, and 'tis late for her to be out of her bed. Prithee, prithee, come! And the moment we are out of this foul hole I'll show thee a treasure thou hast gotten and knowest naught on't, or sure hadst never fled from us so. Alas, what is to do? What have I ignorantly said, to be regarded thus?"

For he had drawn himself all up into a heap, and was looking at her with a strange gaze of fear and suspicion blended.

"Unhappy girl," said he, solemnly, yet deeply agitated, "would you have me risk my soul and yours for a miserable vicarage and the flowers that grow on it? But this is not thy doing. The bowelless Fiend sends thee, poor simple girl, to me with this bait. But oh, cunning Fiend, I will unmask thee even to this thine instrument, and she shall see thee, and abhor thee as I do. Margaret, my lost love, why am I here? Because I love thee."

"Oh, no, Gerard, you love me not, or you would not have hidden from me. There was no need."

"Let there be no deceit between us twain that have loved so true, and after this night shall meet no more on earth."

"Now God forbid!" said she.

"I love thee, and thou hast not forgotten me, or thou hadst married ere this, and hadst not been the one to find me, buried here from sight of man. I am a priest, a monk. What but folly or sin can come of you and me living neighbors, and feeding a passion innocent once, but now (so Heaven wills it) impious and unholy? No, though my heart break I must be firm. 'Tis I that am the man, 'tis I that am the priest. You and I must meet no more till I am schooled by solitude, and thou art wedded to another."

"I consent to my doom, but not to thine. I would ten times liever die, yet I will marry, ay, wed misery itself, sooner than let thee lie in this foul dismal place with yon sweet manse a-waiting for thee."

Clement groaned. At each word she spoke out stood clearer and clearer two things—his duty, and the agony it must cost.

"My beloved," said he, with a strange mixture of tenderness and dogged resolution, "I bless thee for giving me one more sight of thy sweet face, and may God forgive thee, and bless thee, for destroying in a minute the holy peace it hath taken six months of solitude to build. No matter. A year of penance will, *Dei gratiâ*, restore me to my calm. My poor Margaret, I seem cruel, yet I am kind. 'Tis best we part, ay, this moment."

"Part, Gerard? Never. We have seen what comes of parting. Part? Why, you have not heard half my story, no, nor the tithe. 'Tis not for thy mere comfort I take thee to Gouda manse. Hear me!"

"I may not. Thy very voice is a temptation, with its music, memory's delight."

"But I say you shall hear me, Gerard, for forth this place I go not unheard."

"Then must we part by other means," said Clement, sadly.

"Alack, what other means? Wouldst put me to thine own door, being stronger?"

"Nay, Margaret, well thou knowest I would suffer many deaths rather than put force on thee. Thy sweet body is dearer to me than my own, but a million times dearer to me are our immortal souls, both thine and mine. I have withstood this direst temptation of all long enow. Now I must fly it. Farewell! Farewell!"

He made to the door, and had actually opened it and got half out when she darted after and caught him by the arm.

"Nay, then another must speak for me. I thought to reward thee for yielding to me, but unkind that thou art, I need his help, I find. Turn then this way one moment."

"Nay, nay."

"But I say ay! And then turn thy back on us an thou canst." She somewhat relaxed her grasp, thinking he would never deny her so small a favor. But at this he saw his opportunity and seized it.

"Fly, Clement, fly!" he almost shrieked, and, his religious enthusiasm giving him for a moment his old strength, he burst wildly away from her, and after a few steps bounded over the little stream and ran beside it, but finding he was not followed, stopped and looked back.

She was lying on her face, with her hands spread out. Yes, without meaning it, he had thrown her down and hurt her. When he saw that, he groaned and turned back a step; but suddenly, by another impulse, flung himself into the icy water instead.

"There, kill my body," he cried, "but save my soul!"

While he stood there up to his throat in liquid ice, so to speak, Margaret uttered one long, piteous moan, and rose to her knees. He saw her as plain almost as in midday. Saw her face pale and her eyes glistening, and then in the still night he heard these words:

"Oh, God, Thou that knowest all, Thou seest how I am used. Forgive me, then! For I will not live another day."

With this she suddenly started to her feet, and flew like some wild creature, wounded to death, close by his miserable hiding-place, shrieking:

"Cruel!—Cruel!—Cruel!—Cruel!"

What manifold anguish may burst from a human heart in a single syllable! There were wounded love, and wounded pride, and despair, and coming madness all in that piteous cry. Clement heard, and it froze his heart with terror and remorse, worse than the icy water chilled the marrow of his bones. He felt he had driven her from him forever, and in the midst of his dismal triumph, the greatest he had won, there came an almost incontrollable impulse to curse the Church, to curse religion itself, for exacting such savage cruelty from mortal man.

At last he crawled half-dead out of the water and staggered to his den. "I am safe here," he groaned. "She will never come near me again, unmanly, ungrateful wretch that I am." And he flung his emaciated, frozen body down on the floor, not without a secret hope that it might never rise thence alive.

But presently he saw by the hourglass that it was past midnight. On this he rose slowly and took off his wet things and, moaning all the time at the pain he had caused her he loved, put on the old hermit's cilice of bristles, and over that his breastplate. He had never worn either of these before, doubting himself worthy to don the arms of that tried soldier. But now he must give himself every aid. The bristles might distract his earthly remorse by bodily pain, and there might be holy virtue in the breastplate.

Then he knelt down and prayed God humbly to release him that very night from the burden of the flesh. Then he lighted all his candles and recited his psalter doggedly. Each word seemed to come like a lump of lead from a leaden heart, and to fall leaden to the ground; and in this mechanical office every now and then he moaned with all his soul. In the midst of which he suddenly observed a little bundle in the corner he had not seen before in the feebler light, and at one end of it something like gold spun into silk. He went to see what it could be, and he had no sooner viewed it closer than he threw up his hands with rapture,

"It is a seraph," he whispered, "a lovely seraph. Heaven hath witnessed my bitter trial, and approves my cruelty; and this flower of the skies is sent to cheer me, fainting under my burden."

He fell on his knees and gazed with ecstasy on its golden hair and its tender skin and cheeks like a peach.

"Let me feast my sad eyes on thee ere thou leavest me for thine ever-blessed abode, and my cell darkens again at thy parting, as it did at hers."

With all this the hermit disturbed the lovely visitor. He opened wide two eyes, the color of heaven; and seeing a strange figure kneeling over him, he cried piteously: "*Mum—ma! Mum—ma!*" And the tears began to run down his little cheeks.

Perhaps, after all, Clement, who for more than six months had not looked on the human face divine, estimated childish beauty more justly than we can. And in truth this fair Northern child, with its long golden hair, was far more angelic than any of our imagined angels. But now the spell was broken.

Yet not unhappily. Clement, it may be remembered, was fond of children, and true monastic life fosters this sentiment. The innocent distress on the cherubic face, the tears that ran so smoothly from those transparent violets, his eyes, and his pretty, dismal cry for his only friend, his mother, went through the hermit's heart. He employed all his gentleness and all his art to soothe him, and as the little soul was wonderfully intelligent for his age, presently succeeded so far that he ceased to cry out, and wonder took the place of fear while in silence, broken only in little gulps, he scanned with great tearful eyes this strange figure that looked so wild, but spoke so kindly, and wore armor, yet did not kill little boys, but coaxed them.

Clement was equally perplexed to know how this little human flower came to lie sparkling and blooming in his gloomy cave. But he remembered he had left the door wide-open, and he was driven to conclude that owing to this negligence, some unfortunate creature of high or low degree had seized this opportunity to get rid of her child forever.[1] At this his bowels yearned so over the poor deserted cherub that the tears of pure tenderness stood in his eyes, and still beneath the crime of the mother he saw the divine goodness which had so directed her heartlessness as to comfort his servant's breaking heart.

"Now bless thee, bless thee, bless thee, sweet innocent, I would not change thee for e'en a cherub in Heaven."

"At's pooty," replied the infant, ignoring contemptuously, after the manner of infants, all remarks that did not interest him.

"What is pretty here, my love, beside thee?"

"Ookum-gars,"[2] said the boy, pointing to the hermit's breastplate.

"There are prettier things here than that," said Clement. "There are little birds. Lovest thou birds?"

"Nay. Ay. En um ittle, ery ittle? Not ike torks. Hate torks, um bigger an baby."

He then confided, in very broken language, that the storks, with their great flapping wings, scared him, and were a great trouble and worry to him, darkening his existence more or less.

"Ay, but my birds are very little, and good, and oh, so pretty!"

"Den I ikes 'm," said the child authoritatively. "I ont my mammy."

"Alas, sweet dove! I doubt I shall have to fill her place as best I may. Hast thou no daddy as well as mammy, sweet one?"

Now not only was this conversation from first to last, the relative ages,

---

[1]More than one hermit had received a present of this kind.
[2]Query? "looking-glass."

situations, and all circumstances of the parties considered, as strange a one as ever took place between two mortal creatures, but at or within a second or two of the hermit's last question, to turn the strange into the marvelous, came an unseen witness, to whom every word that passed carried ten times the force it did to either of the speakers.

Since, therefore, it is with her eyes you must now see, and hear with her ears, I go back a step for her. Margaret, when she ran past Gerard, was almost mad. She was in that state of mind in which affectionate mothers have been known to kill their children, sometimes along with themselves, sometimes alone, which last is certainly maniacal. She ran to Reicht Heynes pale and trembling, and clasped her round the neck. "Oh, Reicht, oh, Reicht!" and could say no more. Reicht kissed her and began to whimper, and—would you believe it?—the great mastiff uttered one long whine; even his glimmer of sense taught him grief was afoot.

"Oh, Reicht!" moaned the despised beauty as soon as she could utter a word for choking. "See how he has served me," and she showed her hands that were bleeding with falling on the stony ground. "He threw me down, he was so eager to fly from me. He took me for a devil. He said I came to tempt him. Am I the woman to tempt a man? You know me, Reicht."

"Nay, in sooth, sweet Mistress Margaret, the last i' the world."

"And he would not look at my child. I'll fling myself and him into the Rotter this night."

"Oh, fie, fie! Eh, my sweet woman, speak not so. Is any man that breathes worth your child's life?"

"My child! Where is he? Why, Reicht, I have left him behind. Oh, shame! Is it possible I can love him to that degree as to forget my child? Ah, I am rightly served for it!"

And she sat down, and faithful Reicht beside her, and they sobbed in one another's arms. After a while Margaret left off sobbing and said doggedly, "Let us go home."

"Ay, but the bairn?"

"Oh, he is well where he is. My heart is turned against my very child. *He* cares naught for him, wouldn't see him, nor hear speak of him. And I took him there so proud, and made his hair so nice, I did, and put his new frock and cowl on him. Nay, turn about. It's his child as well as mine, let him keep it awhile. Mayhap that will learn him to think more of its mother and his own."

"High words off an empty stomach," said Reicht.

"Time will show. Come thou home."

They departed, and Time did show quicker than he levels abbeys, for at the second step Margaret stopped, and could neither go one way nor the other, but stood stock-still.

"Reicht," said she, piteously, "what else have I on earth? I cannot."

"Who ever said you could? Think you I paid attention? Words are woman's breath. Come back for him without more ado. 'Tis time we were in our beds, much more he."

Reicht led the way, and Margaret followed readily enough in that direction, but as they drew near the cell she stopped again.

"Reicht, go you and ask him will he give me back my boy, for I could not bear the sight of him."

"Alas, mistress, this do seem a sorry ending after all that hath been betwixt you twain. Bethink thee now, doth thine heart whisper no excuse for him? Dost verily hate him for whom thou hast waited so long? Oh, weary world!"

"Hate him, Reicht? I would not harm a hair of his head for all that is in nature. But look on him I cannot, I have taken a horror of him. Oh, when I think of all I have suffered for him, and what I came here this night to do for him, and brought my own darling to kiss him and call him father! Prithee go forward and get me what *is* my own, my sole joy in the world. Thou knowest I am on thorns till I have him to my bosom again."

Reicht went forward. Margaret sat by the roadside and covered her face with her apron, and rocked herself after the manner of her country, for her soul was full of bitterness and grief. So severe, indeed, was the internal conflict that she did not hear Reicht running back to her, and started violently when the young woman laid a hand upon her shoulder.

"Mistress Margaret," said Reicht, quietly, "take a fool's advice that loves ye. Go softly to yon cave wi' all the ears and eyes your mother ever gave you."

"Why?—What—Reicht?" stammered Margaret.

"I thought the cave was afire, 'twas so light inside, and there were voices."

"Voices?"

"Ay, not one, but twain, and all unlike—a man's and a little child's talking as pleasant as you and me. I am no great hand at a keyhole, for my part, 'tis paltry work. But if so be voices were talking in yon cave, and them that owned those voices were so near to me as those are to thee, I'd go on all fours like a fox, and I'd crawl on my belly like a serpent, ere I'd lose one word that passes *atwixt those twain*."

"Whisht, Reicht! Bless thee! Bide thou here. Buss me! Pray for me!"

And almost ere the agitated words had left her lips Margaret was flying toward the hermitage as noiselessly as a lapwing. Arrived near it, she crouched, and there was something truly serpentine in the gliding, flexible, noiseless movements by which she reached the very door, and there she found a chink and listened. And often it cost her a struggle not to burst in upon them but, warned by defeat, she was cautious and resolute to let well alone. And after a while slowly and noiselessly she reared her head, like a snake its crest, to where she saw the broadest chink of all, and looked with all her eyes and soul, as well as listened.

The little boy, then being asked whether he had no daddy, at first shook his head, and would say nothing. But being pressed, he suddenly seemed to remember something, and said he: "Dad—da ill man, run away and leave poor Mum—ma."

She who heard this winced. It was as new to her as to Clement. Some interfering foolish woman had gone and said this to the boy, and now out it came in Gerard's very face. His answer surprised her. He burst out:

"The villain! The monster! He must be born without bowels to desert thee, sweet one. Ah, he little knows the joy he hath turned his back on. Well, my little dove, I must be father and mother to thee, since the one runs away and t'other abandons thee to my care. Now tomorrow I shall ask the good people that bring me my food to fetch some nice eggs and milk for thee as well; for bread is good enough for poor old good-for-nothing me, but not for thee. And I shall teach thee to read."

"I can yead, I can yead."

"Ay, verily, so young? All the better, we will read good books together, and I shall show thee the way to Heaven. Heaven is a beautiful place, a thousand times fairer and better than earth, and there be little cherubs like thyself, in white, glad to welcome thee and love thee. Wouldst like to go to Heaven one day?"

"Ay, along wi'—my—Mammy."

"What, not without her, then?"

"Nay. I ont my Mammy. Where is my Mammy?"

Oh! what it cost poor Margaret not to burst in and clasp him to her heart!

"Well, fret not, sweetheart, mayhap she will come when thou art asleep. Wilt thou be good now and sleep?"

"I not eepy. Ikes to talk."

"Well, talk we then. Tell me thy pretty name."

"Baby." And he opened his eyes with amazement at this great hulking creature's ignorance.

"Hast none other?"

"Nay."

"What shall I do to pleasure thee, Baby? Shall I tell thee a story?"

"I ikes tories," said the boy, clapping his hands.

"Or sing thee a song?"

"I ikes tongs." And he became excited.

"Choose then, a song or a story."

"Ting I a tong. Nay, tell I a tory. Nay, ting I a tong. Nay—" And the corners of his little mouth turned down and he had half a mind to weep because he could not have both, and could not tell which to forgo. Suddenly his little face cleared. "Ting I a tory," said he.

"Sing thee a story, Baby? Well, after all, why not? And wilt thou sit o' my knee and hear it?"

"Yea."

"Then I must e'en doff this breastplate. 'Tis too hard for thy soft cheek. So. And now I must doff this bristly cilice; they would prick thy tender skin, perhaps make it bleed, as they have me, I see. So. And now I put on my best pelisse, in honor of thy worshipful visit. See how soft and warm it is, bless the good soul that sent it. And now I sit me down, so. And I take thee on my left knee, and put my arm under thy little head, so. And then the psaltery, and play a little tune—so, not too loud."

"I ikes dat."

"I am right glad on't. Now list the story."

He chanted a child's story in a sort of recitative, singing a little moral refrain now and then. The boy listened with rapture.

"I ikes oo," said he. "Ot is oo? Is oo a man?"

"Ay, little heart, and a great sinner to boot."

"I ikes great tingers. Ting one other tory."

Story number two was chanted.

"I ubbs oo," cried the child impetuously. "Ot caft[1] is oo?"

"I am a hermit, love."

"I ubbs vermins. Ting other one."

But during this final performance, Nature suddenly held out her leaden scepter over the youthful eyelids. "I is not eepy," whined he very faintly, and succumbed.

Clement laid down his psaltery softly and began to rock his new treasure in his arms, and to croon over him a little lullaby well known in Tergou, with which his own mother had often set him off. And the child sank into a profound sleep upon his arm. And he stopped crooning and gazed on him with infinite tenderness, yet sadness; for at that moment he could not help thinking what might have been but for a piece of paper with a lie in it. He sighed deeply.

The next moment the moonlight burst into his cell, and with it, and in it, and almost as swift as it, Margaret Brandt was down at his knee with a timorous hand upon his shoulder.

"Gerard, you do not reject us. You cannot."

CHAPTER LV

THE startled hermit glared from his nursling to Margaret, and from her to him in amazement equaled only by his agitation at her so unexpected re-

[1] Craft. He means trade or profession.

turn. The child lay asleep on his left arm, and she was at his right knee—no longer the pale, scared, panting girl he had overpowered so easily an hour or two ago, but an imperial beauty with blushing cheeks and sparkling eyes, and lips sweetly parted in triumph, and her whole face radiant with a look he could not quite read, for he had never yet seen it on her: maternal pride. He stared and stared from the child to her, in throbbing amazement.

"Us?" he gasped at last. And still his wonder-stricken eyes turned to and fro.

Margaret was surprised in her turn. It was an age of impressions, not facts. "What!" she cried. "Doth not a father know his own child? And a man of God, too? Fie, Gerard, to pretend! Nay, thou art too wise, too good, not to have—why, I watched thee, and e'en now look at you twain! 'Tis thine own flesh and blood thou holdest to thine heart."

Clement trembled. "What words are these?" he stammered. "This angel mine?"

"Whose else, since he is mine?"

Clement turned on the sleeping child with a look beyond the power of the pen to describe, and trembled all over as his eyes seemed to absorb the little love.

Margaret's eyes followed his. "He is not a bit like me," said she proudly. "But oh, at whiles he is thy very image in little, and see this golden hair. Thine was the very color at his age, ask Mother else. And see this mole on his little finger. Now look at thine own, there! 'Twas thy mother let me weet thou wast marked so before him. And oh, Gerard, 'twas this our child found thee for me, for by that little mark on thy finger I knew thee for his father when I watched above thy window and saw thee feed the birds." Here she seized the child's hand and kissed it eagerly, and got half of it into her mouth, heaven knows how. "Ah! bless thee, thou didst find thy poor daddy for her, and now thou hast made us friends again after our little quarrel—the first, the last. Wast very cruel to me but now, my poor Gerard, and I forgive thee, for loving of thy child."

"Ah, ah, ah, ah, ah!" sobbed Clement, choking.

And lowered by fasts, and unnerved by solitude, the once strong man was hysterical, and nearly fainting. Margaret was alarmed but having experience, her pity was greater than her fear.

"Nay, take not on so," she murmured soothingly, and put a gentle hand upon his brow. "Be brave! So, so. Dear heart, thou art not the first man that hath gone abroad and come back richer by a lovely little self than he went forth. Being a man of God, take courage, and say He sends thee this to comfort thee for what thou hast lost in me. And that is not so very much, my lamb, for sure the better part of love shall ne'er cool here to thee, though it may in thine, and ought, being a priest, and parson of Gouda."

"I? Priest of Gouda? Never!" murmured Clement in a faint voice, "I am a friar of Saint Dominic. Yet speak on sweet music, tell me all that has happened thee before we are parted again."

Now some would on this have exclaimed against parting at all, and raised the true question in dispute. But such women as Margaret do not repeat their mistakes. It is very hard to defeat them *twice* where their hearts are set on a thing.

She assented, and turned her back on Gouda manse as a thing not to be recurred to. She told him her tale, dwelling above all on the kindness to her of his parents. And while she related her troubles, his hand stole to hers, and often she felt him wince and tremble with ire, and often press her hand, sympathizing with her in every vein.

"Oh, piteous tale of a true heart battling alone against such bitter odds!" said he.

"It all seems small when I see thee here again, and nursing my boy. We have had a warning, Gerard. True friends like you and me are rare, and they are mad to part ere death divideth them."

"And that is true," said Clement, off his guard.

And then she would have him tell her what he had suffered for her, and he begged her to excuse him, and she consented, but by questions quietly revoked her consent and elicited it all. And many a sigh she heaved for him, and more than once she hid her face in her hands with terror at his perils, though past. And to console him for all he had gone through, she knelt down and put her arms under the little boy and lifted him gently up.

"Kiss him softly," she whispered. "Again, again! Kiss thy fill if thou canst, he is sound. 'Tis all I can do to comfort thee till thou art out of this foul den and in thy sweet manse yonder."

Clement shook his head.

"Well," said she, "let that pass. Know that I have been sore affronted for want of my lines."

"Who hath dared affront thee?"

"No matter, those that will do it again if thou hast lost them, which the saints forbid."

"I lose them? Nay, there they lie, close to thy hand."

"Where, where, oh, where?"

Clement hung his head. "Look in the Vulgate. Heaven forgive me, I thought thou wert dead, and a saint in Heaven."

She looked, and on the blank leaves of the poor soul's Vulgate she found her marriage lines.

"Thank God," she cried, "thank God! Oh, bless thee, Gerard, bless thee! Why, what is here, Gerard?"

On the other leaves were pinned every scrap of paper she had ever sent him, and their two names she had once written together in sport, and the lock of her hair she had given him, and half a silver coin she had broken with him, and a straw she had sucked her soup with the first day he ever saw her.

When Margaret saw these proofs of love and signs of a gentle heart bereaved, even her exultation at getting back her marriage lines was overpowered by gushing tenderness. She almost staggered, and her hand went to her bosom, and she leaned her brow against the stone cell and wept so silently that he did not see she was weeping—indeed she would not let him, for she felt that to befriend him now she must be the stronger, and emotion weakens.

"Gerard," said she, "I know you are wise and good. You must have a reason for what you are doing, let it seem ever so unreasonable. Talk we like old friends. Why are you buried alive?"

"Margaret, to escape temptation. My impious ire against those two had its root in the heart. That heart, then, I must deaden, and, *Dei gratiâ, I* shall. Shall I, a servant of Christ and of the Church, court temptation? Shall I pray daily to be led out on't and walk into it with open eyes?"

"That is good sense anyway," said Margaret, with a consummate affection of candor.

" 'Tis unanswerable," said Clement with a sigh.

"We shall see. Tell me, have you escaped temptation here? Why I ask is, when *I* am alone, my thoughts are far more wild and foolish than in company. Nay, speak sooth, come!"

"I must needs own I have been worse tempted here with evil imaginations than in the world."

"There now!"

"Ay, but so were Anthony, and Jerome, Macarius, and Hilarion, Benedict, Bernard, and all the saints. 'Twill wear off."

"How do you know?"

"I feel sure it will."

"Guessing against knowledge. Here 'tis men folk are sillier than us that be but women. Wise in their own conceits, they will not let themselves see; their stomachs are too high to be taught by their eyes. A woman, if she went into a hole in a bank to escape temptation and there found it, would just lift her farthingale and out on't, and not e'en know how wise she was till she watched a man in like plight."

"Nay, I grant humility and a teachable spirit are the roads to wisdom. But, when all is said, here I wrestle but with imagination. At Gouda she I love as no priest or monk must love any but the angels, she will tempt a weak soul, unwilling, yet not loath, to be tempted."

"Ay, that is another matter. *I* should tempt thee, then? To what, i' God's name?"

"Who knows? The flesh is weak."

"Speak for yourself, my lad. Why, you are thinking of some other Margaret, not Margaret a Peter. Was ever my mind turned to folly and frailty? Stay, is it because you were my husband once, as these lines avouch? Think you the road to folly is beaten for you more than for another? Oh, how shallow are the wise, and how little able are you to read me, who can read you so well from top to toe. Come, learn thy A B C. Were a stranger to proffer me unchaste love, I should shrink a bit, no doubt, and feel sore, but I should defend myself without making a coil; for men, I know, are so, the best of them sometimes. But if you that have been my husband, and are my child's father, were to offer to humble me so in mine own eyes, and thine, and his, either I should spit in thy face, Gerard, or, as I am not a downright vulgar woman, I should snatch the first weapon at hand and strike thee dead."

And Margaret's eyes flashed fire, and her nostrils expanded that it was glorious to see, and no one that did see her could doubt her sincerity.

"I had not the sense to see that," said Gerard quietly. And he pondered. Margaret eyed him in silence, and soon recovered her composure.

"Let not you and I dispute," said she gently. "Speak we of other things. Ask me of thy folk."

"My father?"

"Well, and warms to thee and me. Poor soul, a drew glaive on those twain that day, but Jorian Ketel and I we mastered him, and he drove them forth his house forever."

"That may not be. He must take them back."

"That he will never do for us. You know the man, he is dour as iron. Yet would he do it for one word from one that will not speak it."

"Who?"

"The Vicar of Gouda. The old man will be at the manse tomorrow, I hear."

"How you come back to that."

"Forgive me, I am but a woman. It is us for nagging. Shouldst keep me from it wi' questioning of me."

"My sister Kate?"

"Alas!"

"What, hath ill befallen e'en that sweet lily? Out and alas!"

"Be calm, sweetheart, no harm hath her befallen. Oh, nay, nay, far fro' that." Then Margaret forced herself to be composed, and in a low, sweet, gentle voice she murmured to him thus: "My poor Gerard, Kate hath left her trouble behind her. For the manner on't, 'twas like the rest. Ah, such as she saw never thirty, nor ever shall while earth shall last. She smiled in pain, too. A-well, then, thus 'twas. She was took wi' a languor and a loss of all her pains."

"A loss of her pains? I understand you not."

"Ay, you are not experienced. Indeed, e'en thy mother almost blinded herself, and said, ' 'Tis maybe a change for the better.' But Joan Ketel, which is an understanding woman, she looked at her and said, 'Down sun, down wind!' And the gossips sided and said, 'Be brave, you that are her mother, for she is halfway to the saints.' And thy mother wept sore, but Kate would not let her. And one very ancient woman, she said to thy mother, 'She will die as easy as she lived hard.' And she lay painless best part of three days, a-sipping of Heaven aforehand. And, my dear, when she was just parting, she asked for 'Gerard's little boy,' and I brought him and set him on the bed, and the little thing behaved as peaceably as he does now. But by this time she was past speaking, but she pointed to a drawer, and her mother knew what to look for. It was two gold angels thou hadst given her years ago. Poor soul! She had kept them till thou shouldst come home. And she nodded toward the little boy, and looked anxious. But we understood her, and put the pieces in his two hands, and when his little fingers closed on them, she smiled content. And so she gave her little earthly treasures to her favorite's child—for you *were* her favorite—and her immortal jewel to God, and passed so sweetly we none of us knew justly when she left us. Welladay, welladay!"

Gerard wept. "She hath not left her like on earth," he sobbed. "Oh, how the affections of earth curl softly round my heart! I cannot help it, God made them, after all. Speak on, sweet Margaret. At thy voice the past rolls its tides back upon me, the loves and the hopes of youth come fair and gliding into my dark cell and darker bosom, on waves of memory and music."

"Gerard, I am loath to grieve you, but Kate cried a little when she first took ill at you not being there to close her eyes." Gerard sighed. "You were within a league, but hid your face from her." He groaned.

"There, forgive me for nagging—I am but a woman. You would not have been so cruel to your own flesh and blood knowingly, would you?"

"Oh, no."

"Well then, know that thy brother Sybrandt lies in my charge with a broken back, fruit of thy curse."

"*Mea culpa! Mea culpa!*"

"He is very penitent. Be yourself and forgive him this night!"

"I have forgiven him long ago."

"Think you he can believe that from any mouth but yours? Come, he is but about two butts' length hence."

"So near? Why, where?"

"At Gouda manse. I took him there yestreen. For I know you, the curse was scarce cold on your lips when you repented it." Gerard nodded assent. "And I said to myself, Gerard will thank me for taking Sybrandt to die under his roof. He will not beat his breast and cry *mea culpa*, yet grudge three footsteps to quiet a withered brother on his last bed. He may have a bee in his bonnet, but he is not a hypocrite, a thing all pious words and uncharitable deeds."

Gerard literally staggered where he sat at this tremendous thrust.

"Forgive me for nagging," said she. "Thy mother too is waiting for thee. Is it well done to keep her on thorns so long? She will not sleep this night. Bethink thee, Gerard, she is all to thee that I am to this sweet child. Ah, I think so much more of mothers since I had my little Gerard! She suffered for thee, and nursed thee, and tended thee from boy to man. Priest, monk, hermit, call thyself what thou wilt, to her thou art but one thing, her child."

"Where is she?" murmured Gerard in a quavering voice.

"At Gouda manse, wearing the night in prayer and care."

Then Margaret saw the time was come for that appeal to his reason she had purposely reserved till persuasion should have paved the way for conviction. So the smith first softens the iron by fire, and then brings down the sledge hammer. She showed him, but in her own good straightforward Dutch, that his present life was only a higher kind of selfishness, spiritual egotism. Whereas a priest had no more right to care only for his own soul than only for his own body. That was not *his* path to Heaven.

"But," said she, "whoever yet lost his soul by saving the soul of others? The Almighty loves him who thinks of others, and when He shall see thee caring for the souls of the folk the Duke hath put into thine hand, He will care ten times more for thy soul than He does now."

Gerard was struck by this remark. "Art shrewd in dispute," said he.

"Far from it," was the reply, "only my eyes are not bandaged with conceit.[1] So long as Satan walks the whole earth, tempting men, and so long as the sons of Belial do never lock themselves in caves, but run like ants to and fro corrupting others, the good man that skulks apart plays the Devil's game, or at least gives him the odds. Thou a soldier of Christ? Ask thy comrade Denys, who is but a soldier of the Duke, ask him if ever he skulked in a hole and shunned the battle because forsooth in battle is danger as well as glory and duty. For thy sole excuse is fear, thou makest no secret on't. Go to, no duke nor king hath such cowardly soldiers as Christ hath. What was that you said in the church at Rotterdam about the man in the parable that buried his talent in the earth and so offended the giver? Thy wonderful gift for preaching, is it not a talent, and a gift from thy Creator?"

"Certes, such as it is."

"And hast thou laid it out? Or buried it? To whom hast thou preached these seven months? To bats and owls? Hast buried it in one hole with thyself and thy once good wits. The Dominicans are the friars' preachers. 'Tis for preaching they were founded, so thou art false to Dominic as well as to his Master.

"Do you remember, Gerard, when we were young together which now

¹I think she means prejudice. Author's note.

are old before our time, as we walked handed in the fields, did you but see
a sheep cast, ay, three fields off, you would leave your sweetheart (by her
goodwill), and run and lift the sheep for charity? Well, then, at Gouda is
not one sheep in evil plight, but a whole flock—some cast, some strayed,
some sick, some tainted, some a-being devoured, and all for the want of a
shepherd. Where is their shepherd? Lurking in a den like a wolf, a den in
his own parish, out fie! out fie!

"I scented thee out, in part, by thy kindness to the little birds. Take note,
you, Gerard Eliassoen, must love something, 'tis in your blood, you were
born to't. Shunning man, you do but seek earthly affection a peg lower than
man."

Gerard interrupted her. "The birds are God's creatures, his innocent
creatures, and I do well to love them, being God's creatures."

"What, are they creatures of the same God that we are, that he is who
lies upon thy knee?"

"You know they are."

"Then what pretense for shunning us and being kind to them? Sith man
is one of the animals, why pick him out to shun? Is't because he is of animals
the paragon? What, you court the young of birds and abandon your own
young? Birds need but bodily food and, having wings, deserve scant pity if
they cannot fly and find it. But that sweet dove upon thy knee, he needeth
not carnal only, but spiritual food. He is thine as well as mine, and I have
done my share. He will soon be too much for me, and I look to Gouda's
parson to teach him true piety and useful lore. Is he not of more value than
many sparrows?"

Gerard started and stammered an affirmation. For she waited for his reply.

"You wonder," continued she, "to hear me quote Holy Writ so glib. I
have pored over it this four years, and why? Not because God wrote it, but
because I saw it often in thy hands ere thou didst leave me. Heaven forgive
me, I am but a woman. What thinkest thou of this sentence? 'Let your work
so shine before men that they may see your good works and glorify your
Father which is in Heaven!' What is a saint in a sink better than 'a light
under a bushel'?

"Therefore, since the sheep committed to thy charge bleat for thee and
cry, 'Oh desert us no longer, but come to Gouda manse'—since I, who know
thee ten times better than thou knowest thyself, do pledge my soul it is for
thy soul's weal to go to Gouda manse—since duty to thy child, too long
abandoned, calls thee to Gouda manse—since thy sovereign, whom Holy
Writ again bids thee honor, sends thee to Gouda manse—since the Pope,
whom the Church teaches thee to revere, hath absolved thee of thy monkish
vows, and orders thee to Gouda manse—"

"Ah?"

"Since thy gray-haired mother watches for thee in dole and care, and turneth oft the hourglass and sigheth sore that thou comest so slow to her at Gouda manse—since thy brother, withered by thy curse, awaits thy forgiveness and thy prayers for his soul, now lingering in his body, at Gouda manse —take thou up in thine arms the sweet bird wi' crest of gold that nestles to thy bosom, and give me thy hand, thy sweetheart erst and wife, and now thy friend, the truest friend to thee this night that ere man had, and come with me to Gouda manse!"

"*It is the voice of an angel!*" cried Clement loudly.

"Then hearken it, and come forth to Gouda manse!"

The battle was won.

Margaret lingered behind, cast her eye rapidly round the furniture, and selected the Vulgate and the psaltery. The rest she sighed at, and let it lie. The breastplate and the cilice of bristles she took and dashed with feeble ferocity on the floor. Then, seeing Gerard watch her with surprise from the outside, she colored and said: "I am but a woman. 'Little' will still be 'spiteful.' "

"Why encumber thyself with those? They are safe."

Oh, she had a reason. And with this they took the road to Gouda parsonage. The moon and stars were so bright it seemed almost as light as day.

Suddenly Gerard stopped. "My poor little birds!"

"What of them?"

"They will miss their food. I feed them every day.'

"The child hath a piece of bread in his cowl. Take that and feed them now, against the morn."

"I will. Nay, I will not. He is as innocent, and nearer to me and to thee."

Margaret drew a long breath. " 'Tis well. Hadst taken it, I might have hated thee. I am but a woman."

When they had gone about a quarter of a mile, Gerard sighed. "Margaret," said he, "I must e'en rest, he is too heavy for me."

"Then give him me, and take thou these. Alas, alas! I mind when thou wouldst have run with the child on one shoulder and the mother on t'other."

And Margaret carried the boy.

"I trow," said Gerard, looking down, "overmuch fasting is not good for a man."

"A-many die of it each year, wintertime," replied Margaret.

Gerard pondered these simple words, and eyed her askant, carrying the child with perfect ease. When they had gone nearly a mile, he said, with considerable surprise, "You thought it was but two butts' length."

"Not I."

"Why, you said so."

"That is another matter." She then turned on him the face of a Madonna. "I lied," said she, sweetly. "And to save your soul and body, I'd maybe tell a worse lie than that, at need. I am but a woman. Ah, well, it is but two butts' length from here, at any rate."

"Without a lie?"

"Humph. Three, without a lie."

And sure enough, in a few minutes they came up to the manse. A candle was burning in the vicar's parlor.

"She is waking still," whispered Margaret.

"Beautiful, beautiful!" said Clement, and stopped to look at it.

"What, in heaven's name?"

"That little candle, seen through the window at night. Look an it be not like some fair star of size prodigious. It delighteth the eyes and warmeth the heart of those outside."

"Come, and I'll show thee something better," said Margaret, and led him on tiptoe to the window.

They looked in, and there was Catherine kneeling on the hassock, with her "hours" before her.

"Folk can pray out of a cave," whispered Margaret. "Ay, and hit Heaven with their prayers. For 'tis for a sight of thee she prayeth, and thou art here. Now, Gerard, be prepared. She is not the woman you knew her, her children's troubles have greatly broken the brisk, lighthearted soul. And I see she has been weeping e'en now; she will have given thee up, being so late."

"Let me get to her," said Clement hastily, trembling all over.

"That door! I will bide here."

When Gerard was gone to the door, Margaret, fearing the sudden surprise, gave one sharp tap at the window, and cried, "Mother!" in a loud, expressive voice that Catherine read at once. She clasped her hands together and had half risen from her kneeling posture when the door burst open and Clement flung himself wildly on his knees at her knees, with his arms out to embrace her. She uttered a cry such as only a mother could. "Ah, my darling, my darling!" And clung sobbing round his neck. And true it was, she saw neither a hermit, a priest, nor a monk, but just her child, lost and despaired of, and in her arms. And after a little while Margaret came in, with wet eyes and cheeks, and a holy calm of affection settled by degrees on these sore troubled ones. And they sat all three together, hand in hand, murmuring sweet and loving converse. And he who sat in the middle drank right and left their true affection and their humble but genuine wisdom, and was forced to eat a good nourishing meal, and at daybreak was packed off to a snowy bed, and by-and-by awoke, as from a hideous dream, friar and hermit no more, Clement no more, but Gerard Eliassoen, parson of Gouda.

CHAPTER LVI

Margaret went back to Rotterdam long ere Gerard awoke, and actually left her boy behind her. She sent the faithful, sturdy Reicht off to Gouda directly with a Vicar's gray frock and large felt hat, and with minute instructions how to govern her new master.

Then she went to Jorian Ketel; for she said to herself, "He is the closest I ever met, so he is the man for me," and in concert with him she did two mortal sly things—yet not, in my opinion, virulent, though she thought they were. But if I am asked what were these deeds without a name, the answer is that as she, who was "but a woman," kept them secret till her dying day, I, who am a man—

She kept away from Gouda parsonage. Things that pass little noticed in the heat of argument sometimes rankle afterward, and when she came to go over all that had passed, she was offended at Gerard's thinking she could ever forget the priest in the sometime lover. "For what did he take me?" said she. And this raised a great shyness which really she would not otherwise have felt, being downright innocent. And pride sided with modesty and whispered, "Go no more to Gouda parsonage."

She left little Gerard there to complete the conquest her maternal heart ascribed to him, not to her own eloquence and sagacity, and to anchor his father forever to humanity. But this generous stroke of policy cost her heart dear. She had never yet been parted from her boy an hour, and she felt sadly strange as well as desolate without him. After the first day it became intolerable, and what does the poor soul do but creep at dark up to Gouda parsonage, and lurk about the premises like a thief till she saw Reicht Heynes in the kitchen alone.

Then she tapped softly at the window and said, "Reicht, for pity's sake bring him out to me unbeknown." With Margaret the person who occupied her thoughts at the time ceased to have a name, and sank to a pronoun. Reicht soon found an excuse for taking little Gerard out, and there was a scene of mutual rapture, followed by mutual tears when mother and boy parted again.

And it was arranged that Reicht should take him halfway to Rotterdam every day, at a set hour, and Margaret meet them. But when these stolen meetings had gone on about five days Margaret began to feel the injustice of it, and to be irritated as well as unhappy.

And she was crying about it when a cart came to her door, and in it, clean as a new penny, his beard close-shaved, his bands white as snow, and a little color in his pale face, sat the Vicar of Gouda in the gray frock and large felt hat she had sent him. She ran upstairs directly and washed away all traces of her tears and put on a cap—which, being just taken out of the drawer, was cleaner, theoretically, than the one she had on—and came down to him. He seized both her hands and kissed them, and a tear fell upon them. She turned her head away at that to hide her own which started.

"My sweet Margaret," he cried, "why is this? Why hold you aloof from your own good deed? We have been waiting and waiting for you every day, and no Margaret."

"You said things."

"What! When I was a hermit, and a donkey."

"Ay, no matter, you said things. And you had no reason."

"Forget all I said there. Who hearkens the ravings of a maniac? For I see now that in a few months more I should have been a gibbering idiot: Yet no mortal could have persuaded me away but you. Oh, what an outlay of wit and goodness was yours! But it is not here I can thank and bless you as I ought. No, it is in the home you have given me, among the sheep whose shepherd you have made me—already I love them dearly—there it is I must thank 'the truest friend ever man had.' So now I say to you as erst you said to me, come to Gouda manse."

"Humph! We will see about that."

"Why, Margaret, think you I had ever kept the dear child so long but that I made sure you would be back to him from day to day? Oh, he curls round my very heartstrings, but what is my title to him compared to thine? Confess now, thou hast had hard thoughts of me for this."

"Nay, nay, not I. Ah, thou art thyself again, wast ever thoughtful of others. I have half a mind to go to Gouda manse, for your saying that."

"Come, then, with half thy mind. 'Tis worth the whole of other folk's."

"Well, I dare say I will, but there is no such mighty hurry," said she coolly (she was literally burning to go). "Tell me first how you agree with your folk."

"Why, already my poor have taken root in my heart."

"I thought as much."

"And there are such good creatures among them, simple, and rough, and superstitious, but wonderfully good."

"Oh, leave you alone for seeing a grain of good among a bushel of ill!"

"Whisht, whisht! And, Margaret, two of them have been ill friends for four years, and came to the manse each to get on my blind side. But, give the glory to God, I got on their bright side and made them friends and laugh at themselves for their folly."

"But are you in very deed their vicar? Answer me that."

"Certes. Have I not been to the bishop and taken the oath, and rung the church bell, and touched the altar, the missal, and the holy cup before the churchwardens? And they have handed me the parish seal. See, here it is. Nay, 'tis a real vicar inviting a true friend to Gouda manse."

"Then my mind is at ease. Tell me oceans more."

"Well, sweet one, nearest to me of all my parish is a poor cripple that my guardian angel and his (her name thou knowest even by this turning of thy head away) hath placed beneath my roof. Sybrandt and I are that we never were till now, brothers. 'Twould gladden thee yet sadden thee to hear how we kissed and forgave one another. He is full of thy praises, and wholly in a pious mind. He says he is happier since his trouble than e'er he was in the days of his strength. Oh, out of my house he ne'er shall go to any place but Heaven!"

"Tell me somewhat that happened thyself, poor soul! All this is good, but yet no tidings to me. Do I not know thee of old?"

"Well, let me see. At first I was much dazzled by the sunlight, and could not go abroad (owl!), but that is past, and good Reicht Heynes—humph!"

"What of her?"

"This to thine ear only, for she is a diamond. Her voice goes through me like a knife, and all voices seem loud but thine, which is so mellow-sweet. Stay, now I'll fit ye with tidings. I spake yesterday with an old man that conceits he is ill-tempered, and sweats to pass for such with others, but oh, so threadbare, and the best good heart beneath."

"Why, 'tis a parish of angels," said Margaret ironically.

"Then why dost thou keep out on't?" retorted Gerard. "Well, he was telling me there was no parish in Holland where the Devil hath such power as at Gouda, and among his instances, says he: 'We had a hermit, the holiest in Holland, but, being Gouda, the Devil came for him this week and took him, bag and baggage—not a ha'porth of him left but a goodish piece of his skin, just for all the world like a hedgehog's, and a piece o' old iron furbished up."

Margaret smiled.

"Aye, but," continued Gerard, "the strange thing is, the cave has verily fallen in, and had I been so perverse as resist thee, it had assuredly buried me dead there where I had buried myself alive. Therefore in this I see the finger of Providence condemning my late, approving my present, way of life. What sayest thou?"

"Nay, can I pierce the like mysteries? I am but a woman."

"Somewhat more, methinks. This very tale proves thee my guardian angel, and all else avouches it, so come to Gouda manse."

"Well, go you on, I'll follow."

"Nay, in the cart with me."

"Not so."

"Why?"

"Can I tell why and wherefore, being a woman? All I know is I seem—to feel—to wish—to come alone."

"So be it then. I leave thee the cart, being, as thou sayest, a woman, and I'll go afoot, being a man again with the joyful tidings of thy coming."

When Margaret reached the manse the first thing she saw was the two Gerards together, the son performing his capriccios on the plot, and the father slouching on a chair in his great hat, with pencil and paper, trying very patiently to sketch him.

After a warm welcome he showed her his attempts. "But in vain I strive to fix him," said he, "for he is incarnate quicksilver. Yet do but note his changes, infinite but none ungracious. All is supple and easy, and how he melteth from one posture to another." He added presently: "Woe to illuminators! Looking on thee, Sir Baby, I see what awkward, lopsided, ungainly toads I and my fellows painted missals with and called them cherubs and seraphs." Finally he threw the paper away in despair, and Margaret conveyed it secretly into her bosom.

At night when they sat round the peat fire he bade them observe how beautiful the brass candlesticks and other glittering metals were in the glow from the hearth. Catherine's eyes sparkled at this observation. "And oh, the sheets I lie in here!" said he. "Often my conscience pricketh me and saith, 'Who art thou to lie in lint like web of snow?' Dives was ne'er so flaxed as I. And to think that there are folk in the world that have all the beautiful things which I have here, yet not content. Let them pass six months in a hermit's cell, seeing no face of man; then will they find how lovely and pleasant this wicked world is, and eke that men and women are God's fairest creatures. Margaret was always fair, but never to my eye so bright as now." Margaret shook her head incredulously. Gerard continued: "My mother was ever good and kind, but I noted not her exceeding comeliness till now."

"Nor I neither," said Catherine. "A score years ago I might pass in a crowd, but not now."

Gerard declared to her that each age had its beauty: "See this mild gray eye," said he, "that hath looked motherly love upon so many of us. All that love hath left its shadow, and that shadow is a beauty which defieth time. See this delicate lip, these pure white teeth. See this well-shaped brow, where comeliness just passeth into reverence. Art beautiful in my eyes, Mother dear."

"And that is enough for me, my darling. 'Tis time you were in bed, child. Ye have to preach the morn."

And Reicht Heynes and Catherine interchanged a look which said, "We two have an amiable maniac to superintend, calls everything beautiful."

The next day was Sunday, and they heard him preach in his own church. It was crammed with persons who came curious; but remained devout. Never was his wonderful gift displayed more powerfully. He was himself deeply moved by the first sight of all his people, and his bowels yearned over this flock he had so long neglected. In a single sermon, which lasted two hours and seemed to last but twenty minutes, he declared the whole Scripture. He terrified the impenitent and thoughtless, confirmed the wavering, consoled the bereaved and the afflicted, uplifted the hearts of the poor, and when he ended, left the multitude standing rapt, and unwilling to believe the divine music of his voice and soul had ceased. Need I say that two poor women in a corner sat entranced, with streaming eyes?

"Wherever gat he it all?" whispered Catherine with her apron to her eyes. "By our Lady, not from me."

As soon as they were by themselves Margaret threw her arms round Catherine's neck and kissed her.

"Mother, Mother, I am not quite a happy woman, but oh, I am a proud one!"

And she vowed on her knees never by word or deed to let her love come between this young saint and Heaven.

History, though a far more daring storyteller than romance, presents few things so strange as the footing on which Gerard and Margaret now lived for many years. United by present affection, past familiarity, and a marriage irregular but legal; separated by Holy Church and by their own consciences which sided unreservedly with Holy Church—separated by the Church, but united by a living pledge of affection, lawful in every sense at its date.

And living but a few miles from one another, and she calling his mother "Mother." For some years she always took her boy to Gouda on Sunday, returning home at dark. Go when she would, it was always fête at Gouda manse, and she was received like a little queen. Catherine was nearly always with her, and Eli very often. Tergou had so little to tempt them compared with Rotterdam, and at last they left it altogether, and set up in the capital. And thus the years glided, so barren now of striking incidents, so void of great hopes, and free from great fears, and so like one another that without the help of dates I could scarcely indicate the progress of time.

However, early next year, 1471, the Duchess of Burgundy, with the open dissent but secret connivance of the Duke, raised forces to enable her dethroned brother, Edward the Fourth of England, to invade that kingdom. Our old friend Denys thus enlisted, and passing through Rotterdam to the ships, heard on his way that Gerard was a priest, and Margaret alone. On this he told Margaret that marriage was not a habit of his, but that as his comrade had put it out of his own power to keep troth, he felt bound to offer to keep it for him; "for a comrade's honor is dear to us as our own," said he.

She stared, then smiled, "I choose rather to be still thy she-comrade," said she. "Closer acquainted, we might not agree so well." And in her character of she-comrade she equipped him with a new sword of Antwerp make, and a double handful of silver. "I give thee no gold," said she, "for 'tis thrown away as quick as silver, and harder to win back. Heaven send thee safe out of all thy perils. There be famous fair women yonder to beguile thee with their faces, as well as men to hash thee with their axes." He was hurried on board at La Vere, and never saw Gerard at that time.

In 1473, Sybrandt began to fail. His pitiable existence had been sweetened by his brother's inventive tenderness and his own contented spirit, which, his antecedents considered, was truly remarkable. As for Gerard, the day never passed that he did not devote two hours to him—reading or singing to him, praying with him, and drawing him about in a soft carriage Margaret and he had made between them. When the poor soul found his end near, he begged Margaret might be sent for. She came at once, and almost with his last breath he sought once more that forgiveness she had long ago accorded. She remained by him till the last, and he died, blessing and blessed, in the arms of the two truelovers he had parted for life.

1476 and 1477 were years of great trouble to Gerard, whose conscience compelled him to oppose the Pope. His Holiness, siding with the Gray Friars in their determination to swamp every palpable distinction between the Virgin Mary and her Son, bribed the Christian world into his crotchet by proffering pardon of all sins to such as would add to the Ave Mary this clause: "and blessed be thy Mother Anna, from whom, without blot of original sin, proceeded thy virgin flesh."

Gerard, in common with many of the Northern clergy, held this sentence to be flat heresy. He not only refused to utter it in his church, but warned his parishioners against using it in private, and he refused to celebrate the new feast the Pope invented at the same time, the Feast of the Miraculous Conception of the Virgin. But this drew upon him the bitter enmity of the Franciscans, and they were strong enough to put him into more than one serious difficulty, and inflict many a little mortification on him.

In emergencies he consulted Margaret, and she always did one of two things. Either she said, "I do not see my way," and refused to guess, or else she gave him advice that proved wonderfully sagacious. He had genius, but she had marvelous tact. And where affection came in and annihilated the woman's judgment, he stepped in his turn to her aid. Thus, though she knew she was spoiling little Gerard, and Catherine was ruining him for life, she would not part with him, but kept him at home, and his abilities uncultivated. And there was a shrewd boy of nine years, instead of learning to work and obey, playing about and learning selfishness from their infinite unselfishness, and tyrannizing with a rod of iron over two women, both of them sagacious and spirited, but reduced by their fondness for him to the exact level of idiots.

Gerard saw this with pain, and interfered with mild but firm remonstrance, and after a considerable struggle prevailed, and got little Gerard sent to the best school in Europe, kept by one Haaghe at Deventer. This was in 1477. Many tears were shed, but the great progress the boy made at that famous school reconciled Margaret in some degree, and the fidelity of Reicht Heynes, now her partner in business, enabled her to spend weeks at a time hovering over her boy at Deventer.

And so the years glided, and these two persons subjected to as strong and constant temptation as can well be conceived were each other's guardian angels, and not each other's tempters. To be sure, the well-greased morality of the next century, which taught that solemn vows to God are sacred in proportion as they are reasonable, had at that time entered no single mind, and the alternative to these two minds was self-denial or sacrilege. It was a strange thing to hear them talk with unrestrained tenderness to one another of their boy, and an icy barrier between themselves all the time.

Eight years had now passed thus, and Gerard, fairly compared with men in general, was happy. But Margaret was not. The habitual expression of her face was a sweet pensiveness, but sometimes she was irritable and a little petulant. She even snapped at Gerard now and then. And when she went to see him, if a monk was with him, she would turn her back and go home. She hated the monks for having parted Gerard and her, and she inoculated her boy with a contempt for them which lasted him till his dying day. Gerard bore with her like an angel. He knew her heart of gold, and hoped this ill gust would blow over.

He himself being now the right man in the right place this many years, loving his parishioners and beloved by them, and occupied from morn till night in good works, recovered the natural cheerfulness of his disposition. To tell the truth, a part of his jocoseness was a blind. He was the greatest peacemaker, except Mr. Harmony in the play, that ever was born. He reconciled more enemies in ten years than his predecessors had done in three hundred, and one of his maneuvers in the peacemaking art was to make the quarrelers laugh at the cause of quarrel. So did he undermine the demon of discord. But independently of that, he really loved a harmless joke.

He was a wonderful tamer of animals, squirrels, hares, fawns, and so on. So half in jest, a parishioner who had a mule supposed to be possessed with a devil gave it him, and said, "Tame this vagabone, Parson, if ye can." Well, in about six months, Heaven knows how, he not only tamed Jack, but won his affections to such a degree that Jack would come running to his whistle like a dog. One day, having taken shelter from a shower on the stone settle outside a certain public house, he heard a toper inside, a stranger, boasting he could take more at a draft than any man in Gouda. He instantly marched in, and said: "What, lads, do none of ye take him up for the honor of Gouda? Shall it be said that there came hither one from another parish a greater sot than any of us? Nay, then, I your parson do take him up. Go to, I'll find thee a parishioner shall drink more at a draft than thou."

A bet was made. Gerard whistled. In clattered Jack—for he was taught to come into a room with the utmost composure—and put his nose into his backer's hand.

"A pair of buckets!" shouted Gerard. "Let us see which of these two sons of asses can drink most at a draft."

On another occasion two farmers had a dispute whose hay was the best. Failing to convince each other, they said, "We'll ask Parson!" for by this time he was their referee in every mortal thing.

"How lucky you thought of me!" said Gerard. "Why, I have got one staying with me who is the best judge of hay in Holland. Bring me a double handful apiece."

So when they came, he had them into the parlor, and put each bundle on a chair. Then he whistled, and in walked Jack.

"Lord a-mercy!" said one of the farmers.

"Jack," said the parson, in the tone of conversation, "just tell us which is the best hay of these two."

Jack sniffed them both, and made his choice directly, proving his sincerity by eating every morsel. The farmers slapped their thighs and scratched their heads. "To think of we not thinking o' that." And they each sent Jack a truss.

So Gerard got to be called the Merry Parson of Gouda. But Margaret, who like most loving women had no more sense of humor than a turtledove, took this very ill. "What!" said she to herself. "Is there nothing sore at the bottom of his heart that he can go about playing the zany?" She could understand pious resignation and content, but not mirth, in truelovers parted. And whilst her woman's nature was perturbed by this gust (and women seem more subject to gusts than men) came that terrible animal, a busybody, to work upon her. Catherine saw she was not happy, and said to her: "Your boy is gone from you. I would not live alone all my days if I were you."

"*He* is more alone than I," sighed Margaret.

"Oh, a man is a man, but a woman is a woman. You must not think all of him and none of yourself. Near is your kirtle, but nearer is your smock. Besides, he is a priest, and can do no better. But you are not a priest. He has got his parish, and his heart is in that. Bethink thee! Time flies, over-stay not thy market. Wouldst not like to have three or four more little darlings about thy knee now they have robbed thee of poor little Gerard and sent him to yon nasty school?" And so she worked upon a mind already irritated.

Margaret had many suitors ready to marry her at a word or even a look, and among them two merchants of the better class, Van Schelt and Oost-wagen. "Take one of those two," said Catherine.

"Well, I will ask Gerard if I may," said Margaret one day with a flood of tears, "for I cannot go on the way I am."

"Why, you would never be so simple as ask *him?*"

"Think you I would be so wicked as marry without his leave?"

Accordingly she actually went to Gouda, and after hanging her head, and blushing, and crying, and saying she was miserable, told him his mother wished her to marry one of those two. And if he approved of her marrying at all, would he use his wisdom, and tell her which he thought would be the kindest to the little Gerard of those two; for herself she did not care what became of her.

Gerard felt as if she had put a soft hand into his body and torn his heart out with it. But the priest with a mighty effort mastered the man. In a voice scarcely audible he declined this responsibility.

"I am not a saint or a prophet," said he. "I might advise thee ill. I shall read the marriage service for thee," faltered he, "it is my right. No other would pray for thee as I should. But thou must choose for thyself, and oh, let me see thee happy! This four months past thou hast not been happy."

"A discontented mind is never happy," said Margaret.

She left him, and he fell on his knees and prayed for help from above. Margaret went home pale and agitated.

"Mother," said she, "never mention it to me again, or we shall quarrel."

"He forbade you? Well, more shame for him, that is all."

"He forbid me? He did not condescend so far. He was as noble as I was paltry. He would not choose for me for fear of choosing me an ill husband. But he would read the service for my groom and me, that was his right. Oh, Mother, what a heartless creature I was!"

"Well, I thought not he had that much sense."

"Ah, you go by the poor soul's words, but I rate words as air when the face speaketh to mine eyes. I saw the priest and the truelover a-fighting in his dear face, and his cheek pale with the strife, and oh, his poor lip trembled as he said the stouthearted words—oh, oh, oh, oh, oh, oh, oh!" And Margaret burst into a violent passion of tears.

Catherine groaned. "There, give it up without more ado," said she. "You two are chained together for life, and if God is merciful, that won't be for long, for what are you? Neither maid, wife, nor widow."

"Give it up?" said Margaret. "That was done long ago. All I think of now is comforting him, for now I have been and made him unhappy too, wretch and monster that I am."

So the next day they both went to Gouda. And Gerard, who had been praying for resignation all this time, received her with peculiar tenderness as a treasure he was to lose. She was agitated and eager to let him see without words that she would never marry, and she fawned on him like a little dog to be forgiven. And as she was going away she murmured: "Forgive! And forget! I am but a woman."

He misunderstood her, and said: "All I bargain for is, let me see thee content. For pity's sake, let me not see thee unhappy as I have this while."

"My darling, you never shall again," said Margaret with streaming eyes, and kissed his hand.

He misunderstood this too at first, but when month after month passed, and he heard no more of her marriage, and she came to Gouda comparatively cheerful, and was even civil to Father Ambrose, a mild benevolent monk from the Dominican convent hard by—then he understood her, and one day he invited her to walk alone with him in the sacred paddock. Before I relate what passed between them, I must give its history. When Gerard had been four or five days at the manse looking out of window, he uttered an exclamation of joy. "Mother, Margaret, here is one of my birds—another, another, four, six, nine. A miracle! A miracle!"

"Why, how can you tell your birds from their fellows?" said Catherine.

"I know every feather in their wings. And see, there is the little darling whose beak I gilt, bless it!"

And presently his rapture took a serious turn, and he saw Heaven's approbation in this conduct of the birds, as he did in the fall of the cave. This wonderfully kept alive his friendship for animals, and he enclosed a paddock, and drove all the sons of Cain from it with threats of excommunication. "On this little spot of earth we'll have no murder," said he. He tamed leverets and partridges, and little birds, and hares, and roe deer. He found a squirrel with a broken leg; he set it with infinite difficulty and patience, and during the cure showed it repositories of acorns, nuts, chestnuts. And this squirrel got well and went off, but visited him in hard weather and brought a mate, and next year little squirrels were found to have imbibed their parents' sentiments. And of all these animals each generation was tamer than the last. This set the good parson thinking, and gave him the true clue to the great successes of medieval hermits in taming wild animals.

He kept the key of this paddock, and never let any man but himself enter it, nor would he even let little Gerard go there without him or Margaret. "Children are all little Cains," said he.

In this oasis, then, he spoke to Margaret, and said: "Dear Margaret, I have thought more than ever of thee of late, and have asked myself why I am content and thou unhappy."

"Because thou art better, wiser, holier, than I, that is all," said Margaret promptly.

"Our lives tell another tale," said Gerard thoughtfully. "I know thy goodness and thy wisdom too well to reason thus perversely. Also I know that I love thee as dear as thou, I think, lovest me. Yet am I happier than thou. Why is this so?"

"Dear Gerard, I am as happy as a woman can hope to be this side the grave."

"Not so happy as I. Now for the reason. First, then, I am a priest, and this, the one great trial and disappointment God giveth me along with so many joys, why I share it with a multitude. For alas, I am not the only priest by thousands that must never hope for entire earthly happiness. Here then, thy lot is harder than mine."

"But Gerard, I have my child to love. Thou canst not fill thy heart with him as his mother can. So you may set this against yon."

"And I have ta'en him from thee. It was cruel, but he would have broken thy heart one day if I had not. Well then, sweet one, I come to where the shoe pincheth, methinks. I have my parish, and it keeps my heart in a glow from morn till night. There is scarce an emotion that my folk stir not up in me many times a day. Often their sorrows make me weep, sometimes their perversity kindles a little wrath, and their absurdity makes me laugh, and sometimes their flashes of unexpected goodness do set me all of a glow, and I could hug 'em. Meantime thou, poor soul, sittest with heart—"

"Of lead, Gerard, of very lead."

"See now how unkind thy lot compared with mine. Now how if thou couldst be persuaded to warm thyself at the fire that warmeth me?"

"Ah, if I could!"

"Hast but to will it. Come among my folk. Take in thine hand the alms I set aside, and give it with kind words. Hear their sorrows. They shall show you life is full of troubles and, as thou sayest truly, no man or woman without their thorn this side the grave. Indoors I have a map of Gouda parish. Not to o'erburden thee at first, I will put twenty housen under thee with their folk. What sayest thou? But for thy wisdom I had died a dirty maniac, and ne'er seen Gouda manse, nor pious peace. Wilt profit in turn by what little wisdom *I* have to soften her lot to whom I do owe all?"

Margaret assented warmly, and a happy thing it was for the little district assigned to her. It was as if an angel had descended on them. Her fingers were never tired of knitting or cutting for them, her heart of sympathizing with them. And that heart expanded and waved its drooping wings, and the glow of good and gentle deeds began to spread over it. And she was rewarded in another way, by being brought into more contact with Gerard, and also with his spirit.

All this time malicious tongues had not been idle. "If there is naught between them more than meets the eye, why doth she not marry?" and so forth. And I am sorry to say our old friend Joan Ketel was one of these coarse skeptics. And now one winter evening she got on a hot scent. She saw Margaret and Gerard talking earnestly together on the Boulevard. She whipped behind a tree. "Now I'll hear something," said she, and so she did. It was winter; there had been one of those tremendous floods followed by a sharp frost, and Gerard in despair as to where he should lodge forty or fifty houseless folk out of the piercing cold. And now it was: "Oh dear, dear Margaret, what shall I do? The manse is full of them, and a sharp frost coming on this night."

Margaret reflected, and Joan listened.

"You must lodge them in the church," said Margaret quietly.

"In the church? Profanation."

"No, charity profanes nothing, not even a church—soils naught, not even a church. Today is but Tuesday. Go save their lives, for a bitter night is coming. Take thy stove into the church, and there house them. We will dispose of them here and there ere the Lord's Day."

"And I could not think of that. Bless thee, sweet Margaret, thy mind is stronger than mine, and readier."

"Nay, nay, a woman looks but a little way, therefore she sees clear. I'll come over myself tomorrow."

And on this they parted with mutual blessings. Joan glided home remorseful. And after that she used to check all surmises to their discredit. "Beware," she would say, "lest some angel should blister thy tongue. Gerard and Margaret paramours? I tell ye they are two saints which meet in secret to plot charity to the poor."

In the summer of 1481 Gerard determined to provide against similar disasters recurring to his poor. Accordingly he made a great hole in his income, and bled his friends (zealous parsons always do that), to build a large xenodochium to receive the victims of flood or fire. Giles and all his friends were kind, but all was not enough, when lo, the Dominican monks of Gouda, to whom his parlor and heart had been open for years, came out nobly and put down a handsome sum to aid the charitable Vicar.

"The dear good souls," said Margaret. "Who would have thought it!"

"Anyone who knows them," said Gerard. "Who more charitable than monks?"

"Go to! They do but give the laity back a pig of their own sow."

"And what more do I? What more doth the Duke?"

Then the ambitious Vicar must build almshouses for decayed true men in their old age, close to the manse that he might keep and feed them as well as lodge them. And his money being gone, he asked Margaret for a few thousand bricks and just took off his coat and turned builder. And as he had a good head, and the strength of a Hercules, with the zeal of an artist, up rose a couple of almshouses Parson built.

And at this work Margaret would sometimes bring him his dinner, and add a good bottle of Rhenish. And once, seeing him run up a plank with a wheelbarrow full of bricks which really most bricklayers would have gone staggering under, she said, "Times are changed since I had to carry little Gerard for thee."

"Ay, dear one, thanks to thee."

When the first home was finished, the question was who they should put into it, and being fastidious over it like a new toy, there was much hesitation. But an old friend arrived in time to settle this question.

As Gerard was passing a public house in Rotterdam one day, he heard a well-known voice. He looked up, and there was Denys of Burgundy, but sadly changed. His beard stained with gray, and his clothes worn and ragged; he had a cuirass still, and gauntlets, but a staff instead of an arbalest.

To the company he appeared to be bragging and boasting, but in reality he was giving a true relation of Edward the Fourth's invasion of an armed kingdom with two thousand men, and his march through the country with armies capable of swallowing him looking on, his battles at Tewkesbury and Barnet, and reoccupation of his capital and kingdom in three months after landing at the Humber with a mixed handful of Dutch, English, and Burgundians. In this, the greatest feat of arms the century had seen, Denys had shone, and whilst sneering at the warlike pretensions of Charles the Bold, a Duke with an itch but no talent for fighting, and proclaiming the English King the first captain of the age, did not forget to exalt himself.

Gerard listened with eyes glittering affection and fun. "And now," said Denys, "after all these feats, patted on the back by the gallant young Prince of Gloucester, and smiled on by the great captain himself, here I am lamed for life by what? By the kick of a horse, and this night I know not where I shall lay my tired bones. I had a comrade once in these parts that would not have let me lie far from him. But he turned priest and deserted his sweetheart, so 'tis not likely he would remember his comrade. And ten years play sad havoc with our hearts, and limbs, and all." Poor Denys sighed, and Gerard's bowels yearned over him.

"What words are these?" he said, with a great gulp in his throat. "Who grudges a brave soldier supper and bed? Come home with me!"

"Much obliged, but I am no lover of priests."

"Nor I of soldiers, but what is supper and bed between two true men?"

"Not much to you, but something to me. I will come."

"In one hour," said Gerard, and went in high spirits to Margaret and told her the treat in store, and she must come and share it. She must drive his mother in his little carriage up to the manse with all speed, and make ready an excellent supper. Then he himself borrowed a cart, and drove Denys up rather slowly, to give the women time.

On the road Denys found out this priest was a kind soul, so told him his trouble, and confessed his heart was pretty near broken. "The great use our stout hearts, and arms, and lives, till we are worn out, and then fling us away like broken tools." He sighed deeply, and it cost Gerard a great struggle, not to hug him then and there, and tell him. But he wanted to do it all like a storybook. Who has not had this fancy once in his life? Why, Joseph had it—all the better for us. They landed at the little house. It was as clean as a penny, the hearth blazing, and supper set.

Denys brightened up. "Is this your house, Reverend Sir?"

"Well, 'tis my work, and with these hands, but 'tis your house."

"Ah, no such luck," said Denys with a sigh.

"But I say ay!" shouted Gerard. "And what is more, I—" (gulp) "say—" (gulp) *"Courage, camarade. Le diable est mort!"*

Denys started, and almost staggered. "Why, what," he stammered, "w—wh—who art thou that bringest me back the merry words and merry days of my youth?" And he was greatly agitated.

"My poor Denys, I am one whose face is changed but naught else. To my heart, dear trusty comrade, to my heart!" And he opened his arms, with the tears in his eyes. But Denys came close to him, and peered in his face, and devoured every feature; and when he was sure it was really Gerard, he uttered a cry so vehement it brought the women running from the house, and fell upon Gerard's neck, and kissed him again and again, and sank on his knees, and laughed and sobbed with joy so terribly that Gerard mourned his folly in doing dramas. But the women with their gentle soothing ways soon composed the brave fellow, and he sat smiling and holding Margaret's hand and Gerard's. And they all supped together, and went to their beds with hearts warm as toast, and the broken soldier was at peace, and in his own house, and under his comrade's wing.

His natural gaiety returned, and he resumed his consigne after eight years' disuse, and hobbled about the place enlivening it, but offended the parish mortally by calling the adored Vicar comrade, and nothing but comrade. When they made a fuss about this to Gerard, he just looked in their faces and said: "What does it matter? Break him of swearing, and you shall have my thanks."

This year Margaret went to a lawyer to make her will, for without this she was told her boy might have trouble some day to get his own, not being born in lawful wedlock. The lawyer, however, in conversation, expressed a different opinion.

"This is the babble of churchmen," said he. "Yours is a perfect marriage, though an irregular one."

He then informed her that throughout Europe, excepting only the southern part of Britain, there were three irregular marriages, the highest of which was hers—a betrothal before witnesses.

"This," said he, "if not followed by matrimonial intercourse, is a marriage complete in form but incomplete in substance. A person so betrothed can forbid any other banns to all eternity. It has, however, been set aside where a party so betrothed contrived to get married regularly and children were born thereafter. But such a decision was for the sake of the offspring, and of doubtful justice. However, in your case the birth of your child closes that door, and your marriage is complete both in form and substance. Your course, therefore, is to sue for your conjugal rights. It will be the prettiest case of the century. The law is on our side, the Church all on theirs. If you come to that, the old Batavian law, which *compelled* the clergy to marry, hath fallen into disuse but was never formally repealed."

Margaret was quite puzzled. "What are you driving at, sir? Who am I to go to law with?"

"Who is the defendant? Why, the Vicar of Gouda."

"Alas, poor soul! And for what shall I law him?"

"Why, to make him take you into his house and share bed and board with you, to be sure."

Margaret turned red as fire. "Gramercy for your rede," said she. "What, is yon a woman's part? Constrain a man to be hers by force? That is men's way of wooing, not ours. Say I were so ill a woman as ye think me, I should set myself to beguile him, not to law him." And she departed, crimson with shame and indignation.

"There is an impracticable fool for you," said the man of art.

Margaret had her will drawn elsewhere, and made her boy safe from poverty, marriage or no marriage.

These are the principal incidents that in ten whole years befell two peaceful lives which in a much shorter period had been so thronged with adventures and emotions. Their general tenor was now peace, piety, the mild content that lasts, not the fierce bliss ever on tiptoe to depart, and, above all, Christian charity.

On this sacred ground these two truelovers met with a uniformity and a kindness of sentiment which went far to soothe the wound in their own hearts. To pity the same bereaved, to hunt in couples all the ills in Gouda, and contrive and scheme together to remedy all that were remediable; to use the rare insight into troubled hearts which their own troubles had given them, and use it to make others happier than themselves—this was their daily practice. And in this blessed cause their passion for one another cooled a little, but their affection increased. From the time Margaret entered heart and soul into Gerard's pious charities that affection purged itself of all mortal dross. And as it had now long outlived scandal and misapprehension, one would have thought that so bright an example of pure self-denying affection was to remain long before the world, to show men how nearly religious faith, even when not quite reasonable, and religious charity, which is always reasonable, could raise two truelovers' hearts to the loving hearts of the angels of Heaven. But the great Disposer of events ordered otherwise.

Little Gerard rejoiced both his parents' hearts by the extraordinary progress he made at Alexander Haaghe's famous school at Deventer. The last time Margaret returned from visiting him she came to Gerard flushed with pride. "Oh, Gerard, he will be a great man one day, thanks to thy wisdom in taking him from us silly women. A great scholar, one Zinthius, came to see the school and judge the scholars, and didn't our Gerard stand up, and not a line in Horace or Terence could Zinthius cite but the boy would follow him with the rest. 'Why, 'tis a prodigy,' says that great scholar, and there was his poor mother stood by and heard it. And he took our Gerard in his arms and kissed him, and what think you he said?"

"Nay, I know not."

"'Holland will hear of thee one day, and not Holland only, but all the world.' Why, what a sad brow!"

"Sweet one, I am as glad as thou, yet am I uneasy to hear the child is wise before his time. I love him dear, but he is thine idol, and Heaven doth often break our idols."

"Make thy mind easy," said Margaret. "Heaven will never rob me of my child. What I was to suffer in this world I have suffered. For if any ill happened to my child or thee I should not live a week. The Lord He knows this, and He will leave me my boy."

A month had elapsed after this, but Margaret's words were yet ringing in his ears when, going his daily round of visits to his poor, he was told quite incidentally and as mere gossip that the plague was at Deventer, carried thither by two sailors from Hamburgh.

His heart turned cold within him. News did not gallop in those days. The fatal disease must have been there a long time before the tidings would reach Gouda. He sent a line by a messenger to Margaret, telling her that he was gone to fetch little Gerard to stay at the manse a little while, and would she see a bed prepared, for he should be back next day. And so he hoped she would not hear a word of the danger till it was all happily over. He borrowed a good horse and scarce drew rein till he reached Deventer, quite late in the afternoon. He went at once to the school. The boy had been taken away.

As he left the school he caught sight of Margaret's face at the window of a neighboring house she always lodged at when she came to Deventer. He ran hastily in to scold her and pack both her and the boy out of the place. To his surprise the servant told him with some hesitation that Margaret had been there, but was gone.

"Gone, woman?" said Gerard, indignantly. "Art not ashamed to say so? Why, I saw her but now at the window."

"Oh, if you saw her——"

A sweet voice above said, "Stay him not, let him enter." It was Margaret.

Gerard ran up the stairs to her, and went to take her hand. She drew back hastily. He looked astounded.

"I am displeased," said she, coldly. "What makes you here? Know you not the plague is in the town?"

"Ay, dear Margaret, and came straightway to take our boy away."

"What, had he no mother?"

"How you speak to me! I hoped you knew not."

"What, think you I leave my boy unwatched? I pay a trusty woman that notes every change in his cheek when I am not here and lets me know. I am his mother."

"Where is he?"

"In Rotterdam, I hope, ere this."

"Thank heaven! And why are you not there?"

"I am not fit for the journey. Never heed me, go you home on the instant, I'll follow. For shame of you to come here risking your precious life!"

"It is not so precious as thine," said Gerard. "But let that pass, we will go home together, and on the instant."

"Nay, I have some matters to do in the town. Go thou at once, and I will follow forthwith."

"Leave thee alone in a plague-stricken town? To whom speak you, dear Margaret?"

"Nay, then, we shall quarrel, Gerard."

"Methinks I see Margaret and Gerard quarreling! Why, it takes two to quarrel, and we are but one."

With this Gerard smiled on her sweetly. But there was no kind responsive glance. She looked cold, gloomy, and troubled. He sighed, and sat patiently down opposite her with his face all puzzled and saddened. He said nothing, for he felt sure she would explain her capricious conduct, or it would explain itself.

Presently she rose hastily and tried to reach her bedroom. But on the way she staggered and put out her hand. He ran to her with a cry of alarm. She swooned in his arms. He laid her gently on the ground, and beat her cold hands, and ran to her bedroom and fetched water and sprinkled her pale face. His own was scarce less pale, for in a basin he had seen water stained with blood. It alarmed him, he knew not why. She was a long time ere she revived, and when she did she found Gerard holding her hand and bending over her with a look of infinite concern and tenderness. She seemed at first as if she responded to it, but the next moment her eye dilated, and she cried: "Ah, wretch, leave my hand! How dare you touch me?"

"Heaven help her!" said Gerard. "She is not herself."

"You will not leave me, then, Gerard?" said she, faintly. "Alas, why do I ask? Would I leave thee if thou wert— At least, touch me not, and then I will let thee abide and see the last of poor Margaret. She ne'er spoke harsh to thee before, sweetheart, and she never will again."

"Alas, what mean these dark words, these wild and troubled looks?" said Gerard, clasping his hands.

"My poor Gerard," said Margaret, "forgive me that I spoke so to thee. I am but a woman, and would have spared thee a sight will make thee weep." She burst into tears. "Ah, me," she cried, weeping, "that I cannot keep grief from thee! There is a great sorrow before my darling, and this time I shall not be able to come and dry his eyes."

"Let it come, Margaret, so it touch not thee," said Gerard, trembling.

"Dearest," said Margaret, solemnly, "call now religion to thine aid and mine. I must have died before thee one day, or else outlived thee and so died of grief."

"Died? Thou die? I will never let thee die. Where is thy pain? What is thy trouble?"

"The plague," said she, calmly. Gerard uttered a cry of horror and started to his feet. She read his thought. "Useless," said she, quietly. "My nose hath bled. None ever yet survived to whom that came along with the plague. Bring no fools hither to babble over the body they cannot save. I am but a woman, I love not to be stared at. Let none see me die but thee."

And even with this a convulsion seized her, and she remained sensible but speechless a long time. And now for the first time Gerard began to realize the frightful truth, and he ran wildly to and fro, and cried to Heaven for help as drowning men cry to their fellow creatures. She raised herself on her arm and set herself to quiet him. She told him she had known the torture of hopes and fears, and was resolved to spare him that agony.

"I let my mind dwell too much on the danger," said she, "and so opened my brain to it, through which door when this subtle venom enters it makes short work. I shall not be spotted or loathsome, my poor darling. God is good and spares thee that, but in twelve hours I shall be a dead woman. Ah, look not so, but be a man, be a priest! Waste not one precious minute over my body, it is doomed, but comfort my parting soul."

Gerard, sick and cold at heart, knelt down and prayed for help from Heaven to do his duty. When he rose from his knees, his face was pale and old, bent deadly calm and patient. He went softly and brought her bed into the room, and laid her gently down and supported her head with pillows. Then he prayed by her side the prayers for the dying, and she said Amen to each prayer. Then for some hours she wandered, but when the fell disease had quite made sure of its prey, her mind cleared, and she begged Gerard to shrive her. "For oh, my conscience it is laden," said she, sadly.

"Confess thy sins to me, my daughter. Let there be no reserve."

"My father," said she, sadly, "I have one great sin on my breast this many years. E'en now that death is at my heart I can scarce own it. But the Lord is debonair. If thou wilt pray to Him, perchance He may forgive me."

"Confess it first, my daughter."

"I—alas!"

"Confess it!"

"I deceived thee. This many years I have deceived thee."

Here tears interrupted her speech.

"Courage, my daughter, courage," said Gerard, kindly, overpowering the lover in the priest.

She hid her face in her hands, and with many sighs told him it was she who had broken down the hermit's cave with the help of Jorian Ketel. "I, shallow, did it but to hinder thy return thither, but when thou sawest therein the finger of God, I played the traitress, and said, 'While he thinks so he will ne'er leave Gouda manse,' and I held my tongue. Oh, false heart!"

"Courage, my daughter, thou dost exaggerate a trivial fault."

"Ah, but 'tis not all. The birds."

"Well?"

"They followed thee not to Gouda by miracle but by my treason. I said, 'He will ne'er be quite happy without his birds that visited him in his cell,' and I was jealous of them, and cried, and said, 'These foul little things, they are my child's rivals.' And I bought loaves of bread, and Jorian and me we put crumbs at the cave door and thence went sprinkling them all the way to the manse, and there a heap. And my wiles succeeded, and they came, and thou wast glad, and I was pleased to see thee glad. And when thou sawest in my guile the finger of Heaven, wicked, deceitful I did hold my tongue. But *die* deceiving thee? Ah, no, I could not. Forgive me if thou canst, I was but a woman, I knew no better at the time. 'Twas writ in my bosom with a very sunbeam, ' 'Tis good for him to bide at Gouda manse.' "

"Forgive thee, sweet innocent!" sobbed Gerard. "What have *I* to forgive? Thou hadst a foolish froward child to guide to his own weal, and didst all this for the best. I thank thee and bless thee. But as thy confessor, all deceit is ill in Heaven's pure eye. Therefore thou hast done well to confess and report it, and even on thy confession and penitence the Church through me absolves thee. Pass to thy graver faults."

"My graver faults? Alas, alas! Why, what have I done to compare? I am not an ill woman, not a very ill one. If He can forgive me deceiving thee, He can well forgive me all the rest ever I did."

Being gently pressed, she said she was to blame not to have done more good in the world. "I had just begun to do a little," she said, "and now I must go. But I repine not, since 'tis Heaven's will. Only I am so afeard thou wilt miss me." And at this she could not restrain her tears, though she tried hard.

Gerard struggled with his as well as he could; and knowing her life of piety, purity, and charity, and seeing that she could not in her present state realize any sin but her having deceived *him,* gave her full absolution. Then he put the crucifix in her hand, and while he consecrated the oil, bade her fix her mind neither on her merits nor her demerits, but on Him who died for her on the tree.

She obeyed him, with a look of confiding love and submission. And he touched her eye with the consecrated oil, and prayed aloud beside her. Soon after she dozed. He watched beside her, more dead than alive himself. When the day broke she awoke, and seemed to acquire some energy. She begged him to look in her box for her marriage lines, and for a picture, and bring them both to her. He did so. She then entreated him by all they had suffered for each other to ease her mind by making a solemn vow to execute her dying requests. He vowed to obey them to the letter.

"Then, Gerard, let no creature come here to lay me out. I could not bear to be stared at, my very corpse would blush. Also I would not be made a monster of for the worms to sneer at as well as feed on. Also my very clothes are tainted, and shall to earth with me. I am a physician's daughter, and ill becomes me kill folk, being dead, which did so little good to men in the days of health. Wherefore lap me in lead, the way I am, and bury me deep! Yet not so deep but what one day thou mayest find the way, and lay thy bones by mine.

"Whiles I lived I went to Gouda but once or twice a week. It cost me not to go each day. Let me gain this by dying, to be always at dear Gouda—in the green kerkyard. Also they do say the spirit hovers where the body lies. I would have my spirit hover near thee, and the kerkyard is not far from the manse. I am so afeard some ill will happen thee, Margaret being gone.

"And see, with mine own hands I place my marriage lines in my bosom. Let no living hand move them, on pain of thy curse and mine. Then when the angel comes for me at the last day, he shall say, 'This is an honest woman, she hath her marriage lines' (for you know I am your lawful wife though Holy Church hath come between us), and he will set me where the honest women be. I will not sit among ill women, no, not in Heaven, for their mind is not my mind, nor their soul my soul. I have stood, unbeknown, at my window and heard their talk."

For some time she was unable to say any more, but made signs to him that she had not done. At last she recovered her breath, and bade him look at the picture. It was the portrait he had made of her when they were young together, and little thought to part so soon. He held it in his hands and looked at it, but could scarce see it. He had left it in fragments, but now it was whole.

"They cut it to pieces, Gerard. But see, Love mocked at their knives. I implore thee with my dying breath, let this picture hang ever in thine eye.

"I have heard that such as die of the plague unspotted, yet after death spots have been known to come out, and, oh, I could not bear thy last memory of me to be so! Therefore as soon as the breath is out of my body, cover my face with this handkerchief, and look at me no more till we meet again—'twill not be so very long. Oh, promise!"

"I promise," said Gerard, sobbing.

"But look on this picture instead. Forgive me, I am but a woman. I could not bear my face to lie a foul thing in thy memory. Nay, I must have thee still think me as fair as I was true. Hast called me an angel once or twice, but be just, did I not still tell thee I was no angel, but only a poor simple woman that whiles saw clearer than thou because she looked but a little way, and that loves thee dearly, and never loved but thee, and now with her dying breath prays thee indulge her in this, thou that art a man."

"I will. I will. Each word, each wish is sacred."

"Bless thee! Bless thee! So then the eyes that now can scarce see thee, they are so troubled by the pest, and the lips that shall not touch thee to taint thee, will still be before thee as they were when we were young and thou didst love me."

"When I did love thee, Margaret! Oh, never loved I thee as now!"

"Hast not told me so of late."

"Alas! Hath love no voice but words? I was a priest, I had charge of thy soul. The sweet offices of a pure love were lawful, words of love imprudent at the least. But now the good fight is won, ah me! Oh, my love, if thou hast lived doubting of thy Gerard's heart, die not so, for never was woman loved so tenderly as thou this ten years past."

"Calm thyself, dear one," said the dying woman with a heavenly smile. "I know it, only being but a woman, I could not die happy till I had heard thee say so. Ah, I have pined ten years for those sweet words! Hast said them, and this is the happiest hour of my life. I had to die to get them. Well, I grudge not the price."

From this moment a gentle complacency rested on her fading features. But she did not speak. Then Gerard, who had loved her soul so many years, feared lest she should expire with a mind too fixed on earthly affection.

"Oh, my daughter," he cried, "my dear daughter, if indeed thou lovest me as I love thee, give me not the pain of seeing thee die with thy pious soul fixed on mortal things. Dearest lamb of all my fold, for whose soul I must answer, oh, think not now of mortal love, but of His who died for thee on the tree. Oh, let thy last look be heavenward, thy last word a word of prayer."

She turned a look of gratitude and obedience on him. "What saint?" she murmured, meaning, doubtless, what saint should she invoke as an intercessor.

"He to whom the saints themselves do pray."

She turned on him one more sweet look of love and submission, and put her pretty hands together in prayer like a child.

"Jesu!"

This blessed word was her last. She lay with her eyes heavenward, and her hands put together. Gerard prayed fervently for her passing spirit. And when he had prayed a long time with his head averted, not to see her last breath, all seemed unnaturally still. He turned his head fearfully. It was so. She was gone. Nothing left him now but the earthly shell of as constant, pure, and loving a spirit as ever adorned the earth.

A priest is never more thoroughly a priest than in the chamber of death. Gerard did the last offices of the Church for the departed just as he should have done them for his smallest parishioner. He did this mechanically, then sat down stupefied by the sudden and tremendous blow, and not yet realizing the pangs of bereavement. Then in a transport of religious enthusiasm he knelt and thanked Heaven for her Christian end. And then all his thought was to take her away from strangers, and lay her in his own churchyard. That very evening a covered cart with one horse started for Gouda, and in it was a coffin, and a brokenhearted man lying with his arms and chin resting on it. The mourner's short-lived energy had exhausted itself in the necessary preparations, and now he lay crushed, clinging to the cold lead that held her.

The man of whom the cart was hired walked by the horse's head, and did not speak to him, and when he baited the horse spoke but in a whisper, respecting that mute agony. But when he stopped for the night, he and the landlord made a well-meaning attempt to get the mourner away to take some rest and food. But Gerard repulsed them, and when they persisted, almost snarled at them, like a faithful dog, and clung to the cold lead all night. So then they drew a cloak over him, and left him in peace.

And at noon the sorrowful cart came up to the manse, and there were full a score of parishioners collected with one little paltry trouble or another. They had missed the Parson already. And when they saw what it was, and saw their healer so stricken down, they raised a loud wail of grief, and it roused him from his lethargy of woe and he saw where he was, and their faces, and tried to speak to them. "Oh, my children, my children!" he cried, but choked with anguish could say no more.

Yet the next day, in spite of all remonstrances, he buried her himself, and read the service with a voice that only trembled now and then. Many tears fell upon her grave. And when the service ended he stayed there standing like a statue, and the people left the churchyard out of respect. He stood like one in a dream till the sexton, who was, as most men are, a fool, began to fill in the grave without giving him due warning.

But at the sound of earth falling on her, Gerard uttered a piercing scream. The sexton forbore. Gerard staggered and put his hand to his breast. The sexton supported him, and called for help. Jorian Ketel, who lingered near, mourning his benefactress, ran into the churchyard, and the two supported Gerard into the manse.

"Ah, Jorian, good Jorian," said he, "something snapped within me. I felt it, and I heard it. Here, Jorian, here," and he put his hand to his breast.

CHAPTER LVII

A FORTNIGHT after this pale, bowed figure entered the Dominican convent in the suburbs of Gouda, and sought speech with Brother Ambrose, who governed the convent as deputy, the Prior having lately died and his successor, though appointed, not having arrived.

The sick man was Gerard, come to end life as he began it. He entered as a novice, on probation; but the truth was he was a failing man, and knew it, and came there to die in peace near kind and gentle Ambrose his friend, and the other monks to whom his house and heart had always been open. His manse was more than he could bear, it was too full of reminiscences of her.

Ambrose, who knew his value, and his sorrow, was not without a kindly hope of curing him and restoring him to his parish. With this view he put him in a comfortable cell over the gateway, and forbade him to fast or practice any austerities.

But in a few days the new Prior arrived, and proved a very tartar. At first he was absorbed in curing abuses and tightening the general discipline, but one day, hearing the Vicar of Gouda had entered the convent as a novice, he said: " 'Tis well, let him first give up his vicarage, then, or go. I'll no fat parsons in my house." The Prior then sent for Gerard, and he went to him, and the moment they saw one another they both started.

"Clement!"

"Jerome!"

Jerome was as morose as ever in his general character, but he had somewhat softened toward Gerard. All the time he was in England he had missed him more than he thought possible, and since then had often wondered what had become of him. What he heard in Gouda raised his feeble brother in his good opinion—above all, that he had withstood the Pope and the Minorites on "the infernal heresy of the Immaculate Conception," as he called it. But when one of his young monks told him with tears in his eyes the cause of Gerard's illness, all his contempt revived. "Dying for a woman?"

He determined to avert this scandal. He visited Clement twice a day in his cell, and tried all his old influence and all his eloquence to induce him to shake off this unspiritual despondency, and not rob the Church of his piety and his eloquence at so critical a period.

Gerard heard him, approved his reasoning, admired his strength, confessed his own weakness, and continued visibly to wear away to the land of the leal. One day Jerome told him he had heard his story, and heard it with pride.

"But now," said he, "you spoil it all, Clement, for this is the triumph of earthly passion. Better have yielded to it and repented than resist it while she lived and succumb under it now body and soul."

"Dear Jerome," said Clement, so sweetly as to rob his remonstrance of the tone of remonstrance, "here, I think you do me some injustice. Passion there is none, but a deep affection, for which I will not blush here, since I shall not blush for it in Heaven. Bethink thee, Jerome. The poor dog that dies of grief on his master's grave, is he guilty of passion? Neither am I. Passion had saved my life, and lost my soul.

"She was my good angel. She sustained me in my duty and charity, her face encouraged me in the pulpit, her lips soothed me under ingratitude. She interwined herself with all that was good in my life, and after leaning on her so long, I could not go on alone. And, dear Jerome, believe me I am no rebel against Heaven. It is God's will to release me. When they threw the earth upon her poor coffin, something snapped within my bosom here that mended may not be. I heard it and I felt it. And from that time, Jerome, no food that I put in my mouth had any savor. With my eyes bandaged now I could not tell thee which was bread and which was flesh, by eating of it."

"Holy saints!"

"And again, from that same hour my deep dejection left me, and I smiled again. I often smile—why? I read it thus: He in whose hands are the issues of life and death gave me that minute the great summons, 'twas some cord of life snapped in me. He is very pitiful. I should have lived unhappily, but He said: 'No, enough is done, enough is suffered. Poor, feeble, loving servant, thy shortcomings are forgiven, thy sorrows touch thine end. Come thou to thy rest!' I come, Lord, I come."

Jerome groaned. "The Church had ever her holy but feeble servants," he said. "Now would I give ten years of my life to save thine. But I see it may not be. Die in peace."

And so it was that in a few days more Gerard lay a-dying in a frame of mind so holy and happy that more than one aged saint was there to garner his dying words. In the evening he had seen Giles, and begged him not to let poor Jack starve, and to see that little Gerard's trustees did their duty, and to kiss his parents for him, and to send Denys to his friends in Burgundy. "Poor thing, he will feel so strange here without his comrade." And after that he had an interview with Jerome alone. What passed between them was never distinctly known, but it must have been something remarkable, for Jerome went from the door with his hands crossed on his breast, his high head lowered, and sighing as he went.

The two monks that watched with him till matins related that all through the night he broke out from time to time in pious exclamations, and praises, and thanksgivings. Only once, they said, he wandered, and thought he saw her walking in green meadows with other spirits clad in white, and beckoning him, and they all smiled and beckoned him. And both these monks said (but it might have been fancy) that just before dawn there came three light taps against the wall, one after another, very slow, and the dying man heard them, and said, "I come, love, I come."

This much is certain, that Gerard did utter these words and prepare for his departure, having uttered them. He sent for all the monks who at that hour were keeping vigil. They came, and hovered like gentle spirits round him with holy words. Some prayed in silence for him with their faces touching the ground, others tenderly supported his head. But when one of them said something about his life of self-denial and charity, he stopped him, and addressing them all said,

"My dear brethren, take note that he who here dies so happy holds not these newfangled doctrines of man's merit. Oh, what a miserable hour were this to me an if I did! Nay, but I hold with the Apostles and their pupils in the Church, the ancient Fathers, that 'we are justified not by our own wisdom, or piety, or the works we have done in holiness of heart, but by faith.' "[1]

Then there was a silence, and the monks looked at one another significantly.

"Please you sweep the floor," said the dying Christian in a voice to which all its clearness and force seemed supernaturally restored. They instantly obeyed, not without a sentiment of awe and curiosity.

"Make me a great cross with wood ashes."

They strewed the ashes in form of a great cross upon the floor.

"Now lay me down on it, for so will I die."

And they took him gently from his bed, and laid him on the cross of wood ashes.

"Shall we spread out thine arms, dear brother?"

"Now God forbid! Am I worthy of that?"

He lay silent, but with his eyes raised in ecstasy. Presently he spoke half to them, half to himself.

"Oh," he said with a subdued but concentrated rapture, "I feel it buoyant. It lifts me floating in the sky whence my merits had sunk me like lead."

Day broke, and displayed his face cast upward in silent rapture, and his hands together; like Margaret's. And just about the hour she died he spoke his last word in this world.

"Jesu!"

And even with that word—he fell asleep.

They laid him out for his last resting-place.

Under his linen they found a horsehair shirt. "Ah!" cried the young

[1] He was citing from Clement of Rome. Author's note.

monks, "behold a saint!" Under the haircloth they found a long thick tress
of auburn hair. They started, and were horrified, and a babel of voices
arose, some condemning, some excusing. In the midst of which Jerome
came in, and hearing the dispute, turned to an ardent young monk called
Basil, who was crying scandal the loudest.

"Basil," said he, "is she alive or dead that owned this hair?"

"How may I know, Father?"

"Then for aught you know it may be the relic of a saint?"

"Certes it may be," said Basil skeptically.

"You have then broken our rule, which saith 'Put ill construction on
no act done by a brother which can be construed innocently.' Who are
you to judge such a man as this was? Go to your cell, and stir not out
for a week by way of penance."

He then carried off the lock of hair. And when the coffin was to be
closed, he cleared the cell, and put the tress upon the dead man's bosom.

"There, Clement," said he to the dead face. And set himself a penance
for doing it, and nailed the coffin up himself.

The next day Gerard was buried in Gouda churchyard. The monks followed him in procession from the convent. Jerome, who was evidently
carrying out the wishes of the deceased, read the service. The grave was
a deep one, and at the bottom of it was a lead coffin. Poor Gerard's, light
as a feather, so wasted was he, was lowered, and placed by the side of it.
After the service Jerome said a few words to the crowd of parishioners
that had come to take the last look at their best friend. When he spoke
of the virtues of the departed, loud wailing and weeping burst forth, and
tears fell upon the coffin like rain.

The monks went home. Jerome collected them in the refectory and spoke
to them thus:

"We have this day laid a saint in the earth. The convent will keep his
trentals, but will feast, not fast. For our good brother is freed from the
burden of the flesh, his labors are over, and he has entered into his joyful
rest. I alone shall fast, and do penance, for, to my shame I say it, I was
unjust to him, and knew not his worth till it was too late. And you, young
monks, be not curious to inquire whether a lock he bore on his bosom was
a token of pure affection or the relic of a saint, but remember the heart
he wore beneath. Most of all, fix your eyes upon his life and conversation, and follow them an ye may, for he was a holy man."

Thus after life's fitful fever these truelovers were at peace. The grave,
kinder to them than the Church, united them forever, and now a man of
another age and nation, touched with their fate, has labored to build their
tombstone and rescue them from long and unmerited oblivion. He asks
for them your sympathy, but not your pity. No, put this story to a whole-

some use. Fiction must often give false views of life and death. Here, as it happens, curbed by history, she gives you true ones. Let the barrier that kept these true lovers apart prepare you for this, that here on earth there will nearly always be some obstacle or other to your perfect happiness.

I ask your sympathy then for their rare constancy, and pure affection, and then cruel separation by a vile heresy[1] in the bosom of the Church, but not your pity for their early, but happy end.

Beati sunt qui in Domino moriuntur.

CHAPTER LVIII

In compliance with a custom I despise, but have not the spirit to resist, I linger on the stage to pick up the smaller fragments of humanity I have scattered about—some of them, for the wayside characters have no claim on me.

Eli and Catherine lived to a great age, lived so long that both Gerard and Margaret grew to be dim memories. Giles also was longevous. He went to the court of Bavaria, and was alive there at ninety, but had somehow turned into bones and leather, trumpet-toned.

Cornelis, free from all rivals and forgiven long ago by his mother, who clung to him more and more now all her brood was scattered, waited, and waited, and waited for his parents' decease. But Catherine's shrewd word came true. Ere she and her mate wore out, this worthy rusted away. At sixty-five he lay dying of old age in his mother's arms, a hale woman of eighty-six. He had lain unconscious a while, but came to himself *in articulo mortis,* and seeing her near him, told her how he would transform the shop and premises as soon as they should be his. "Yes, my darling," said the poor old woman, soothingly, and in another minute he was clay, and that clay was followed to the grave by all the feet whose shoes he had waited for.

Denys, brokenhearted at his comrade's death, was glad to return to Burgundy, and there a small pension the court allowed him kept him until unexpectedly he inherited a considerable sum from a relation. He was known in his native place for many years as a crusty old soldier who could tell good stories of war when he chose, and a bitter railer against women.

Jerome, disgusted with Northern laxity, retired to Italy and, having high connections, became at seventy a mitered Abbot. He put on the screw of discipline. His monks revered and hated him. He ruled with iron rod ten years. And one night he died, alone, for he had not found the way to a single heart. The Vulgate was on his pillow, and the crucifix in his hand,

[1] Celibacy of the clergy, an invention truly fiendish. Author's note.

and on his lips something more like a smile than was ever seen there while he lived; so that methinks at that awful hour he was not quite alone. *Requiescat in pace.* The Master he served has many servants, and they have many minds, and now and then a faithful one will be a surly one, as it is in these our mortal mansions.

The yellow-haired laddie, Gerard Gerardson, belongs not to fiction but to history. She has recorded his birth in other terms than mine. Over the tailor's house in the Brede Kirk Straet she has inscribed:

"Haec est parva domus natus quâ magnus Erasmus,"[1] and she has written half a dozen lives of him. But there is something left for her yet to do. She has no more comprehended *magnum Erasmum* than any other pigmy comprehends a giant, or partisan a judge.

First scholar and divine of his epoch, he was also the heaven-born dramatist of his century. Some of the best scenes in this new book are from his medieval pen, and illumine the pages where they come. For the words of a genius so high as his are not born to die. Their immediate work upon mankind fulfilled, they may seem to lie torpid, but at each fresh shower of intelligence Time pours upon their students, they prove their immortal race. They revive, they spring from the dust of great libraries, they bud, they flower, they fruit, they seed, from generation to generation, and from age to age.

[1]This is the poor house in which the great Erasmus was born.